THE SHADOW MAKER

BOOK 1 IN THE **SHADOWMAKER** SERIES

T.J. CHAMPITTO

WILDBLUE PRESS

WildBluePress.com

THE
SHADOW
MAKER

Acknowledgments

Thanks to my most ardent supporter, my agent Linda Langton who continues to find the perfect homes for my stories. To my beautiful wife Tisha for always believing, no matter what. Michael Cordova, Ashley Kaesemeyer, and the entire team at WildBlue Press for their unwavering support and dedication. Jenn Waterman for her remarkable insight and for pushing me to the finish line. And to my readers, you give me purpose, every last one of you.

For Tisha—*sei il mio tutto.*

CHAPTER 1

He'd planned this day for so long—carefully and methodically. He'd accounted for every waking second, every tiny detail, and now, standing in the atrium of the Montreal Museum of Fine Arts, Henry Sirola took one last calming breath and began a slow march across the polished tile floor. He'd done it thousands of times before in his head.

The Hornstein Pavilion was nearly empty now, the last of the day's visitors slowly fizzling out onto the cold sidewalk.

"Tomahawk Two in place," a voice crackled in his ear.

Henry kept pace as he crossed the atrium and continued past the lecture hall to a flight of open stairs. He ascended to the second floor and took up position.

"We've got three tangos holding on level one," he whispered. "Somebody get eyes on number four, please."

After a tense pause, another voice clamored into his ear. "Tango number four just came out of the service elevator on one."

"Copy that." Henry looked down at his wristwatch. "Launch the harpoon."

On the first floor, just beyond the corridor connecting the Bourgie Concert Hall to the Hornstein Pavilion, a rather tall tourist casually strolled along. His deep-set blue eyes studied a folded pamphlet gripped in his hand. As he passed beneath a stone archway, he stuffed the pamphlet into his coat pocket. He ran his hand gently against the marble wall, then stopped just short of the corridor. His fingertips massaged a metal guide rail that ran vertically from floor to ceiling. The tourist checked over his shoulder before placing a magnetized block of iron—which had been machined to the perfect dimensions—neatly into place along the inside of the rail.

"Harpoon is away," the man said quietly into the air.

Perched on the second-floor balcony overlooking the atrium, Henry watched as three security officers scurried toward the elevators below in a frantic rush to find whatever had just blocked the emergency door and set off the silent alarm.

He reached into his jacket and pulled out a roll of red caution tape. "Looks like there's one left in the guard room. Tomahawk Three, you're up," he whispered.

The museum felt quiet and serene, just as it was supposed to. Henry turned and made his way through the first of four exhibition galleries. As he reached the second, he taped off the entrance and slipped inside. He paused for a moment to appreciate the sixteenth-century collection from Joachim Patinir—something he'd allotted an additional ten seconds for. It was a brilliant display of the Dutch artist's most infamous work, he thought, and well worth the precious time.

Satisfied, he produced a small handheld device and carefully placed it against the glass that entombed the first painting—*Charon Crossing the Styx*, a piece he'd chosen personally. He pressed his thumb against a small button and the glass splintered outward in a perfectly chiseled spiderweb across the canvas. With a gentle tap, the collage of broken glass fell to the hardwood floor in a prattling crash.

He placed the gadget back into his pocket and exchanged it for a small switchblade. The canvas was cut with precision, just inside the frame, leaving no more than a millimeter behind—a sacrifice he was willing to make for such a prize.

As the last cut was made, he reached up and gently peeled the painting from its display. There would only be time for three, he reminded himself. With calculated intent, he moved on to the next, and then the next.

The paintings were rolled up individually and secured with rubber bands. As he set them onto an empty visitors' bench, a man ducked beneath the red tape and stepped into the room.

"Bring them here," Henry instructed.

His teammate walked across the gallery and set three plexiglass tubes onto the bench. "I've got Tango number four demobilized in the guard room. We have twenty seconds," the man warned as he retreated back to the main hall.

Henry stuffed the three paintings into the tubes one by one, then capped them with plastic lids. Each tube had a thin leather strap attached from end to end. He secured them over his shoulder and darted out of the hall.

"Spartan is in custody," he whispered as he paused at the top of the staircase. "Tomahawk Two, I need an update."

"Levels one and two secure," the voice responded.

Henry smiled. He lunged toward a third exhibit hall, separated from the others by a wide catwalk. At a quickened pace, he crossed the gallery to a set of service elevators.

"Everyone out. Exfil, exfil," he commanded under his breath.

The seconds were ticking by faster now. From the corner of his eye, he could see the silhouettes of Tomahawks Two and Three pacing briskly to the main entrance and out onto the colonnaded portico.

Henry stared at himself in the polished nickel of the elevator door until it opened with a light *BING*. He stepped inside and clasped his hands in front of his light brown sportscoat.

The elevator brought him two stories up to a maintenance hall, where a steel exit door led him to the pavilion rooftop. Outside, he inhaled the cool, crisp air and tightened the three straps around his collar.

He could hear them now—the pulsing, high-pitched whines of the alarm system blaring from below.

In a quickened stride, he made his way to the ledge.

The metallic crash of the door bursting open behind him was followed by the sound of boots rushing across the gravel in hot pursuit.

"*Arrêter!*" a voice shouted.

Henry glanced down into the alley between the museum and the gothic stone façade of the adjacent church.

"Show me your hands!" the security guard sharply instructed.

Henry peered over his shoulder to size the man up, then returned his gaze to the narrow alley below. He took a long, soothing breath and leaned his head back into the wind.

As the officer drew his revolver and carefully approached, Henry gripped the leather straps against his shoulder and thrust himself from the ledge.

The guard raced across the gravel and stared with shock into the alley below.

The thief was gone.

CHAPTER 2

The city of Atlanta glimmered in the cool night air. Its lights hung across the skyline, strewn from building to building all the way to the horizon. A few hand-cut ice cubes melted away in Henry's glass. He sat alone at an outside table, buried in his smartphone, sipping vodka.

His attention waned as three drunk sorority sisters giggled their way past. But he couldn't be bothered. Henry was waiting for someone.

His waitress, a cute brunette with full lips and long legs, drifted over to check on him. With a slow grin, he ordered another drink, then placed his phone into his pocket, enjoying the soft breeze that pushed across the patio bar.

Another vodka on the rocks landed on the table.

Finally, his guest arrived.

Henry stood to greet the man and the two embraced in a quick, tight hug. "How was Miami?" Henry asked.

Darius Martović considered a snarky response—something about thongs and beaches and tourists—but just smiled and rocked his head. "Same as always."

The leggy brunette appeared again.

"Vodka tonic," Darius requested. "Stolichnaya, not that organic crap."

"Yes, sir. Anything else?"

Darius smiled pleasantly. "No, we're all set."

"So, what do you feel like getting into tonight?" asked Henry.

"I can't tonight. I'm sorry, brother, I'm too tired."

"Oh please. It wasn't even a two-hour flight. What, are you jet-lagged?"

"I wish I could," Darius leveled. "The boys kept me up late last night… and the night before that and the night before that. I need some rest."

Henry swept his brown hair back into place and tugged at the collar of his Italian leather jacket. "That's the worst excuse I've heard in a while."

"Give me a break, man. I'm too old to be clubbing until sunrise."

The waitress returned and set Darius' drink on the table. With a spin of her hips, she floated off to the next group of patrons.

"Fair enough," Henry conceded. "How's Anton doing these days?"

"He's great. He wanted me to tell you hello. I bragged about your work in Montreal."

"I appreciate that. And speaking of Montreal, I know it's been a couple weeks, but this is a little down payment for all your help. I'll have the rest soon." Henry produced a large white envelope, neatly stuffed with twenty thousand dollars in cash, and placed it on the table in front of his captain.

"Yeah, that was a lotta fun. Glad we could work it out." Darius beamed as he casually slipped it into his coat.

Henry plucked the lime wedge from his glass and took a long pull. "So what did Miami turn up this time?"

"Anton needs me to set up some potential buyers."

"For what?"

"I have no idea. But whatever it is, it's expensive."

"How expensive?" Henry pressed.

Darius leaned in closer, narrowing his deep-set blue eyes across the table. "*Very* expensive."

"You need a crew?"

"It's not like that. But I could use some help setting up a fence. You interested?"

Henry tried to play it cool, twirling the half-empty glass in his hand. "Sure. I think I could handle that."

"Good. Let's do breakfast Friday. I'll get you all caught up."

"And you have no clue what it is?"

"Probably another set of stones. Who the hell knows what Anton's gotten himself into this time." Darius downed his drink and stood from the table.

"Get some sleep, princess," Henry teased. "I'll see you Friday."

With a tired grin, Darius patted him on the shoulder and disappeared into the brisk night.

Henry polished off his drink and paid the tab. Outside, he tucked his hands into his pockets and began a light stroll past the High Museum of Art, then the Swiss consulate. A few blocks further brought him to the entrance of the Forty West building, where he paced across the hardwood to a set of elevators.

On the twenty-sixth floor, he got off and stepped into his penthouse. The crisp, white walls were adorned with original paintings from some of his favorite contemporary artists: Kiefer, Saville, Barcelo, and others he'd grown fond of over the years.

With a deep groan, he took off his jacket and tossed it onto a black leather sofa.

Henry was a handsome fellow, just over six feet tall with a sharp jawline and chiseled biceps. His clothes were always perfectly tailored and his skin was flawless and smooth. And at the ripe old age of thirty-three, the lifelong criminal had built a career stealing valuable art, antiquities, and precious jewels from the world's most renowned museums and galleries.

It was the only life he'd ever known.

With the stench of vodka wafting from his pores, Henry stumbled up the hallway to his room and collapsed into bed.

The next morning, he awoke to the sound of his automated coffee machine chirping from the kitchen. He lifted himself from the bed and dropped to the floor for a set of push-ups.

A cold shower helped shake the cobwebs loose and by eight o'clock, Henry was fully dressed, sipping coffee on the back balcony. Under a soft morning breeze, he stared out at the bustling city below.

Atlanta had treated him well over the years. The relationship had always been one of discretion and immorality, but it was also symbiotic in some strange way. The city needed people like Henry. He was part of its cultural makeup and alluring identity. And in return, Henry needed Atlanta and the wealth of opportunity it presented him.

With a formidable sigh, he walked back inside and set his mug on the kitchen counter. He continued to the foyer, where he snatched his pistol from a buffet drawer and slipped it into his gray sportscoat.

As the morning news rattled in the background, Henry checked his watch. He stepped into the elevator and descended to a private underground parking garage.

"Good morning, Mr. Sirola," the valet greeted as Henry walked past.

"Morning, John," Henry politely replied.

Ahead of him, a midnight blue Maserati Ghibli waited in the shadows. With the press of a button, the car roared to life.

Seconds later, the Maserati pulled out of the garage and shot eastbound onto Twelfth Street. He continued to the interstate, where he drifted several miles before veering off the highway. Under the low hum of a supercharged V8, Henry turned left and pulled into a lot behind a small brick building.

He stepped out of the car and walked across the pavement to the entrance, where a sign above the door read SCRANTON

& BROOKS—an architectural firm owned by Darius. Henry had worked here—or at least pretended to—for the past six years.

He greeted a few smiling faces as he made his way up the hall to his corner office. Inside, perfectly placed in the center of the room, sat a rosewood desk flanked by a wet bar and a foosball table. The drapes were drawn shut—as they always were—and a couple of black-and-white prints set in thin wooden frames hung against the wall behind his desk.

Henry walked across the room and stood in front of a tall bookshelf. It was an impressive collection of first-edition classics and small, ancient artifacts, mostly of Roman and Greek origins.

He took a moment to appreciate the treasures. He then pulled his hands from his pockets and carefully placed them on the third shelf from the top. With a gentle nudge, the entire unit slowly collapsed into the wall, revealing a dark, empty passageway. He stepped through the entry and descended a flight of stairs, which brought him to a narrow tunnel nestled between two brick walls. Above him, the shelf quietly closed, encasing the corridor in complete darkness.

There was a time when he needed to count his steps, but those days were long gone. By now, he'd committed every square inch of the subterranean tunnels to memory.

He continued on for another hundred feet until he reached a second staircase. This one, however, took him three levels up, back to the surface. At the top of the steps, he pushed through a metal door and emerged into the boiler room of the Capital Transit Building. His hands felt blindly through the darkness for a light switch on the wall, and as the bulb above him flickered to life, Henry stepped out into a sprawling warehouse.

CHAPTER 3

The Capital Transit Building was the heartbeat of the Ružaro clan's operations in the southern United States. From this location, random household goods were stuffed with stolen artwork and priceless gems, then packed and loaded onto trucks, destined for various distribution points around the country. And for years, the entire operation had eluded the wandering eyes of law enforcement.

This was Henry's domain—the hub from which he planned daring heists and managed the international sales of his spoils. It was the one place where he felt most at home.

He sauntered across the concrete floor with more vibrancy than usual. Today, he knew, three very special pieces of artwork were set to arrive from Montreal. It was a shipment he'd been patiently anticipating for weeks.

The museum job had been Darius' idea—an ambitious heist that would ultimately net them a quarter of a million dollars.

For the next several hours, he paced the loading dock, answering phone calls and texting associates, until a large tractor-trailer turned the corner of Krog Street and backed into one of the bays. The driver got out and hustled back to the loading area, where he stepped onto the platform and unlocked the cargo doors. He opened them with flare as a forklift rushed inside and pulled the first pallet from the truck.

A few members of Henry's team began unraveling the thick layer of packing wrap, which revealed a bulky metal turbine that had been stripped from an airplane engine. Henry stepped to the pallet with measured excitement. His eyes examined it carefully and, after a brief pause, he reached his arm into a ventilation shaft. His fingers grasped the tip of a plastic tube as a devilish grin swept across his face.

The forklift continued to retrieve pallets from the trailer, one after the other, each loaded with random, useless airplane parts. A small group of men gathered around and began rifling through the assemblage of rusted metal until the other two paintings were located and removed.

Henry now stood with his hands on his hips, gazing down at the three plastic tubes laying in front of him. He wouldn't dare open them—a command that chewed away at his curiosity.

For the next hour, a small team repacked the three tubes into barrels of grain and loaded them onto a tractor-trailer, this time destined for the port of Savannah. From there, the paintings would be transferred onto a cargo ship and sent to Portugal, where a buyer anxiously awaited.

As the semi pulled away, Henry gazed out at the debris field around him, a collection of greasy machinery and other large, unrecognizable lumps of metal.

"What do you want to do with all this stuff?" a young worker shouted.

Henry inhaled with a sense of accomplishment. "Get it to the scrap yard," he instructed. "Darius will flip out if he sees this mess."

With that, he ambled across the warehouse to the boiler room. The small victory had stirred his appetite. Through the darkness of the tunnels, he navigated back to his office at Scranton and Brooks, where he slipped through the lobby and out onto Irwin Street. A two-block hike took him to his favorite microbrewery, a local hipster joint clinging to the fringes of society with wildly named menu items and a socially awkward staff.

Henry found a stool at the bar and ordered a cheeseburger and fries and a cold beer. Afterwards, the Ružaro lieutenant made his way back to his office, only this time, he opted for the scenic route through Old Water Tower Park.

The sky above him closed in with the onset of clouds and a looming storm. With his three prizes now safely on their way across the world, Henry returned to the lot behind Scranton and Brooks and climbed into his Maserati.

He arrived home just after two o'clock. He changed into a t-shirt and a pair of athletic shorts and hit the gym downstairs, followed by a light jog through Winn Park.

That evening, Henry rewarded himself with a few drinks at Club Trinidad. Perched high above the dance floor in a private booth, he watched the dazzling display of miniskirts and glow sticks. It was Thursday night, and between the velvet ropes and flashing strobe lights, Buckhead's most beautiful were out in full force.

By one in the morning, he'd seen enough. With a brush of his expensive navy-blue suit, he left the raucous club and returned home. He poured a nightcap and stood on his balcony overlooking Piedmont Park and the lights of the city's surrounding enclaves.

Nights like this often reminded him of his humble beginnings. He'd arrived in Atlanta at a young age, with little memory of his parents. He often fought desperately to remember them—the way they looked, the way they sounded. But nothing ever came. Henrick Lucian Sirola had been orphaned, scooped up by his aunt and uncle, then brought to the United States along with several other families from the village of Krasno. Thousands had fled that year, escaping the Homeland War in search of a better life.

He and Darius had been recruited in their early teens. They learned at a young age how to brew the perfect cup of coffee and avoid getting hit by cars while delivering packages on skateboards. It wasn't long before they graduated to stealing motorcycles and credit cards. Along the way, they were trained in espionage and tradecraft, as well as hand-to-hand combat, a skill they'd honed in nightclub parking lots during their early twenties.

Henry's career had blossomed over the years. There wasn't a vault or museum in the world that could keep him out.

He downed the last of his drink and slithered to his bedroom, where he passed out against the mattress.

Hours later, the sun broke through the window and forced his eyes open. Through a light hangover, he rousted himself from bed and slipped into a pair of blue slacks and a white shirt.

He left his apartment on foot and walked several blocks to a small diner. Tucked in a booth in the far corner, Darius sat idly, sipping his coffee.

"*Dobro jutro*," Henry greeted as he sat down.

"And good morning to you," his friend replied. "Why do you always do that?"

"Do what?"

"Speak Croatian. It's weird."

"Don't let my Aunt Sara hear you utter those words," Henry warned.

"Oh, I wouldn't dare. How's she doing these days?"

"She's doing great," said Henry, his eyes glued to the menu. "So what are we having?"

"I already ordered for us."

"Cool. Now tell me what's going on with this new project."

Darius shook his head. "Do you ever just chill out? Can we at least enjoy some breakfast first?"

"No," Henry coldly replied. "So what's the deal?"

Darius paused as the waitress brought two plates of fresh fruit and croissants. She refilled their coffee with a pensive smile before drifting away. "Anton's on to something big," Darius quietly revealed.

Henry leaned over his plate. "What the hell is it?"

"I don't actually know all the details yet. Everybody's being super hush-hush about it."

"Oh c'mon. You expect me to believe that?"

"Seriously. I don't know anything about it."

"Fine," Henry conceded. "Specs?"

"No. But listen to me; based on the type of buyers we're lining up, I think it's something serious. I won't know for sure until I get my hands on it."

Henry sat back and cast a discerning glare across the table. "Well, thanks for bringing me in. Sounds like fun. What else is Anton cooking up these days?"

Darius shrugged. "You know him, he's juggling a few ops right now. Nothing too crazy."

"The guy never slows down."

"Nope." Darius set his fork down and reached for his coffee, gazing at Henry over the rim of his mug.

"What?" Henry asked. "I know that face… what is it?"

"Don't get pissed off at me…"

"Oh great. Let me guess; you're sending me to Dubai, aren't you? Are you pairing me up with someone? Who is it, Carlos? Please don't tell me it's Carlos."

"No," Darius replied. "But also, yes. And no."

"What the hell does *that* mean?"

"No, you're not going to Dubai. Yes, I'm pairing you up with someone. And no, it's not Carlos."

"Is it Bender?"

"Worse."

"C'mon, dude, I'm tired of playing. Just tell me."

Darius took a deep breath. "It's Isabell."

Henry sat frozen in his chair. He blinked several times in disbelief before diving back into his breakfast. "It's too early to be fucking with me," he growled.

"I wish I was. I'm sorry, man. Anton's orders. She's the only decent tour guide we have available right now."

"She's my ex-girlfriend! Why would you do that to me?"

An awkward hush fell over the diner. Darius nodded and smiled at the curious patrons now eyeing them with contempt.

"You promised you'd never do this to me," Henry hissed.

"She was already on board, bro. You asked to get involved… so here we are." Darius took another pull of his coffee. "One big happy family."

"This is bullshit," Henry groaned under his breath. He took a final bite of croissant and stood from the table. "Thanks for breakfast."

"Don't be mad. Are you still in?"

"Of course I'm in. I'll see you tonight," he shouted over his shoulder as he exited the diner.

CHAPTER 4

A black Suburban followed him to the corner of Peachtree and Twelfth, then continued past, northbound through Inman Park, then Emory Village, and into the suburbs. Twenty minutes later, the SUV pulled into the FBI field office just outside the city. Special Agent Miles Brennan made his way up the stairs to the second floor and pushed through the bullpen. Before he could make it to his desk, David Tisdale caught his attention.

"Brennan, a minute please!" the special agent-in-charge called from across the floor.

Miles kept his eyes on the worn carpet and continued to his cubicle, where he set his belongings on his desk. "Sure thing, be there in a sec."

Every morning was the same: upon his arrival, Tisdale would bark at him from across the bullpen, ordering the agent into his office with some melodramatic story about Atlanta's escalating crime problem. Everything was a crisis.

Miles wondered what today's cataclysm was. He maneuvered through the maze and popped his head into Tisdale's office. "What's up?"

"Come in. Close the door."

David Tisdale was a tall, lumbering Black man with a stern gaze and a thick mustache. He was in his early fifties, Miles guessed, but didn't look a day older than forty-five. The special agent-in-charge had three pre-teen daughters and a bad habit of bringing his parental anxieties to the workplace.

Miles closed the door as he ran a hand through his messy brown hair. His black suede jacket tightened against his back as he stood at attention.

Tisdale glanced down at Miles' stained gray slacks. "When's the last time you took a shower? Or washed your clothes?"

Miles had to think about it for a moment. "Monday. No… Tuesday."

Tisdale rolled his eyes. "Any updates on our Korean friends on the north side?"

"Same old, same old," Miles replied. "I'm still running down some footage from the crime scene, should have a lineup ready by the end of the week."

"Good. I've got a new assignment for you."

"Give me a break, David. You know I'm already juggling—"

"Don't worry, I'm not piling any more work onto your plate," Tisdale assured. "We can pass some of these other cases off to the team, but you've been specifically requested for a new operation."

"A new operation? Requested by who?"

"Come with me."

Tisdale slapped a manila envelope into Miles' chest as he walked by. He paced out of his office and through the bullpen to a long, dark hallway. It was an area of the building typically reserved for interviews and closed meetings. Miles followed closely behind, doing his best to pull documents from the envelope. Ahead of him, Tisdale shouldered into one of the doors lining the hallway.

Two strangers waited inside. Miles noted their suits— they were expensive and professionally tailored. These men weren't with the bureau.

"Miles, I'd like to introduce you to Jonathan Harwick from NSA and Antonio Garza from DCIS," Tisdale announced with little enthusiasm. "Agent Harwick is heading up a new task force and has enlisted our help."

Miles eyed the men with caution.

"Special Agent Brennan, we've heard a lot about you," the NSA man greeted. His hair was perfectly combed into position and his face, while clean-shaven, was sallow and pitted.

Miles raised an eyebrow and mustered a smile. "That's great."

"Agent Brennan has extensive experience with all the major crime organizations active in the area," Tisdale promised.

"We're excited to have you," Harwick granted. "Officer Garza has been running an operation over at DCIS that has overlapped with an ongoing NSA surveillance program. With the help of the FBI, we thought it would be a good time to combine our resources and assemble a joint task force."

"Nice to meet you both," Miles offered. "I certainly hope I can be of assistance, but who exactly are we targeting here?"

Jonathan Harwick set his hands on his hips and gazed across the room. "We're opening an investigation into the Ružaro crime organization."

"I see. So you're here to steal my sources and information, right?"

"It's not like that, Miles," Tisdale interrupted. "We're going to be rolling our investigation in with the new task force. This isn't about stealing intel, this is operational. We need you on board."

"Give me a break," snapped Miles. "I'm happy to turn over everything I have, but there's no reason for you guys to waltz in here and hijack my investigation."

"Let's not get territorial here," Tisdale said, attempting to diffuse the situation. "The Ružaro crew is the biggest thing you've worked on in years. This is your chance to take them down… once and for all."

Miles darted his eyes at the NSA agent. "You sure you guys want me on this? Have you seen my file?"

"We've seen your record," Harwick confirmed. "And I honestly don't care about any of that garbage. Your file also reveals a decorated career—a Silver Star in Iraq, top of your class at Quantico, and you're one of the best field agents in the bureau. I can assure you there wasn't any hesitation on our part."

Miles blinked at the candor, then searched for a good reason to say no. But there wasn't one. "Yeah, okay," he finally muttered. "We're good."

Harwick nodded with appreciation. "The task force will be made up of myself, Officer Garza, Special Agent Tisdale, Agent Brennan, and a small team of NSA analysts. We're very anxious to get started."

"What's the objective?" asked Miles as he took a seat next to Garza.

Agent Harwick opened his intelligence brief and cleared his throat. "Anton Krunoslav," he began. "As you all know, the Ružaro crew is one of three clans that make up the international syndicate known as *Čopor Vukova*, which loosely translates to *Pack of Wolves*. Their leadership council resides somewhere in the Balkans, most likely Bucharest. But at the moment, Ružaro is our only focus since they're the ones operating in the United States."

"Any plans to move on to the other two—Demiri and Laskaris?" asked Tisdale.

"Not at the moment," confirmed Harwick. "Now, Anton Krunoslav has been in charge of Ružaro for more than thirty years. He's an ethnic Croat, born in Šibenik, emigrated to the US in '91 with several other members. He assumed leadership shortly thereafter. Operations are currently run right here out of Atlanta. However, Krunoslav also likes to spend a lot of his time in Miami."

"He's never returned to Croatia?" asked Garza.

"Croatia gained its independence in 1995," Harwick answered. "He's been back a total of three times since then. Twice in '97 and a short trip in 2001."

"Why not since?" the DCIS officer pressed.

"Because he's wanted for war crimes," Miles interjected. "He took those trips under a fake passport, but that became harder to do after 9/11, especially for a world-class celebrity like him. But it doesn't matter; modern technology has allowed him to manage ops all over the world without ever stepping foot out of the country."

"*War crimes*?" Garza repeated as he flipped through his brief. "There's no indication of that. There haven't been any formal charges."

Miles took a heavy breath. "Horrible atrocities were committed during the Croatian War of Independence. Krunoslav was targeted by the Serbs for assassinating their officers. He was also wanted by his own Croatian generals for murdering civilians. With the fall of Yugoslavia, the new Croatian government did its best to erase any criminal charges that would have reflected poorly on their own army."

"What about the international tribunal?" Garza wondered.

"They had bigger fish to fry," replied Miles. "Krunoslav and a lot of other low-level officers slipped through the cracks."

Harwick nodded in agreement. "We have reason to believe he's currently being sought by SOA. Croatian intelligence. There's an extradition treaty in place between Croatia and the US, but SOA won't share any of their intel with us and they haven't asked us to turn him over. Which means he's free to operate here until we can charge him with crimes on American soil."

"That shouldn't be hard," Garza scoffed.

Miles pressed his elbows onto the table. "In addition to being wanted for war crimes, SOA wants him for dozens of murders, not to mention extortion, racketeering, and grand larceny. The rub is, most of those crimes are being committed in Croatia, so living here gives him plausible deniability. All they can do is arrest his lieutenants working overseas, and believe me, those guys aren't cooperating."

Garza closed his notebook. "I didn't see that in any of the reports either."

"That's because it's not in any of the reports," said Miles. "Listen, this is an organization unlike any you've ever run across. Anton Krunoslav's reach is immeasurable; he owns judges and members of Congress, and anybody else you can think of. His officers practice countersurveillance better than most intelligence agencies, and their network of communications and planning is remarkably sophisticated. These aren't a bunch of Italian thugs running numbers out of the pool hall, or Mexican cartels smuggling coke over the border—those are fucking Boy Scouts compared to the Ružaro clan. We're dealing with a legitimate international organization made up of assassins, thieves, and spies—all with the technology and resources to back it up."

A sly grin slipped across Harwick's face. "And now you see why we wanted you, Agent Brennan."

"Look," Miles argued, "I respect your interest in the Ružaro organization, but why now? Krunoslav's been causing headaches here for a long time. We have reason to believe he ordered hits on two federal judges a few years back. Luckily, he failed. Since then, he and his crew have been persons of interest in multiple grand thefts and trafficking cases. We could've used your help a long time ago… so why the sudden interest?"

Harwick flared his nostrils as he and Garza exchanged looks of concern. The NSA agent stepped over to the wall and lowered the lights, then snatched a tiny remote from the table. The wall in front of them was now illuminated with the first slide of the agent's presentation. It was a mugshot of the Ružaro leader.

"You've all seen him before. Anton Krunoslav, aged sixty-two," Harwick explained. He clicked to the next slide. "Seven weeks ago, he met with this man—Arthur Neilson. This is a photo our surveillance team snapped at Bayside Marketplace in Miami. Neilson and Krunoslav sat on this bench together for fourteen minutes and exchanged two large envelopes."

"And why do we care about Arthur Neilson?" asked Miles.

Harwick nodded to Officer Garza, who rose to his feet. "Neilson is a rather pesky entrepreneur and activist," Garza began. "His sweet spot is illegal oceanic mining and recovery operations. His organization, Deep Lyra, went so far as to build an offshore drilling rig twenty miles off the coast of Guatemala back in 2017. He was within days of actually pulling crude oil from the seabed before authorities shut him down."

"That doesn't answer the question," Tisdale chimed from the back.

Garza kept a strong poker face. "The meeting of these two men is not only rare but quite problematic. The head of a major crime organization and a deviant billionaire with an endless bank account—it's a recipe for disaster."

"Maybe Krunoslav is just getting a loan?" Miles wondered aloud.

"That's what we thought too," said Harwick. "Until we saw this." He clicked to the next set of slides. Brennan and Tisdale narrowed their eyes at the image on the wall.

"This is the research vessel *RV Tiger Claw*, formerly *USS Melville* until the navy sold her to Deep Lyra ten years ago. And guess who manages it?"

"Arthur Neilson," Tisdale guessed knowingly.

"You got it. The big man himself."

Miles sat upright in his chair. "Where was this photo taken?"

"This was taken last Monday over the South Atlantic Ocean, roughly five hundred miles off the coast of Brazil. We began circling drones over the location once the *Tiger Claw* dropped anchor and began sending submersibles down."

"Why isn't the CIA involved?" wondered Miles. "This seems right in their wheelhouse."

"Where do you think we got the drones?" Harwick revealed with a sharp wink. "This is a multi-agency initiative. We're calling it Operation Evergreen."

Miles wrinkled his face. "Cool name. But where does Krunoslav fit in?"

"Thought you'd never ask," the NSA agent replied. "We have reason to believe Krunoslav is leasing the vessel through Neilson."

Another image snapped in front of them. "This next shot is Krunoslav, Neilson, and several Ružaro associates gathered at a pier in Santos, Brazil, as the *RV Tiger Claw* set sail a couple weeks ago." Several more photos of the men roaming the docks flashed against the wall. "They were treating it like some kind of party—a christening of sorts."

"What are they celebrating?" asked Miles. "Is Krunoslav suddenly in the treasure hunting business?"

"That's what we're here to find out. Our fear is that he may be trying to recover a historic shipwreck, or worse, a nuclear warhead."

"A nuclear warhead?" Miles echoed.

Harwick confirmed with a nod. "You'd be surprised how many Balkan warlords not only find, but recover, sunken nuclear missiles, most of which were lost by Soviet fleets during the Cold War."

"Well, that wouldn't be good." Miles placed his palms against the table and tapped his fingers. "So what's the plan?"

Harwick brought the lights back up. "Our plan is to establish a surveillance network on high-value Ružaro targets, identify anyone involved in the operation, *and* develop residents, all while keeping eyes on the research vessel." The agent made his way back to the table and froze in front of Miles. "We understand you have an informant on the inside."

Miles turned his eyes to Tisdale, then back to Harwick. "I do," he confirmed reluctantly.

Garza pulled another file from his messenger bag. "We've had the opportunity to read some of your field reports from the last couple years," he began as he thumbed through documents. "You've had a lot of contact with members of the Ružaro clan. It's very impressive. But as I sifted through these intel reports, I wasn't able to find a name. You only refer to your informant as *the Shadowmaker*."

"He doesn't have a name," Miles replied softly.

Harwick looked to Tisdale for assistance.

"I wish I could help you guys," the special agent-in-charge answered coldly. "Agent Brennan has kept that information off the record to protect the informant. Krunoslav has eyes and ears all over the city, in every building, courthouse, and jail. Needless to say, we practice some pretty hefty security measures."

"That's all fine and well," Harwick acknowledged. "But if we're going to be working together, I need the identification of your informant." He took a moment to shift uncomfortably in his expensive suit. "Cut us some slack, Agent Brennan. We're all on the same side here."

"Is that what this is?" Miles struck. "You bring me in here and tell me how talented I am and what an added value I'll bring to your little task force… just to shake a name out of me?"

"That's not an accurate assessment," Harwick corrected. "And I'm not going to stroke your ego any further. Now let's cut the bullshit; if you're not comfortable giving us a name… fine. But your informant could play a big role in this investigation.”

“You drove all this way for one goddamn name? You guys are dumber than I thought.” Miles stood from the table.

“Sit down, Agent Brennan!” ordered Tisdale.

Harwick shook his head in disappointment. “Okay, you want me to pat you on the head like a little puppy?”

Miles snorted. “Fuck you, pal.”

“Here’s the truth,” the NSA agent leveled, his voice now raised with frustration. “Without you, we don’t have access to anyone on the inside. Is that what you want to hear? You need me to tell you that you’re the linchpin of this entire operation?”

“That’d be a good start.”

“Is this guy for real?” Harwick bemoaned into the air. “David, a little help here?”

“Miles, I need you to pull your shit together,” the special agent-in-charge warned. “You need to know your place here—at the FBI *and* on this team.”

Miles’ pulse slowed. He rocked his head back and forth, considering whether to play along. “Sure,” he finally mocked. “Keep those drones over the boat and I’ll see what I can shake out of my guy.”

Harwick forced a tight smile. “I appreciate that, Special Agent Brennan. I can’t thank you guys enough for all the cooperation. We’ve set up a command post on the twenty-first floor of the Marriott Buckhead across from Krunoslav’s residence. Now, considering our target is located on the forty-second and forty-third floors of the Park Avenue building, all we’ll be able to put eyes on is a set of balconies and the building’s entrance.” Harwick paused for effect. “Gentlemen, welcome to Operation Evergreen.”

With that, Miles got up and exited the room.

Harwick cut his gaze to Tisdale. “I hope your boy is everything you say he is, David. So far, I’m not impressed.”

“He’ll be fine.”

CHAPTER 5

Henry finished his three-mile jog and began pacing the sidewalk in front of the Woodruff Arts Center. Nearly out of breath, he shuffled past a Rodin sculpture with his arms raised above his head. He continued along Peachtree Street until he reached the intersection of Fourteenth. There, stapled to an old, wooden electrical pole, he noticed a familiar item—a white business card with a large orange logo stamped across the top. Printed in blue text was the name of a salesman at a local tech firm: DON MATHIS, THE NEELY GROUP.

He rolled his head back and shut his eyes. It was a signal he rarely received.

Within a small crowd of pedestrians, he crossed the street and continued south to the Forty West building, where he took the elevator up to his penthouse.

After a warm shower and a bowl of leftover linguine, he plucked a suit from his closet and combed his hair neatly into place.

Under a canopy of low-hanging clouds, Henry drove to Club Trinidad and left his car with the valet. He brushed past the doorman and was quickly ushered upstairs to a private booth tucked in the corner. A handful of Ružaro gang members were peppered throughout the second-floor lounge, each of them sipping expensive liquor as women in short skirts sat in their laps, giggling at whatever nonsense fell from their mouths.

Henry offered a few smiles as he made his way to the corner. Resting on the table were a pair of candles dancing wildly in the shadows. He unbuttoned his coat and sat down. Within seconds, a college-aged woman in a halter top, black-laced shorts, and little else stepped to the table.

"Vodka on the rocks," he shouted over the music.

She winked at him through a set of long fake lashes and slid away.

On the dance floor below, a young, sweaty mob cavorted to the beats of hardcore techno music thumping from an arsenal of speakers. Most of the kids were high as hell, but it never kept him from coming. Henry enjoyed being surrounded by the uninhibited energy of reckless humans. Years ago, he was just like them—an intoxicated dissenter stalking the dance floor in search of a warm body to grind himself against.

But things had changed since then. The cocaine didn't taste as good as it used to and the endless parade of women slipping in and out of his penthouse had lost its luster. Nowadays, his bank account wasn't being drained every Saturday night, and the last time he woke up in Mexico, it wasn't by mistake.

Right as his drink hit the table, Henry caught a glimpse of Darius coming up the stairs. He checked his watch—five minutes late.

Behind his friend, in the shimmer of fluorescent lights, was the silhouette of a small woman. Her black minidress hugged every curve with tenacity. Her eyes, smoked with shadow, darted around the lounge with a palpable combination of confidence and disgust. As the two approached, Henry wrinkled his brow. It was her.

"Henry! I hope you haven't been waiting long," Darius offered as they strolled up to the booth. "Parking's a bitch over here."

"You live five blocks away," Henry noted dryly.

"Yeah, well, I had to pick up Isabell. I'm sure there's no need for introductions."

"None whatsoever," Henry allowed. He lifted his eyes and stood from the table, doing his best not to look her up and down. She hated that.

"Henry, it's nice to see you," said Isabell, clutching her tiny purse at her side.

"It's been a while," he replied. "You look… stunning."

Isabell did in fact look stunning. Her dark hair was pulled back in a bun—a few loose strands fell around her face. The straps of her dress revealed the flawless skin of her shoulders and, of course, she smelled as wonderful as he remembered.

"Well, let's not make this weird," she snapped. "It's just a job. And I'm sorry you got paired with me."

He wanted to fire something back—something snarky, but intelligent. But he chose instead to proceed with caution. She was volatile now; he could see it in her face. Isabell no more wanted to be here than he did.

"I'm sure it'll be just fine," he finally said.

Her eyes wrinkled with amusement. "Wonderful. And you look good too, Henry."

"Okay," Darius interrupted. "Glad that wasn't totally awkward. Isabell, can I grab you a drink?"

"We have a waitress," Henry implored. "She'll be back any minute."

"It's fine. I have a running tab at the bar," Darius argued. "Isabell, what can I get you?"

She sat down and clasped her hands on the table. "Thank you, Darius. A mojito, please."

"You got it. I'll be right back." Darius disappeared into the darkness.

Henry and Isabell were now sitting alone for the first time in nearly two years. "So how have you been?" she asked politely.

"I'm well," he said with a nod. "Staying busy."

"That's good. Me too."

Henry's eyes searched for something to latch onto. Anything but her.

"I told you not to make this weird," she scolded.

But he couldn't respond. He'd been pulled into the hypnotic glint of her green eyes.

"Henry?"

"Yeah. I'm sorry, it's been a long day. And no, I promise not to… make this weird or whatever."

"Good." Isabell straightened her back and glanced around the lounge. The black fabric of her dress, wrapped snugly around her body, was doing its best to contain her ample breasts.

But Henry remained strong, his eyes refusing to fall.

Finally, Darius returned with Isabell's mojito and a vodka for himself.

"Thank you, love," she remarked. "So, what are we doing here?"

"Anton needs a new buyer," Darius answered as he sat down between them.

"A buyer for what?" she asked.

The Ružaro captain smiled. "Take a breath, Isabell. Have a sip of your drink."

She raised her brow, then pulled the mojito to her lips.

"I know neither of you wants to be here," Darius began. "So I'll make this as painless as possible. Anton has some precious stones coming in from South America… probably in a week or two."

Henry was paying close attention now. "Where in South America?"

"It doesn't matter."

"What's wrong? Anton doesn't trust you with that information?" Henry teased.

Isabell allowed a tiny laugh to escape her lips. "I don't care where it's from. What's the take?"

Darius eyed them with discretion. The pulsing of dance music blasted through the lounge as he searched for an appropriate response. "This may very well be the most lucrative job any of us will ever take," he finally announced.

Henry reached for his highball glass. "You can't be serious. Don't fuck with me like that."

"I need you both in Sorrento, Italy," Darius continued. "There's a potential buyer there. You're just couriers at this stage, which means no fuckin' around. Got it?"

"Couriers?" Henry retorted. "You're kidding, right? I'm supposed to believe this job is so big you're sending senior operatives to act as couriers?"

"For now. Once we secure a buyer, you'll be in charge of the transaction. But for this trip… you're couriers."

"You still haven't answered my question regarding the take," Isabell reminded him. "And don't give me this bullshit about 'biggest job ever' and 'you'll be set for life.' I'm not interested in any of that. I'm interested in real numbers."

Darius' eyes quickly scanned the lounge. "Anton's putting a lot of responsibility on my plate. This is the biggest op I've ever been a part of. And I need people I can trust, people like the two of you. So, please, I need your absolute commitment before I go any further."

"The *take*, Darius," she repeated. "How much money am I walking away with?"

"Are you in?"

"Of course I'm in," she confirmed. "My only two questions are, how much are you paying me and when am I leaving for Italy?"

A boyish grin appeared on Darius' face. "Good. I'm paying you each two million dollars."

Henry choked on his vodka. He casually reached for a napkin and wiped his mouth.

Isabell, however, sat like a statue, completely motionless. There was obviously a lot Darius wasn't telling them, but for some reason, she didn't seem to care. "And when do we fly out?" she pressed.

"Tomorrow afternoon."

The brunette bore her eyes into the two men sitting with her. "Fine."

"You'll be posing as business partners," Darius explained. "Entrepreneurs scouting potential investments on the Amalfi Coast."

"What type of investments?" asked Henry.

"Hotels and restaurants." Darius pulled two thick envelopes from his jacket. "Here are your passports, a buyer profile, hotel info, and plenty of spending cash."

Henry pulled out a passport and examined it closely. "Why are you being so dodgy?"

"What the hell does that mean?"

"Why are you beating around the bush? You're still not telling me what it is we're offloading. What's the big secret, Darius? Because on the surface, it sounds like some bullshit setup."

Darius rolled his eyes. "Give me a break, Henry. I told you it's stones."

"Answer him," said Isabell. "What kind of stones? I'm curious."

The Ružaro captain took a deep breath, then leveled his gaze at his two accomplices. "Okay, here's the deal," he confessed. "We're looking to move over a hundred and thirty carats."

"Is this some kind of a joke?" Henry scoffed.

"No, it's not."

"That's a nice haul," Isabell noted. "Why only a single buyer?"

Darius took a slow sip of his vodka.

"It's a package," Henry appraised. "We're fencing something that's worth more as a collection, aren't we?"

Darius confirmed the notion with a sly wink, then patted his friend on the shoulder. "Listen, this is a solid deal. Quit being so difficult."

"So what's our objective in Italy?" Henry asked.

"Tomorrow you'll check in to Hotel Palazzo Guardati and hold a pattern. The buyer is Hamad bin Thani Al Hassani—a Qatari billionaire. Made his fortune in commercial real estate and gun trafficking. You're meeting with him at seven o'clock at Ristorante Syrenuse. He'll probably have a security detail with him. There's a private room in the back; they'll be waiting for you there. Deliver the package, then get your asses home. This isn't a negotiation, you're just messengers."

Isabell wasn't impressed. "Messengers of what exactly? What *package* are you referring to?"

"This." Darius reached into his pocket and retrieved a small metal capsule, then placed it on the table.

Henry eyed the object curiously. "Is that what I think it is?"

"No," Darius replied sharply. "It's not that kind of mission. This capsule contains a message that can only be delivered to Hassani in person. But if at any point you're detained, swallow it without hesitation, understand?"

"Sure," Henry confirmed as he slipped the capsule into his pocket. "But I have to ask: why is this all happening so fast? I mean, you spend two weeks in Miami and now you've suddenly got the score of a lifetime?"

"Would I ever screw you over?"

"No. You're smart enough to know I'd cut off your head and hang it from the I-85 overpass."

They shared a quiet laugh as Isabell watched, judging them.

"Okay, you two lesbians," she finally jolted, "I'm heading home. I didn't come here to watch you goons molest each other all night."

"Oh c'mon! One more drink, Isabell!" Darius urged. "Henry won't bite, I promise."

"I actually like biting," she retorted. "But Henry already knew that."

"All right, all right. Just one more thing before you go," Darius argued as he lifted his glass into the air. "To one big happy family," he toasted.

Henry and Isabell raised their drinks above the table to meet Darius'.

"Maybe this won't be so bad after all," Isabell said as she downed the last of her mojito and stood from the table. "And thanks for picking me up, Darius, but I'll grab an Uber home. Henry, I'll see you at the airport."

"Good night," Henry offered as she turned and walked away.

He and Darius remained frozen in the booth, watching her perfect legs reach the staircase and disappear into the vapor below.

"How did you ever screw that up?" asked Darius.

Henry released a deep, agonizing groan. "I have no idea. Biggest mistake of my life."

"What? Losing her?"

"No. Getting involved with her."

"Are you two gonna be okay?"

"Of course."

Darius nodded. "Cool. What about you? Are you okay?"

"Yeah. But it's not Isabell I'm worried about," Henry confessed.

"What's the problem?"

"I'm worried about this new op. I mean, two million dollars? You act like this is perfectly normal, Darius. A hundred and thirty carats? The numbers don't add up—those must be some flawless stones."

"It doesn't matter," replied Darius. "We each have a job to do. Let's just get it done and we'll be sipping daiquiris in Fiji this summer."

"I don't drink daiquiris. We've talked about this."

"It's just a metaphor."

"For what?"

Darius huffed with frustration. "For whatever it is you're into, bro. Seriously, in my multi-million-dollar fantasy, I'm sipping daiquiris. Maybe in your fantasy, you're poppin' wheelies on a diamond-studded crotch rocket with Isabell hanging off the back."

Henry laughed as he envisioned the ridiculous scene. "Does it have to be Fiji?"

"Yes," Darius affirmed as he motioned for two more drinks. "Fiji is non-negotiable."

Henry pursed his lips in consideration. "Fiji it is."

CHAPTER 6

The next morning, Henry got up at sunrise and skipped his morning run. He donned a pair of tattered jeans and a t-shirt before topping off the costume with an old, worn Atlanta Braves cap. He then shoved his keys and cell phone into his pockets and exited the penthouse.

A short walk north brought him to the Arts Center Transit Station. He rode for several stops before getting off at the Civic Center, where he kept his head down and marched up the concrete stairs to street level. He continued on foot to the Atlanta Aquarium and meandered around the ticketing booth before circling back to the station—a countersurveillance measure that had become as instinctual to him as breathing.

Satisfied, he boarded the southbound line and found an empty seat against the window. He sat quietly for a half hour before getting off at Hartsfield-Jackson International Airport. From there, he rented a car and drove south along I-85 to Macon, then east on I-16. An hour later, he exited the highway in a desolate, rural area of south Georgia, where large bales of hay rested against an endless green landscape.

He rolled down the window and inhaled the aroma of wheatgrass and sunshine. The air smelled different here, he thought, as if sweetened by the dense pines gathered along the roadside.

Henry pulled onto a dirt trail that wove deep into the forest. His gaze tightened over the steering wheel as the small rental car crawled around a sharp bend, then came to a stop.

A black Suburban sat ominously ahead of him, parked in the middle of a sprawling field, shielded from any nearby roads or homesteads. The SUV flashed its headlights three times.

Henry responded with three flashes of his own, then exited the car. He approached cautiously through the grass and opened the passenger door of the Suburban. With a silent nod, he hoisted himself into the seat.

"So what's the big deal?" he pressed. "We never meet out here."

Miles' gaze remained fixed against the windshield. "You sure are making a lot of noise these days, don't ya think?"

"Business never sleeps," Henry admitted with a hint of sarcasm.

"Listen, I'm really pushing the envelope on the Hartsfield case. Everyone knows it was your crew."

The criminal scoffed. "Don't bluff me, Miles. Of course everyone knows it was Ružaro. But nobody except you knows it was *my* crew."

"Two hundred Cartier watches is a solid take."

"Are you asking me for a cut, Agent Brennan?"

Miles turned to face him. "We've been doing this a long time, Henry. You know I can only protect you to a certain point. Once the hounds get your scent, I have to do my job." He paused to choose his next words carefully. "Don't put me in a position where I have to make all this official and force you to testify, then put you into federal protection… it'll be a whole thing. Neither of us wants that."

"Fine," Henry relented. "The watches left Atlanta a week ago. There's no trace to me, everything was clean. All you technically have to go on is an assumption. I can handle a surveillance team for a few months. Not a problem."

"It's more than that."

"What do you mean?"

"I mean there's a multi-agency task force setting up shop in Buckhead. You guys are a hot ticket all of a sudden."

Henry scowled. "Task force? Are you serious?"

"Yeah."

"What triggered that?"

"Anton's crazy ass, that's what triggered it."

Henry threw his head back against the seat. "Damn! I knew something was up. I saw you tailing me yesterday." He took a moment to think. "All right, I'll start sanitizing a few things."

"You're just a lieutenant. There's only so much you can do."

"I'll tell Darius I was approached by the feds. He'll batten down the hatches for a while."

Miles rubbed his chin in thought. "Anything big coming down the pipe? Anything I should know about?"

"I don't know," Henry said hesitantly. "Anton's got Darius and me working on a buyer for some new trophy. I hear it's diamonds or something, but I'm not exactly sure yet."

"Any chance it's a nuke?"

"A nuke?" Henry sat upright in his seat. His mind tried to rationalize a scenario where Anton would be peddling nuclear weapons. "No," he finally stated. "Not a chance."

"All right. Can you think of anything else he's trying to recover from the bottom of the ocean?"

Henry was thoroughly confused now. Miles must've been off his meds, or drinking, or both. "I don't know anything about ocean ops," the informant assured. "Besides, even if Anton picked up a warhead, he wouldn't be asking me or Darius to offload it. There's obviously more you're not telling me. You've got something."

Miles confirmed with a silent nod. "I do. The new task force has eyes on an active operation in the South Atlantic. Research vessels and submarines, an entire crew of engineers and divers."

Henry shook his head. "No idea what you're talking about."

"What was Darius doing in Brazil two weeks ago?"

"Darius? He wasn't in Brazil. He was in Miami." Henry's eyes wandered the dash. He needed to be careful now. Miles was playing him. "I honestly have no idea," Henry said after further consideration. "I've never heard anything about it."

Miles produced two photographs from a manila envelope and held them in the air for Henry to see. "These were taken in Brazil."

The images showed Anton Krunoslav pacing a pier at some unknown harbor. There were several men with him, and Henry knew each of them well. And there, standing next to Anton, was his best friend. Darius Martović.

It was clear now: Darius had lied to him. Or, at the very least, kept it from him. But Henry wasn't about to reveal that to his handler.

"All right," Miles finally granted. "Keep your ears open. If you hear anything about a research vessel operating in the Atlantic, I want to know about it."

Henry nodded, still absorbing what he'd just learned. "Sounds good."

"And keep me posted on these new buyers you're talking about."

"Don't spoil this one for me," Henry warned. "I'm not in the mood."

Miles chuckled under his breath. "You know the drill—keep it clean."

Henry reached for the handle and exited the Suburban. He then traipsed back to the rental car and pulled away through the thick foliage.

The long ride back to Atlanta allowed his mind to spin recklessly through a series of next moves and potential scenarios. It was apparent now that Darius and Anton were working on something—something big enough to keep from a senior officer like himself.

He knew that all Ružaro operations were handled with tactical secrecy—information only flowed through the ranks on a need-to-know basis.

For now, he'd focus on locating a buyer for Darius and pretending as if he'd never heard anything about a research vessel or secret trips to Brazil.

By the time he returned home, it was all a distant memory.

As he stood in his bedroom, Henry checked his watch—his flight would begin boarding in less than three hours. He packed a small duffle bag and changed into something more comfortable: a cable-knit cashmere sweater, blue slacks, and a pair of Converse sneakers.

Soon, a car arrived to take him to the airport. The driver was a large Russian he'd seen a few times before. Henry thought his name was Boris but wasn't sure.

"The traffic is fairly light today, Mr. Sirola," the man announced with a heavy accent. "We should arrive a little earlier than expected."

"Sounds good," said Henry as he climbed into the back of the Audi.

"Is there anything you need before your flight?"

"No, I'm all set. But we're not going directly to the airport."

"I'm sorry?" Boris asked, confused.

"There's another car waiting for me at a parking garage in Grant Park. I'll need you to drop me off there."

"The one on Cherokee Avenue?"

"That's the one," Henry confirmed.

"Very well, Mr. Sirola. I'll have you there in twenty minutes."

The Audi bucked off the curb and merged into a pocket of traffic. They rode in silence as the Russian navigated across town with his burly hands gripping the wheel.

Henry gazed out the window, lost in his thoughts, until the car arrived in Grant Park and darted to the third level of the Cherokee Avenue parking garage.

Boris parked at the end of a row and got out to open Henry's door. "Have a safe flight, Mr. Sirola. Would you like me to pick you up when you return?"

"No thank you. That won't be necessary."

Henry grabbed his bag and walked over to an old white pickup truck and unlocked the driver's side door. He tossed his bag across the tattered bench seat and hoisted himself inside.

CHAPTER 7

He'd taken extra precautions, knowing there was a federal task force monitoring his every move. There was the zig-zagging route he'd driven from the parking garage to the MARTA station and the extra stops he'd gotten off and on at. Hopefully, it was enough to keep him cloaked from Miles and his team of federal agents.

Now, with a single bag strapped over his shoulder, Henry took his ticket from the Delta check-in kiosk and meandered to a nearby café, where he ordered a black Americano.

As he blew across the top of his Styrofoam cup and continued toward the gates, he noticed her. On the other side of the terminal, Isabell sat at a high-top outside Pecan Bistro, picking at a warm bagel.

He approached with caution, remembering that she wasn't exactly fond of airports.

"Hey, how's it going?" he asked.

She inhaled with boredom, then expelled a dramatic sigh.

Henry set his bag down and posted up in the chair next to her. He checked their surroundings—a habit he'd formed long ago.

"Flight starts boarding in thirty minutes," she said as she grabbed her carry-on and stood up.

He noticed something different about the way she wore her makeup, but he couldn't quite put his finger on it. "You still afraid of flying?" he asked.

"No. My fear of flying miraculously went away," she snapped with heavy sarcasm.

Henry managed a phony smile and nodded.

"Do we *have* to sit together?" she complained.

"Yes. It's part of our cover."

"Fine. I want the aisle seat."

"It's all yours."

With fake passports in hand, they wove their way through the security line to the first checkpoint. Henry passed their tickets and passports over to the young TSA agent, who ran the documents under a light sensor and handed them back.

They moved further along until they reached the next agent, this one armed with a handheld infrared thermometer, which was pointed at Henry's forehead, then Isabell's. "Thank you, enjoy your flight," the woman offered.

Henry and Isabell continued to Concourse F and arrived at their gate just as the overhead speakers began calling for first-class passengers. They boarded through the jetway in a slow, torturous march like a herd of cattle, found their seats, and settled in for a long flight.

For the next several hours, Henry and Isabell slept in their first-class recliners as the Airbus 350 streaked across the skies over the Atlantic. Eventually, a young blonde appeared in the aisle. "Would you care for coffee or tea?" she asked politely.

Isabell raised her head from the seat. "A coffee would be great. Black, please."

"Yes, ma'am. And for you, sir?"

"Same," Henry replied.

The attendant offered a friendly wink before walking away to the front of the plane. Isabell rolled her eyes with repulsion. The woman returned minutes later with two hot cups of coffee resting on small white plates. Her red lips formed a playful smile as she moved on to the next set of passengers.

Henry sipped his coffee and fumbled with the buttons of a tiny LED television mounted in front of him. He stretched his legs onto the floor and found a channel with current news coverage and weather reports.

"When do we land?" Isabell asked through a tired yawn.

Henry checked his watch. "An hour and forty-five minutes."

She narrowed her eyes at the window beyond him, staring vacantly through it. "Do you trust Darius?"

"Of course I do. We grew up together, we're from the same village. Why, don't you?"

"I have no reason not to," she admitted. "He's always been straight with me. But you Ružaro guys are remarkably shady people. I mean, who the hell just drops a"—she checked over her shoulder and lowered her voice—"a two-million-dollar job on somebody like that? Out of the blue?"

"Oh come on. Darius is fine. He's just trying to make a name for himself. He and Anton have grown close. It's good for him; he deserves it."

"I remember when you two idiots were stealing cars and running insurance scams," she said. "Now look at you, trotting around the globe like criminal masterminds."

A small grin appeared on Henry's face. "He's like a brother to me, you know?"

"Yes, I know. I've heard all the stories. But I think I liked you both better when you were just a couple two-bit thieves terrorizing the suburbs."

The smile slipped away. He turned to the window and stared out into the endless horizon. "You know as well as I do: the risks go up when the price goes up. We just need to do our jobs."

Without replying, she pulled a pair of wireless earbuds from her hoodie pocket and slipped them into her ears. Under the soothing melodies of Ludovico Einaudi, Isabell closed her eyes and focused on her assignment. She envisioned the unhurried energy of Sorrento and its maze of alleys and side streets, piazzas and parks. She drew a map of the city in her mind, then the route from the train station to the hotel—something she'd done in person over a dozen times before.

Isabell didn't have the luxury of being a world-class thief or sharpshooter. She couldn't rappel through the roof of a museum or fend off attackers with her bare hands. She was a freelancer—a person the Ružaro clan referred to as a *tour guide*.

A graduate of Vanderbilt University, the stunning brunette spoke six languages, was an expert in Eastern European cultures, and had long ago mastered the art of modern tradecraft. Depending on her mission, she could either be the Duchess of Edinburgh or a shadow in a dark corner—the choice was hers.

As she drifted off into some brilliant trance, the Airbus began its final approach to Naples International Airport. The grinding metal of the landing gear clamored from beneath the plane. Isabell removed her earbuds and straightened in her chair, her hands gripping the armrest with paralyzing fear.

The aircraft touched down safely on the runway and taxied through the darkness to their gate.

"You okay?" Henry asked.

Isabell got up and snatched her bag from a bin at her feet. "I'm fine. Let's just get off this death trap."

After exiting the plane, they navigated their way through the concourse to the customs checkpoint, where their passports were stamped by a tired agent working the tail end of a night shift.

With no additional luggage to claim, they walked through a wide atrium to the transportation depot outside. As they were greeted by the crisp Mediterranean air, Isabell motioned to a waiting taxi, which promptly pulled up beside them.

A ten-minute ride brought them to Napoli Garibaldi Stazione where they boarded the Circumvesuviana—a local commuter train that wove along the coast connecting Naples to the small, upscale town of Sorrento.

It was nearly six o'clock in the morning as the empty train rambled southbound through the Italian countryside, offering glimpses of the gulf through the hazy darkness. Finally, they arrived at the last stop on the line. Henry and Isabell shouldered their bags and stepped out onto the concrete platform. He followed her through the station and down a series of concrete stairs to the street below. As dawn began to break, they strolled the sidewalk along Corso Italia until they reached Piazza Tasso.

"That's it, over there," Isabell said as she motioned toward Hotel Palazzo Guardati looming from across the main square. They made their way across the street and stepped through the grand entrance into the lobby.

Isabell walked to the counter and shared a few pleasantries with the concierge. After the man checked them in, the two jet-lagged "investors" trudged up a flight of stairs to a white hallway with red carpet.

Isabell stopped halfway up the corridor and slipped her keycard into a door. "I'm going to sleep," she proclaimed. "You're the next room down."

"Sweet dreams," Henry said dryly. "Just come get me when you're ready."

But she'd already closed her door.

He continued to his room where he found a perfectly made bed and an ensemble of spotless furniture. Through the large glass window, the first slivers of sunlight rose over the Picentini Mountains. Henry set his bag onto a dresser and shuffled into the bathroom. He splashed some cold water on his face before retreating to the bed, taking off his clothes, and crawling beneath the sheets.

He slept for several hours until there was a sharp knock at his door. He lifted his head from the pillow and, with a tired yawn, got up and made his way across the room. Through the peephole, he could see the top of Isabell's brown hair, bobbing impatiently, as she waited to be let in. He threw on a pair of slacks and opened the door.

"It's almost noon," she pointed out while brushing quickly past him. "Let's get some fresh air and something to eat."

He pretended not to hear her as he retrieved a blue polo shirt from his bag and pulled it over his head. He searched the floor for a pair of sneakers, then slid them onto his feet.

They left the room and descended through the lobby, then out onto the sidewalk.

Not far from the hotel, they found a table at the outside patio of a wine bar and ordered a plate of local meats and cheeses and warm bread. And after a couple slow glasses of pinot, they paid their tab and strolled the surrounding blocks.

It was an opportunity for Henry to familiarize himself with the operational zone. From behind his sunglasses, he carefully studied the alleyways and fire escapes and other nooks that could serve as an escape route—should he ever need one. He took mental notes of which churches kept their doors open during the day and which businesses had storefront security cameras. It was a task he'd grown used to over the years.

They circled the sidewalks along Porto di Sorrento, overlooking the sea, as a light breeze blew in from the waters below. Henry stared out to the horizon. He couldn't help but feel the romantic energy that swept through the picturesque coastal town.

"What are you thinking so hard about?" Isabell asked.

"Nothing. Just admiring the beauty of this place. It's gorgeous."

"I've always enjoyed coming here. Is this your first time?"

His mind reeled back through an avalanche of memories. "No. I was here once before. But I didn't stay long."

She pushed a strand of loose hair from her face. "Well, hopefully, this op is more fun for you."

"I'm sure it will be."

"Are you worried about tonight?"

"No. Are you?"

"Not really. I just know that these things rarely go as planned."

Henry cut his eyes to the sidewalk beneath his feet. "Well, that's precisely why they sent us and not some new recruits. We'll be fine."

"That's what you said in Monaco," she teased.

"Monaco was different."

"How?"

Henry stopped walking and grabbed her gently by the arm. "Listen, that was a long time ago. And things were very different then."

"You're right. They were." With a swing of her arm, Isabell continued along the sidewalk.

As they reached the marina, she turned up a narrow staircase that brought them to a paved, winding road on the east side of the city. They continued in silence back to the square at Piazza Tasso. There, Isabell ducked beneath a row of hanging vines, emerging onto the patio of a tiny café.

Henry followed her in. "What is this place?"

"It's the best espresso in town," she said as she sat down at a cast-iron table against a stucco wall.

Henry took a seat next to her and folded his arms. "You get one espresso. I don't need you getting jumpy tonight."

She rolled her eyes and signaled the waitress.

They sat quietly for the next half hour as Isabell sipped from her tiny cup. Satisfied, she set four euros on the table and got up from her chair. "I have some work to do," she announced, sliding her sunglasses over her eyes. "I'm going back to the hotel."

Henry nodded without looking up at her. "I'll see you in the lobby at five thirty. I'd like to get to the restaurant early and grab some dinner."

"Are you trying to trick me into a date?" she chided playfully.

"Absolutely not."

"Good. Then I'll see you at five thirty." She turned and walked away, crossing the piazza back to the hotel.

Henry sat for a moment, leering out at the processional of tourists parading through the main square. He eventually got up and circled the block one last time before retreating back to the hotel for a short nap. By five thirty, he was standing in the lobby, waiting patiently with his hands tucked into his charcoal peacoat.

Isabell descended the staircase in a knitted sweater and fuzzy scarf that cascaded down to a pair of designer chinos that hugged her hips perfectly. She'd worn her hair down tonight, he noted with a devious smile. The young brunette played along, winking at him as they came together in the middle of the lobby.

"You look quite dapper," she granted.

"Thank you. But we're business partners, remember?"

Isabell scowled. "We're in Italy, *remember*? The least you could do is pretend you're having a nice time."

"I'm sure I will," he remarked as he turned for the large glass doors.

He accompanied her up the block and across Piazza Tasso to the front of Ristorante Syrenuse, where they were greeted by a small woman in a blue dress.

"*Due per cena*," Henry informed the hostess.

"*Cognome?*" the woman asked.

He shuddered, frozen by the simple question.

"Carlotto," Isabell promptly responded.

The woman flashed a courteous smile and ushered them to a table in the main dining hall.

"Sorry," he apologized under his breath.

Isabell chuckled. "It's fine, you did good."

"Don't let me talk anymore."

"We're American entrepreneurs," she reminded him. "So act like it; mess up your Italian, insult someone by mistake, whatever… it's all perfectly normal."

"I'll do my best," he said as he sat down and glanced at the menu in front of him. "I'm absolutely starving."

"Me too. So where is this private room we're supposed to meet our contact in?" Isabell wondered, craning her neck around the restaurant.

"Behind me, to your right. The hallway leads to at least two private rooms."

"Got it."

His eyes wandered the restaurant, taking note of the patrons and the flow of the room: how many waiters were on staff, the locations of kitchens and bathrooms, which diners were most likely to be members of Hassani's advance team.

It didn't take long to spot them.

"The gardeners are here," he alerted quietly.

"Are you sure?"

"Yes."

It was a two-man team, and he was happy to see them. Their presence was a sign things were on schedule. Anything otherwise would have been peculiar. And Henry didn't like peculiar.

"Now that we've got that solved, let's eat some proper Italian food," he suggested.

"In *Italiano, per favore*," she challenged.

Henry scrunched his face. "*Mangiamo cibo Italiano*," he managed after a moment.

"Very good."

As their eyes met briefly above the table, a waiter slid up beside them. "Ciao," the man offered.

Isabell ignited into a frenzy of Italian—a nauseating volley of conversation between her and the dashing young waiter. Henry watched with disdain. She was just showing off now. Finally, the guy smiled and walked away.

"I hope there was a vodka in there," said Henry. "I don't think I heard vodka."

"The Italian word for vodka is *vodka*," she teased. "And yes, I ordered you one."

"Good."

Henry sat quietly until their drinks arrived. He cast his gaze beyond Isabell's right shoulder to Hassani's men sitting at a table at the front of the restaurant. The big one he named Larry. The smaller one, Moe. The goons were obvious professionals and had quickly identified Henry and Isabell as well.

"Okay, looks like they've made us," Henry whispered as his eyes returned to the table. "The bigger guy is making a phone call."

"Good. Hopefully, we can get this over with sooner than later."

"We're just the couriers," he reminded her.

"I know. But this part always gives me the creeps."

"Hassani will be here soon. Just chill out and enjoy your dinner."

"Fine." Isabell sat back and relaxed her shoulders. "So… what have you been up to?"

"Working, mostly. Trying to keep the dream alive. And you?"

She'd always admired his casual confidence. It was the thing that originally hooked her. "Same. Just working," she answered. "I took a gig with XT Security."

"So, like, what… you're a mercenary now?"

"No," she corrected. "A linguistics instructor."

"Not bad," he said after a sip of vodka. "You've always had a way with words."

"It's stable work. In addition to the rare instances I hear from Darius."

"Did you know I was going to be part of this op?"

"I had a feeling you might be. But I'm a big girl, Henry. I would never let my personal life get in the way of work."

"Of course not," he said with a hint of sarcasm. "Are you gonna quit your gig with XT after this?"

"I have no expectations of Darius coming through with the money," she confided into her wine glass. "Something about this job doesn't add up."

He tightened his brow. "You're talking in circles."

"Am I? This is a ridiculous amount of money just to come here and act as mid-level couriers. Something's not right."

"This is only the first stage; there'll be plenty more for us to do down the road. Besides, if you don't expect to get paid, what are you doing here?"

"I'm a slut for curiosity," she boldly admitted.

Henry dipped his eyes, unable to argue the fact. He unfolded his napkin and placed it on his lap as their food arrived. Isabell had ordered him a plate of tortellini, which she knew he liked. She, however, opted for a cioppino seafood bowl, adorned with fresh herbs and gremolata toast. They ate their meal in comfortable silence, the way they always had, with the light sounds of classical Italian music drifting overhead.

Henry chewed his tortellini and stared at her. A slight movement in the background—just over her shoulder—caught his attention. Larry and Moe were on the move. His eyes shifted to the front of the restaurant where a group of men in tailored suits had just entered. One of them stopped to speak with Larry, who whispered something into the man's ear.

The newcomer was a large Middle Easterner with a short haircut and broad shoulders. He darted his eyes to Henry.

"They're here. I think I just made eye contact."

Isabell shook her head. "Why would you do that?"

"I might've even smiled."

She set her fork on the table and slowly reached for her wine glass. "You're impossible."

As Larry and Moe exited Syrenuse, the four well-dressed men walked toward Henry and continued past, making their way to the back hall.

"Hassani was the third from the front," Henry noted. "Blue suit, white shirt."

"The bartender's with them too," she added. "That makes seven in total."

Henry glanced at his watch. It was three minutes until seven. He wiped his mouth and dropped a hundred euros onto the table. Isabell rose to her feet and joined him in a slow yet determined walk to the back of the restaurant. As they pushed up the hallway, Henry arrived at a door on his right. It was wide open, and the bulkiest of Hassani's men halted them before they could enter.

"You know who we are," Henry said in a light, forceful tone.

The man eyed them cautiously. "Hold out your arms," he instructed. Henry stepped forward and allowed the guard to grope him from chest to ankle. Satisfied, the bruiser moved on to Isabell. "Ma'am, I'm very sorry."

Isabell huffed, then held up her arms. "Make it quick."

The man gently patted her rib cage and waist, swept his hands up her legs, stopping just short of her crotch. He stepped to the side and extended his arm into the room.

Hamad Al Hassani sat at a table in the middle of the large private dining area. In addition to the door man, two other bodyguards lurked threateningly around them.

"Thank you for coming," Hassani greeted. "I'm always happy to hear from Anton Krunoslav and his friends."

"We appreciate you taking time from your busy schedule," Henry replied. "And Anton sends his regards. I can assure you he values the relationship."

Hassani was a bristly, unpolished man, well into his sixties. His thick neck and scarred knuckles revealed a lifetime of backroom deals and street brawls. "So," the billionaire began as he eyed Henry, then Isabell. "Who is the girl?"

"My name is Isabell DiMarco," she answered. "I'm the tour guide."

"I see. And what have you two brought me?"

Henry could feel the prying eyes of Hassani's men bearing down on him. He slowly reached into his coat pocket, pulled out the small capsule, and gently set it on the table.

With a look of disdain, Hassani reached for it and quickly twisted off the top. He pulled a tiny scroll from inside and discarded the metal pill on the table. Slowly and methodically, he began to unroll it.

Hassani took a moment to read the message, then retrieved a Zippo from his pants pocket. He set the small papyrus on fire and tossed it onto the table where it disintegrated into black dust.

"I'm sure you didn't come all this way to tease me," Hassani apprised.

Henry cleared his throat. "I'm afraid I don't know what you mean."

"Is the item secure? It is in Anton's possession?"

"I'm terribly sorry, sir, but I cannot speak to that."

Isabell stood like a statue, keeping close tabs on the wandering guards.

"Where did it come from?" Hassani asked.

Henry smirked. "You know better than that, Mr. Hassani." He could sense one of the guards drawing closer, slithering up behind him like a snake in the grass.

"I think it's time we go," Isabell requested firmly.

Hassani's grin grew wider. "Please, stay and have a drink!"

"No, thank you," Henry refuted. "We have a plane to catch. Anton sends his best wishes and he'll be anxious to hear back from you."

Hassani's smile suddenly vanished and his face was now flush with anger. "You have no idea what it is, do you?"

"We're just the couriers," Henry assured.

But before he could explain any further, the cold, steel barrel of a nine-millimeter was pressed into the back of his head. Henry calmly raised his hands.

"I asked you a fucking question!" Hassani roared.

Isabell shook her head in disappointment. "Respectfully, sir, you're making a huge mistake."

The billionaire raised an eyebrow. "Is that right?"

"Yes," she said with a sharp nod.

An awkward silence hung in the air.

In a sudden flash, Henry spun from the pistol and snatched it from the bodyguard's grasp. He then pulled the man against his chest—using him as a shield—and pointed the nine-millimeter directly at Hamad Al Hassani.

The others had been too slow to react, but one of them now had his sidearm drawn and aimed at Isabell's head.

"Shoot him, Henry," she instructed calmly.

Henry stood firm, his pistol trained on Hassani's body mass as the Qatari sat frozen in his chair.

"My tour guide is no more than collateral damage," Henry threatened. "I promise I'll be the only person to walk out of this room alive."

Hassani sat in silence. After a few tense moments passed, he motioned into the air and the second guard lowered his pistol from Isabell's head and holstered it into his jacket.

"I'm going to need proof of possession," Hassani demanded. "Until then, tell Anton I don't want to hear from him or his couriers."

Henry removed the magazine from the gun, ejected the chambered round, and engaged the release lever, pulling free the slide and barrel. He then tossed the pieces onto the table, where they landed with a metallic *CLANK*. "Thank you for your time, Mr. Hassani. I'll notify Anton that the information has been delivered. But rest assured, you're not the only buyer we have lined up."

Henry pulled a business card from his breast pocket and set it on the table next to the disassembled nine-millimeter. With that, he turned and extended his elbow toward Isabell.

Her face dazzled with pride. She placed her hand against his bicep as he led her out of the room. They slipped through the dining hall and exited the restaurant before disappearing into the shadows of Piazza Tasso.

CHAPTER 8

"I think I've seen enough of Sorrento," she joked quietly as they walked back to their hotel. But instead of going inside, Henry ushered her past the front doors without stopping. "Is everything all right?" she asked.

"We've got a tail—fifty yards behind us. One of Hassani's men from the restaurant."

Isabell tried to gather her senses. Everything inside of her wanted to run as fast as she could—to grab her belongings from the room and hustle out of town in a dizzying sprint. But she knew better. She held his arm firmly and smiled for the sake of any onlookers.

As they approached Basilica di Sant'Antonino, Henry checked the reflection in a shop window; the strange man was still slinking behind them, lurking in the shadows.

He guided Isabell into an alley beside the church, where they followed the cobblestone path around a corner and further into the darkness. They reached the rear entrance of Hotel Palazzo Guardati and dashed up the stairs to their room.

After quickly packing, they grabbed their bags and retreated to the hallway. Downstairs, Isabell crossed the lobby to the front counter and informed the concierge there had been a last-minute change of plans and that they would be leaving for Amalfi immediately.

The man looked her over before taking her key. "*Buonasera, signora*," he said vibrantly as his fingers returned to the keyboard in front of him.

She turned and followed Henry back to the rear exit, where they burst through the door and into the alley, then around the corner toward the bay.

After several blocks, they reached a series of restaurants that overlooked the Tyrrhenian Sea. A set of stairs, carved by hand long ago, led them down to the beachhead. There, Henry peered over his shoulder, then out to the gulf, where the full moon cast its reflection onto the glassy waters.

Isabell stood guard while he jumped over the railing and teetered along a stone seawall. He dropped to one knee and placed his hand on the outside of the façade, blindly feeling for a particular stone as the waves splashed gently beneath him.

There. He felt it.

With an eager tug, Henry removed a rock from the wall and set it in front of him. He reached down again, and this time pulled a .40-caliber Glock from the open crevice. With a beholden exhale, he set the small stone back into place and returned to the stairs, where Isabell breathlessly awaited.

It was a cache that had been set up long ago for Ružaro members operating in Sorrento, and Henry had hoped he would never have to use it.

"What time is it?" Isabell asked.

Henry checked his cell phone. "Seven forty-five."

"Shit!"

"What?"

"The last train leaves in eight minutes."

He shook his head. "We're ten blocks away; we'll never make it."

"Great. Any idea what the hell happened back there?"

"I don't know," Henry said as they began their climb back up the steps. "Maybe Hassani didn't like whatever was written down on that piece of paper."

"Or maybe he didn't like your asshole face."

"I don't think my asshole face had anything to do with it. I have a feeling Hassani doesn't believe we have the stones."

"That's the funny thing," she remarked. "He kept referring to it in singular form."

Henry replayed the conversation in his head. Isabell was right; Hassani had used the words *it* and *the item*. "Yeah, I guess that was a little weird," he mumbled. "But it's the least of our concerns right now. Hassani thinks he's some kind of badass gangster and the last thing I need is to spend the rest of my life in an Italian prison for killing a bunch of Arabs."

"He's not that stupid."

"The hell he isn't!" Henry snapped back. "He just pulled a gun on a Ružaro lieutenant and a tour guide. Nobody's that fucking stupid! And now he's got some asshole tailing us." They reached the top of the steps and turned left at the patio of La Villa Bar. "Let's sit down and have a drink. Figure out how to get back to Naples."

"No, we need to keep moving. If they're as dumb as you say they are, the only way to deescalate the situation is to remove ourselves from the operational zone. Hassani's trying to spook us; we don't need to give him a reason to react."

Henry shook his head in frustration. "Everything has to be by the book, doesn't it? Fine. We'll keep going."

Isabell pulled her cell phone from her purse and dialed a number. After a brief, quiet exchange in Italian, she tucked it away. "The port. Ten minutes," she said.

Henry turned and darted his eyes east, toward the flickering lights of the port below. They navigated the sidewalk overlooking the sea—past groups of drunk tourists gathered along the patio bars—until they reached an elevator that took them back down to sea level.

"Who's your contact?" Henry asked as they reached the bottom and stepped onto a long pier.

"An old friend."

"An old friend? You have to be more specific than that."

Isabell sighed with annoyance. "I hate to break it to you, but your authority ended as soon as we survived the meeting, Henry. We are now in exfil mode—*my* domain. Do you understand?"

"Of course."

She turned and continued to the end of the pier; the low hum of an outboard motor echoed from somewhere in the distance. As it grew louder, Henry could now see the silhouette of a small fishing boat skimming across the water. A man with a medium build rested at the helm as the vessel crept through the darkness and docked at their feet.

"Ciao, Giovanni!" Isabell called into the night.

"Ciao, *bella*!" the man responded gleefully. He held out his hand and guided her aboard.

Henry stood cautiously on the pier. He checked over his shoulder and stared up at the lights of Sorrento looming above them.

"Is he coming with us?" the Italian asked impatiently.

Isabell smirked. "Let's go, Henry. We're on the clock."

After a brief pause, he climbed aboard the craft and studied Giovanni's eyes. The Italian met his gaze and motioned for him to take a seat. Henry found an empty crab cage and dropped onto it as the small boat sputtered from the dock. Through the desolate night, they pushed further into the gulf toward Naples—a mere sixteen miles away.

He sat in silence while Isabell and Giovanni caught up and shared a few laughs. The spectral hush of the sea seemed to calm Henry's nerves, and after a few minutes, he managed to let down his guard and relax.

As the lights of Naples drew closer, Isabell joined him against the cage. She brushed her hair from the wind and tucked it gently behind her ear.

"Everything okay?" she asked.

"Yeah, we're good," Henry replied.

"Good."

"Who's Giovanni?"

She let out a scant laugh before straightening her face. "Why? Are you jealous?"

"Why would I be? He's old enough to be your father."

"And what if he was a gorgeous young stallion with perfect pecs and a chiseled jaw?"

It was an obvious trap. "I wouldn't care any less than I do now," he responded defiantly. The answer seemed to satisfy her. "I'm guessing this is your Italy network?"

"Yes. Giovanni was one of my infil-exfil residents when I worked here with Leffler. I haven't spoken with him in years. We're lucky he's still around."

"Bullshit," Henry charged. "You had him on standby before we even left, didn't you?"

She allowed a guilty shrug. "So I made a few calls. Big deal. It's standard operating procedure. It's also why you guys pay me so well. Besides, I wanted to make sure we weren't operating completely alone out here."

"That's the thing, Isabell. We're *not* operating. We're couriers."

"When guns get drawn, we're operating."

"Fine. I can't argue with that. Either way, I appreciate you staying on your toes."

"Don't mention it," she replied as she cast her eyes across the dark waters. "So I've been meaning to ask, how's Aunt Sara these days?"

The question caught him off guard. "She's doing well. Still living in the same house on the north side. Trying to keep the hardware store going."

"That's good to hear."

"I don't know why she even bothers with that store anymore. Her house is paid off and I take care of everything else. I guess it just reminds her of Luka. He used to work so hard to keep that thing going.”

Isabell smiled as her hair tousled in the wind. “I’m sure it brings her a certain level of peace. She’s a wonderful woman.”

“She asks about you a lot,” he confessed. “Well, not as much as she used to, but every now and then, your name comes up.”

“Well, please tell her I said hello.”

“I will.”

“Are you seeing anyone? Maybe if you were seeing someone, she’d leave you alone.”

“No, not really. You?”

“Yeah,” she said with a nod. “He’s a nice guy. I met him through a friend.”

“What’s his name? What’s he do?”

Her eyes drifted to the floorboard. “His name’s Jacob— he’s a recruiter for the US Marines.”

“Sounds impressive. Are you happy?”

“Of course I’m happy.”

“Good.”

“And you? Are *you* happy?”

“Yeah,” he said into the salty air. “I can’t complain.”

As the boat cut across the water, Isabell nestled closer to him, shielding herself from the wind.

Eventually, the city of Naples began closing in, its fluorescent lights sparkling against the water. Giovanni guided the vessel toward a marina just below Ovo Castle— an imposing seaside fortress that hovered above them like an ancient sentinel.

Henry reached out and grabbed hold of a wooden post and guided the craft against the slip. He leapt onto the dock and panned his eyes across the marina.

Isabell thanked Giovanni for his trouble, kissing him softly on both cheeks. “*Grazie mille. Tante belle cose,*” she told him as she stepped off the boat and found her footing on the dock.

"*In bocca al lupo*!" the captain yelled over the idling engine.

And just as quickly as it had arrived, the boat roared back out to sea. Henry and Isabell watched as it melted into the darkness.

"What does that mean?" Henry asked. "*In bocca al lupo*?"

"In the mouth of the wolf," she answered.

"Sounds reassuring. I'm sure that's a perfectly normal thing to say to someone."

"You'd be surprised."

With a measured sense of relief, they made their way up the gangway to the sidewalk surrounding Ovo Castle. From there, they drifted toward downtown Naples, passing small bistros and bars along the way. As they reached the intersection at Via Partenope, the Grand Hotel Vesuvio leered at them from across the road.

"It's as good as any," suggested Henry.

He led her up the steps and through the infinity doors to the main lobby, where Isabell checked them in under fake names. With room cards in hand, she drifted from the counter to the elevators while Henry waited impatiently, pacing the marble floor.

"I may just get some actual sleep tonight," he grumbled as he pressed the button on the wall.

Isabell looked him over, appreciatively. "You did great tonight, by the way. Really. I mean it. Had you not kept your composure, we might both be dead."

"Well… *you'd* be dead for sure," he noted playfully.

"No, I'm serious, Henry. Thank you."

"You're very welcome," he granted as the elevator opened.

They reached the third floor and lugged their bags into the hallway.

"Now, if you don't mind, I'm going to bed," Isabell announced as she slid her card into the door.

"What's the matter? Too much excitement for one night?"

"Honestly, I found the whole thing to be quite boring. *Buonanotte*, Henry."

"Goodnight," he whispered as she shut the door. Henry continued up the hall to his room. He went inside, slung his bag onto the carpet, and dropped face-first onto the bed. Turning over, he stared at the ceiling—envisioning her perfect emerald eyes—until he fell asleep.

CHAPTER 9

Darius eyed them from across the kitchen table. "So what's the problem?"

"Hassani drew guns on us!" Henry snarled.

"We're not selling insurance here, bro. This is one of the largest shadow market deals to ever go down. The asset is essentially priceless; you have to expect things to get a little tense."

Isabell leaned in with a discerning look. "It's not priceless if there's a number attached to it, Darius."

"Fine," the captain conceded. "But Hassani isn't going to just cough up hundreds of millions of dollars without—"

"Without what?" she interrupted.

"Without testing us," admitted Darius. "Quit acting like babies. Christ, Henry's had at least six guns pointed in his face this year alone!"

Henry confirmed with a reluctant nod.

Isabell wasn't impressed. "So what now?"

"You both look like hell. Why don't you go home and get some sleep."

Henry stood from the table and began pacing the kitchen floor. "How about a drink first?"

"It's eight o'clock in the morning," Darius reminded him.

"You two enjoy yourselves," Isabell granted. "I'm going home."

Darius stood up and gave her a warm hug. "I'll be in touch in a few days. Thanks for everything, Isabell."

"Let me know how everything goes," she said as she marched through the living room and out the front door.

Henry pinned his elbows on the table. "Hassani doesn't think we have it," he revealed quietly.

"Do you blame him?"

"Tell me what it is, Darius. I mean, this has to be one hell of a load… you're using *me* as a goddamn courier. And Hassani? The whole thing stinks."

Darius threw his head back. He glared at Henry with a sense of apathy. "I can't tell you what it is yet."

"Are you serious with this shit right now?"

"I'm sorry, Henry. My hands are tied." Darius shook his head, searching for cover.

"Fuck it. I see how it is. You don't trust me anymore."

"Trust can be a double-edged sword, bro. I don't want to put you in any unnecessary danger right now. But at the next stage, I promise you'll know everything."

"It doesn't really matter." Henry feigned disinterest. "And obviously Isabell couldn't care less, so why should I?"

"Good. Then there's nothing to be upset about."

Henry locked eyes with his best friend. "Yeah, you're right. Now, if you don't mind, I'm going home to clean up before heading over to the warehouse."

"All right, I'll meet you over there this afternoon."

Henry ambled out to the driveway and into his car. He returned home and took a long, hot shower, followed by a fresh cup of coffee on the balcony. He rehearsed in his mind the conversation he'd have with Miles. Surely, his handler would send another signal soon.

With a stretch of his arms, he went back inside and pulled a navy-blue suit from his closet.

It was late Monday morning and the last of the rush hour commuters were slithering downtown. He arrived at

Scranton and Brooks and navigated his way underground—to the opposite side of the block—and emerged in the maintenance room of the Capital Transit Building.

He stepped onto the warehouse floor and looked out at his crew, who buzzed around like a swarm of worker bees. A fleet of forklifts hurried from the loading bay to the storage depot—then back again—under the loud droning whine of their engines. The slamming of pallets and cargo boxes clamored from every direction. It was the sound of progress.

"Henry!" a voice shouted from across the floor.

It was Hudson Rukov—a tall, stocky, ruthless member of Anton's gang. He'd been promoted to captain years before Darius had, but he was often seen as the weaker of the two. Regardless, Henry maintained a high level of respect for the man.

"Hudson, good to see you," he greeted with a firm handshake. "How's the west side treating you?"

"Not bad. Is Darius around today?"

"He'll probably be here before too long. Anything I can help with?" Rukov's devious grin was a dead giveaway. "Ah," Henry said with a glint of acknowledgment. "The stabilizer fins."

The tall Croatian nodded.

"Arrived yesterday from Houston," Henry announced as he began marching deeper into the warehouse.

Rukov followed closely behind. "They shipping back out today?"

"Where's your buyer?" Henry asked as he examined a tall stack of wooden crates.

"Thailand."

"All right, let's have a look." He continued to examine the wooden crates as he opened an app on his cell phone and began scrolling. "We should have it out of here this evening, Hudson. She'll set sail from Savannah on Wednesday. Final destination: Bangkok."

Hudson patted him on the shoulder. "That's perfect. Thank you."

"Top-of-the-line hardware you got here," Henry noted as he scanned the shipping label with his phone. "Nice score."

"You have no idea what we went through to get these bad boys. Thanks again for the update."

"Anytime. Just give me a call next time. I could've given you that over the phone."

"Nah, I wanted to see them with my own eyes." Hudson turned and headed for the exit. "Give Darius my best!"

"Will do!" Henry shouted back.

He watched the man disappear, then made his way to the other side of the warehouse to the break room. It was a small lounge with worn carpet and a wide window that offered a view of the loading docks. Against the back wall, Henry slammed his fist against a soda machine, which quickly dropped a cold can of Coke into the shoot. He pulled it out, popped open the top, and took a long, satisfying drink.

With a deep exhale, he stepped over to the window and gazed out at his tiny empire. As his eyes panned across the warehouse, he was reminded of his early days coming up in the organization—working long hours loading and unloading trucks, one after the other, until the morning shift melted into the night shift. He used to wonder how so many products could come and go through a single building, how so many boxes of random goods could be controlled by one man.

But those days were behind him.

As his mind drifted, a familiar face appeared on the warehouse floor. Henry set his soda can on a foldout table and watched as Darius navigated his way toward the break room.

The captain burst in with a wide grin. "Hey, brother, you feeling better?"

"I'm surviving," Henry replied. "You just missed Rukov. He came to check on those stabilizing fins for the RPGs he picked up in Boston."

"Right on. What'd you tell him?"

"I told him they'd be leaving the port by Wednesday."

"Perfect. I know he was excited about those things."

Henry paced the room, eyeing his friend with an impatient gaze. "Any updates on our new prize?"

"Maybe."

"What do you mean *maybe*?"

"Anton's coming in from Miami tomorrow," Darius revealed as he sat down in an orange plastic chair. "He wants to see us."

"Tomorrow? What time?"

"Seven. Why don't I pick you up at five thirty? We'll grab some dinner first."

"Sounds like a plan," Henry said with little enthusiasm.

An uneasy hush fell over the room.

"Is everything okay?" Darius finally asked.

Henry's eyes shifted to the window. "Yeah, I'm good. Just a lot going on."

"I'm sorry about the whole Isabell thing. It just… I don't know… the crew just got put together like that. My hands were tied, I didn't have a choice."

"It's no big deal. We actually got along just fine."

"Well, I'm glad to hear it. And I had no idea Hassani would pull a stunt like that. I'm sure it was all—"

"Darius," Henry cautioned. "I said it was no big deal."

"Fine. I'll leave it alone."

"Thank you."

"Well, on to more pressing issues. Anton's pretty excited about the upcoming score. It'll be good to catch up with him—get you more involved."

"What's he so excited about?" Henry retorted. "We don't even have a buyer yet. Sorrento was an epic failure."

"Hassani's still in play," assured Darius. "Besides, if he bails, we just line up someone else. Relax, brother. We're good here."

Henry turned up the corner of his mouth and glanced at his friend. "I trust you. If you say it's right… then it's right."

"It's right. Now listen, I hate to do it, but I've gotta run upstairs and make a few calls. I'll see you tomorrow around five thirty?"

"I'll be ready." Henry took one last swill from the can before tossing it into the trash. For the next hour, he watched through the glass as the warehouse team hauled televisions, solar panels, and other random items from the trailers to the depot. As the last of the afternoon's trucks pulled away from the loading dock, Henry slipped unnoticed into the cavernous tunnels below.

Minutes later, he emerged from the bookshelf in his office at Scranton and Brooks. As the wall behind him slowly melted back into place, Henry sat down at his desk and retrieved a small key from his sportscoat. He slipped it into a keyhole in the top drawer and turned it clockwise. Inside was a field laptop, protected on all sides with polished titanium and black rubber padding. He set it on the desk and peeled it open.

His fingertips danced along the keyboard as he logged in to a secure portal and began scrolling through a lengthy index of code. After several minutes, he found a line he liked. He clicked on it and watched as the screen uploaded a live video link, intercepted from a Chinese satellite orbiting above the Atlantic.

He leaned in closer, squinting at the high-resolution images of the Brazilian coastline. There was a fleet of shipping vessels spread across the vast blue ocean, coming and going from South America's array of ports.

With a sense of discouragement, Henry sat back and rubbed his eyes. It was pointless, he told himself. He didn't even know what he was looking for, and even if he did, he wouldn't be able to distinguish it from any other normal oceanic activity.

He minimized the satellite window and brought up the Ružaro distribution database. He entered several keywords into the search bar: BRAZIL. ATLANTIC. DIAMONDS.

Nothing.

He checked the internal manifests but couldn't find a single shipment that he didn't already know about. There were no items or assets that had been flagged for increased security or special treatment.

Whatever was coming in from Brazil was being moved covertly.

The whole thing aggravated him. There were no pieces to put together, no clues to follow, or red flags to identify. All he had to go on was Darius' word—and for some reason, that didn't feel as comforting as it once did.

He closed the laptop, returned it to the drawer, and locked it away. He then left his office and, with a few quiet goodbyes, passed through the lobby and outside to his car.

As he pulled out of the lot, he saw Miles' signal. Only this time, it was in the form of a pink-and-turquoise bicycle resting ominously across the street, chained to the bike rack outside Maggie's Coffee House. It was the same old Schwinn cruiser he'd seen a handful of times before.

His Maserati detoured east through Virginia Highlands, then south toward Little Five Points. He found a parking space on the curb in front of a produce market on Moreland Avenue and set out on foot. A brisk walk south took him to one of his favorite food trucks. He ordered a cheesesteak and bottled water.

He strolled to the intersection of Euclid Avenue and crossed the street. Nearby, an iron bench rested beneath a canopy of trees. Henry took a seat and unwrapped his sandwich.

Minutes later, a grizzled man in torn jeans and a t-shirt—with a newspaper under his arm—ambled up the sidewalk and sat down beside him.

"How we doing today?" Miles asked from behind a dark pair of sunglasses. He opened his newspaper and began scanning the headlines.

"Not bad," Henry replied with a mouthful of cheesesteak.

"Anything on the research vessel?"

"No."

"And your new buyers?"

Henry scoffed. "Yeah, a Qatari business mogul. Real nice guy."

"I'll bet."

"So, how are your friends at the task force?"

"They're doing well, keeping busy."

"Are there eyes on us right now?"

"No," Miles assured from behind the newspaper. "We're good."

"And you'll let me know when that changes?"

"Absolutely. You have my word."

"Darius lied to me about Brazil," Henry confessed abruptly. "He never told me he was down there."

Miles took it in—the information was curious. "Why would he do that?"

"Operational protocol, I guess."

"I see. And does that upset you?"

Henry shifted on the bench. His eyes remained locked ahead of him. "Not really. He's just protecting me."

"So tell me about this Qatari. What's his name?"

"I told you not to jam me up on this," Henry quietly urged. "And you know I'm not going to give you a name. I'm sure you can figure it out on your own."

"Have you met with him yet?"

"Yesterday. Southern Italy."

Henry and Miles had been working together for a little over four years. They'd formed a strong bond, but it had always been a complex game of chess. Henry would offer vague information—just enough to send Miles on a scavenger hunt of hotel records and flight lists that would eventually lead him to places like Sorrento and people like Hamad Al Hassani.

Miles allowed a smirk. "I'll be sure to check it out."

"And in case you're wondering, it didn't go well. Isabell was with me."

The agent dropped the newspaper into his lap, but recovered quickly and pulled it back to his face. "You have to be shitting me."

"Nope. She was there."

"What was that like?"

Henry smiled into his sandwich. "The meeting with the buyer pretty much fell apart. But everything went well between her and me."

"She really screwed you over, Henry. I'm shocked you didn't kill her."

"Well, I didn't."

"And how's she doing?"

"She seems good. Working in linguistics, dating some marine recruiter named Jacob."

"That doesn't burn you up?"

"I'm over her, Miles. I've been over her for quite some time."

"Whatever you say."

"Are we done?" snapped Henry.

Miles checked over his shoulder, then the other. "What's the price tag on your package?"

"I actually don't know. But it's a lot."

"I'm sure it is," the agent noted. "Listen, if you're trying to pull off grand larceny right under my nose, especially one that's going to end up on my desk anyways, our relationship's gonna fizzle real fast. Should I remind you of our agreement?"

"No."

"And that Hartsfield shit was brazen betrayal, by the way. You're making me look like a fool."

"I've already apologized for that. It won't happen again. But believe me, this one isn't coming up on anyone's radar."

"Let's keep it that way." Miles turned the page of his paper. "All right, I guess we're done. Be safe out there, Henry."

"You too, Miles."

Henry rose from the bench and began hiking back up Moreland Avenue to the market, where he got into his Maserati and drove away.

CHAPTER 10

The next morning brought heavy rains. The stench of fast food and body odor filled the suite on the twenty-first floor of the Marriott Buckhead. Miles entered with caution, unsure of what to expect.

"Agent Brennan," Harwick announced. "Thanks for joining us."

Miles paced over to the broad reflection windows at the end of the room and greeted the NSA agent with a firm handshake.

Nearby, Officer Garza sat idly behind two high-focus lenses aimed at Anton Krunoslav's residence.

"He won't be home until tonight," Harwick began. "We don't have the best visual from here, but we can at least keep track of general movement—who's coming and going, that sort of thing."

"Looks good," Miles granted. "Anything from the drones over the Atlantic?"

"Nothing yet. The crew sends a submersible down twice a day but we still have no idea what they're looking for. Anything from your end?"

"Well, I may have something. It seems an upper-level lieutenant met with a foreign associate in Sorrento, Italy, the other night. I think Anton is setting up a fence."

Harwick leaned back and tapped his chin. "Interesting. A fence for what, though?"

"No idea."

"You think it's connected to our ocean expedition?"

"I think it's highly probable. I stumbled across one of Anton's guys leaving the country under a fake passport; he landed in Naples on Sunday. That same day, Hamad Al Hassani—a former politician from Qatar who's been known to dabble in the arms market—checked into a hotel in Sorrento with an entourage. I'm pretty sure the two connected at some point."

Harwick grunted. "Seems flimsy. Who's Anton's lieutenant?"

"A guy by the name of Henry Sirola, professional art and jewel thief."

The task force leader drifted deep into thought, trying his best to connect the dots. "I don't see it," he said at last, shaking his head. "But who knows. If Krunoslav's mining anything of value, which he likely is, he'll be looking to unload it. And while this Sirola kid going to Italy is worth noting, we still don't know what Krunoslav's searching for at the bottom of the Atlantic. Until we do, we have to assume it's just another fence being set up for some stolen cell phone parts or something."

"You're probably right," Miles agreed. "So what's next?"

"Have you spoken with your informant?"

"I have."

"And? Any new intel?"

Miles tilted his head. "No, sir. Just the tip-off on Sirola's Italy trip."

"At some point, whatever's going on with that research vessel is going to trickle its way through the organization. And I want to know when it does."

"You and me both. I'll keep my ear to the ground and make sure we're getting regular updates from the Shadowmaker."

Harwick stared blankly out the window. "Good. In the meantime, we're placing surveillance on two Ružaro captains who were photographed with Krunoslav in Brazil: Hudson Rukov and Darius Martović."

"That sounds like a good call. They're both pretty high-level guys."

"I'm assigning you and Garza to Martović."

Miles nodded. "Perfect. I'll set everything up this afternoon. We've got a utility van outfitted with some decent gear."

"It'd be nice to have ears inside his house. Any chance we can get something installed?"

Miles sighed with apprehension. "We've tried bugging a few of these guys' residences in the past. Just getting *in* is damn near impossible most of the time. But… Martović lives in a single-family residence, much easier than the high-rises most of these guys stay in. We might be able to pull something off."

"If you hit any snags, I can put in a call and have my guys get it done."

Miles raised an eyebrow. "Is that some sort of interagency jab, Agent Harwick?"

The NSA man grinned.

Miles wandered over to the window and gazed out at the Park Avenue building. The top two floors were empty—for now.

Across the room, Garza fidgeted in his chair. The DCIS officer leaned over his laptop, his eyes darting from pixel to pixel. "You guys may want to check this out," he alerted. "We have divers."

Harwick's head swiveled with surprise. "Divers?"

"Yes, sir. *RV Tiger Claw* has four divers in the water."

Miles and Harwick rushed across the room and hovered over Garza's shoulder. They watched the grainy black-and-white footage: four men bobbing in the water. Suddenly, they dropped beneath the waves.

"They were gearing up on the deck," said Garza. "At first, I couldn't exactly tell what they were doing. Then I noticed the oxygen tanks."

"Four of them?" asked Harwick.

"Yes, sir."

Miles squinted at the screen. "Is this video in real time?"

"It is. Three-second delay, at best."

"Have the divers ever gone down before?"

"No. Up until now, it's just been the sub."

Miles and Harwick locked eyes. Whatever Anton Krunoslav was looking for, he'd found it.

For the next thirty minutes, they watched the screen in captivated silence, until the divers finally reemerged from the water. But they weren't carrying anything nor had they attached any lines to the crane mounted to the deck. They simply pulled themselves aboard and began shedding their diving gear.

The agents kept their eyes glued to the monitor, quietly observing the divers and crew huddled on the ship's deck; there had to be ten of them now.

Then it happened. The small crowd that had gathered on the screen began celebrating wildly, high-fiving one another and dancing around the deck like wild savages.

Miles leaned in closer. "Whatever their mission was, they just accomplished it."

"How? Are they sending the submersible back down to retrieve something?" Harwick wondered.

"I don't think so, sir." Garza reached over and pointed to the corner of the screen. "They're firing up the engines and pulling anchor."

"Fuck!" Harwick snapped. He loosened his tie and began pacing around the room. "You two go ahead and get Martović under surveillance. I'll put another team on Rukov. I'm sure this will trigger some kind of movement, so we need to be ready."

Miles chewed at his bottom lip. "Can we intercept any of the transmissions coming from the ship?"

"No," said Harwick. "I don't have anything active in that area other than the drone. But asking the CIA to go from overhead surveillance to radio intercepts is a big jump. They'll never go for it."

Miles stood upright with his hands on his hips. "All right, I'll go ahead and get everything set up at Martović's residence. Garza, can you go get a tail on him?"

Garza nodded. "Sure, where should I start looking?"

"More than likely he's still at work over at the Capital Transit warehouse."

The DCIS officer rose from the desk, gathered his backpack, and bolted for the door. "I'll let you know when I've got him."

Miles stayed behind, his gaze fixated on the Park Avenue building across the street. "What do you think they found?" he asked quietly. "I know you have a theory."

Harwick sat down in front of the window and clasped his hands in front of his chin. "I honestly have no idea," he confessed after a while. "At first I thought it was something sinister: a dirty bomb or a piece of top-secret military technology."

"But you don't think that anymore?"

"No. The more I learn about Anton Krunoslav, the less I think he's a national security threat. He's more likely to be salvaging an old shipwreck for treasure chests and ancient pottery."

Miles chuckled. "Yeah, that sounds more like Ružaro to me."

"Whatever it is, it may give us something to shake him down with. As much as I'd like to throw a wrench in his little oceanic expedition, the real objective is to bring him down for larceny, racketeering, and about a dozen murder charges. We just need a foot in the door. If we can pull just one tiny pebble, the whole damn castle will collapse."

Miles strode with determination toward the door. "I'll check in with you later, Harwick." He hurried downstairs and climbed into his Suburban. As he coasted into Midtown, he reached toward the center console and pressed a name on the screen. The line rang twice through the car speakers before Tisdale answered. "Hey, David, we've got movement on the research vessel. I need the plumbing truck ready within the next hour. Is that possible?"

"Sure, I think we can accommodate that. Are you on your way now?"

Miles pumped his fist into the air. "I sure am."

"Okay, give us twenty minutes. What happened with the boat?" Tisdale asked.

"Divers went down, then came back up. Next thing you know, they're pulling anchor and heading back to Brazil."

"Divers? Sounds like they found something."

"Yeah, I'd say so. I think something big is coming down the pipe, David. I'll see you in a bit." Miles ended the call and floated the SUV east through the city.

He arrived at the FBI field office and hustled into the building. He took the stairs to the second floor and barreled into Tisdale's office. "David, how we looking?"

The special agent-in-charge gazed up from a stack of paperwork. "Your van should be ready in five. The techs are just wrapping up now."

"Thanks. Any chance I can get a bug in Martović's house?"

"Under what evidence am I supposed to get a warrant for that?"

"FISA maybe?"

"Please," Tisdale said with a snort. "You're going to need more than a research vessel and a team of divers for that."

"How about a meeting in Italy between a Ružaro lieutenant and Hamad Al Hassani?"

"Hamad who?"

Miles shook his head in defeat. "Never mind."

"Listen, I know you want these guys, but we can't go throwing warrants around because of shady meetings and research vessels."

"Meetings," Miles echoed under his breath. "That's it! His meeting with Neilson!"

Tisdale scowled. "I'm not following."

"I think the previous meeting between Krunoslav and Arthur Neilson is enough to get a warrant. Especially considering Krunoslav's ties to Croatia and the possibility he's hunting a lost nuclear warhead."

Tisdale furrowed his brow. "Did you actually *see* a nuclear warhead?"

"No. But we can't exactly rule it out, can we? There isn't a judge in the country that would turn down a warrant request for that type of threat. The potential consequences are too dangerous to ignore."

"Do you really think the man's pulling a nuclear warhead from the ocean?"

"Of course not, but it doesn't matter what I think. I just need a judge to consider the possibility."

Tisdale stared a hole in him. "Fine. I'll try to get a warrant. Give me two hours. In the meantime, go ahead and get in position; we'll send in the AV team once we get a judge to sign off."

A wide grin swept across Miles' face. "Thank you, David!" he shouted as he rushed out of the room.

He took the elevator to the basement, where a team of technicians was putting the final touches on a mobile communications post. It was an old white van with a peeling blue logo on each side that read Anderson Plumbing.

A skinny technician stepped out of the sliding door and handed Miles a set of keys. "She's all yours, Agent Brennan. You've got everything you need from the receiving end. The hardware team will meet you on location as soon as possible."

"Best crew in the country, I swear to God," Miles declared as he snatched the keys and climbed behind the steering wheel.

The tech wiped his brow and shook his head. "Just bring her back in one piece."

Miles fired up the engine. Through a cloud of exhaust, the old van rumbled out from beneath the FBI building and onto a side street that took him back to the interstate. He exited a few miles north of downtown, then wove through Piedmont Heights to the upscale neighborhood of Ansley Park. He pulled a dark blue ball cap onto his head as he drove slowly past Darius' house. The old van continued for a few more blocks, then turned around. On the second pass, he found a spot against the curb two houses away. The rain was coming in waves now.

Miles pulled out his radio and brought it to his lips. "Phantom Two, are you in place?"

"Affirmative. Phantom Two is on location at the warehouse," Garza reported.

"You have eyes on target?"

"Roger that, Phantom One. Target is here."

"Copy that," said Miles. "Let me know when he leaves. Phantom One out."

"Good, copy. Phantom Two out."

Miles set the handheld onto the dash and relaxed in his seat. He tapped his fingers against the steering wheel and rocked his head to a song that wasn't playing. After several minutes of boredom, he ducked into the back of the van and slipped into a pair of blue coveralls.

Moments later, the bay doors flung open and the plumber stepped out into the pelting rain. He set a large compression pump on the pavement, then laid a long piece of yellow tubing down next to it. The final touch was a pair of orange traffic cones strategically placed at both ends of the vehicle.

Satisfied, he crept back into the van, shut the bay doors, and settled onto a metal stool in front of three computer monitors. The compression pump he'd left outside was equipped with a small camera, offering a clear view of Darius' property.

The next thirty minutes passed with little excitement. Miles sat restlessly in the back of the van, staring through the screen at an empty house.

His cell phone buzzed. He checked the screen; it was a text message from Tisdale.

GOT THE WARRANT. LANDSCAPERS ETA 5 MIN

Excitement swelled through Miles as a wave of thunder crashed above the van. He waited patiently for the AV team to arrive, and five short minutes later, a landscaping truck with a trailer full of mowers, trimmers, and other equipment came to a stop in front of Darius' house.

A ragtag crew emerged from the truck and went to work. Among them was a large, athletic Black man who wandered over to the gate and injected a small wire into the keypad. Within seconds, the iron gates slowly began to open.

As Miles watched from the van, three of the landscapers slipped around the side of the house and in through an open first-floor window. It took the technicians no more than eight minutes to set a series of microphones around Darius' residence. They accessed the home security cameras, erased the last eight minutes of footage, and ran an interceptor line from the main box.

Outside, live footage from the inside of Darius' home appeared on one of the monitors in front of Miles.

"Video check," a voice rattled over the radio.

"Affirmative," Miles responded. The FBI agent watched the screen as one of the technicians stepped to the center of the living room and stared into the camera.

"Audio?" the man asked into the air.

"Affirmative," Miles said again. "All systems go. Get your asses out of there."

The men gathered their gear and quickly left the same way they'd entered. Miles peered anxiously through the windshield as they climbed back into their truck and drove away.

The agent watched the monitors with anticipation. Suddenly, the radio came to life in the front passenger seat.

"Phantom One, this is Phantom Two. Do you copy?"

Miles reached for the handheld. "Copy that, Phantom Two. Go ahead."

"Delta Target has left the warehouse. We're merging northbound onto I-85. Headed your way."

"Got it. Peel off at Sixteenth and meet me at the Artmore Hotel."

"Roger that. Phantom Two out."

Miles opened the back door and leapt onto the pavement. He tugged the bill of his hat against his brow and grabbed the compression pump. He loaded it into the van, followed by the yellow tubing and both orange cones.

Moments later, the old plumbing van pulled off the curb and made its way south through Ansley Park. As it crested the intersection of Peachtree Street, Miles noticed Darius' Porsche in the opposite lane, coming toward him. He kept his head down as the sportscar blew past.

The agent turned right onto Sixteenth Street, then parked the van behind the Artmore Hotel. He cut the engine and ducked into the back to watch the monitors.

He waited for several minutes before Garza's SUV pulled into the lot and parked next to him. The DCIS officer jumped out and quickly hoisted himself into the back of the van. He swept the rain from his shoulders and tossed his backpack onto the table.

"Nice to see you, Officer Garza." Miles pulled a second stool from beneath the thin table. "Have a seat. We've got live audio and video from his living room, garage, first-floor hallway, and the front and back doors."

Garza sat down and narrowed his eyes at the screen. He and Miles watched intently as Darius parked his car in the garage and continued to his expansive living room. They sat in silence, fixated on the monitors, observing Darius' every move: to the fridge for a bottled water, to the foyer to sift through some mail, then to the couch where he sat, then sat some more.

Garza shifted anxiously on his stool. "Your AV guys got in and out pretty quick. Any issues?"

"No. Eight minutes flat. Bang, bang."

"That's impressive. So now what?"

Miles looked at him curiously. "What do you mean?"

"Sorry. I guess now we wait."

"Is this your first time in the field, Garza?"

The DCIS officer lowered his eyes. "With the exception of Afghanistan, yes. I don't spend a lot of time in the field."

"Afghanistan? Really?"

"Yes. Really."

"Where in Afghanistan?"

Garza removed his rain-soaked jacket and folded it over his leg. "Look, I'm a profiler, Agent Brennan. But I did five months with a small task force at Bagram when we were hunting al-Zawahiri. They needed a few analysts on the ground… so there I was."

"That's pretty damn cool," said Miles. "I did a few tours in Iraq when I was younger."

"Yeah, I remember seeing that in your bio."

"You did, huh?"

"Anbar Province was no joke back then," acknowledged Garza. "You were a war hero."

Miles shook off the compliment. "Hardly."

"Saving the lives of six Rangers is nothing to scoff at. Fallujah, right?"

"Yeah."

"First or second battle?"

"The first," Miles replied mawkishly. "It was a fucking nightmare." He sat for a moment in silence, taking himself back to a time he'd rather forget. "We were doing door-to-door just after sunset, blowing holes in the sides of these brick homes to avoid booby traps at the front entrances. We hit this one house and rushed in through the rubble—dust was everywhere, the molecules floating around the room were covered in it. We pretty much walked into a hornet's nest. Luckily, no one was killed."

"There was a sniper," added Garza, remembering what he'd read in the report.

"Yeah, there was a sniper."

"I still don't know how you did it."

Miles chuckled. "It's funny what your mind and body will do in the heat of a firefight."

"What happened next?"

"You read the report. You know what happened."

Garza smiled and turned his attention back to the monitors. "Yes, I do. You raced to the top of an adjacent building and ambushed a sniper who had six of your friends pinned down in an alley. They found three bullets in you when they pulled you out."

Miles shook his head. "I don't really remember much of it, to be honest."

"You're a brave man, Agent Brennan. I respect that."

"Well, you shouldn't. Three of those six soldiers were KIA within the next week, so it really didn't matter."

"I'm sorry to hear that. And the other three?"

"They survived the war. But one was killed in a bar fight in Mexico, another hanged himself from a bridge when he got home, and the third is now homeless somewhere in Nebraska."

They sat in silence—allowing the tragic weight of reality to hang in the air—as a set of dark clouds gave way to a sliver of sunlight. Slowly, the sky above them peeled open.

A familiar voice crackled over the radio. "Phantom One, this is Evergreen. Do you copy?"

Miles snatched the device from the table. "Go ahead, Evergreen."

"What's your status?" Harwick asked brusquely.

"I'm with Phantom Two near Delta Target's residence. We've got AV linked up, all eyes on location."

"Good. Let us know if you get any movement."

"Roger that," Miles confirmed. "Phantom One out."

For the next few hours, they watched the Ružaro captain eat leftovers, swim laps in the pool, drink beer, and peck away at his smartphone. To their growing irritation, Darius Martović was a remarkably normal human being.

Miles huffed at the monitors and threw his hands on top of his head. "What do you think they found at the bottom of the ocean?"

Garza leaned back in his chair, rubbing at his face with exhaustion. "Who the hell knows. I wouldn't even be able to make an educated guess at this point."

"It's not a nuke. And we all know it isn't."

"No. It's not a nuke."

"So what are we chasing here, Garza? I feel like there might be something you guys aren't telling me."

"Look, Agent Brennan, these guys are unpredictable. Anton Krunoslav has his hands in multiple markets and underground networks. Your guess is as good as mine. But I promise there's nothing we're keeping from you."

"How long have you been working with Agent Harwick?"

"Two weeks," answered Garza. "I got a call, out of the blue, that some intel we were collecting on an arms dealer in Mexico somehow tied back to that meeting between Krunoslav and Arthur Neilson. Originally, we thought Neilson was trading top-secret defense technology to the cartels. Turns out he was simply acting as a middleman between Krunoslav and the Brazilian Port Authority. They were paying a fee for the safe passage of the research vessel."

Miles quickly began connecting the dots. "And they were running the whole operation out of Atlanta and Miami?"

"Bingo," said Garza. "Which is what brought us to you."

Outside the van, the sun beat down against the wet asphalt, producing a thin layer of mist above the road.

As Miles stared at the screens, one of them went blank, then another. "What the fuck?" he blurted.

Garza checked the cables on the back of the monitors. "I got nothing."

"Shit! The goddamn cams went out!"

"How is that possible?"

Miles scrunched his face. "Who knows."

"What kind of hardware did you guys install?"

"The FBI kind. Do we still have audio?"

Garza leaned over and transferred the audio cable to a small speaker on the utility shelf. "Yeah, we've still got audio."

"So the only video I have left is his hallway? What good is that gonna do?"

"I guess we can watch him walk to his bedroom before he falls asleep," Garza remarked dryly.

Miles slammed his palm against the table and stood up.

"Luckily, the weather just cleared up," Garza noted as he reached for his backpack.

"And how does that help us, exactly?"

The DCIS officer set a plastic case onto the table, opened it, and produced a small aerial drone. It was no bigger than a cell phone with four tiny propellers mounted to its top. "This has a 4K camera and can read a newspaper from a thousand feet away," Garza explained. "It also has a range of twelve miles and, with a full charge, can operate for up to five hours."

"And let me guess: a person wouldn't be able to hear drone blades from a thousand feet away, would they?"

Garza's face beamed with pride. "No, they would not."

The officer reached back into his bag and pulled out a handheld controller with several buttons and a joystick. He pushed open the back door of the van and tossed the small drone into the air, where its propellers quickly engaged and lifted it above the pavement.

As the little gadget zipped upward into the clouds, Garza flipped a switch on his remote and the overhead footage came to life on the monitors.

Miles watched with excitement while Garza maneuvered the drone across Sixteenth Street and over the treetops of Ansley Park. Finally, Darius' home appeared on the screen.

"Climbing to one thousand feet," Garza announced.

The drone's camera zoomed in and they could now see Darius Martović sitting in a chair on his back deck, enjoying the clear skies and sunshine. The agents watched for nearly an hour as the Ružaro captain toiled with his digital tablet and sipped a can of beer. Then, the hushed ring of a cell phone chimed through the tiny speakers on the van's shelf.

Garza leaned forward, examining the screen with intensity. "He's getting a call."

"From who?"

"I don't know."

"Is it Krunoslav?"

Garza shook his head. "I can't tell. I wish he'd go inside; our audio still works in there. All we've got now is what the drone's picking up."

Their eyes remained fixated on the monitor. They watched with eager curiosity—Darius was speaking quietly to someone on his phone. But they couldn't hear a single word.

"Headphones!" Miles demanded. "Crank it up through the headphones!"

Garza ripped two sets of headphones off the shelf, handed one to Miles, then plugged them both into the back of the monitor.

"I can't believe you found it!" they could hear Darius shouting. *"How deep was it?"*

Miles held his breath, pressing the headset tighter against his ears. "Who the hell's he talking to?"

"I have no idea."

"Wow!" the Ružaro captain continued. *"That's great news... All right, I'll see you tonight."*

With that, the call came to an abrupt end.

Their headphones fell silent.

"Was that who I think it was?" Garza quietly asked.

"Yeah, I'm pretty sure it was."

"Martović asked how 'deep' it was."

"He sure as shit did." Miles reached for his radio and brought it to his mouth. "Evergreen, this is Phantom One. Do you copy?"

"What's your status, Phantom One?"

"Delta Target just received a call. We think it was from Alpha Target."

"Are you sure?"

Miles looked to Garza, who confirmed with a nod. "We're almost certain."

"What did they discuss?"

"They were excited about something. Delta Target asked Alpha how 'deep' it was. He said he 'couldn't believe' they 'found it.'"

"Found what?"

"They didn't mention anything specific. Are you still with the team in Buckhead?" Miles asked.

"Affirmative. We're just waiting on Alpha Target to arrive. He must've made the call from his car."

"The two of them are meeting later tonight."

"Do we have a time and location?"

"Negative," replied Miles. "But we're staying on top of him."

"Copy that. Do you need any backup?"

"No, sir. I think we've got it."

"Good. I want to know when your target is on the move. Evergreen out."

CHAPTER 11

Henry rifled through his closet in search of his favorite suit—the one that made him feel most confident. It was a snug, charcoal number made from fine Italian fabric—tailored by an old Puerto Rican woman in Brookhaven—and he liked the way it looked with his brown leather shoes.

He took the elevator downstairs and floated across the lobby to the main entrance. Outside, Darius' Porsche rumbled pretentiously in front of the building. Henry unbuttoned his jacket and dipped into the passenger seat.

They took Twelfth Street north for several miles and pulled into La Grotta Ristorante, where the maître d' had a table waiting for them in the back corner. After a quiet meal, Darius slipped the valet a fifty-dollar bill and they sped away in the Porsche.

Ten minutes later, they arrived in Buckhead, where the Park Avenue building towered over the city with a menacing presence. Darius parked in a private space below ground, and he and Henry took the elevator to the forty-second floor.

As they stepped through the doors and into a magnificent foyer wrapped in red carpet and red walls, they were greeted by Asa Petrovi—the "general" of the Ružaro security arm. The old warhorse stood well over six feet, his body chiseled from stone. The scars on his face and neck revealed a lifetime of violent scuffles and disagreements.

"Gentlemen, it is wonderful to see you," he said with a sharp Croatian accent.

Henry and Darius smiled and nodded, forcing themselves to appear equally excited. But they'd known Asa since childhood and were familiar with his explosive temper and frail ego.

"Good to see you too, Asa," Henry greeted quickly. "How did Miami treat you?"

"As wonderful as always," the burly general asserted. Asa shook their hands and examined them both closely before waving them further into the penthouse.

They strolled through the foyer and into a sprawling living room, where several more men stood around, each of them armed with a slim-cut suit and a submachine gun. Henry knew that Asa's band of misfit soldiers were a treacherous lot, so he offered nothing more than a steely gaze as he brushed past.

They continued to the grand hall, which was adorned with accented blue wallpaper and white trim. A statue of Perun—undoubtedly the most powerful god of the Slavic pantheon—stood triumphantly in a finely carved fountain in the center of the hall.

"Have a seat, gentlemen," Asa instructed. "Anton will be with you in just a moment."

"Thank you," said Darius as he and Henry dropped onto a leather settee against the wall.

Asa quickly disappeared, off to do whatever devious things he was hired to do.

They sat in silence for several minutes until two French doors carved from solid oak swept open with flare.

Anton Krunoslav burst into the hall with his arms open to the heavens. His red-and-gold smoking jacket flowed behind him as a brilliant smile burst through his perfectly trimmed graying beard. Everything about him was dashing and exuberant. Even his hair had been neatly combed back against his skull.

"My boys!" the man roared, his voice echoing against the cathedral ceiling.

Darius rose to his feet with a broad grin.

"How are you?" Anton asked with a rigorous hug. "And Henry!" he shouted, extending his arms further outward.

Henry hugged him back. "So good to see you, Anton. You look well."

"Thank you, my boy. You always know just the right thing to say. Now, please, join me in the study."

The spacious room was lined with floor-to-ceiling bookshelves, expensive tapestries, and one-of-a-kind works of art. It was extraordinary, even to the most ardent collector. No matter how many times Henry stepped inside, it always awed him.

"Have a seat, gentlemen," Anton offered graciously.

Henry and Darius sat down on a midcentury chesterfield sofa, complete with genuine hand-painted leather and gold tacks.

"So tell me," the boss began. "How are things with my friend, Hamad Al Hassani?"

"It's progressing nicely," Darius replied.

"No problems in Sorrento?"

"None."

The lie made Henry nervous.

"Very good. And who else are we lining up?"

"I have a shortlist already prepared," said Darius.

"Is Nomari on it?"

"He is."

Anton leveled a prideful glare. "Good. Thank you, Darius. You know how important this is to me." He reached for a decanter of Scotch and three crystal glasses. "Henry, how is everything going here in Atlanta?" he asked as he poured a round of drinks.

"Good," replied Henry. "We've had over five million in product leave the warehouse so far this month. The Montreal job went smoothly. Everything else is on track."

Anton seemed pleased. He handed them each a glass, then sat down behind his desk. His fingers tented securely in front of him.

The men knew better than to refuse the Scotch—or anything else for that matter. Others had been killed for far less. Anton's explosive rage and appetite for violence came in various forms, as evidenced by two failed marriages and an estranged relationship with his only child, a daughter, who retreated long ago to the safe confines of California.

"When does our treasure arrive?" Darius asked anxiously.

Anton's eyes cut across the room. "It will be here very soon. Obviously, privacy is a concern, so we're using various well-guarded means of transportation."

Darius took a sip of his Scotch. "Well, we're all very excited. This is going to be a wonderful opportunity."

"That it is," Anton agreed. His eyes shifted to his lieutenant. "I was happy to hear Darius brought you in, Henry. You've always been a good earner. Your parents would be proud."

Henry crooked the corner of his mouth. "Thank you, sir. That means a lot."

"Each crew is working independently on this one," Anton explained. "Asa will handle transport security; Rukov's team will be safeguarding the asset; and you boys are in charge of the transaction. No procedural details are to trickle from one crew to the next, do you understand?"

Henry nodded sharply before taking a sip from his glass. He hated Scotch.

"Good," the old man allowed. "Darius?"

"Yes, sir. I completely understand."

Anton examined his two protégés carefully. "The asset is in transport from South America as we speak. Darius, I'll alert you as soon as it arrives. Until then, I expect a buyer to be set up without delay."

Darius nodded profusely. "Yes, sir. Right away."

After a light pause, Anton clapped his hands in conclusion. "Very well. I think we're all set here. If either of you run into any problems, just get with Asa."

Henry and Darius lifted themselves from the sofa and gave Anton another round of warm embraces before retreating back to the grand hall.

Asa returned, as if on cue, and ushered them back through the living room to the elevator.

Minutes later, the Porsche roared out of the garage.

"That went well," remarked Henry.

"Yeah, I think so too. I can't wait to get my hands on this thing."

Henry shifted his eyes through the windshield. The city lights gleamed ahead of him, tucked beneath a canopy of purple sky. Suddenly, an extraordinary theory formed in his mind.

"Darius," he said softly, "is it a single stone?"

His friend sat silent, steering the car through the enclaves of northeast Atlanta.

"Darius?"

"Yes."

"Yes, what?"

"Yes, it's a single stone."

Henry closed his eyes and took a calming breath. "You can't be serious!" he quietly exclaimed. "There's only a handful of diamonds that size in existence—and they're all accounted for. Are you telling me Anton's gotten his hands on one of the biggest stones on the planet? Is that what you're telling me?"

"Yes, Henry. That's what I'm telling you. We're going to be rich."

"We're *already* rich. What's the price tag? You have to tell me!"

"It doesn't matter," Darius grumbled. "Your reward is going to be a hell of a lot more valuable than two million dollars. You're going to be a captain—a very *wealthy* captain with unlimited resources. Say goodbye to the Forty West penthouse, bro."

"Oh come on! That's a nice apartment!"

"Of course it is. Speaking of which, are you going to invite me up for a drink?"

"Sure. But all I have is Scotch."

They shared a spirited laugh as the Porsche dipped into the underground lot beneath the Forty West building.

Upstairs, Henry stood in the kitchen and poured them each a glass of Rogaska, neat. He then walked out to the balcony where Darius waited patiently, his hands resting on the rail.

"Beautiful view," the captain noted.

Henry glanced up at the hints of pink light that brushed against the clouds as the sun melted below the skyline. "And you think I'm gonna get rid of this place? You're crazy."

Darius took his glass and raised it into the air. "*Živjeli*," he toasted.

"*Živjeli*," Henry echoed before taking an easy pull.

They stood on the balcony and finished their drinks in comfortable silence, staring out at the city.

Eventually, Henry grabbed their empty glasses and ambled back into the kitchen. Darius followed him in and snatched his keys from the table. "Thanks for all your help, Henry. You know we couldn't have gotten here without you."

Henry allowed a tiny grin. "Don't mention it. I wouldn't have it any other way, brother."

With a knowing nod, Darius turned and headed for the elevator. "I'll see you tomorrow!" he shouted before disappearing behind a set of nickel-plated doors.

Henry set the two glasses into the dishwasher and made his way to the living room.

Thirty minutes into the nightly news, he got up from the sofa and lumbered into the hallway to start a load of laundry. As he poured his detergent and closed the lid, his cell phone rang.

It was Darius.

He pulled the device to his ear. "Hey, buddy, what'd you forget?"

Darius' voice was low and reserved. "I need you to meet me downstairs."

"Is everything all right?" Henry asked.

"I'm pulling back in now. Just get your ass down here."

"Okay, be down in a sec."

Henry shoved the phone into his pocket and marched up the hallway. He got off the elevator at the basement level and began a slow pace across the concrete floor. Darius' car was parked against the back wall, deep within the shadows.

"What's up?" Henry asked as he approached.

Darius stood rigidly against his Porsche, his arms crossed in front of him. "I just got a call from Asa. Something's happened… we need to move out."

"What are you talking about? What happened?"

"Our asset's been held up."

"Where?"

"Santos, Brazil."

Henry furrowed his brow. "What's the stone doing in Brazil, Darius?"

"We pulled it from some old wreckage at the bottom of the ocean. It was a whole thing, bro—research vessels, divers, subs, the works. Apparently, the boat got picked up by customs and the stone was confiscated."

"Why didn't I know about this operation?" challenged Henry.

"Do you think I have a choice? Because I don't! I don't get to decide who's in on shit like that. I'm just like you; I follow orders."

"All right, all right. It doesn't matter." Henry took a breath and tried to think. "Why didn't we have Brazilian Customs on payroll? Seems like a security flaw."

"We did. The port at Santos is under the control of the Cardoso cartel. Anton had already paid for safe passage—half a million dollars, to be exact."

"So we've been double-crossed?"

"Who the hell knows. Either way, we have to get it back. And I can't make that happen without you. We're wheels up in one hour."

Henry flinched. "That's impossible. There's no way Isabell can get flights ready that fast. Besides, we'll never make it to the airport in time."

"We're not flying commercial. And Isabell's not coming. This is as covert as it gets, bro. Ružaro only."

"What's the plan?"

Darius checked his watch and climbed back into his car. "We'll have plenty of time for briefing once we're in the air. And pack light—we'll be jumping over Santos."

"What? Darius, we haven't jumped in like six or seven years, man. I don't even have a parachute anymore."

The Porsche's engine roared to life. "Everything's taken care of," Darius assured. "Brown Field, one hour."

Before Henry could argue, the sportscar darted out of the garage.

He rushed back to the elevator and barged inside, counting the floors as the small, illuminated numbers flashed above the door. He arrived at his penthouse and rushed to the bedroom, where he slipped into a pair of black cargo pants and a black tactical jacket. He then gathered his lock pick set, a pair of gloves, and a lightweight hoodie, and shoved them into a backpack.

After running through a quick mental checklist, he ran back to the elevator and descended to the garage.

Forty minutes later, Henry's Maserati pulled through the main gate of Brown Field—a small regional airport on the fringes of town that served as a hub for private jets and piston planes. Henry coasted along the tarmac, then pulled into one of the hangars.

Nearby, under the bright glow of halogen ceiling lights, sat a midnight blue Gulfstream G500.

He grabbed his backpack from the passenger seat and slung it over his shoulder. In a steady march across the floor, he offered a nod to the two uniformed pilots giving the aircraft its final inspection.

On the other side of the hangar, Darius waved his arm high in the air. "Henry! You all set?" he shouted.

"Let's hope so. Who's on the team tonight?"

"Jack Veselko. He should be here any minute."

"And?"

"And *what*?"

"Who else?" Henry pressed.

"That's it. Just you, me, and Veselko."

"Darius, if you're talking about breaking into a Brazilian Customs House to steal a priceless diamond, we're going to need a hell of a lot more than three operators."

"Listen, we don't have the time or resources to put a full team together. If we don't get there before Cardoso's men move our asset to a new location, this whole thing goes to shit. No money. No diamond. Nothing. Understand?"

Henry nodded. "I got it."

"Good. Now get your ass on the plane."

CHAPTER 12

As the Gulfstream streaked through the night sky somewhere over Cuba, Henry opened his pack and set it on the floor. Next to him was a nefarious collection of tools and hardware neatly laid out on a small table. He began sifting through the items: climbing rope, carabiners, knives, suction cups, bolt cutters, blow torch, and a pistol fitted with a silencer. One by one, he stuffed them into his backpack.

A few feet away, sitting in a swivel chair and chewing his fingernails, was Jack Veselko. He was an athletic guy in his mid-twenties, who happened to be one of Ružaro's up-and-coming stars. Henry had worked with him on a handful of previous missions, and he respected the man's intelligence and fearless tenacity.

"Where are we jumping?" Henry asked over the low hum of the engines.

Darius stood in the back of the cabin, packing the last of his surveillance cameras into a large metal suitcase. "Off the coast of Santos," he replied. "We'll take the inflatable and make a beach landing just south of the port. From there, a truck will pick us up and drive us into the city. Hopefully all before sunrise." Darius pulled a laptop from his bag and opened it up on the table. "This is an overhead view of the shoreline. We drop in the water *here*, land on the beach *here*, our ride picks us up *here*."

"Who's our ride?" asked Jack.

"We've got a few friendlies with the Red Command."

Henry shook his head nervously. "I don't know, Darius. They're fucking drug smugglers, which means they're about as loyal as a tree stump. Besides, haven't they been at war with the Cardoso cartel for like ten years?"

"Yes. And that's exactly why they're helping us. Relax, bro, everything's in place. We just have to get in, get out, and go home."

"You make it sound easy," Henry chided.

Darius quickly typed into the keyboard and pulled up a photo of a large gray building.

Henry leaned over his friend's shoulder and squinted at the monitor; the place looked cold and unwelcoming. "I'm guessing this is the Customs House?" he asked.

"It is," confirmed Darius. "Three stories, the outside shell is reinforced concrete, four feet thick. The holding rooms are on the second floor against the south wall. Four in total."

Jack gazed at the screen, scrutinizing every detail. "Do we know which room our target is in?"

"Holding room number two."

"And how exactly do we know that?" asked Henry.

Darius began typing again. "Asa got us into the government mainframe. The Customs database has an item registered on its books that was confiscated from our boat, the *RV Tiger Claw*."

"Cool name," noted Jack. "How big is this target we're after?"

"The research team had it in a small black safety case—about the size of a shoebox. Only Anton has the code to open it, but I doubt the Cardoso guys have figured that out yet."

Jack let out a deep grunt. "Can I ask what's in this little box?"

"No. Our only objective is to retrieve it," said Darius. "Now, once we get into Santos, there's a safe house on the northwest corner of the city where we can set up shop. But we need to hit this thing quick and we don't have a lot of time to surveil and plan. It's gotta be *bang-bang*, understood?"

Henry and Jack offered confirming nods.

"Once we have the asset, there's an airstrip in the village of Campinas to the north. A private jet is already on standby, waiting to take the asset to Caracas, where it'll get put on a ship destined for Miami."

"And what about us? How are we getting back?" asked Henry.

"Don't worry. After our package is safely on that ship, we'll fly home."

"And what about customs?"

"Well, luckily, we won't have to worry about customs when we land in Caracas, but obviously, the US is a little trickier."

"We're jumping twice, aren't we?"

"Yes," Darius replied.

Jack stood next to them, his eyes wide with excitement. "Two jumps? Oh man, this could not get any better!"

"Calm down, princess, we've got a ways to go," Henry teased.

"All right, I've got blueprints of the building," Darius continued. "So the only unknown at this point is security. Which means we're going to be surveilling the place in real time, on the ground. Once we get a bead on that, we should be able to strategize a way in."

Henry's chest tightened with apprehension. "This thing could easily go sideways, Darius. I feel like our plan is held together by a thread."

"I never promised it was going to be easy. What are you gonna do, back out?"

"No. Absolutely not."

"I didn't think so. Now, the skydiving gear is in the back. The pilot will alert us twenty minutes from the drop zone. The water's gonna be cold as shit and we'll be jumping from over thirty thousand feet, so it's wetsuits and full respirators." Darius stood with his hands on his hips, examining the packs of gear scattered around the cabin. "I think we're all set. Four hours until go time."

Henry tucked his bag into a safety bin before returning to his plush leather recliner.

It was just past two o'clock in the morning, and the endless black sky beyond his window seemed to taunt him. He hated jumping at night.

The next few hours passed in heavy silence until a bright red light illuminated at the front of the cabin.

Henry got up from his seat and followed his teammates to the rear of the plane.

In a small chamber, they slipped into their wetsuits and secured their parachute packs.

Henry reached for his bag and strapped it backwards onto his chest, then pulled a respirator mask over his face.

Slowly, the back cargo door began to lower.

The red standby light flashed against Henry's face shield as he gazed through the back of the plane and into the dark abyss.

Darius stepped to the ledge first. He held three fingers into the air as the cargo door locked into position.

Two fingers.

One finger.

The red light turned green just as Darius closed his fist, and just like that, he disappeared into the hazy night.

Jack was next. The young operator lunged away and thrust himself from the platform.

Henry checked his pressure gauge one last time. He took a firm step forward, then another, and with a deep breath, he spread his arms and dove into the darkness.

The wind blasted against his shield as he dropped through the sky at over a hundred miles per hour. The loss of control was immediate. He steadied his breathing and checked the elevation meter on his wrist: twenty-five thousand feet.

He'd lost sight of Darius and Jack, but knew they were somewhere beneath him. He tucked his arms and lowered his head, boring through the sky like a human missile.

He could sense his body reaching terminal velocity, and it suddenly felt as if he was floating.

With a sliver of purple haze lining the horizon, the faint silhouettes of his teammates came into view. For the next ninety seconds, the three men plummeted through the darkness toward the ocean.

Henry's gauge now read six thousand feet. The gray outline of Darius' chute blossomed below him as he reached for the small orange handle against his chest. He braced himself for the coming jolt and pulled.

As the chute opened above him, he could now see the waves of the Atlantic rippling far below. He lifted his legs and prepared for a plunge into the icy waters.

He hit with a sharp splash and vanished below the waves. His hands quickly guided him back to the surface, where he detached his chute and pulled it in, wrapping it into a tight ball through the murky water.

As hints of sunlight broke on the horizon, Henry tore the mask from his face and filled his lungs with cool air.

Nearby, Darius bobbed in the water, craning his head in search of the shoreline.

"How we looking, boss?" Henry shouted.

"Looking real good," Darius replied. "Nice jump, boys!"

Not far from them, Jack Veselko floated on his back with a valiant grin.

Darius reached for the large rubber tube that had been tethered to his waist. With the flip of a tiny lever, a seven-foot dinghy inflated from the water and popped open on the surface.

One by one, they climbed inside and began pulling off their gear. The wetsuits, respirators, and parachutes were quickly stuffed into a large weighted bag and tossed into the ocean, where they sunk beneath the waves.

Darius lowered a small trolling motor into the water and guided the boat toward the lights of Brazil.

After a thirty-minute ride into a strong headwind, they ran the dinghy onto a deserted beach slightly south of Santos and tucked it beneath a canopy of overgrown brush.

As daylight broke over the Atlantic, they secured their packs and vanished into the nearby tree line. A short hike brought them to a gravel road that wove from the bay to the mainland. Under the shadows of daybreak, they waited silently in the stockyard of a tile factory that had been abandoned long ago.

Darius checked his watch. The minutes ticked by with a sense of unease.

Finally, a light beige compact pickup truck appeared in the distance. Its headlights beamed through the fog as the truck raced into the stockyard. It came to a sudden, dramatic halt on the gravel in front of them.

Within a cloud of dust, a large, portly Brazilian man with a thick beard stepped out and bore his beady eyes across the landscape. "Are you lost?" he grumbled as the three Ružaro members slithered from their hide.

"We're looking for the library," Darius replied cryptically.

The man stood there, cautiously examining the strangers from head to toe. "The library is closed for renovations," he finally granted.

"Thanks for picking us up, friend," Darius greeted with a handshake.

The grizzled farmer got back into his vehicle. He started the engine and waved them aboard. Henry, Jack, and Darius climbed into the back and sat down against the cold, rusted steel of the bed. The truck wove several miles into the wilderness, making its way north along a dirt road.

Henry gazed out at a makeshift village of tents and hastily constructed shanties that lined the path.

As the fog lifted, the pickup truck veered onto a thin trail that wove deeper into the forest. They continued on, pushing further into the jungle until they reached a sprawling compound hidden within a canopy of towering pines. Beyond a scrapyard and a crumbling water tower was a small single-story building. Its roof had caved in and the exterior walls were held together with sheet metal and plywood.

They got out, unloaded their packs, and hustled into the building as the truck sped away, retreating back into the dense woodland.

"Okay, boys, this is it," Darius announced as he swiped a collection of empty bottles from a nearby table and set down his laptop.

"How far are we from the Customs House?" asked Henry.

"Three miles. There's an old Jeep parked in the barn out back. Jack, go make sure the damn thing runs."

Jack bolted out the door and made his way through the tall grass to a decaying barn in the backyard.

Meanwhile, Darius pulled a satellite image up on his laptop. "This is a view of the Customs House and surrounding blocks. We need to find a place to set up surveillance."

Henry leaned over and narrowed his gaze. "There," he said, pointing to the screen. "Zoom in on that."

Darius pushed his finger across the touchpad and a tall brick building came into view.

"What is that?" Henry asked.

"I have no idea. It's not an apartment complex, but it looks taller than the Customs House."

"There's an antenna rig on the roof and a few HVAC systems. It's gotta be an office building or something."

"Only one way to find out."

As they stared at the mysterious structure, Jack burst through the back door. "The Jeep's good to go. You guys ready?"

Darius shut the laptop and stuffed it into his pack. "Let's move."

They bolted outside and crept across the field to the barn. Inside, tucked between a pile of scrap wood and mounds of straw, they climbed into an old blue Jeep with bald tires and dented rollbars. Under the deep rumble of its rusted V6 engine, they pulled out of the barn and raced through the forest toward Santos.

Soon, the skyline of the port city began to lift against the horizon. Darius put on his sunglasses and coasted the Jeep down a barren road. They entered a maze of slums and dilapidated buildings and continued south, deeper into Santos.

Finally, they crossed the Santana River and descended into the São Vicente District—the eastern edge of the island that made up the port city.

Darius bucked the old Jeep left onto Perimetral Avenue and after several minutes, the monotonous gray exterior of the Customs House materialized in the distance, daring them to enter.

Henry glanced across the street to the tall brick building adjacent to them, the one he'd pinpointed on the laptop. "That's our perch," he announced.

Darius examined the place with curiosity. "There's no signage. For all we know, it's an army barracks."

"It's definitely not an army barracks," Jack chimed from the backseat. "The electrical's already been gutted and the windows on the top three floors are all smashed out. Hate to break it to you guys, but this is probably a flop house for the homeless."

Darius yanked the steering wheel left and pulled in behind the brick building.

They got out and scanned the area for any visible threats. Satisfied, the three operators entered through the shredded remnants of a back door.

Inside, the walls dripped with condensation and a litany of empty wire looms hung from the ceiling where electrical lines had once been.

They carefully made their way to the other side of the floor to a staircase that wound upward. As they ascended through the darkness, a deep groan emanated from the foundation beneath their feet.

Henry froze on the platform between the fourth and fifth floors. "What the hell was that?" he whispered into the shadows.

"It's an old building," Jack replied with amusement. "Just keep moving. Three more flights."

Henry continued his trek upwards until they reached the top floor. He pushed through a metal door and into a hallway. The brisk air brushed against his face as he walked toward an empty room on his left.

He stopped for a moment and retrieved the pistol from his backpack, then trained it in front of himself. Together, they slithered into the room one at a time.

Henry panned his weapon from left to right before lowering it to his side. "All clear," he called out.

Darius slowly edged to the far window and braced himself against the wall next to it. With a light breath, he craned his neck and peered out at the Customs House across the road. "This is perfect," he said as he pulled a camera and a pair of binoculars from his pack.

Henry and Jack joined him at the window while Darius began snapping photos of the building. For the next hour, they observed the government complex from their perch.

Henry scanned the area with his binoculars, counting the number of guards and staff and examining the security fence that was meant to keep curious thieves at bay. "Where's our target exactly?" he asked.

"Second floor, third room from the northeast corner," said Darius.

Henry brought the binoculars back to his eyes for another look, panning the lens across a row of second-floor windows. The place was an absolute fortress—there were no soft points of entry or flaws in the architecture, no ledges along the façade or alleys hidden from view.

He exhaled with apprehension. "You weren't kidding, Darius; this is no walk in the park. Jack, what are the chances of getting you inside?"

"Inside?" Jack questioned. "What do you mean?"

"These delivery trucks coming in through the main gate. Can you get in through there?"

Jack took a moment to think. He gazed down at the two young security guards pacing around their post, waiting for the next truck to arrive. "Maybe," he mumbled. "Depends."

"On what?"

"Whether or not you can get me a truck and a driver's uniform."

"We don't have time for that," Darius reminded them. "Maybe we can get you hidden inside one of the trucks."

"No," said Jack. "But I think I might be able to get under one."

Henry's eyes flashed with approval. "I like it. I like it a lot."

"So we get one guy into the building under a truck, then what?" asked Darius.

Henry grabbed hold of the window frame and tested its strength. "I can zipline in from right here."

"You sure about that?"

"A hundred percent. I'll drop onto the roof, Jack gets inside the building to kill the lights, and you stay right here as our eyes and ears. It's our only option."

Darius dropped the camera into his lap and exhaled nervously into the air. "All right, but how are you getting from the roof to the second floor?"

"Easy," said Henry. "The ventilation duct on the roof should get me into the elevator shaft on the northeast corner. As long as the power's out, all I have to do is walk three doors up the hallway to holding room number two."

"How do you know there's an elevator shaft on the northeast corner?" Darius asked.

Henry pulled the binoculars back to his eyes. "Because I can see the electrical box mounted on the roof, which means there's an elevator underneath it."

Darius nodded. "Let's pack it up. We'll come back tonight and get this thing done."

They quickly loaded their gear and returned to the staircase, where they circled their way to the bottom.

Minutes later, the old Jeep pulled onto Perimetral Avenue and darted away. They stopped at a roadside stand in São Vicente for a bag of barbecue beef *kibe* before crossing the river, winding through the slums, and returning to their safe house.

CHAPTER 13

It was nearly three in the morning and the crescent moon dangled above him, high in the night sky. Henry cradled the harpoon launcher in his arms and gazed out from the eighth-floor window of the old brick building on Perimetral Avenue.

A voice crackled in his ear. "Tomahawk Three on approach."

"Copy that," replied Henry. "We'll be watching for you."

Darius sat on the floor next to him, his back pressed against the wall.

After a few tense minutes, Jack's voice again came through their earpieces. "Tomahawk Three at the gate."

Darius lifted his infrared binoculars and peered into the street below. He focused the lens on the guards standing at the gate, then the cargo truck waiting to be let in. Somewhere beneath its steel frame, clinging to the undercarriage, was Jack Veselko.

Henry glanced out the window, holding his breath as the two guards gave the vehicle a close inspection. Finally, the men waved the driver in and returned to their post.

As the truck rumbled through the gates and into the complex, Henry stood in the window and brought the harpoon to his shoulder. He gripped the handle firmly, his eyes searching for a target. Then, with a firm exhale, he pulled the trigger. The metal grappling hook launched from the window and arched into the darkness toward the Customs House.

Darius watched through his binoculars as the projectile landed on the adjacent roof. "Direct hit," he whispered.

Henry leaned down and grabbed the black line resting at his feet. He gently tugged out the slack and mounted it to the exposed door frame on the opposite wall. Satisfied, he secured his harness to the zipline with a set of carabiners and tightened his gloves. "Tomahawk One incoming," he announced as he lunged toward the window.

In a full sprint, Henry propelled himself through the opening feet first and vanished into the cold night.

Darius stood in the window as the faint buzzing of the zipline hissed through the darkness.

As the wind whipped against Henry's face, the roof of the Customs House drew closer. He grabbed the top of the line with his hand to slow his approach. Then, with the snap of a carabiner, he dropped onto the rooftop. "Tomahawk One is on the LZ," he reported quietly.

"Copy that," said Darius. "Tomahawk Three, what's your status?"

After a few seconds, Jack's voice buzzed over the channel. "Walking through the basement now. Gonna try to make my way upstairs to the main atrium."

"Copy that. All right, boys, let's move on to Birch Phase."

Henry rose to his feet and peered through the darkness. With a calming breath, he marched toward the northeast corner of the roof and tore the grate from a ventilator duct. He entered the tube left foot first, then his right, then wriggled his way inside. Inch by inch, he slid down through the tight canal until he reached the bottom, where the duct redirected him horizontally above the third-floor ceiling.

After a sixty-foot crawl on his stomach, he reached the end. With a closed fist, he punched the grill gate out of the duct, hurling it into the deep abyss of the elevator shaft. He stuck his head out and examined the four walls that descended into the darkness. There was no sign of an elevator car and the components of the pulley system looked as if they'd been torn out long ago.

He reached his arms out of the duct and felt around for something to grab hold of. His fingers found a thin steel rail that offered just enough grip to pull himself from the duct. He slid his chest out first, then his hips, until he was clinging to the side of the shaft.

With a peek over his shoulder, he lowered himself along the cement wall until his feet landed on a metal runner just above the second-floor opening. A searing burn tore through his forearms as he gripped the rail and leaned back into the air.

"I'm ready for those lights," he said under his breath. "Where you at, Tomahawk Three?"

"Thirty more seconds," replied Jack. "Entering the mechanical room now."

Henry steadied his breathing as he hung several stories above the floor.

"Fifteen seconds," alerted Jack. "Ten seconds. Prepare for blackout."

Henry waited on the wall until the thin light seeping through the cracks in the door just below his feet went dark. With a rush of relief, he shimmied himself down and stood on the ledge of the elevator doors. He slipped his fingertips between the metal sliders and pulled them open.

The corridor ahead of him was pitch black, but he could hear the faint voices of staff members grumbling from somewhere in the distance. He hurried up the hallway to the third door on his right and pulled a small pick set from his back pocket. The two picks slipped into the doorknob and gently set into position. With a slight turn, the lock disengaged and the door sprang open.

Henry ducked inside and closed himself in.

Against the far wall were a pair of utility shelves stuffed with bins, boxes, and other random items.

"Tomahawk One moving to Cherry Phase," he said into the air.

"Copy that," answered Darius. "The item number is Charlie, Hotel, Tango, Seven, Three, Five, Two."

Henry stepped to the wall and scanned through the index numbers posted above each shelf. He ran his fingers along the ledge until he found one marked CHT7352. His heart pounded through his jacket as he pulled a large plastic bin from the shelf.

Henry gazed inside, squinting through the darkness. "Guys, we got a serious problem."

"Tomahawk One, please repeat," Darius screeched into his ear. "What's your status?"

"The asset isn't here. There's nothing here."

"Bad copy, Tomahawk One. Please confirm: did you just say it isn't there?"

"Affirmative. The asset's gone."

"Fuck! Get your asses outta there," Darius instructed.

"Roger that. Tomahawk One on exfil. See you boys at the go zone." Henry shoved the container back onto the shelf and rushed toward the door.

There were still whispers outside in the hallway and they seemed to be coming closer. He pinned himself against the wall just behind the door and held his breath.

He counted three voices in total—one man and two women. As they walked past the door outside, Henry clenched his eyes and leaned his head back against the concrete.

The three staff members continued on and were now standing in the hallway between Henry and the elevator shaft—his only escape.

He waited patiently until he heard the voices dissipate. With no other option, he reached for the door and slowly pulled it open. He peered into the dark, empty hallway before breaking into a light jog toward the elevator.

As he passed the last door on his left, he could see the silhouettes of the staff members inside the room.

"*Que é aquele?*" one of them said as he rushed past.

Henry reached the end of the hall and ripped the elevator doors open with his hands. As he struggled to get himself into the shaft, he could hear a set of footsteps rushing toward him. He grabbed hold of the runner above his head and lifted himself from the platform to the ledge.

After a short climb, Henry dipped into the ventilation duct and slithered his way back to the roof. He emerged minutes later and broke into a full sprint toward the black horizon ahead of him. As he reached the ledge, he closed his eyes and leapt from the building.

The zipline attached to his harness whipped against his chest as he plummeted through the air. He tightened the handbrake just before slamming his feet against the outside wall. He rappelled the last two stories and hit the ground with a thud.

Under the cover of night, Henry tossed his harness to the ground and sprinted toward the back fence. As he ran, he reached for the bolt cutters in his backpack. Then, two gunshots burst into the air behind him.

"*Pare! Pare!*" a voice shouted through the darkness.

Henry froze.

"*Você está encrencado!*" the voice roared.

Henry raised his hands as the barrel of a pistol was placed against the back of his head. "Listen, I don't speak Portuguese," he tried. "How about some English, huh?"

"Fuck you and your English!"

"Okay… I can deal with that. No problem."

Henry's hands were quickly forced behind his back and handcuffed. He was then thrown against the fence and patted down. The guard grabbed Henry's backpack from the dirt and tossed it over his arm before hustling the prisoner into the building.

Henry was taken down a long hallway and thrust into an empty room. The door closed behind him as he struggled to free himself from the handcuffs.

He paced the floor for nearly an hour before the guard returned and took him back into the hall and through another door. This one, however, led to an outside courtyard, where two men in street clothes waited next to a white Cadillac Escalade. Their eyes widened at the sight of their new prize.

"Hey! What the hell is going on here?" Henry yelled as they shoved him into the backseat and slammed the door in his face.

A rush of adrenaline spiked through his body. These weren't customs agents, he knew. They were members of Cardoso. He sat silent as the two men piled in and drove him to the outer limits of the city. Eventually, they arrived at a small marina tucked along the north shore, far from the lights of Santos.

With his hands still cuffed behind his back, Henry was yanked out of the SUV and led down a long pier. His feet shuffled against the planks as his captors pushed him along.

They reached the bottom platform, where a large fishing boat bobbed in the dark water. Henry stepped aboard and was forced into a chair on the back deck.

One of the men ducked beneath the transom and disappeared into the main cabin. Seconds later, the twin Mercury outboard engines sputtered to life. The boat slowly backed away from the pier and vanished into the dark, icy waters of the Atlantic.

The fifteen-minute ride felt like an eternity. As Henry sat in the swivel deck chair, he gazed up at the stars and searched for a soothing memory—anything to calm his mind.

The boat's engines finally cut off, and, for a brief moment, all he could hear was the calm sound of water splashing against the hull.

His pulse began to race and his hands suddenly went numb behind his back. A black hood was slipped over his head as he was lifted to a standing position. Henry tried to remain strong, but the fear of certain death proved to be too much.

"No! No, please don't!" he screamed.

His captors remained silent, holding him firmly by the arms.

With a deep breath, Henry mustered what little energy he had left and tried to lunge away. But the men were quick to grab hold of him. They yanked him back into position and slammed him down to his knees.

With his hands clasped behind his back, his eyes began to well beneath the hood. "Please don't kill me," he begged.

He tried one last time to free himself, but the cuffs were simply too tight. Through an uncontrollable instinct to survive, he thrashed himself violently against the deck. Then, with nothing left, Henry's body went still. The two men lifted him back to his knees, and for a single, tranquil moment, he surrendered to his fate.

Under a blanket of silence, he filled his lungs with the fresh, salty air of the ocean and tried to find comfort in the fact that he would die in such a peaceful place.

As he exhaled one final breath, the sound of a bullet being chambered into a pistol echoed behind him. He closed his eyes and cleared his mind.

Two loud pops broke the crisp air as Henry fell to the floor.

He opened his eyes and blinked. The gunshots were followed by a single thud against the deck.

As the boat gently rocked from side to side, he listened carefully. There were footsteps nearby and he could hear the sound of a body being dragged to the edge, followed by a sharp splash.

Henry fought to catch his breath. "H-h-hello?" he stuttered. "Is someone there?"

He was grabbed from under his arms and lifted to his feet. The hood was ripped from his head. Henry looked up to see the bigger of the two men standing before him. The other thug was nowhere to be found.

"What just happened?" he grumbled.

With the first rays of sun now rising over the ocean, the man smiled and walked back to the cabin. Seconds later, the outboard engines came to life and the boat began moving.

Handcuffed and stunned, Henry steadied himself in the chair as the vessel picked up speed and darted across the waters toward Santos.

They reached the marina as darkness gave way to dawn. Beyond their wake, the boundless blue waters of the Atlantic clashed with an orange sky that struggled to free itself from the horizon.

Henry was lifted onto the pier by the large Brazilian, then stuffed into the waiting Cadillac. "Where are you taking me?" he asked as the SUV tore out of the lot and onto a dirt road. The man didn't respond. "Is this a language barrier thing? Do you speak English?"

Still no response.

After a moment, Henry nodded acceptingly. "Okay. All right. Who do you work for? You're with Cardoso, right?"

The man reached for the dash and turned on the radio. He quickly found a channel he liked and turned it up.

Henry tried to rationalize the strange series of events as the Cadillac dashed through the forest with the sounds of Brazilian salsa music blaring through its open windows.

An hour's drive brought them to a deserted outpost at the base of a large, densely wooded mountain. Henry knew they had been driving north and were probably somewhere just outside the small city of Cubatão. Surely, he was being sold to a rival gang: or worse, the authorities.

He was pulled from the backseat and guided into a decades-old building with a blue tarp draped over its roof.

Inside, Henry squinted through the shadows. The Brazilian drew his pistol cautiously as they entered, panning it from side to side with his eyes trained down its barrel. Suddenly, a door burst open on the far end of the building. The man pulled Henry closer, using him as a human shield.

The silhouettes of two figures stood at a distance.

One of them began marching forward.

Henry narrowed his eyes. "Darius?"

"Henry! Holy shit!" his friend shouted as he ran up and wrapped Henry in a bear hug. "Get these goddamn cuffs off of him, will ya, pal?"

The heavy-set Brazilian pulled a key from his pocket and unlocked the handcuffs from Henry's wrists.

"What the absolute hell is going on, Darius? What the fuck?"

"I can't believe it! I totally thought we lost you, bro."

As the two stared at each other in bewilderment, Jack Veselko emerged. He dropped a duffle bag onto the ground and unzipped it, revealing stacks of US currency.

"What are you guys doing here?" Henry screeched. "And what's with the whole, you know, thing with this guy?"

"We planted a seed with some low-level Cardoso soldiers," Darius explained. "A reward for anyone who brought us the tall white guy who was captured at the Customs House. You're lucky, bro. Cardoso gave the order to have you killed. Did they take you out to the ocean? What happened?"

"Yes, they took me out to the fucking ocean!" Henry roared. "They put a hood over my goddamn face and I was about to be executed! Do you have *any* idea what that feels like?"

Darius fought the urge to laugh. "I'm sorry, Henry. But that was close. I mean, even Jack said the odds of getting you back alive were really, really bad."

"I told him there was no way," the young operator added.

Henry shook his head. "I'm sure you did."

As the three of them reveled in their reunion, the Brazilian reached for the duffle bag and slung it over his shoulder.

"How much?" asked Henry.

Darius rocked his head. "What do you mean?"

"How much did you pay this dude to bring me here?"

"Two hundred thousand."

"That's it? That's *all* my life is worth? Are you fucking kidding me right now?"

Darius and Jack erupted with laughter.

"I would've taken less," the Brazilian said with a boyish grin.

"I'm sorry, where are my manners?" Darius muddled aloud. "Henry, I'd like you to meet Caesar. You should at least thank him for saving your life."

"Thank you, Caesar," Henry quipped. "Now what the hell are we gonna do about the asset?"

Darius straightened his back and inhaled conspicuously. "I don't know."

"Are you guys talking about the box they took from your boat?" asked Caesar.

"Yes," Darius replied. "Any idea where it went?"

The man nodded. "They took it last night, around midnight. It left on an old transport truck with the number EIGHT painted on the back. I helped load it."

"Where's this truck going exactly?" asked Darius.

"Rio de Janeiro."

Henry did a quick calculation in his head. "That's gotta be like an eight-hour drive. If it left at midnight that means it'll arrive in a couple hours. We'll never make it."

"I have an idea," uttered Jack. His eyes darted from side to side. "Caesar, is there an airport around here?"

The Brazilian thought for a moment before nodding. "Yes. There's a private airport in Santo Andrè, maybe thirty minutes from here."

"And where the hell are we supposed to find a pilot?" asked Henry.

Darius gently raised his hand.

"No, absolutely not."

"We don't have any other choice," the captain argued. "And if we don't leave right now, we'll never be able to intercept that truck before it reaches Rio."

Henry shook his head begrudgingly. "This is ridiculous."

"Caesar, can you get us to that airstrip?"

The big man crossed his arms over his broad chest.

"How much?" asked Darius.

"Ten thousand."

"Fine. Jack, do we have ten grand left?"

Jack slid a backpack from his shoulder and opened it up. He pulled out a stack of bills and handed them to Caesar.

Moments later, the Cadillac burst onto the open road and coasted north, weaving through a swath of mountains and dense forest.

They arrived at the old airfield and came to a stop at the end of a crumbling runway. They stepped out and glared across the vast expanse. Caesar waved his arm wildly out the window as the Cadillac sped away.

"So what happens to him?" asked Henry.

"Two hundred thousand US dollars goes a long way in this part of the world," said Darius. "I'm sure he'll make a nice life for himself and his family somewhere."

"You don't think Cardoso will come after him?"

"I doubt it. It'll look like you killed him and his partner at sea. Which means the cartel is sure to put a bounty on your head."

"Great. That's exactly what I need right now."

Further up the tarmac, Jack was pulling open the large bay door of an old hangar. "Over here!" he yelled.

Darius and Henry jogged over and set their eyes on an early-edition PS-28 Cruiser.

"So what's the plan here?" Henry asked as he set his palm against the fuselage. "We just gonna land this thing in the middle of nowhere?"

"Something like that," Darius answered.

Jack inspected the wings and landing gear, then glanced out at the runway. "There's a problem; this is only a two-seater."

"I'm sure we can find something else," Henry said as he stared out at a half dozen other planes scattered haphazardly along the tarmac.

Jack shook his head. "I'm not so sure about that. All these other birds are either missing parts or too old to get off the ground. This is it."

"We'll be fine," assured Darius. "Henry, you're coming with me. Jack, you need to get to the rendezvous point in Campinas. It's probably a half-day hike from here; can you make it?"

"Yeah, I'll make it."

"Good. Just wait for us there. If we're not back in forty-eight hours, get your ass on that jet and go home. You got it?"

Jack nodded. "Yeah, I got it, boss."

With that, Darius climbed into the cockpit of the small plane and shoved his hand beneath the dash. He ripped two ignition wires from the circuit box and tapped them together. As he entwined the wires and set them back into place, the Rotax 100-horsepower engine slowly sputtered to life.

Henry lifted himself into the co-pilot seat and pulled the safety belt over his shoulder.

The tiny, single-engine aircraft pulled away from the hangar, turned toward the horizon, and began accelerating up the runway. After a turbulent one-hundred-yard dash, the

PS-28 lifted off the ground and climbed into the clouds over Santo Andrè.

Darius kept the plane at a low altitude, skimming along the coastline as the ocean gently rolled beneath them.

The grinding hum of the engine prattled through the cockpit as Henry tried to focus on the mission ahead. He knew their lives were already at risk, and that the fate of Anton's priceless diamond rested solely on their shoulders.

He only hoped their reckless abandon and stupidity would be enough to keep them alive.

CHAPTER 14

As the PS-28 glided over the Brazilian coast, a long, two-lane highway came into view below. It was the only road that connected the port city of Santos to Rio de Janeiro.

Henry was getting nervous now. They were only twenty miles from Rio and they still hadn't seen a single car.

Then, after cresting over a patch of treetops, they caught sight of a large military truck racing along the highway ahead of them, its tattered canvas cover flapping in the wind.

Henry squinted through the windshield at the dusty vehicle rambling below. As they roared above it, he could make out the number eight spray-painted onto the back gate.

"That's it!" he yelled excitedly. "I can't freakin' believe it!"

Darius brought the stick gently to his left, guiding the craft inland. Just ahead of them, beyond a cluster of bristling palms, the highway straightened into a long, narrow strip.

"Whatchya think?" Darius asked over the clamor of the engine.

"I think it's as good as any. Just don't kill us, okay?"

"I'll try my best. But I have a confession to make! I have no idea how to land!"

Henry shut his eyes. "Of course you don't."

Darius steadied the yolk and pulled the thrust back. As the aircraft zeroed in on the thin road ahead, the wings tilted from side to side in a slow, uneasy motion.

A bead of sweat fell from Henry's brow. He leaned into the windshield and braced his hands against the dash.

The plane's landing gear clipped the treetops before finally straightening out. As they glided above the asphalt, Darius dropped the thruster and, in a flailing descent, the airplane plunged toward Earth.

The rear wheels hit the grass first, followed by the nose, which slammed violently against the ground. The left wing cut through the dirt as the plane charged into the thick brush and crashed into a cluster of trees. It eventually came to a stop within a chaotic assemblage of broken branches, leaves and pine needles.

Henry lifted his head and glanced through the hole where a window had once been. He kicked out the door and stepped onto the muddy ground. "Darius, you okay?"

Darius sat in the pilot's seat, his hands still gripped to the stick.

"Darius?"

"Yeah. I'm good. I guess we can add that to the list."

"What list?"

"The list of things we should never do again."

Henry glanced out at their surroundings. The PS-28 was in shambles, its propeller wrapped around the trunk of an aging pine.

They were at least seventy yards into the brush, he guessed. He peered into the forest at the smoldering trail of debris that had been left in their wake. The smell of petrol filled his nostrils and somewhere in the distance, he could hear the sound of waves crashing against the shore.

Darius slowly pulled himself from the wreckage. After a quick body check, he grabbed his pack and slung it over his shoulder. "We all set?" he shouted.

"Yeah. Let's get moving."

They hustled through the woods, emerging minutes later at the roadside. Henry tossed his hands on top of his head and paced in the tall grass, trying to catch his breath.

Darius stood next to him, studying the road to the south. "It'll be here any second," he huffed.

"What's the plan?"

The Ružaro captain pulled a .44-caliber pistol from its thigh holster. He chambered a round and held it menacingly at his side.

"Darius? What's the plan here, brother?" Henry tried again.

"I didn't go through all that just to come out here and play nice. The plan is to put a bullet in anyone that stands between me and that little black box."

"Careful, Darius. You're going to start a war if you do anything stupid."

Before they could debate any further, the old truck hurtled around the bend ahead of them. Darius slipped the pistol behind his back and tucked it under his shirt. As the vehicle approached, Henry could make out two men sitting in the front cab.

With a deep breath, Darius stepped into the road and began waving his arms in the air. The truck began to slow and eventually came to a complete stop. The two men inside glanced coldly through the windshield.

"*Ajuda! Ajuda!*" Darius shouted excitedly. "We crashed our plane into the trees! Please, we need help!"

The men looked at each other, then back to Darius. After a moment, the driver opened his door and climbed out of the old truck. And just as his feet hit the ground, he pulled a gun from his side holster.

But it wasn't fast enough. Darius snapped the .44 from his waistband and released two blistering shots into the quiet air. The man dropped to the pavement and slumped into a disheveled mound of flannel and denim.

As Darius trained his weapon on the passenger, Henry bolted into the road and began dragging the fresh corpse into the grass.

"Get out of the fucking truck!" Darius screamed. "Get out right now!"

The passenger raised his hands in surrender and slowly stepped out of the vehicle.

"On your knees, motherfucker!"

The young man followed Darius' orders and dropped to his knees. He then clasped his hands on top of his head.

With the dead body out of sight, Henry rushed over and pulled a set of zipties from his pants. He strapped the guy's wrists together and kicked him into the dirt.

"C'mon, help me find this thing!" Darius shouted from the truck bed.

Henry gazed up the road in each direction before jumping into the bay in a frantic search for the little box. He tore through crates—one after the other—as seconds ticked by. Finally, he opened one that held a small black metal box. "I think I've got it!"

Darius rushed to his side and peered into the crate. "Holy shit."

"Is that it?"

"That's it."

Henry reached in and pulled out the tiny safe. He tucked it under his arm and leapt off the back of the truck.

They raced around to the front and climbed into the cab.

As Darius threw the old truck into gear, it jolted into the grass, then turned around and sped south along the narrow highway.

Henry glanced into the side mirror at the reflection of the young man sitting on the roadside with his hands tied behind his back. Against the horizon, a plume of black smoke rose from the crash site and billowed above the trees.

The truck hugged the coastline for several miles before turning inland toward the small village of Rialto. They sputtered into town and parked in the shade behind a shredded billboard.

"We're probably a good two hundred miles from our rendezvous point," Henry noted as he got out of the truck.

Darius stepped onto the gravel and peered up at a smattering of roadside stands and old dust-covered cars that stretched for hundreds of yards. "I got about five grand left," he noted. "You think it'll be enough?"

"I do," said Henry with a sly grin.

Minutes later, they were buckled into the front of a late-eighties Chevy Camaro with a peeling coat of light blue paint and a missing hood. The car tore through the open roads, winding deeper into the Mantiqueira Mountains. They continued a grueling climb to the peak of a long range before making their final descent into the valley.

After stealing a tank of gas from a roadside shed, they drove for several more hours until they reached the picturesque village of Campinas.

The rendezvous point was a small farmhouse tucked along the Capivari River on the southern edge of town.

As dusk began to hover across the sky, Darius crept the Camaro onto a private dirt road and guided it around a series of random potholes and downed trees. Finally, they came to a stop at a metal stock gate.

"You sure this is it?" Henry asked.

"Yeah. This is it. I'm guessing some weird little foot soldier will spring from the woods any minute now."

Just as Darius had predicted, a short, frail Brazilian with a thick mustache and an assault rifle emerged from the trees, eyeing them with vigilance.

"Just give him the damn password and let's get on with it," Henry grumbled.

The disheveled soldier approached the truck and glared at them through the windshield.

"*Eu sou a cobra preta!*" Darius shouted out the window.

The man didn't blink. But after a stern examination of the two visitors, he opened the gate and waved them in.

The old sportscar rumbled onto the property and came to a stop in front of a decaying farmhouse. Henry and Darius got out and scanned the mountain range to the north, then the dirt road to the south.

The front door of the home suddenly sprang open and a tall man in a baseball cap and a stained brown suit stepped onto the porch. He raised his arms to the heavens and smiled. "Hello! Hello, my friends!"

"Who the hell is *this* guy?" Henry asked under his breath.

"It's our contact. His name's Miguel."

The man hurried down the steps to meet them in the yard, his ridiculous grin fixed to his russet face.

"Miguel, my name's Darius and this is my partner, Henry. Has Jack Veselko made it in yet?"

The man's grin quickly vanished. "No, my friends. I'm so sorry, but no one else has arrived."

"That's fine," said Darius. "He'll be here soon. Let your men know we've got an operator coming in on foot."

Miguel nodded profusely. "Yes, my friend. We'll keep an eye out for him."

Henry returned to the Camaro and retrieved the metal box from the floorboard. He followed Darius into the house and set it on the kitchen counter.

"So?" he asked.

"So what?"

"I want to see what we just risked our lives for."

"It doesn't work like that. And you know it." Darius reached into the refrigerator and pulled out two cans of beer. He tossed one to Henry. "Listen to me, bro, you did amazing today. But we can't open the thing. Besides, only Anton has the code. Let's just keep our eyes on the prize, okay?"

"That's the thing," Henry argued. "I don't even know what the prize is."

Darius popped his beer and took a long drink. "The prize is millions and millions of dollars. Now stop busting my balls and focus. Our only objective is to wait for Jack, then put that thing on a cargo ship, and get the fuck outta here! Got it?"

Henry dropped into a chair behind a makeshift table in the corner of the room. "Yeah. I got it," he snarled.

"Good. Now open your beer and have a drink. What happened today was nothing short of incredible. And if we get Veselko back, it'll be remembered as one of the greatest Ružaro ops of all time."

Henry cracked his beer and raised it into the air. "To wild rides and reckless nonsense," he toasted.

"That's what I'm talking about! Cheers, my brother!"

As they slugged their beers, Miguel rushed into the kitchen, tugging at the lapel of his jacket. "Gentlemen," he began in accented English. "I am honored that you have called upon the Red Command for assistance. And if there is anything I can do for you and your men, please do not hesitate to ask."

Darius let out an exhausted laugh. "Thank you, Miguel. Just make sure your men are ready to take us to the airport. As soon as our colleague arrives, we'll be leaving."

"Yes, sir. I will make sure everything is ready to go." With that, Miguel smiled proudly and disappeared from sight.

As the evening wore on, they anxiously paced the kitchen. And when they grew tired of pacing the kitchen, they went outside and paced in the grass.

Just after eight o'clock, one of Miguel's men came running toward the house from the front gate, shouting excitedly in Portuguese.

Miguel spilled out the front door and down the steps.

"What the hell's he saying?" Henry demanded.

Miguel caught his breath. "He says a truck just dropped a man off at the end of the road!"

Henry and Darius turned toward the main entrance and began running. As they reached the stock gate, a strange figure appeared in the road ahead of them.

"This isn't what I signed up for!" the voice shouted through the darkness.

A weary grin lifted from the corner of Henry's mouth.

With a backpack slung over his shoulder, Jack Veselko lumbered up the trail and through the metal gate.

"What a nice surprise!" Henry greeted. "I was just telling Darius that the odds of you surviving were really, really bad."

Jack was completely out of breath but managed a tiny laugh. He fell to his knees and dropped his pack into the dirt.

Miguel and one of his men rushed over and helped the young operator back to his feet. They handed him a bottled water and stood by, eager to help in any way they could.

Jack finally caught his breath. "So? Tell me this wasn't all for nothing."

"This wasn't all for nothing," Darius proudly confirmed.

Jack's booming battle cry echoed across the valley as he lunged at Darius and wrapped his arms around him. "Oh, thank you, tiny baby Jesus!" he wailed. "I can't believe it! You found the truck?"

"We found the truck," Henry confirmed. "We also crashed an airplane and stole a priceless package from the largest cartel in Brazil. But all in all, everything worked out well."

"You two are the craziest motherfuckers I've ever met. That's insane!"

Henry nodded reluctantly. "Yeah, it sorta feels like that sometimes."

"All right, Jack, go clean yourself up," Darius ordered. "We leave for the airport in ten."

Jack turned and limped inside as Henry and Darius stood beneath a canopy of stars.

"He's a good guy," said Henry.

"Yes, he is. Keep him in mind someday; he'll make a good lieutenant."

Henry snickered to himself and shook his head. "I'm sure he will."

"So… whaddya think? You ready to go home, bro?"

"Never been more ready."

"Good. Let's pack it up."

Henry made his way into the old farmhouse and gathered his things. As he and Darius hustled the gear out to Miguel's white sedan, Jack stepped off the porch dressed in a purple tracksuit he'd taken from a closet, his hair still wet from a cold shower.

Miguel fired up the car's engine and the three Ružaro members piled in.

After a short drive through the darkness, they wove into the valley and arrived at a small airport south of Campinas. Miguel cut the headlights and pulled the sedan onto the runway.

As Henry squinted through the windshield, a white Learjet slowly came into view on the tarmac. The plane was much smaller than the Gulfstream they'd flown in on, but he couldn't have cared less. He got out and lugged his pack up the staircase before flopping into the first seat he could find. Minutes later, the small jet lifted off the runway and streaked into the cold, dark sky.

CHAPTER 15

He'd survived a cartel kidnapping, a plane crash, and two high-altitude jumps. And now, exhausted and grateful to be alive, Henry dropped onto his couch, slipped off his sneakers, collapsed against the cushions, and drifted into a deep sleep.

* * *

Special Agent Miles Brennan sipped his coffee in the driver's seat of his Suburban. He made a left turn onto Weuca, then pulled the SUV into the rear lot of the Marriott Buckhead hotel.

He took the elevator to the twenty-first floor and trudged up the hallway to the command center. Inside, Agent Harwick and Officer Garza waited at a table against the far window.

"Good morning, Special Agent Brennan," Harwick greeted. "I see your target is back on the grid."

Miles set his coffee on the counter and rubbed his eyes. "Yep. Martović returned early this morning. Sirola was with him."

"Any idea where they might have gone?"

"None. Their flight out of Brown Field was destined for Buenos Aires. Only they weren't on it. Officially speaking, that is."

"Of course they weren't," scoffed Harwick. "You think it's related to the research vessel?"

The FBI agent nodded slowly. "I do. Krunoslav sent Martović down to check on something. If I had to guess, I'd say he was down there setting up a transport channel to get whatever the hell they found back home unnoticed."

"Keep your eyes open and give me an update by sundown. I want to know what these assholes are up to."

"You and me both, sir." Miles snatched his coffee and headed for the door. "Garza, you coming?"

With a roll of his brown eyes, Garza grabbed his things and charged after his partner, who was now in the hallway waiting for the elevator.

* * *

Henry had cocooned himself within a large blanket, where he remained for the better part of the day. A little after four o'clock, he pulled himself from the couch and walked into the kitchen. He made a cup of coffee and stood motionless at the window, lost in his thoughts.

As the world stood ominously still, the sound of his cell phone snapped him from a distant trance. He let it go to voicemail.

But it rang again.

And then again.

He shuffled out of the kitchen and into the living room where the device buzzed against the coffee table. He held it up and glared at the screen.

It was Darius.

"Hello?"

"How you feeling?"

"I'm great," he lied. "How about you?"

"Anton wants to see us in an hour. Just a quick debrief, nothing serious. Want me to pick you up?"

Henry pushed his hair back against his head and sat down on the sofa. "Sure. Give me thirty minutes."

"You got it. See you then."

With a light sigh, he tossed the phone back onto the table, then forced himself up the hallway and into his room. He picked a brown suit with a white shirt, then brushed his hair into place and walked to the elevator.

Downstairs, he waited patiently in the parking lot until the headlights of Darius' Porsche appeared from above.

He got in and buckled up as the car shot out of the garage southbound onto Peachtree Street. They arrived at the Park Avenue building and hurried upstairs where Asa welcomed them in and guided them through the penthouse.

As they approached the grand hall, Anton burst out of his study to meet them. "My boys!" he shouted gleefully. "You are by far the most daring, incredibly talented operators I have ever known! Oh my goodness, please tell me that the stories I hear are true!" He wrapped Darius in his arms, then Henry.

"We found it," Darius said into his shoulder. "We actually found it."

Anton led them into the study and poured a round of Scotch. "So tell me, boys, did you really crash an airplane into the forest?"

"Yes," Darius answered through a tight laugh. "It was quite a sight."

"That's wonderful! Please, come, have a seat."

As the three of them settled in, Asa left the room and closed the door behind himself.

"The asset is on its way to Miami," Darius reported. "Everything went smoothly."

Anton was delighted. He sipped his Scotch and looked upon them as if they were his own sons. He raised his glass and offered a toast. "To the next generation."

Henry and Darius hoisted their glasses into the air, unable to contain their excitement.

"Now, listen to me very carefully," Anton instructed. "I'm giving you both danger pay for what happened in Brazil. And I don't want to hear a word about it. As long as you're both safe and sound and working for this organization, there isn't a price I wouldn't pay to keep you both happy. Soldiers have to eat, am I right?"

Henry nodded his head softly. "Thank you, Anton. That's very generous of you."

"Well, I didn't ask you here just so I could stuff your pockets. We're ramping up the operation. This *business* with Cardoso just amplified everything—security, distribution, the transaction, all of it."

"So what's that mean for us?" asked Darius.

"While Rukov's crew prepares safety measures, I need to make sure there are no more setbacks."

Darius shook his head. "It won't be a problem, Anton. We put it on a cargo ship in Caracas ourselves. And half of the Miami Port Authority is on our payroll. We're good to go. No more setbacks."

"And after it arrives in Miami?" Anton pressed.

"Once it gets through customs, they'll load the entire container onto one of our trucks. Then it's just a short, ten-hour drive up the interstate to our doorstep. Asa's men will be guarding it the entire time."

"Perfect. Thank you, both, for staying on top of things." Anton paused with concern. "I want you boys to be very careful from here on out. We're not in the business of making enemies, but things don't always go as planned."

Darius nodded. "Absolutely, Anton. I never intended to stir up trouble by taking out that driver, I just—"

"No need for apologies, my boy. I can assure you the Cardoso cartel is more upset about us retrieving the box from their disgusting, greedy hands than they are about some local foot soldier. But nonetheless, they'll be out for blood."

"We'll keep our eyes open," assured Henry.

A wide smile appeared on Anton's face. "I'm proud of you both, and I just had to see your faces with my own eyes.

Now go prepare your crew. Everyone needs to be on high alert until our package arrives."

Henry and Darius downed what was left of their Scotch and got up from their seats.

Anton walked them to the door, into the grand hall where Asa patiently waited. "Now you boys get some rest, then back to work," the boss ordered. "I'll see you on Monday."

Henry stuck his hands into his pockets. "Yes, sir. And thank you again."

As Anton returned to his study, Asa ushered them back to the elevator.

"Did the old man not think we'd survive?" Darius wondered aloud.

"No," Asa revealed as he paced up the long, red hallway. "Once we found out Henry had been captured, Anton put in a call to the cartel, but they assured us it was too late. We were certain all three of you were as good as dead."

"Thanks for the vote of confidence," Darius joked. "What would you have done if they killed us?"

The husky Croatian stopped at the elevator and grinned. "We would have burned their entire organization to the ground," he confessed. "If it makes you feel better, Anton takes your safety very seriously. As do I."

"I knew you loved us," teased Henry. "That means a lot, Asa. It really does."

Asa allowed a meager chuckle as the elevator opened and the two operators stepped inside. "I'll post a few of my men outside your homes for the next few days," the general promised as the doors began to close. "And don't lose track of that fucking stone!"

Henry and Darius rode to the parking garage with a pair of grins firmly attached to their faces. Downstairs, they got into the Porsche and sped away. As the sportscar darted through the city back to Midtown, Henry fidgeted in his seat, chewing away at one of his fingernails.

"What's wrong?" Darius asked, sensing his friend's trepidation.

"Nothing."

"*Something.*"

Henry looked away, through the window into a simple world that seemed to be passing him by. "I'm just ready for this whole thing to be over," he said somberly.

"Well, I hate to break it to you, but we've still got a long way to go."

"I know. I'm just tired, Darius. How much longer can we play the roles of Anton's lunatics?"

Darius laughed. "That's just the way it is, bro. What's the matter, you getting too old for this shit?"

"No, that's not it."

"Are you seriously going to sit here and tell me you didn't enjoy jumping out of those planes and chasing cartel soldiers around Brazil? Bullshit! You loved it."

Henry fought a mischievous smirk. "Yeah, all right, I guess that was pretty fun. But one of these days, our luck's gonna run out. And don't pretend like you don't see it coming."

"You know what your problem is, Henry?"

"What?"

"You think too much. Just enjoy the ride. Other people would kill for this life."

Henry shook his head. "We *do* kill for this life, Darius. And a lot of times it's for no good reason. We're thieves, not murderers."

"Are you talking about that truck driver? C'mon, that guy was a stone-cold killer. He was reaching for his gun! He was gonna blow us both away!"

"No, believe me, I get it. I was there. It's just not my favorite part of the job."

Darius shook his head and grunted with discontent. "Listen, I will always protect you, no matter what. And I'll always protect this crew. You know the rule: nobody gets in our way. It's us versus the world, remember?"

"Yeah, yeah. I just wish more people would stay out of our fucking way, that's all."

"Me and you both. Now, you want to come over and get some work done?"

Henry rocked his head. "I guess that's not a bad idea. We need to get our buyer worked out and coordinate with Rukov's team."

"That's the spirit," Darius cheered as the Porsche veered into Ansley Park and wove along the tree-lined streets.

Minutes later, the iron gates at the top of his driveway slowly opened and the sportscar inched forward and parked in front of the garage. "It's a beautiful night," Darius noted as they got out. "You up for a little walk through the park before we get started?"

Henry glanced up at the stars lingering overhead. "Sure, why not."

They began an easy stroll through Darius' backyard to an illuminated trail that led them into Ansley Park. The soft, faraway sounds of the city whispered against the backdrop of a still hush. They walked the pathway along the grass, their hands tucked into their pockets and their eyes glued to the gravel.

"Have you spoken with Isabell since Sorrento?" Darius asked.

"No. Why?"

"She's a good girl, ya know. You can't hold on to grudges forever. At some point, you'll need to forgive her."

"That's not my style, Darius. You should know that by now."

"Fair enough. But who knows, maybe Sorrento was a step in the right direction?"

Henry was eager to change the subject. He ambled on with a deep, frustrated groan.

"Fine," Darius relented. "I won't bring it up again."

They continued in silence up the trail, around the northeast corner of the park, and over a thin wooden bridge that rose above a small creek.

"I'm really proud of you," Darius finally stated.

Henry stopped, his feet seemingly locked to the ground. "For what?"

"Working in this business alongside your best friend isn't always easy," Darius admitted. "I know you've put up with a lot of my bullshit… and I'm proud of you for maintaining your focus. You're gonna be a legend someday."

Henry fought his modesty and allowed a tiny glint of satisfaction to splash across his face. The gravel beneath his feet crackled as he began moving again. The trail eventually wove them back toward the south end of the park, where they traipsed along, enjoying the cool breeze.

As they cornered the bend to Darius' home, a rustling in the shadows caught their attention.

But before Henry's eyes could adjust, two deep thuds broke the quiet air. He shuddered his shoulders instinctively.

Beside him, Darius slumped forward, then fell to his knees.

Another wispy ping burst from the ground at Henry's feet. Then another. He quickly realized it was the sound of bullets hitting the gravel.

He grabbed Darius by his shoulders and lunged for cover behind a large boulder just off the trail. His pulse quickened beneath his jacket as he pinned himself to the rock.

"Darius? You okay?"

He could see a spot of blood pooling around his friend's stomach. He peered over the stone, trying to get a bead on where the shots had come from.

As Darius groaned in pain, Henry did what he was trained to—he lifted Darius' shirt and pressed his hands against the wound.

"Hang in there, buddy," he growled. "Stay with me."

Darius gasped for air. "My gun," he said through a labored breath.

Henry dropped his eyes to the nine-millimeter holstered inside Darius' jacket. He pulled it out and again gazed over the top of the boulder. As he tried to get into firing position, two more bullets shattered against the granite above him.

"Damn it!" Henry shouted. He raised the pistol over the rock and fired three random shots into the dark night. He then listened for footsteps, but the park had fallen completely silent.

Next to him, Darius' body shivered against the boulder. A stream of blood now ran from his mouth.

"Try to calm your breathing, Darius. You're gonna be all right."

"Henry," Darius whispered as he clutched his stomach. "You need to listen to me very carefully."

But Henry wasn't listening. He was scanning the area for an assassin, cycling through a series of potential escape routes.

"Henry!" Darius snapped.

Henry looked down with concern.

"I need you to do something for me," Darius tried. "You need to find someone."

"What? What are you talking about? Just stay calm, man. We're getting out of here."

"You have to find… a man." Darius was struggling to speak. "A man named Colton Sinclair."

Henry stared at him, shaking his head. "What the hell are you talking about?"

"Colton Sinclair," Darius repeated as he winced in pain. "Find him… as soon as possible."

"You're not making any sense, Darius."

"Laura Bell… she'll help you."

"Laura who?" Henry pleaded. The words seemed like gibberish.

Darius' eyes slowly closed. "The poet," he whispered softly.

"Darius! Darius! Stay with me… don't you fucking pull this shit! Wake up!" Henry was in full panic now.

Darius opened his eyes and looked up. His teeth were stained with blood and his body began to tremble. Then, with a final breath, he leaned his head gently against the rock.

"Darius! Don't do this to me!" Henry screamed.

He checked for a pulse, but it was gone.

Darius' eyes stared vacantly into the night sky.

Through a rush of adrenaline, Henry reached into Darius' pocket and fumbled around for his cell phone and wallet. It was all part of the protocol. With a final, calming breath, he stood from behind the rock and sprinted away through the darkness.

Henry pushed further into the woods until he reached the parking lot of a nearby brewery along the main road. He shoved the nine-millimeter into his waistband beneath his shirt and raced across the pavement.

He tried to catch his breath and think rationally, but he struggled to make sense of what had just happened. With a distant, empty gaze, he looked down at his arms—his shirt and hands were covered in blood.

He tore the white button-up from his body and hurled it into the nearby trees. He then slipped his hands casually into his pockets and began pacing up the sidewalk beneath a hazy row of streetlights.

CHAPTER 16

"Shots fired! Shots fired!" Miles yelled into his radio. "I repeat, we have shots fired. Delta Target is down!"

The front doors of the utility van blew open as he and Garza charged toward the park. Miles sprinted to Darius, who lay motionless against the boulder. The agent checked for a pulse but felt nothing. He gritted his teeth and stared into the nearby forest.

Garza jogged over with his sidearm drawn. "What the hell happened?"

"I don't know," Miles said as he scanned the park. "We need to get a perimeter in place. Get an APB out on Henry Sirola."

"What about the shooter?"

"I didn't see anything, did you?"

Garza huffed with frustration. "No. The shots came from that wooded area over there, but I never saw anyone."

"This is a fucking disaster," Miles grumbled as he lifted the radio to his mouth. "Evergreen, this is Phantom One. I need a perimeter set up around Ansley Park."

"Roger that," Harwick responded. "Are you on location?"

"Yeah, we're at the southeast corner."

"And he's dead?"

"Affirmative. Delta Target is down. We weren't close enough to respond."

The blistering sound of sirens wailed from several blocks away, drawing closer with every passing moment. Miles rose to his feet and marched over to the wooded area where the shots had come from. He pulled out a small flashlight and scanned the ground. There were no bullet casings, no cigarette butts, no footprints. There was absolutely no evidence of a shooter.

Miles paced the grounds, darting his eyes through the park, which was now illuminated with halogen lights. Police helicopters circled above like vultures as local officers ran yellow tape around trees and detectives snapped photos of Darius' body.

Twenty minutes later, Agent Harwick arrived. He examined the area with disgust, his hands clasped to his waist. "Well, let the games begin," he announced casually.

"Has Henry Sirola been picked up?" Miles asked.

Harwick kicked at the pebbles beneath his feet. "No. We have teams at *his* residence, Krunoslav's residence, and everywhere in between. Sirola's in the wind."

"I can't fucking believe this shit."

"Who the hell would've done this?" Harwick wondered.

Miles shook his head. "No idea. He was a high-level captain. The Ružaros don't have a lot of enemies, your guess is as good as mine."

"They left Krunoslav's place an hour ago. Did they stop anywhere on their way over here?"

"No. They went straight to Darius' house, then punched through the backyard on foot and walked around the park for ten minutes. We had to circle around in the van and by the time we got here, all we could see was suppressed gunfire coming from this wooded area. Sirola returned maybe two or three rounds, and that was it; he took off in that direction."

"Unbelievable."

Miles sulked for a moment in the darkness. "Something's not right," he finally offered.

"What do you mean?"

"Well, Martović is put in charge of setting up a fence for Anton's little treasure, and then he's killed? It doesn't add up."

Harwick lowered his voice. "Have you spoken with the Shadowmaker?"

"Not since the other day."

"Well, I suggest you set something up."

"Will do."

"And Miles?"

"Yes, sir?"

"I want to know who your informant is by tomorrow morning. Am I clear?"

"I'm sorry, but that's not going to happen, sir."

Harwick stepped closer. They were now face to face. "You better dig real deep, son, and find a way to make it happen." The NSA agent spun away and darted into the chaos of the crime scene.

As Miles stood alone in the grass, a light breeze swept across the open field. He stared absently into the lights of the city beyond the swaying trees. "Where the hell are you, Henry?"

CHAPTER 17

Isabell sat on her couch with her knees tucked against her chest. She dipped her spoon into a carton of ice cream and flipped through an endless list of channels on her big screen TV.

He watched her through the window, second guessing his decision to come. With a deep sigh into the cool night, he eased through the bushes toward the back of the house. There were a dozen other ways of getting in but none of them would end well for him. This, he figured, was the lesser of multiple evils.

A light knock on the back door startled her from the couch. Isabell set the carton of Moose Tracks on the end table and rose to her feet. Her eyes darted around the room as she listened closely.

Another light knock.

She walked over to the window and peered through the blinds to the front yard. The only car in the driveway was hers, and the street beyond it was empty and still. Whoever was tapping on her back door had arrived on foot.

She rushed to her bedroom and put on her robe, then tiptoed through the hallway and into the kitchen. She grabbed a butcher's knife from the wooden block on the counter and cautiously approached the back door.

"Who is it?" she asked sharply.

"Isabell, it's me," a voice replied. "It's Henry."

She tightened her brow. "Are you alone?"

"Yes. Can I come in?"

The lock disengaged and the door slowly opened.

Isabell stared at him for a moment, then waved him in. She checked behind him before closing the door and locking it. "What are you doing here, Henry? You could've called first."

He turned to face her. His eyes were swollen and damp. There were bloodstains on his hands.

"What the hell happened?" she asked. "What did you do?"

"It's not like that."

"Then whose blood is that?" She was angry now, standing with her arms crossed at her chest.

But Henry didn't answer. He hung his head and began to cry.

"Henry?" she softly murmured.

"He's dead."

"Who's dead?"

Henry took a breath and lifted his eyes. "Darius."

Isabell gasped as her hands shot up to her mouth. "Oh my God! How? What happened?"

"He was shot. He died in my arms. I'm sorry, there was nowhere else for me to go."

"Henry, are we in danger?"

"No."

"No one followed you here?"

"No. I got off the bus in Brookhaven and walked the rest of the way. I wasn't followed." He pulled the gun from his waistband and set it on the counter.

She placed her hands on his shoulders, comforting him with what little empathy she could muster. "Are you hurt?"

"No. No, I'm fine."

As the shock wore off, Isabell allowed her training to take over. She grabbed the nine-millimeter from the counter and rushed into the living room, where she shut the blinds and turned off the television. She used her robe to wipe down the grip and the trigger before shoving it into a bookshelf and out of sight.

"Take off that shirt!" she demanded.

Henry pulled off his white undershirt, which still held a few splatters of blood. She ripped it from his hands and disappeared down the hallway.

He could hear the door of the washing machine slam shut before she reappeared with a gray sweatshirt. "Here, put this on."

Henry slipped it over his head and followed her back to the living room. "They killed him. They fucking killed him," he uttered in a low, distant tone.

"Who did this?"

Henry shook his head. "I don't know. I didn't see them."

"Have you called Anton? Does he know about this?"

"No. Probably not."

"Why are you here, Henry?" she finally asked. "I know you guys have a protocol. And there's no way this is it."

He sat down on the couch and dropped his head into his hands.

Isabell went to the kitchen and returned with a bottle and two glasses. She twisted off the top and poured a couple fingers of bourbon, handing one to Henry.

He brought it to his lips and took a swig. "I just don't know who I can trust right now."

"Tell me what happened."

"We had a meeting tonight—"

"With who?"

"Anton. Afterwards, we went to Darius' place and walked into Ansley Park. On our way back, somebody opened fire on us."

"*Opened fire*? You mean someone just appeared and started shooting?"

"They were hidden, I couldn't see anything. But yeah… they just started shooting."

"What kind of gun?"

"I don't know, I didn't really hear the shots. They must've been using a silencer."

"Pistol or rifle?"

Henry thought for a moment. "I don't know…a pistol, I think."

"How many shots?"

"Two… at first."

Isabell's mind tried desperately to recreate the scenario. "Both shots hit Darius?"

"Yes."

"Then what?"

"I threw him behind a big rock and we took cover."

"Henry, this was a hit."

"Yeah, no shit!" he snapped, his voice rising with anger. "I'm glad you're keeping up!"

"No, I mean, this was a professional, calculated hit. Someone big wanted Darius dead."

Henry shook his head and leaned back into the sofa. "Darius never had enemies like that… until now."

"What do you mean *until now*?"

"I mean, we got into some trouble this week. In Brazil."

She tightened her lips with frustration. "What were you doing in Brazil?"

"It's a long story. There was a problem with the asset."

"What kind of a problem?"

"A customs problem. Darius and I had to go down and… retrieve it."

"From who?"

Henry lifted his gaze and locked in to her sparkling green eyes. "Cardoso," he quietly revealed.

"What? Are you *insane*?"

"Yes. I'm starting to think I am."

"You have to go to Anton," she urged. "I don't see any other options."

"I will. I just need to clear my head and—"

"And what?"

"I don't know." He took another sip. "This is all so fucked."

Isabell sat down on the couch and inched closer to him. "I'm truly sorry, Henry."

"He was like a brother to me. I'm gonna kill whoever did this."

"I know," she said soothingly. "Anton will take care of everything. He'll find out who did this and make sure they pay."

Henry clenched his eyes, holding back the tears that were fighting to come out.

She pulled him into her shoulder and rubbed his arm. "Everything's going to be okay. I promise."

"You know better than to tell me that," he muttered.

"Yeah, I guess you're right. I shouldn't make those kinds of promises. But you're going to be all right. You'll get through this, Henry. You always do."

He downed his bourbon and set the glass on the table. "Let's just keep drinking," he suggested with a wave of his arm.

She was reluctant at first, but then reached for the bottle and refilled their glasses, this time much higher than before. "Did anyone else see you in the park with Darius?" she asked.

"No. Just the shooter."

"So nobody's looking for you? They didn't give chase?"

"No, Izzy," he groaned. "Nobody is looking for me. And nobody followed me."

The nickname caught her off guard. She hadn't heard him call her that in years. "Okay, I believe you. But there are probably investigators all over that crime scene by now, and at some point, they'll figure out that Darius was with someone. And then they'll start looking for that someone."

He raised his glass into the air, pretending not to hear her. "To Darius," he solemnly toasted.

"To Darius," she echoed.

They sat together on the sofa for nearly an hour. He regaled her with tales of his and Darius' childhoods, mostly for his own sake, she knew. Eventually, he ran out of stories and just sat quietly, staring into the nothingness of her living room.

Isabell was giving him the space he needed—the comfortable, delicate silence that only she could afford him.

"Can I stay here tonight?" he asked.

"Of course."

"I can't tell you how much I appreciate this. I'm really sorry."

"It's fine. And stop apologizing. You can sleep in the guest room, stay as long as you need."

Henry stared into her eyes. "Will your boyfriend mind? What's his name, Jacob?"

Her eyes suddenly widened. "Y-y-yes. Jacob," she stuttered. "And no, he won't be back for a few days. Just get some rest, we'll figure everything out in the morning." Isabell got up from the couch and drifted up the hallway to the guest room, where she drew the curtains and tossed an extra pillow on the bed.

"Thanks for letting me crash," he said from the doorway. "I really, really appreciate it."

"Well, from a tactical standpoint, it's not the worst idea you've ever had."

He stepped into the room and took off his sweatshirt before dropping onto the bed.

"I'll see you in the morning," she said as she slipped out of the room and closed the door.

Henry laid there quietly, trying to wrap his head around the fact that Darius was no longer out there—that his corpse was lying alone in the shadows of Ansley Park. The thought made him furious.

When the trauma and fatigue and anger had finally worn off, Henry fell into a light sleep.

As morning broke, the first rays of light peeked through the window. He pulled himself out of bed and paced up the hallway to the bathroom, where he stepped into the shower and let the hot water beat down on his face and chest.

After slipping into his clothes, he went to the kitchen and found Isabell sitting quietly at the breakfast table. A freshly brewed pot of coffee rested on the counter.

"You sleep okay?" she asked.

He took a seat next to her and tried to steady his thoughts. "No. I can't say that I did."

"How about some coffee and breakfast?"

Henry nodded half heartedly. While Isabell scrambled eggs and buttered toast, he sat like a vacant statue.

"Do you think anyone from Ružaro was behind this?" she asked as she set their plates on the table. "Is that why you haven't called Anton?"

Henry shrugged it off. "No, that's absurd. It had to be the Cardoso cartel. Besides, why would Anton do something like this?"

"If there's one thing I've learned, Henry, it's that you can't make assumptions. Ever."

"The only way Anton would have any of us killed is if we betrayed him. And Darius would *never* betray him."

"Okay. What about the Dominicans? Darius used to do a lot of work with the Molinas gang. Maybe something went sideways?"

"No way. The Molinas are stupid, but not that stupid. Taking out Darius is a direct attack on Anton. The Molinas would never bite the hand that feeds."

She picked at her eggs, trying to consider every option. "So that makes Cardoso suspect number one. Other than the new diamond haul you just stole back from them, what else was Darius working on?"

Henry shook his head. "I don't know."

"What do you mean you don't know? You guys worked together."

"Yeah, but the flow of information isn't always…"

"Isn't always what?"

"I recently found out that he had already been to Brazil a couple weeks ago… without me. But he never told me about it."

"Seems out of character for Darius to lie to you, don't you think?"

"He didn't exactly lie. He just didn't mention it. And I have no idea what else he might've been working on."

"He never mentioned anything? Maybe he was doing contract work for someone else. Maybe he was double-crossed."

Henry's mind flashed back to the previous night, hunkered behind the boulder as Darius bled out next to him. "You know, Darius said some weird shit last night after he was shot."

Isabell's forehead wrinkled with bemusement. "Like what?"

"Names," Henry recalled. "He was mentioning these names."

"What names?"

"I don't know… Cole or Colton." He sighed heavily into his plate. "Yeah, it was Colton something."

"That's weird. You've never heard the names before?"

"Colton Sinclair," Henry blurted into the air.

"Who?"

"He told me to find some guy named Colton Sinclair. And then he mentioned someone else." Henry pursed his lips in thought. His eyes wandered the table.

"Colton Sinclair," Isabell slowly repeated. She pulled out her phone and typed the name into the search field. "Hmm, I don't see anything when I Google it. Who was the other person he mentioned?"

A tight grin splashed across Henry's face. "Laura Bell," he whispered.

"Who's Laura Bell?"

"His favorite poet. He used to read all of her books when we were younger."

Isabell let out a tiny laugh. "A poet? Darius was into poetry? C'mon, I don't buy it."

"It's true, I swear. But he would never confess that to anyone."

"Anyone except for you."

"Yeah. Anyone except for me," he noted dryly.

"Great, so she's a poet. I don't understand what that has to do with anything. Was Darius coherent when he said this stuff or do you think he was just in shock?"

"He said Laura Bell could help me find Colton Sinclair."

Isabell again took to her smartphone. "Well, that's not going to happen. Laura Bell died in 1972."

"Exactly. And the only way she can talk to us is through her words. We need to get to Darius' house."

Isabell wasn't biting. She eyed him curiously from across the table. "I think you should just talk to Anton first."

"Look," Henry implored, "Darius used his dying breath to tell me to find this man. I think Laura Bell was just a clue."

"A clue? What are you playing detective now?"

"I don't know. Maybe."

"Fine." She set her fork down and huffed with aggravation. "Let me get dressed and we'll drive over to Darius' house. But it's probably crawling with cops by now."

She cleaned up the kitchen and disappeared into her room. Ten minutes later, she glided up the hallway and through the front door to her midnight blue SUV parked in the driveway. Henry quickly followed.

They left the suburbs along the interstate and drifted south into downtown before exiting at Piedmont Avenue. Within minutes, they entered the Ansley Park residential area.

"Pull over here," he instructed as they wove deeper into Darius' neighborhood. Isabell found a spot against the curb and tucked her SUV between two other vehicles. "Just wait for me," he said. "If I'm not back in fifteen minutes, go directly back to your house."

"And then what?"

Henry smiled at her. He'd always loved her argumentative logic. "Pretend you never met me and enjoy the rest of your life."

Before she could answer, he leapt out of the SUV and disappeared into the woods behind a row of homes. He emerged minutes later behind Darius' house along the same pathway the two had walked the night before.

As he peered around the brick façade, he could see two agents sitting in a blue van parked out front. One was taking a nap, the other seemed lost in his smartphone. With an amused look, Henry tightened his collar and peered into a nearby window. Inside, he could see the faint green light of the security keypad blinking in the hallway—an indication it had been disabled.

He pulled a small metal pick from his back pocket and slid it carefully between the window panes. With a gentle lift, he opened it up and crept inside.

A few of Darius' things lay strewn around in the kitchen—the last book he ever read, the last beer he ever drank, and a sheet of notebook paper containing the last words he would ever write: a scribbled grocery list of cheese slices, tonic, dish detergent, and jelly.

Henry continued up the hallway to the study, where he walked to a tall bookshelf against the wall. He quickly scanned the book spines in search of a particular author. There, on the bottom shelf, he set his index finger on a copy of *Listen to the Warmth* by Laura Bell. It was a small book by comparison—a collection of short poems and essays. He took a moment to search for other books by the author but didn't find any.

With an anxious breath, he rose to his feet and left the house the same way he'd come in.

Two blocks away, Isabell sat in her SUV, humming the tune to a song she couldn't quite place. She tapped her fingers against the steering wheel and peered out into the street. It had been eleven minutes since Henry had gotten out of the car and darted into the woods, which left a mere four minutes before she would pull away and never see him again. The thought bothered her for reasons she wasn't ready to face.

Another minute passed. Then another. Finally, the passenger door sprang open.

Isabell let out a tiny gasp. "You scared the shit out of me!"

"I think I found it. Let's go," he commanded as he strapped himself in.

She pulled the SUV off the curb and drove away.

Henry began thumbing through the small book page by page.

"So what are you looking for?" she asked.

"I don't know exactly."

"But you think there's a clue in there?"

"Maybe." He was distracted now, almost afraid of what he might find.

After a short ride through the suburbs, they pulled into Isabell's driveway and into the garage. Henry raced inside, sat down at the kitchen table, and turned the book back to page one. His eyes devoured the text, skimming each line with careful precision. He tried to remember if Darius had ever mentioned a favorite passage, but couldn't recall anything specific.

Isabell grabbed her laptop and sat down next to him. She ran a quick search for the author and examined the litany of results. "Laura Bell wrote twelve collections of poetry," she read from her screen. "How do you know we have the right one?"

"It was the only Laura Bell book in his library." His eyes continued to scan until a notation on page thirty-six caught his attention. There were two letters scribbled into the side margin: *H.S.* Henry squinted closer. "I think I found something."

Isabell peered over his shoulder "H.S.? What's that?"

He lifted his eyes from the page. "They're my initials."

Beside the two letters was a hand-drawn arrow that pointed to a passage further down the page. He followed it with his index finger and read the words aloud. "*In toilsome times, we must not draw back. For the lunar stones shall guide your path.*"

Isabell crinkled her nose. "What does that mean?"

"I have no idea."

She ripped the book from his grasp and eyed the page intently, searching for more context or side notes. "It's just a poem about moons and rivers," she mumbled.

"This isn't about the poem, it's about that line. He picked it for a reason."

"*Lunar stones?*" she repeated. "What lunar stones?"

Henry shut his eyes and tried desperately to come up with a reasonable answer. But there wasn't one.

She set the book down in front of him. "Maybe you're overthinking it, Henry. I mean, there's no telling what was going through Darius' mind after he'd been shot. It could be nothing."

"No, this means something. I just don't know what exactly." He quickly flipped through the rest of the book, then stopped at the last set of pages. "There's more here," he said.

"What is it?"

Henry peered down at a series of numbers that had been scrawled across a blank page in blue ink. "It's a code."

Isabell hardened her gaze deeper into the book.

10.1 12.4 19.2

23.1 8.2 8.3 4.3 20.1 20.4 23.2 1.3 20.2 14.4

"Any idea what it means?" she asked.

"No." The wheels in his head were spinning at reckless speeds.

"Maybe they're coordinates?"

His eyes jumped from one set of numbers to the next. "It almost looks like an Arnold Cipher but the structure isn't right."

"An Arnold Cipher? I haven't seen that before, you'll have to enlighten me."

"It was a code that Benedict Arnold invented for his network of spies during the Revolutionary War—a series of numbers in sets of three that can only be deciphered using a specified book."

"I'm not following."

Henry sat back in his chair and rubbed his forehead. "The three numbers of each set are separated by a period," he explained. "They signify a page number, a line number, and a word number. With the right book, you can decipher the code."

"Okay, but these sets only include two numbers."

"Yeah, that's the problem."

"Why would someone put a cipher in the same book used to decipher?" she asked. "Sort of defeats the whole purpose, don't you think?"

Henry moaned into the air. "I don't know. I'm at a total loss."

"So we have a senseless passage of poetry and an incomplete cipher code." She reached over and grabbed his hand. "I'm sorry, Henry. I really am. I'm sorry about Darius and this whole thing. All of it."

"It's okay. I'll go see Anton this afternoon. He'll want to hear from me."

"Good. I'm sure he'll know what to do."

CHAPTER 18

Asa Petrovi glared at Henry through his dark, empty eyes. The young lieutenant sat restlessly on the settee, tapping his sneaker against the carpet as he waited for Anton. After several minutes, the door to the study slung open.

"My boy!" Anton greeted. "I was worried about you. Please come in."

Henry stepped inside the expansive room as Anton closed the doors behind them.

"I can't believe what happened," the boss stated with grief. He pulled Henry in for a hug. "I'm so sorry. Darius was like a son to me, and a brother to you. Come, let's sit and talk."

Henry paced over to the fireplace, where a couple of hand-stitched barrel back chairs faced each other. "The shots came out of nowhere," Henry explained as he sat down. "We took cover but Darius had already been hit."

"Yes, I know," Anton replied. "I was able to get my hands on the police report. They still haven't found the shooter."

"Who could've done this?"

"I promise you, my boy, Asa has an entire army out there trying to figure it out. It won't take long."

"And then what?"

"It depends on who it was, of course. Each outcome determines the next, you understand."

"What if it was the Cardoso cartel?"

Anton scoffed. "Obviously, Cardoso makes sense—they had the motive and the means. But we have nothing to go on right now, Henry. You just need to relax. The worst is over now. Maybe you should take some time off; you've been through a lot."

Henry shifted in his seat. "Thank you, Anton. I'll take that into consideration."

"Tell me, did Darius mention anything to you last night? Maybe some trouble he was having with someone other than Cardoso?"

"No," Henry answered, a bit distracted.

"What were the two of you discussing in the park?"

"Well, we had just gotten back from meeting with you, and Darius wanted to take a stroll and chat for a little bit."

"Chat about what?"

Henry shook his head, trying to remember the last few minutes before the shooting. "We talked about our security assessment and coordinating with Rukov's team… stuff like that."

"Anything else?"

Henry froze in his chair, suddenly uncomfortable with Anton's line of questioning.

"Henry?" Anton tried again. "Was there anything else he said that may be of help to us?"

"No. That was it. Just small talk, nothing that really sticks out."

"All right, my boy. Is there anything I can do for you? Anything at all?"

"No, sir. I think I'm all set. I'm going to take your advice and lay low for a few days. Maybe go visit my Aunt Sara."

Anton flashed his flawless white teeth, but only for a moment. "How is she doing, by the way? I know losing Luka was hard on her."

"She's doing well. I think each day is a little easier. Thank you for asking."

"You know, I remember the old country, when you and Darius were just boys. Hell, your Uncle Luka and I were just boys." Anton stared blankly into the air, conjuring spirits of the past. "I remember leaving Krasno that day, driving off in an old military truck with all of our families packed into the back like sardines."

Henry nodded remorsefully. "I wish I could remember."

"No… you don't. It was awful. The war had taken so much from us. But desperate times call for desperate measures. Isn't that what they say?"

"Yeah, I guess they do."

"I want you to know that I'm here for you, Henry. We all are. You're part of this family and I won't let anything happen to you."

"I can't tell you how much that means to me, Anton. Thank you."

"Good. Now, when you're ready to return, you'll be coming back as a captain."

Henry lifted his eyes. "A captain?"

"Yes. Unfortunately, Darius' crew isn't going to run itself. The line of succession falls on you."

"I don't know what to say, Anton."

"Don't say anything. Go get your head straight and come back here ready to work. And Henry?"

"Yes, sir?"

"I'm going to need you to take over the new operation—the deal with Hassani."

"Absolutely. I know it was important to Darius. I'd be honored to see it through."

"I believe you already have Isabell DiMarco set up as the tour guide?"

"I do."

"Good. You'll also need to pick a new lieutenant to fill your role—somebody who can help out with the negotiation."

"I will," Henry replied softly. "I'll let you know as soon as I choose someone."

"Perfect."

"Anton, can I ask you a question?"

"Of course, my boy. Anything."

"Before Darius died, he told me the asset was a single diamond. How is that possible? Where'd it come from?"

A thin smile appeared on the old man's face. "You'll have to see it to believe it. Now, get some rest, we'll be in touch next week. I want you here when it arrives." With that, Anton rose from his chair and escorted Henry to the door.

"Thank you again, Anton. For everything."

"There's nothing in this world I wouldn't do for you. Never forget that."

Henry lowered his head and turned away. He met Asa in the grand hall and was quickly taken to the foyer.

Downstairs, he climbed into his Maserati and drove back to his penthouse in a despondent trance. As he walked into his living room and collapsed onto the sofa, his cell phone rang.

It was Isabell.

"Hello?" he answered.

"Henry, it's me."

"Hey. Everything okay?"

"Yeah, I just wanted to check on you."

"I'm fine," he said softly. "Just got back from Anton's."

"And? How'd it go?"

"Good, I guess. He promised to find out who killed Darius."

"I see. And what are you doing now?"

"I'm about to order some food and watch TV… probably drown myself in alcohol, then pass out on my couch."

"Well, don't bother, I just picked up dinner from the Greek Table. I'm on my way over."

Henry sat upright. "You're on your way here?"

"Don't get any ideas," she scolded. "I'm just worried about you. I want to make sure you're okay."

"I already told you I'm okay."

"So I shouldn't come over?"

He exhaled into the phone. "Did you say you picked up Greek Table?"

"Yep."

"Fine, I'll buzz you up when you get here." He hung up the phone and laid it on the coffee table. Minutes later, she walked through the front door with a plastic takeout bag dangling from her arm.

"You weren't kidding," he joked. "That was fast."

"I was basically here when I called." She set the bag on the table and pulled two small boxes from inside.

"Gyros?" he asked.

"Yep. Your favorite."

"Can I get you something to drink?"

"Do you have wine?"

Henry wandered into the kitchen. "Red or white?"

"Red," she answered. He poured a glass of pinot for her and Rogaska for himself, then joined her at the table. "Any progress on Darius' scavenger hunt?" she asked, eyeing the copy of *Listen to the Warmth* laying open on the table.

"Not since this morning." He pulled it closer and flipped to the last page. "I put some thought into your coordinates theory and typed them into a map. Unfortunately, it just kept landing on remote deserts and oceans."

Isabell took a bite of her gyro and a sip of her wine. "Well, it was worth a shot. Maybe it's still a cipher, just not the one you thought it was."

"If this message was truly intended for me, it would've been an Arnold Cipher."

"Why is that?"

"Because we learned how to use it together—when we were coming up in the organization. Asa made it part of our training. It's easy to use and it doesn't matter if the enemy knows you're using it. It only works if you have the right cipher key, the right book."

"Okay, maybe he didn't need a third number," she surmised. "Maybe there aren't any reference pages."

Henry took a long pull of vodka. "What do you mean?"

"You said each set was comprised of three numbers, right? Page number, line number, and word number."

"Yeah, I'm with you," he replied, hanging on her every word.

"If you think about it, there's only one reason why Darius' code would be missing a number in each set."

He stared at her over his glass for a moment. "Because it's not a book: it's a single document." Isabell snapped a flirtatious wink. "You're a genius!" he exclaimed. "It's just line numbers and word numbers, all from the same page. Could it be that simple?"

"Who knows," she replied. "It seems pretty cloak and dagger to me."

Henry stuffed the rest of his gyro into his mouth. His mind raced to figure out what the cipher key could be: a letter, a document, a poster, anything. He grabbed the book and flipped to the page where his initials had been written in the margin, and more importantly, the passage next to it. He read each word carefully, trying to find meaning in its otherwise pointless prose.

In toilsome times, we must not draw back
For the lunar stones shall guide your path

Isabell listened as he read the passage aloud. "*Lunar stones*," she quietly said. "I keep getting stuck on these stones. What lunar stones is she talking about?"

Henry's mind drifted. "The lunar stones shall guide your path," he repeated. "Lunar stones… guide my path." The answer hung ominously in the air, begging to be discovered. "Guide stones. Holy shit! The guide stones!"

"What guide stones?"

Henry darted from the kitchen to the living room. He opened his laptop on the coffee table and began typing away.

Isabell wiped her mouth and got up to follow him. "Henry? What's going on?"

"When we were younger and first started making money, we bought these Harleys thinking we were total badasses. We used to ride those damn things all over the city on the weekends. But once a month we'd ride out of town… to Elberton."

"Elberton? What's in Elberton?"

"These," he said as he spun the laptop toward her. "The Georgia Guidestones."

Isabell joined him on the sofa. "Oh yeah. I remember hearing about those on the news."

"Well, some idiot blew them up with dynamite a while back, but in 1980, these stone pillars were mysteriously erected out in the middle of some field. There were four of them. And get this: they were each aligned with the lunar declination cycle. They're the lunar stones we're looking for."

"Was there something written on these stones?"

Henry sat back with a knowing grin. "I thought you'd never ask." He clicked on an old image of the structures, then zoomed in. "It's a set of commandments… sort of. Experts think it was a list of rules for the world to follow after the apocalypse."

"Whoa. That seems heavy." She squinted at the screen and began reading aloud from the text inscribed on the granite slab. "*One: maintain humanity under five-hundred million in perpetual balance with nature. Two: guide reproduction wisely—improving fitness and diversity*." She stopped and shook her head. "Henry, this is weird."

"Sure, maybe a little," he granted.

"How do we know which stone to use?"

"Well, that's the good news; they each say the same thing, just in different languages."

Henry spun the laptop back to himself and set the book down next to it. He pulled a pen and notepad from the end table and handed it to Isabell. "Here, write this down as I go."

She grabbed the pen and began jotting down letters as Henry used the cipher to locate them. One by one, the text began to form a message. When he was done, Isabell set the notepad on the table. They glared at it with intrigue.

PROTECT THE TRUTH
LEAVE ALL THINGS AND SEEK THE ROOM
UNDER 6 HARMONY COURT

Henry scowled at the notepad. "Well, I'd say that's pretty clear," he mumbled.

"This is scary," Isabell whispered. "There's something really creepy about all of it, Henry. I don't like it."

He quickly typed the address into his laptop. "It says there's over a dozen matches in the United States. But only one nearby."

Isabell lifted herself from the couch and walked over to the sliding glass door overlooking the city.

"Don't you want to know where it is?" he asked.

"Henry, how do we know this is safe? I mean, what kind of trouble was Darius in that he had to leave you some cryptic message like this?"

"I don't know. But I plan on finding out."

Her eyes remained fixated on the skyline in the distance. "Where is it? Six Harmony Court?"

"Waleska. About an hour north of here."

Isabell released an anxious breath and returned to the coffee table. She then grabbed the poetry book and marched over to a buffet against the wall.

"What are you doing?" asked Henry.

"I'm putting this somewhere safe," she replied as she removed a drawer from the buffet and placed it on the floor. "I need some duct tape."

Henry went to the kitchen and rattled around for a few seconds before returning with a roll of thick gray tape. He handed it to her with a look of concern. "Don't you think you're overreacting?"

"Absolutely not." She tore a long piece from the roll, then taped the book to the back of the drawer. With a final push, she set the drawer back into its slot.

Henry looked down at the deciphered message and pulled a lighter from his pocket. He tore the page from the pad, then set it on fire and dropped it onto the table. "So, when do we leave?"

Isabell darted her eyes at the sliding glass door. "There's a black Suburban parked across the street. You're under surveillance, Henry."

He stared at the table as the small blaze turned to ash. "Give me thirty minutes," he said.

"Thirty minutes for what?"

He put on his coat and turned for the door. "I need to sweep the block, see if I catch a tail."

"And if you do?"

"I didn't do anything wrong," he corrected. "If they want to talk to me about Darius' murder, I'll be more than happy to tell them exactly what happened."

"Fine," she conceded. "Just be careful. I'll wait for thirty minutes… then I'm leaving."

CHAPTER 19

He stepped out into the cool October air and tucked his hands into his pockets. With a quick glance across the street, he lumbered south along the sidewalk. He continued on for two more blocks before dipping into an old, rundown pub. A set of Christmas lights hung over the bar and the soft melodies of country music resonated from a nearby jukebox.

As Henry took a seat on a wooden stool, he noticed a bearded drunk in a plaid flannel shirt slumped against the bar a few seats down from him. The bartender—an older gal hardened by years of mixing cocktails—acknowledged his presence with a slight nod.

"Vodka on the rocks," he said pleasantly.

She spun the cap from a gallon of Stolichnaya and dipped a highball glass into a well of ice. The drink landed in front of him atop a small white napkin. As Henry pulled it to his lips, a tiny bell on the front door rang. A brisk wave of cold followed the newcomer in as he approached the bar and found a stool next to Henry.

"What took you so long?" Henry said under his breath.

Miles raised his index finger at the bartender. "Whiskey. Neat." After a moment of silence, another highball glass hit the bar in front of them. "I'm sorry about Darius," the agent offered. "Anything you want to tell me?"

"Stop fucking around," Henry quietly charged. "Were you there? Did you see it go down?"

"No. We had you up to the driveway. By the time I circled the block to the park, it was over. Listen, we have all of sixty seconds to wrap this up, so you need to tell me everything you know."

"Are there any more of you assholes outside?"

Miles slugged his whiskey. "I have a new partner. DCIS officer—solid guy. He's parked in front of your building on Peachtree. Late-model maroon Pathfinder."

"But you parked on Twelfth Street. Why? So I would see you?"

"Maybe."

"All right, all I can tell you is that Darius and I met with Anton just before we went back to his place. He wanted to take a walk and chat about some things. Then he was killed. I never saw the shooter."

"Henry, you know how this works. You were a witness to murder."

"I'm talking to you, aren't I?"

"No, not like this. You need to go to local law enforcement. Once they identify you, they'll notify someone from the bureau to take your statement. But it's gotta be by the book."

Henry shook his head and slouched over his drink. "Well, I'm kinda busy right now."

"Is that Isabell upstairs?"

"Yes, but it's not what you're thinking. I just watched my best friend get gunned down in a park. She stopped by to make sure I was okay."

"*Are* you okay?"

"Of course I am."

Miles stood from his stool and dropped a ten-dollar bill on the bar. "I expect to get a call tomorrow that you're sitting at an APD station ready to give a witness statement. Don't make me come knocking on your door."

"Fine. I'll pay them a visit as soon as I can."

"Oh, and, Henry, one more thing. There isn't a marine recruiter named Jacob within five hundred miles of here. Thought you should know."

Henry furrowed his brow as the agent slipped out the front door. After finishing his drink, he settled the tab and took the same route back to his apartment.

"How'd it go?" Isabell asked as he entered the penthouse.

"Yeah, it's definitely the feds."

"I knew it. Whoever was sitting in that Suburban got out and walked down Twelfth Street right after you left."

"Total amateur. I made him at the corner of Crescent."

"All right," she huffed, "so what now?"

"Now we slip out of the building unnoticed and drive to Waleska."

"Tonight? You want to do this tonight?"

"Absolutely. I won't be able to sleep until I find Colton Sinclair. If there's someone out there who can tell me what happened to Darius, I need to find them. Tonight."

"Fine. And how do you expect to get out of here without the feds following us?"

"You're the tour guide—you tell me."

With a roll of her green eyes, she reached for her purse and marched to the elevator.

Minutes later, Isabell's blue Pathfinder pulled out of the parking lot.

Antonio Garza watched from his vehicle as she turned left onto Peachtree. "I've got Isabell DiMarco leaving the property," the DCIS officer called into his handheld radio.

"Is she alone?" Miles asked.

"Affirmative, she's alone."

"That means Echo Target's still in his apartment. I think we can call it a night. If he doesn't file a police report in the next twenty-four hours, we'll bring him in."

"Roger that."

As the two agents pulled their vehicles away from the property and headed back to FBI headquarters, Isabell's SUV was miles away, merging onto I-75 North.

"Okay, we're all clear," she called out as her eyes scanned the rearview mirror.

Henry popped up from the back seat and crawled to the front. "The oldest trick in the book," he proclaimed.

"Well, if we'd done it your way, I'd be rappelling down the side of your apartment building scared shitless right now."

He managed a quick smile. In some strange way, he missed it—the pithy banter and light-hearted insults. No matter how much he fought it, he enjoyed being around her again.

They continued north out of the city and drove for another hour before getting off in Waleska. Nestled in the foothills of the Blue Ridge Mountains, it was a seemingly endless landscape of rolling hills, old plantation homes, and fields of grazing cattle.

Under a setting sun, her GPS guided them west toward the historic downtown. Most of the businesses had been permanently boarded up. The few remaining signs of life included an old tavern, a hardware store, and a train depot that had been converted into a weekend farmers market, among other things.

"Sure is quiet out here," Henry noted.

"Yeah, looks like Darius' friend lives in the sticks."

They pushed through the square and followed a long, dark road out of town, flanked by rows of expansive corn fields and farmhouses. After a few miles, Isabell turned right onto a dirt road—Harmony Court.

She crept the SUV up the path before coming to a stop and cutting the lights.

"That's it up there," she said, motioning up the road to an old black mailbox with the number six painted on it.

Henry peered out through the scant darkness. "Stay here. If you hear gunshots, leave."

"Wait a second. What's the plan here?"

"I'm going inside."

"What if someone's home? Henry, we don't even know if this is the right place."

"Either way, I'm going in. And I hope someone *is* home. I might finally get some answers."

"I don't like any of this," she tried.

But there was no use.

"Just wait here. I'll be fine."

As he stepped out and examined the surrounding area, he could hear a dog barking somewhere in the distance. He paced across the dirt road and dipped into a thick forest, pushing further into the brush toward the homestead. It was a charming southern plantation house with peeling white paint and a crumbling chimney. Just beyond it, an old rickety barn rested in a field, struggling to hold itself upright.

There were no lights on inside the house and, like every other building in town, the place seemed cold and abandoned. There were no vehicles in the driveway, just a decades-old tractor rotting in the grass. Thick vines clung to its deflated tires and rusted side panels, pulling it slowly into the earth. Henry continued along the tree line toward the rear of the home. With one last gaze across the field, he lunged out into the tall grass and hurried to the back porch. He crouched through the shadows and pulled a pistol from his shoulder holster. With his back pressed against the house and his weapon secure in his hands, Henry peered into a window. Inside was a small room with two chairs and nothing more. Beyond it, a narrow hallway was blanketed in darkness.

He slid further along the side of the house until he reached the back door. He tucked the pistol away and retrieved the metal picks from his front pocket. His hands steadied as he slipped the two picks into the lock. It was almost too easy.

Under the light creak of the hinges, Henry crept into the home. He quickly retrieved his nine-millimeter and inched carefully through the kitchen. He reached the same hallway he'd seen through the window and craned his neck in each direction. As he took his first step onto the brown carpet, he heard an unmistakable sound: the pump action of a shotgun.

He was careful not a move a muscle. With a cautious exhale, he slowly held his pistol in the air.

"Drop it," a voice instructed. The pistol fell to the carpet at his feet. "Hands on your head. Turn around and face me."

Henry turned slowly. He could make out the dark silhouette of a man holding a shotgun, standing at the end of the hallway. A set of wind chimes rang ominously from the back porch as Henry stood dumbfounded, waiting for a blast of buckshot to slice him in half. "You must be lost," the man finally asserted.

"I'm looking for someone," Henry replied.

The silhouette stepped out of the shadows. With the shotgun still raised, the man patted Henry from shoulder to ankle with one hand. He then reached down to pick up the nine-millimeter before stepping away.

"Who is it you're looking for?" the man finally asked. He was tall with large shoulders and forearms. He seemed older: mid- to late forties, Henry guessed.

"I'm looking for someone named Colton Sinclair."

The man didn't flinch. His face remained deep and cold—as if he'd done this a million times before. The long barrel of his shotgun hung threateningly in the air.

"Do you happen to know Mr. Sinclair?" Henry tried again.

"You won't find him here. Now, why don't you call your girlfriend parked up the street and tell her to come join us."

"I can't do that," Henry argued. "I was sent here by a friend. He told me I could find Colton Sinclair at this address."

"Who's your friend?"

Henry took a moment to consider his answer. "Darius Martović."

The man's eyes cut to the front door, and then back to Henry. He was visibly nervous now.

"Please," Henry begged. "Are you Colton Sinclair?"

"No. But you said Darius Martović sent you?"

"Yes."

"Okay. Then why isn't he here?"

Henry struggled to find his words. "Darius is dead," he finally stated.

The shotgun slumped to the man's side. "Then so is Colton Sinclair."

CHAPTER 20

Isabell's Pathfinder crawled up the long dirt drive. The headlights beamed ahead of her as Henry and the strange man stood awkwardly on the front porch. She parked on the grass and got out. "Everything all right?" she asked as she approached slowly.

The man on the porch stood motionless. She could see the shotgun hanging at his side.

Henry eyed her with a look of unease. "Yeah, we're good," he said.

She knew there were a set of code phrases that Ružaro members would use as warnings or signals, but Henry wasn't using any of them.

"Get inside before someone sees us," the stranger demanded, his shotgun still clutched in his hand. Henry and Isabell followed him in. "Have a seat," he ordered, motioning with the barrel of the Mossberg toward a tattered couch.

Henry probed the room, scanning every square inch and committing it to memory. The place was simple and modern: a couch, a chair, a glass coffee table, and a bronze floor lamp in the far corner. He joined Isabell on the edge of the couch with his hands clasped in front of him.

"So, you must be Henry," the man said through a thick layer of scruff.

"I am."

"And who's this?"

"This is a friend of mine, Isabell DiMarco."

The man took a moment to examine them both. "I assume Darius left you something?"

"The poetry book," said Henry. "And the cipher code."

"I see."

"May I ask who you are?"

"I'm A.J., a friend of Darius'."

"A.J. what?"

"Just A.J."

Henry wasn't amused. "So tell me, A.J., what am I doing here? The message indicated there's something beneath the house. A room."

"You mind if I ask how Darius died?"

"I do, actually. Why don't we start with you telling me what all this nonsense is about. Whose house is this? And how do you know Darius?"

"The house belongs to Colton Sinclair. And this 'nonsense' is about very important work that's being done here."

"What kind of work?"

"Secret work."

Henry hung his head. He was tired of the wordplay. "You know, it's been a long week and I'm short on patience. Why was Darius using the name Colton Sinclair? And how come I never knew about this place?"

"The pseudonym was for everyone's protection. And the reason you didn't know about this place is because Darius didn't want you to know about it."

"Until now?"

"Yes. Until now."

"All right, A.J., back to my original question: why am I here?"

A.J.'s eyes listed toward Isabell. "Where are my manners? Ma'am, can I get you something to drink?"

"No, I'm fine, thank you."

"And you, Mr. Sirola?"

Henry stood from the sofa. "Enough with the bullshit. Darius was murdered last night, and now you're going to tell me what he was doing up here and why he was killed."

A.J. rose from his chair and met Henry's gaze. He studied his prey carefully, waiting for the perfect moment to strike. Then, with learned precision, he snapped the Mossberg to Henry's face. "Tell me how Darius died or I'll kill you where you stand," he snarled. "I won't ask you again."

Henry took a reluctant step backwards and sat down.

"Why don't we just talk this out," Isabell suggested nervously. "Please, put the gun down before someone gets hurt."

A.J. lowered the weapon and returned to his chair.

"You're not one of us," Henry asserted. "I'm guessing you're former military."

"That would be an accurate assessment."

"What branch?"

"It doesn't matter."

"No, I guess it doesn't. So what, are you, like, Darius' little bodyguard or something?"

A.J was growing more impatient by the second. "Answer my fucking question," he growled.

"Fine," Henry granted. "Darius was shot last night in the park behind his house. I was with him."

"Shot by who?"

"I don't know. But it was a professional hit—suppressed pistol, quiet as the wind, two shots."

"A rival gang maybe?"

Henry shrugged. "Who the hell knows. He died in my arms. I didn't have time to ask him."

"How did *you* survive, Henry? What happened, they just decided to let you live?"

"I don't know. Like I said, all signs point to a hit. Their target was apparently Darius, not me." Henry clenched his fists and gently tapped them on his knees. "So now that I've told you how he died, I think you owe me some answers."

A.J. relaxed in his chair and laid the shotgun across his lap. "Fair enough. Darius hired me three years ago to help him with his work."

"Well, I guess this makes you unemployed then, doesn't it?" Isabell quipped.

"It's not quite that simple," replied A.J. "I was paid upfront for what's going to happen next. In the event of Darius' death, I am supposed to… get things where they need to be. So my apologies, but I'm still technically under contract."

"What does that even mean?" Henry asked. "And stop being so goddamn dismissive about all this. Why am I here?"

"You really have no idea, do you?"

"No. Maybe you should explain it to me."

A.J. stared blankly through a nearby window. "Darius was a collector," he revealed. "And a very good one at that."

"A collector of what?"

"Secrets."

"What kind of secrets?"

A.J. leaned over the shotgun and tented his fingers in front of his mouth. "The kind of secrets that could bring down an entire crime syndicate."

Henry shook his head. "I don't believe you."

"You don't have to believe me. But I'd expect you to believe Darius."

"Why would he be collecting secrets?"

"I guess that's for you to find out."

Henry ran his hands over his face, trying to piece it all together—Darius' murder, the deciphered message, the farmhouse. None of the dots seemed to connect. "I want to know what Darius was doing. He brought me here for a reason."

A.J. allowed himself a smile. He got up from his chair and pulled the pistol from his jeans. "Here," he said as he handed it back to its owner. "Can I trust you not to shoot me?"

"No," Henry replied as he secured it in his shoulder holster.

A.J. crossed the room and disappeared into the hallway. Henry and Isabell got up and quickly followed. At the end of the hall, the man stopped and turned to his guests. He opened a white door and extended his hand into a deep, dark staircase. "After you," he offered.

Henry took a moment to examine the murky abyss. Satisfied, he grabbed the handrail and descended the stairs. Isabell was next, followed by A.J.

As they reached the bottom step and set their feet against the concrete floor, A.J. flipped on a set of recessed lights, revealing a small room with unfinished sheetrock. Built into the far wall was a large steel door.

A.J. stepped forward and placed his thumb against a digital keypad, which disengaged the lock and sprang the thick door slightly ajar. He reached out and pushed it open, which gave way to a deep, cavernous room with a polished floor and cinderblock walls.

In the back corner was a large gun safe and a fold-up bed. To their left sat a long desk with a single laptop resting on its wood-stained top. And running the length of the right wall was a large whiteboard where notes had been scribbled with a dry-erase marker.

Henry was quick to notice it was Darius' handwriting. "What the hell is this place?" he mumbled as he stepped deeper into the room.

"Darius called it the Hornet's Nest."

"Of course he did," Isabell teased. "I'm guessing this is where he managed his fantasy football team?"

"Quit joking around," Henry chided as he examined his surroundings. "The man won three championships in five years. He left behind a legacy."

She rolled her eyes and paced to the center of the room to a small wooden bistro table and two high-top chairs.

"Before we discuss anything," A.J. began, "I need you to understand what's going on here."

Henry circled the room, shifting his eyes from the desk to the whiteboard. "Okay, what exactly am I looking at?"

"You're looking at three years' worth of intelligence gathering. Darius was going to bring the whole thing to the ground," said A.J.

"Bring *what* to the ground?"

"Not just Ružaro, but the entire syndicate—*Čopor Vukova*, as you call it."

"That's impossible."

A.J. leaned his shotgun against the wall. "Is it?"

"I don't understand. I grew up with him. I knew everything about him. How could he keep something like this from me?"

"This wasn't a matter of loyalty or friendship," A.J. assured. "It was about security."

"Then why would he want me to know about this now? After his death?"

"He didn't want you to know about it: he wanted you to finish it."

Henry's eyes widened. "Finish it? Finish what? Taking down the world's largest crime syndicate? Why would I do that?"

"You don't have to do anything. You and Miss DiMarco can walk out that door right now and never look back."

"No, we can't," Henry reasoned. "Darius would've put a protocol in place to keep me from going to Anton with all of this."

"Oh Jesus," Isabell whispered. Her eyes quickly searched the room for anything that could be used as a weapon.

"It's not like that," A.J. said calmly. "If you decide you want nothing to do with this, I simply remove you from the property and everything in this room gets relocated by sunrise."

"What's on the laptop?" asked Henry.

"Everything."

"Everything?"

"Yes."

Henry nodded. "Okay. Tell me more."

"The information we have goes beyond Krunoslav's crew. Like I said, it's about the entire syndicate, from Dubrovnik to Italy, Atlanta to New York. Everything these people have ever done to make this world a darker place… Darius was documenting it."

"Sounds poetic and all, but why would Darius do that? Why would he turn on Anton? The man saved his life, gave him a career, a home, an income!"

"You're criminals," A.J. corrected. "Don't romanticize what it is you guys do for a living, how you earn your money."

Henry's eyes cut across the room. "That's fair. So what made Darius want to burn it all down? He was a criminal just like the rest of us. It's the only life he ever knew."

"Because he did a little digging and didn't like what he found."

"So what was the plan? Turn all this over to the feds?"

"No. SOA."

"Croatian intelligence?" Henry alleged. "You have to be kidding me!"

"And why would I do that?"

"I don't know, maybe because this whole thing is nuts!"

A.J. took a seat in one of the bistro chairs. "This wasn't an official SOA operation, but Darius had a contact there. Let's just say they were aware of his efforts."

"You're part of it, aren't you? You're SOA."

"No, absolutely not. I met Darius through a mutual friend. He offered me a job."

Henry snickered contemptuously. "And what makes *you* so special?"

"Not much," A.J. confessed. "I guess you could say I had the background Darius was looking for: defense and intelligence experience, black ops, that sorta thing."

Henry threw his hands on top of his head. "Why me?"

"Because he trusted you more than anyone else on the planet."

"Fine. What do you want? What did Darius want me to do?"

"For starters, you may want to take a look at some of this stuff. But only you." A.J. cut his eyes to Isabell. "Sorry, Miss DiMarco. Strict orders."

She furrowed her thin brow. "You're kidding, right? I mean, you're just some backwoods redneck with a shotgun who met Darius a few years ago. And now, what, you think you're some kind of superhero? No, fuck this. We need to destroy everything down here. Darius was making a huge mistake!" Her voice was stern and forceful. "We can't even consider turning this over to anyone."

Henry rested his hand gently on her shoulder. "It's fine, Isabell. I just need to check it out. I at least owe Darius that much."

"*Check it out*?" she echoed. "How do we know Anton hasn't already found out about this? For all we know, *he* killed Darius because of it!"

"That's not what happened."

"But you don't know that, Henry. We're not safe here, we need to leave right now!"

"Then go."

"Excuse me?"

Henry walked to the table and slid into a seat across from A.J. "I'll be fine. I have to know what Darius was doing here."

"This is a mistake," she warned. "I'm not leaving you here with this psychopath."

"Yes, you will. There's no way I'm leaving without seeing what's on that laptop."

"Fine! Have your little sleepover!" she shouted as she made her way to the door. "I'll pick you up in the morning."

Henry listened to the sounds of her sneakers ascending the staircase, followed by the slam of the front door. He took a deep breath and looked around the room. "What's in the gun safe?"

A.J. leered over at the large steel box. "Guns," he answered dryly.

"Big guns?"

"Mostly."

"This is crazy, you know that right?"

"I can see how it would seem that way," A.J. agreed.

"So, where do we start?"

"*You* start with the laptop. I'm going upstairs to get some sleep."

"You're just going to leave me down here?"

"Yes," A.J. replied as he got up and snatched his shotgun from the wall.

"Then what?"

"Then you decide what you want to do with all of it. The password is NEPTUNE7482." With that, A.J. drifted up the stairs and disappeared into the old farmhouse.

Henry walked over to the laptop and keyed the password in before he had a chance to forget it. As the home screen opened on the monitor, three folders sat in the upper left corner, each named after a different constellation: ORION, ARIES, and GEMINI.

He clicked on the first one—ORION.

For the next several hours, he read through file after file. They were mostly electronic documents that had been hacked and sourced from various law enforcement databases. Others were simple Word documents, presumably written by Darius, with explicit details and firsthand accounts of crimes that had been committed.

The receipts were all there—names, locations, targets, bank statements, distribution orders. It was a treasure trove of incriminating evidence.

The night melted away as he combed through robberies, money laundering schemes, bribes, and dozens of felonies. There were lists of judges, senators, city council members, and police officers: all of whom were on the Ružaro payroll.

As dawn began to break, Henry shut his eyes and leaned back in his chair.

"Coffee?" a voice called out from the doorway.

"What time is it?"

A.J. checked his wristwatch. "Seven fifteen. I've got breakfast ready in the kitchen."

"Thanks, I'll be up in a minute," replied Henry. He closed the laptop, stood, and stretched his arms high above his head.

He then went upstairs where A.J. was devouring a plate of fresh biscuits and sausage gravy. On the opposite side of the table was another fixed plate with a hot cup of coffee set to the side. Henry sat down and examined it carefully.

"There's creamer in the fridge," A.J. told him through a mouthful of biscuit.

"No, I'm fine."

"So? What do think about everything?"

Henry cut into his biscuit with a metal fork and stuffed it into his mouth.

"Look, if you're not up to the task, I completely understand," A.J. leveled.

"Up to what task?" Henry calmly retorted. "Turning my friends and family over to the authorities? How exactly do you think that would help me?"

"It sounds like you've only scratched the surface."

"I'm going to do a lot more than scratch," threatened Henry. "I'm taking the laptop with me."

A.J. leered across the table, fiddling with the fork in his left hand and the knife in his right. "That's not going to happen," he warned gently.

"I'm a thief, A.J. You think I won't find a way to get that thing out of here?"

"It's not leaving this house. Besides, the files are copy-proof and I can clear the hard drive remotely. What, you don't think Darius and I considered this scenario?"

Henry shoved another bite into his mouth.

"You do know this house belongs to you now, right?" said A.J. "You can come and go as you please. Hell, there's even an old Land Cruiser in the barn out back. That's yours too."

"How is any of this mine?"

"Because you're Colton Sinclair now. Downstairs in the safe, you'll find a passport, driver's license, birth certificate, social security card, the whole package."

"For me?"

"Yes. For you."

Henry took a moment to consider the resources it would've taken to put a package like that together. Not an easy task.

"The combination is thirteen, twenty-one, five, forty-three," said A.J. "Commit it to memory and never write it down. Do you understand?"

"Yeah."

"Good."

Henry finished his plate and pushed it to the side. His head was spinning. "A.J., I have to ask you something."

"Go for it."

"I know how meticulously Darius used to plan things—he was a constant planner. Isabell was right; he would've put a safety measure in place to make sure I don't ruin all of his hard work and take all this shit directly to Anton. And there's no way your orders are to simply wipe the drive and destroy it all. So tell me: what's the protocol if I go rogue?"

A.J. put down his fork and dabbed his mouth with a napkin. "You're right, Henry. There is a protocol. But going to Anton serves absolutely no purpose, except to destroy Darius' good name."

"What's the protocol?"

"The protocol is that I vanish into thin air, the laptop gets wiped, and you look like an absolute fool. Anton would never trust you again… and we all know how that typically ends for people."

"There's a backup, isn't there?"

"Yes. We backed it up onto another drive before the files were locked down. It's in a safety deposit box in a faraway place. And if someone doesn't come to check on it within a certain period of time, the box gets transferred to a third party."

"SOA?"

A.J. nodded.

"That means he wanted me to dig through all this information. He didn't need me to *do* anything!"

"I never questioned the man's intentions," A.J. said as he stood and gathered the empty plates. "Darius was a very intelligent man. He's serving you a brand-new life on a silver platter."

"I never asked for a new life. Darius and I had the best goddamn lives you could imagine. So why exactly did he want me to find this?" Henry pressed.

A.J. set the plates on the kitchen counter and poured the rest of his coffee into the sink. "Because the fantasy of your perfect little lives finally crumbled. He found things."

"What kind of things? Because all I see downstairs is a bunch of shit I already knew about."

"Then you haven't dug deep enough."

"What the fuck is that supposed to mean?" Henry shouted. "Tell me what's down there that's going to change my mind!"

"I don't know what's down there, Henry! I was only hired to get access to a few foreign intelligence websites and put security measures in place to ensure nobody ever got to Darius or this house."

Henry took a pacifying breath and sipped his coffee. "Darius never told you about any of the specifics?"

"Sure, from time to time we'd discuss things, but as far as what ultimately set him on this path to righteousness, I have no idea. It wasn't any of my business." A.J. pulled a cell phone from his pocket and stared at the screen. "Your ride is here," he announced calmly.

"My ride?"

"Miss DiMarco. She just turned onto Harmony Court."

"Of course. You have security cameras."

"How else do you think I got the drop on you last night?"

Henry stood from the table and walked into the living room. He glared out at the sprawling landscape just in time to see a red minivan pull up the driveway with a hazy cloud of dust in its wake.

"When should I expect you back?" A.J. asked.

"I'll be back tonight. Can you pick me up in Sandy Springs?"

"Sure. There's an old pool hall on Roberts. I'll be there at five."

Henry nodded. As the minivan pulled up the drive, he stepped through the door and into the grass.

"Good morning," Isabell greeted as he climbed into the passenger seat.

"Thanks for picking me up," he muttered.

She glimpsed through the windshield at the old farmhouse before turning the van around and darting back to the main road. "So, how'd everything go?" she asked. "Did you shoot that guy and leave his dead body in the house?"

"No."

"I'm shocked. That place had serious *Thunderdome* energy going on. I figured only one of you would survive the night."

Henry allowed a scant laugh. "Yeah, well, A.J.'s just doing his job. What's with the van, by the way? Where's your SUV?"

"Thanks to you, I had to take countersurveillance measures. You've got me spooked with all these feds nosing around. I have a legitimate career, you know?"

"I know, I know."

"So you say A.J.'s just doing his job, huh? Do we even know what that is?"

"To protect Darius' secrets, apparently. Whatever those may be."

"Did you look at the laptop?"

"There's so much there, Izzy," he confessed. "And I'm only a fraction of the way through it. I mean, there are files on just about every crime *Čopor Vukova* has committed in the last ten years."

"The entire syndicate?"

"Yep. DeMiri in Berlin, Laskaris in Tirana, Ružaro in Atlanta. And everything traces back to the high command."

"The Balkans?"

"Yeah."

"Great," she exhaled, "just great."

Henry stared out at the passing trees, lost in the enormity of it all.

"What are you going to do?" she asked. "I mean, we came here to find out who would have wanted Darius dead... and now *this*?"

"No," he corrected. "We came here because Darius wanted me to find something."

Isabell scoffed. "I don't buy it. There's no way Darius would gather up all this evidence just to simply send everyone to prison. Maybe the SOA had something on him?"

"And what? You think he flipped?"

She shrugged. "Maybe he was facing a long prison sentence or something."

"We're trained to handle hard time, Isabell. That wasn't it."

"So one day he just up and decided to start working with Croatian intelligence? To help bring down the entire Wolf Pack? I don't think so."

"There's more to it than that," he argued. "I just don't what it is yet."

"So you're *going back*?"

"Yeah. Tonight."

"Well, I can't help you with that. I have to work," she proclaimed.

"Don't worry, I can take care of myself."

Isabell lowered her head and closed her eyes. She cared for him, no matter how hard she tried not to. "I can pick you up Friday evening," she finally offered.

"That would be great. Thank you."

"A.J. knows more than he's telling us, by the way. A lot more."

"You're probably right," Henry agreed. "He says he and Darius never discussed specifics, but I don't know if I believe him."

"And you don't think Anton found out about this?"

Henry refused to even entertain the insinuation. "No. There's just no way."

"Am I reaching here?" she continued. "Would Anton kill Darius if he knew about all this?"

The pieces fell easily into place—perhaps too easily, he thought. "Yeah, I guess he would."

"That means he wouldn't hesitate to kill us either."

"You're assuming Anton's aware of everything—Darius, the house, all of it. We don't know that right now."

"I'm just saying—"

"I know what you're saying," he struck back. "But we have no idea if Darius' death is even related to any of this. All we know is that Darius wanted me to see it."

"Fine. But I want you to be careful. With Anton, with Asa… all of them. You can't trust anyone right now."

"I can trust *you,* can't I?"

"Of course you can trust me! But at a certain point, I have to watch out for myself."

They merged onto the interstate and continued southbound in complete silence.

Finally, they entered Midtown and she parked the van on a curb five blocks from his building. Henry reached for the door handle and glanced up at her. "Thanks again. See you Friday?"

She offered a knowing wink as he stepped out of the van and onto the sidewalk.

With a tired breath, Henry began a casual stroll back to the Forty West building.

CHAPTER 21

Miles sat in a metal folding chair in front of a large window facing the Park Avenue complex. He pressed his hands together in his lap and stared vacantly at Anton's penthouse across the street. "Were you at the FBI building this morning?" he finally asked.

Garza took a sip from his bottled water, then set it at his feet. "Yeah, why?"

"Any leads on the Martović murder?"

"No, I don't think forensics was able to pull anything from the crime scene. The shooter must've picked up his casings before he fled. All we've got are the ones scattered around the body, which were likely from Martović's gun. Nine-millimeter."

"Do we have the gun?"

Garza rubbed his chin in thought. "No. I imagine Sirola took it. We're gonna need to question him at some point. He's our only witness."

"He'll pop up."

"I'm not so sure about that. Anton's probably got him halfway to Canada by now."

Before Miles could argue, the front door blew open and Agent Harwick stormed into the room. "Brennan, a word please." Miles got up from his post and followed the lead agent into the master bedroom. "So?" Harwick asked impatiently.

"So *what*?"

Harwick closed the door and raised his index finger to Miles' face. "You're out of time, hotshot. We've already got one dead Ružaro captain, and whatever the hell Anton just snatched from the bottom of the ocean is being shipped to Atlanta as we speak. Who's your fucking informant? I'm done playing games!"

Miles had hoped to avoid this confrontation for as long as possible. "Listen, Agent Harwick, I'm really sorry—"

"I don't want to hear how sorry you are, Brennan! Give me a goddamn name!"

Miles kept his eyes ahead of him. "It was Darius Martović," he stated. "The Shadowmaker's dead."

Harwick's face flared with astonishment. "Are you serious?"

"Yes, sir. I'm sorry I didn't tell you sooner."

The NSA agent ran his hand over his head and began pacing the small room. "So we've got nothing. Our informant's dead and we have absolutely fucking nothing to show for it."

"That sounds about right, sir."

"Do you think Krunoslav found out he was an informant and had him killed?"

"Absolutely not," assured Miles. "This is just bad luck."

"I want a full report of your last three interactions with him on my desk by five o'clock."

"Of course. I'll go ahead and put something together."

Harwick continued to pace. The wheels in his mind were spinning furiously. "So what happens now? From their end?"

Miles considered it for a moment. "Well, Anton will have to replace Darius with a new captain."

"Any ideas who that might be?"

"My guess is either Peter Guillen or Henry Sirola."

"Speaking of which, where the hell is Henry Sirola?"

Miles shook his head. "We have no idea, sir. Garza thinks he went to ground, I happen to believe he'll stick his head out sooner than later. There's still work to be done on their end and Anton needs all of his best men operational right now."

"Find him!" Harwick shouted as he marched into the foyer and out the front door, slamming it behind him.

"He seems pleasant today," Garza noted from behind a set of mounted binoculars.

"He'll be fine. Has Anton left his residence yet?"

The DCIS officer squinted into his lens. "Nope. He's sitting in his office alone."

As they watched in silence, Miles' cell phone rang. "Special Agent Brennan," he answered.

"Agent Brennan, this is Sergeant Wilshire with Atlanta PD."

"Morning, Sergeant. What can I do for you?"

"We've got a fella named Henry Sirola down here at the Fifth Precinct, says he wants to give a witness statement concerning the murder of Darius Martović. I was told this was an FBI matter and Special Agent Tisdale gave me your number."

"Sure thing. I can be there in ten minutes."

"That'd be perfect. We'll hold him till then."

"Thank you, Sergeant." Miles shoved the phone back into his pocket. "Ha! What did I tell you!"

"What happened?" asked Garza.

"Henry Sirola."

"Get outta here! Seriously?"

"Yep. He's sitting at the Fifth Precinct ready to give a statement."

"Well, isn't that some dumb luck."

The agents hustled out of the room and down to the back lot where they jumped into Miles' Suburban and sped south onto Peachtree Street.

Minutes later, they arrived at the Fifth Precinct and entered the building with their badges held in the air. A young officer directed them to a desk in the back corner of the bullpen. Sergeant Wilshire sat behind a stack of paperwork with a clean-shaven face and brown eyes, which rested behind a pair of wire-rimmed glasses. "You Brennan?" he asked sharply.

"I am. This is my partner, Officer Garza from DCIS."

Sergeant Wilshire shook both their hands with a firm grip. "All right, gentlemen, your boy's sitting up the hall in Interview Room Three. Let me know if you need anything."

Miles turned for the hallway.

He and Garza arrived at a metal door and peered in through a tiny window, where they could see Henry sitting at a small table with his back to the door.

"That's our guy," Miles said before he barged in and took a seat. He and Henry locked eyes. "You must be Henry Sirola."

"And you must be a rocket scientist," the brash criminal replied.

"Do you know who I am?"

"You've interviewed me before. I've seen you around," Henry granted, trying his best to stay in character.

"I'm FBI Special Agent Miles Brennan, and this is Officer Antonio Garza with the Defense Criminal Investigative Service."

"And I like long walks on the beach. Who the fuck killed my friend?"

Miles tapped his fingers against the table. The game was on. "We're looking into that now actually. I'm very sorry for your loss, Mr. Sirola. I understand you knew the victim well."

"I just hope you two are competent enough to find whoever's responsible."

"I can assure you, we're doing the best we can. Sergeant Wilshire says you're here to submit a witness statement, is that correct?"

"Yes."

"Good. I'm going to turn on this recorder, okay?"

"Sure."

Miles clicked the Record button on a small digital device, then set it on the table. "So, what exactly was your relationship with Darius Martović?"

"I work at Scranton and Brooks. He was my boss."

"The crime scene indicates that Mr. Martović was in the park with another person when he was murdered. I'm assuming that other person was you?"

"Let's cut the shit, Agent Brennan. You know damn well it was me."

"All right, then. Tell us what happened."

Henry turned his eyes to the two-way mirror against the wall, then back to the agents. "Darius and I had dinner together, then went back to his house to work on a new project. When we pulled in, he wanted to take a walk through the park… so we did."

"Where'd you two have dinner?" asked Miles.

"La Grotta."

The agent raised an eyebrow. "Fancy place. So after that, you went straight to the park?"

"We drove around for a while—maybe thirty minutes—before we got back to his house."

"When you walked to the park, did you see anyone else around?"

"No."

"Any strange individuals you may have run across earlier in the night?"

"None that I can think of."

"Did Mr. Martović have any enemies?"

The question almost seemed silly, even to Henry. "Nobody that I was aware of."

"Give me a break," Garza groaned from the corner of the room. "We're not stupid, Henry. We know who you really work for and what you really do. Stop playing games with us."

"I'm a business development specialist for an architectural firm."

"Fine," Garza scoffed. "Tell us what happened when the shooting started."

"Darius was hit twice right away. He fell to the ground and we took cover behind a large boulder."

"Was that it or was there more shooting?" asked Miles.

"I don't know. I think the guy took a few more pot shots at us after that."

"How many?"

Henry was genuinely trying to remember now. "Three."

"Mr. Martović had an empty holster under his arm. Did he have a weapon?"

"Yes. A nine-millimeter."

"Did he return fire?"

"No. I did."

"With Martović's gun?" pressed Miles.

"Yes."

"How many rounds did you get off?"

"Three or four. I just sprayed toward the trees."

"You could've killed somebody!" Garza interrupted.

Henry narrowed his eyes. "Yes, that was my intention."

"Was he dead when you left?" Miles continued.

"What kind of question is that?"

"I'm just curious. Did you leave him to die alone or did you stay there with him?"

"He died next to me."

"And where did you go after that?"

"I went to a friend's place."

"Why not go to the police?"

"I was scared."

Miles crossed his arms at his chest and examined his witness. "So where's this nine-millimeter now?" he carefully asked.

"I tossed it."

"Where?"

Henry bore his elbows into the table and leaned in. "Up your fucking ass."

"Cute. Very cute," Miles snickered.

"Are we done here?"

"Not until I get the location of Darius' gun and the name of the friend whose place you went to after the shooting."

Henry rubbed his eyes, exhausted and frustrated. "Fine. I tossed the nine-mil into a trash can on the north side of the park."

"Can you be more specific?"

"No. It was dark, I was under duress."

Miles granted a phony smile. "And who's the friend you went and stayed with?"

"I'm not giving you a name," countered Henry. "I don't see what that has to do with Darius' murder. Besides, I'm not interested in dragging anyone else into this mess."

Garza stepped forward and set his hands on the table. "Listen, Henry. I know you guys prefer good old-fashioned street justice, but if you know who did this to your friend, you need to tell us. Otherwise, this thing only gets worse from here. We don't need a gang war on our hands."

"It's not like that," Henry asserted. "None of us wants a war. And I truly have no idea who would want Darius dead."

"Okay," Miles concluded. "If you have any other information or you happen to remember anything that might help us out, please don't hesitate to reach out to me." The FBI agent placed a business card on the table and got up from his chair.

"Am I free to go?"

"Of course. But don't go far."

Henry stood and walked through the door and into the hallway. He brushed past several police officers before exiting the precinct and getting into his car.

Miles and Garza followed him out of the building and climbed into the Suburban. "So what now?" Garza asked as they watched him pull away.

"Now that he's resurfaced, I don't want to lose him again. We need to stay on him."

After pulling through an old chain-link gate, the SUV shot north onto Williams Street. The agents caught up with their target in Midtown and followed the Maserati south into Inman Park.

* * *

Henry arrived at Scranton and Brooks, went to his office, and descended into the dark cavernous tunnels belowground. This time, however, he took a different path and emerged in the wine cellar of Ammazza Trattoria on the opposite side of the block.

He reached his hand beneath one of the wooden wine racks and retrieved a small backpack stuffed with a change of clothes. He emptied the bag, then removed his jacket and put on a green hoodie and black ball cap. After shoving his jacket inside and returning the bag to its hiding place, he pushed through a door and into the kitchen, maneuvering past a small army of sous chefs and waiters.

He continued to a rear exit and followed the alley to the street, where a waiting taxi whisked him to the West End MARTA station. He boarded the red line which took him north to the edge of the city. He got off at Sandy Springs and darted up the stairs and into the parking lot.

It was almost four o'clock, and Henry had an hour to burn before meeting with A.J.

He made his way across the lot and began marching up the sidewalk for nearly a half mile before arriving at the Perimeter Shopping Center and dipping into a narrow side street. Ahead of him, a neon sign for Woody's Billiards flickered against the window.

The place was a rundown dump, wedged between a liquor store and a laundromat. He opened the front door and stepped into a dark, musty bar with only a handful of lightbulbs dangling above a few empty pool tables. He noticed an older couple in the corner drinking draft beers and whispering to each other. The man wore an old tattered biker vest and a red bandana across his forehead; the woman's clothes were tight and disheveled, her hair white with streaks of yellow.

Henry kept his eyes down and made his way to a small table against the wall.

A tall, slender woman with greasy hair and stained teeth wandered over. "Thirsty?" she asked.

"Miller Lite," he said quietly.

She pursed her lips and peeled away toward the bar, returning moments later with a cold bottle.

"Open a tab, sweetheart?" she asked with a thick southern drawl.

Henry reached into his pocket and pulled out a few loose bills. He counted them out before setting a twenty on the sticky table. "I'll probably have a couple more. Keep the change."

"Just holler when you're ready," she said as she snatched the money and disappeared.

Henry brought the bottle to his lips, then wiped his mouth and scanned the place over. There was a swing door just beyond the bar that led to what he assumed was the kitchen. Surely there would be an exit there, he thought.

He polished off his beer as a Hank Williams song bellowed from a hidden speaker somewhere nearby. Eventually, the bartender brought him another Miller Lite.

After the jukebox cycled through a few more hits from an out-of-date playlist, A.J. walked through the front door and shuffled over to the table. His wavy hair was neatly combed back, tucked behind his ears, and his biceps filled the arms of a red-and-blue flannel shirt.

"Thanks for coming," Henry greeted.

A.J. took his seat. "How long you been waiting?"

"Thirty, forty minutes, maybe. Is the food any good here?"

"Terrible. Stick with the beer."

The bartender returned and took A.J.'s order—a Red Stripe and a bowl of pretzels—then slipped back to the bar.

"How'd you find this place?" Henry wondered aloud.

"Just lucky, I guess."

Henry took a swig from his beer as A.J.'s Red Stripe landed on the table.

"You boys all set for now?" the woman asked.

"Yes, ma'am," A.J. kindly replied.

Henry watched her walk away with a certain disdain. He hated getting out of the city. "Next time just pick me up at the train station," he complained.

"No can do, man. Cameras everywhere down there."

"Seriously?"

A.J. leaned in and gripped his bottle. "You're under federal surveillance, my friend. You think I'm stupid?"

"No. I don't."

"Good. Then we'll keep everything below deck from here on out."

They sat quietly for the next half hour, pretending to watch the baseball game muted on the television. Finally, the two got up and walked out the front door.

As the skies grew darker, they climbed into an old white Land Cruiser with a steel grill guard and oversized tires. The interior leather had been worn to its last layer of fabric and the smell of dirt and sweat lingered throughout the cab. With the turn of a key, the engine roared to life beneath the hood and a thick cloud of smoke wafted from the exhaust.

They pulled away and headed north on the interstate before stopping at a drive-thru burger joint just outside Waleska. After a quick, greasy meal, they drove the final stretch to Harmony Court. The Land Cruiser rambled up the drive and parked inside the old barn out back. Henry got out, threw his backpack over his shoulder and followed A.J. into the house.

They made their way downstairs, where A.J. set his thumb against the pad and opened the steel door. "Do you need anything?" he asked.

Henry stepped inside and turned on the lights. "No. I think I'm all set."

"Well, make yourself at home. There's food and drink upstairs."

"Thanks, I appreciate it."

With that, A.J. turned and disappeared. As Henry stood alone in the basement, he glanced up at the whiteboard against the wall. He could almost feel Darius' presence—a vaporous hologram of his friend meticulously scribbling notes across the board in black marker. Henry watched him with a heavy heart, wishing it were real.

With a tired blink, the vision quickly faded.

Across the top of the whiteboard were several columns labeled with three-letter abbreviations. Beneath each of them was a list of last names, many of which Henry knew well. Darius had connected several of them with red lines, but the relationships seemed random at best.

With hands on hips, Henry squinted at the board, trying to piece it all together.

He turned his attention back to the laptop and decided to pick up where he'd left off the night before. From the home screen, he clicked the second of the three folders—ARIES. Much like the previous folder, it contained documents from various sources, each outlining some devious plot that Anton and the other heads of the syndicate had hatched. Henry read through each file with ardent concentration, trying to find commonalities and connections between the numerous crimes. Surely, he thought, a pattern would emerge. But as midnight quickly approached, nothing came together.

Another hour passed and he sat back, rubbing his tired eyes. He'd found another set of subfolders buried within

ARIES along with hundreds of seemingly irrelevant files. Deep within each subfolder, it occurred to him that Darius had begun categorizing documents—organizing them according to specific missions, heists, and money trails. His friend had been building individual cases.

The revelation was enough to warrant a short break. He stood from the desk and wandered up the stairs and through the hallway. As he approached the kitchen, the bitter scent of fresh coffee wafted through the air. He stepped into the cramped space and found a set of mugs resting on a wooden shelf above the stove. As he poured himself a cup, he turned to the window and noticed a small campfire burning in the backyard, its flames dancing wildly through the darkness.

Henry smiled to himself and reached for the door.

Outside, next to the fire, A.J. sat in a plastic Adirondack chair with a steaming mug clasped in his hand. He lifted his eyes as Henry approached. "Taking a break?" A.J. mumbled into the dark night.

"Yeah. It's a lot to take in," said Henry as he found another chair and pulled it closer. "I can only imagine what it took to gather all that information."

A.J. lifted himself out of the Adirondack and threw another log onto the fire. He stood over it quietly, sipping his coffee.

"What did you know about the new operation in Brazil?" Henry asked.

"It's Anton's new pet project. Darius thought the old man had been working on it for years."

"How long had Darius been operational on it?"

A.J. rocked his head for a moment. "Since the summer… maybe four months."

"How does the research vessel fit in? The *Tiger Claw*?"

"You know about that?"

"Yeah. I just read a handful of documents that Darius had archived in a subfolder. They all pertain to a deal I'm setting up with some maniac from Qatar. What the hell did they need a research vessel for?"

A.J. chewed at his lip, pondering an appropriate response. "Well, if you're going to pull a priceless diamond from the bottom of the ocean, you're going to need a boat and a submarine, don't ya think?"

"I thought you didn't know any specifics."

"I said I didn't know *a lot* of specifics," A.J. corrected. "But this was a big one. Darius was really excited about putting a case together and returning the stone to its rightful owner."

"Wait a sec," Henry interrupted as he leaned toward the fire. "Which priceless diamond are you talking about?"

A devious grin broke through the stubble on A.J.'s face. "It sounds like you may have missed a file in there."

"What file?"

"The one that describes Anton's little treasure. The one you're preparing to sell for a small fortune. Maybe Darius hadn't properly archived it yet, but somewhere on that laptop is a spec sheet for a diamond the likes of which I've never fuckin' seen before."

Henry sat frozen in his chair as the flames twirled in his eyes. "When Darius told me it was a single stone, I didn't believe him."

A.J. chuckled for a moment, amused by Henry's ignorance.

"Something funny?" Henry asked.

"Darius struggled with all of this as well."

"How so?"

"Well, he felt a strong loyalty to Anton. But along the way, he uncovered a lot of things that broke his trust. The old man has a lot of skeletons in his closet."

"We all have skeletons, A.J."

"Yep. I'm afraid you're right about that."

Henry gazed out beyond the fields to the mountaintops in the distance, barely visible beneath the night sky. In some strange way, he'd found solitude in the quietness of Waleska. And for a brief moment, he appreciated the fact that Darius had sent him here.

"So, what are you going to do with all this information?" A.J. asked quietly.

Henry shuffled his sneakers in the dirt. "I have no idea, honestly."

"It'll come to you in time. It always does."

"Tell me something, A.J., how close were you and Darius?"

"Our relationship was professional. We didn't go out clubbing on the weekends, if that's what you're asking. But I liked him. He was a good man, and it pains me to know he'll never walk through that door again. I'll miss him."

"Me too."

A.J.'s eyes drifted to the sky. "Darius told me the two of you grew up together. What was he like as a kid?"

"He was always getting me into trouble, that's what he was like," Henry revealed with a glint of admiration. "There was something about Darius that drew people to him. He could hatch a plan to steal the Statue of Liberty and a thousand people would blindly follow him."

"That's a striking character trait."

"Yeah, he had a lot of those. We were both born in a small village in Croatia. By the time I was three, the Homeland War was tearing the country apart. Milosévić's army had teamed up with some local Serbian rebels… they destroyed everything in their path."

"From what I've heard, that was a brutal war. Do you remember much of it?"

"No, not at all. Just what I learned in school later on. My first memories are here in the States with my aunt and uncle."

"May I ask what happened to your parents?"

Henry exhaled into the cool air. "Well, my father had been in combat on the outskirts of Zagreb right after the

Yugoslav army began their first assaults. Apparently, he was injured pretty badly and sent home. Soon after, a group of Serbs loyal to Milosévić took over my village. They lined up about thirty people in a field and executed them. My mother and father were among them.”

“I’m sorry to hear that.”

“It’s okay, I never really knew them.”

“Anton brought all of you here, right?”

“Yeah, he and my Uncle Luka were part of a group that managed to escape before the massacre. They returned later and gathered the survivors, mostly children, then put us onto a big truck and drove to the coast. Anton stole a fishing boat in the middle of the night, which we used to cross the Adriatic to Italy. The next day we were on a plane to America.”

A.J. shook his head. “That’s a hell of a story, Henry. You ever been back?”

“No. There’s nothing there for me. All my family either got onto Anton’s truck or were killed by the Serbs.”

“Darius told me his father died before he was born and that his mother was killed in a car crash when he was a kid.”

Henry sipped his coffee. “Yeah, that was tough. He and his mom fled to America with the rest of us. Once we got here, she worked as a secretary for some bank downtown. She was hit by a tractor-trailer on her way home one day. Darius took it really hard. He used to visit her grave every year on the anniversary of her death. From what I remember, she was a kind woman—strong and honest.”

“What happened to him after that?”

“Anton took him in. Raised him as his own.”

A.J.’s gaze remained fixed on the stars. “I see.”

“You know, A.J., you don’t have to stick around. I know Darius paid you and you probably feel some sort of obligation to help me out but—”

"It's not about the money. I made a promise to Darius that if anything ever happened to him, I'd be here to see it through."

"And what if I decide to do nothing? What if I decide to walk away?"

"Then we'll never see each other again. It's that simple."

As the fire began to die out, Henry got up from his chair and meandered through the grass toward the house.

"That sofa down there is a foldout!" A.J. called into the night.

Henry waved his hand in some indolent response before disappearing through the back door. He made his way to the basement and sat down in front of the laptop. A quick search for the word DIAMOND returned more than a dozen results. He scrolled down the list until he found one that caught his attention, then clicked on it.

The file that appeared on the screen was exactly what A.J. had told him it would be: a specifications sheet detailing a large, rare diamond.

He set his coffee mug on the table and inched forward in his seat. With narrowed eyes, he blinked, then blinked again.

This can't be possible.

CHAPTER 22

Henry struggled to sleep. His mind had spun in circles trying to come up with some sinister plot that Anton might have bankrolled—something really evil, beyond the pale of larceny and fraud. Something powerful enough to make Darius want to turn on him.

With a stretch of his legs, he peeled himself off the sofa bed and put on his sneakers and hoodie. He went up the stairs and brewed a pot of coffee, poured himself a cup, and returned to the basement. Under the overwhelming pressure to find something, Henry began organizing as many files as he could into new subfolders, picking up where Darius had seemingly left off. He spent hours categorizing all the documents within the ARIES folder: connecting money transfers, dates, emails, shipping manifests, and anything else he could find.

It was past noon when he finally ran out of gas. As he took a moment to decompress, there was a knock on the steel door. It was A.J. "Why don't you come grab a sandwich and recharge?"

"A.J., why are you always lurking around like some weird butler?"

"Because you haven't given me anything to do. You're down here going through the evidence, which means half of my job is done. You want something to eat or not?"

"Yeah, sure," Henry grumbled as he rose from the desk and followed A.J. back upstairs.

They sat at the kitchen table and ate in a quiet hush, serenaded by the sound of wind chimes on the back porch.

After lunch, A.J. poured two shots of bourbon into a pair of lowballs. "I worked closely with Darius for the past few years," he said as he handed a glass to Henry. His voice was shallow and pressing. "I grew to like him. And I want to know who killed him."

"Yeah, you and everyone else," Henry quipped.

"Did he suffer?"

"Yes. He did. He was shot once through the stomach and once through the lung. He bled out in my arms."

"I'm sorry to hear that. And I'm sorry all this shit came crashing down on you."

Henry cleared his throat and gently ran his fingertips along the grain of the table. "There's something funny about everything I've found down there," he said. "My name comes up in a few files—sporadically, here and there. But for the most part, I seem to be missing from all of it."

"Funny how that works sometimes," A.J. replied with a tight smile.

"Seriously, there's nothing down there about the Hartsfield job or Montreal or the Uffizi Gallery. It's as if none of it ever happened."

"Darius wanted to protect you as much as he could. He was trying to bring down Anton and his bosses. Not you."

Henry shook his head in disagreement. "But that's not how it works. If he brings down Anton, he brings down everyone else around him, including me."

"Not if you're working with federal investigators."

"What's that supposed to mean?"

A.J. leered at him from across the table. "Does Isabell know?"

"Know what?"

"That you're an FBI informant."

Henry's face remained cold and motionless. "What makes you think I'm an FBI informant?"

"Because you are. It's okay, your secret's safe with me."

"Did Darius know?"

"Of course he did."

An awkward silence fell over the kitchen. Henry stared absently out the window, his mind racing uncontrollably.

"He respected you for it," A.J. leveled. "And so do I."

"It's not what you think."

"You don't have to explain yourself."

Henry nodded silently as an avalanche of defeat quickly washed over him, followed by a welcomed sense of relief. "Isabell will be here soon. I should go outside and wait for her."

"Okay. Is there anything I can do while you're gone?" A.J. asked.

"Yes, there is, actually. I want you to help me organize the files from the laptop."

A.J. dropped his head and grunted. "Is that right?"

"Darius had started grouping some documents together—building individual case files. I organized the entire Aries folder this morning. Maybe you could start with the Orion folder while I'm gone?"

"All right," A.J. replied with a hint of uncertainty. "I can give it a go."

"If you're not sure about something, just leave it where it is and I'll archive it when I get back."

"And when will that be?"

Henry tilted his head. "I really have no idea. How can I get in touch with you?"

"I used to communicate with Darius through an encrypted cell phone. He kept a burner at his house."

"Where in his house?"

"There's a hidden compartment in the electrical box in the basement. The upper-left corner of the panel, just give it a little push. My number's saved in the contacts."

Henry nodded. "Perfect. I'll touch base with you as soon as I can."

"By the way, I didn't mean to startle you with the whole informant thing," said A.J. "But it's important that you and I are on the same page here. We have to be able to trust each other."

"That's fair, but you seem to know a lot more about me than I know about you," Henry noted.

A.J. stood from the table with his arms crossed against his burly chest. "Well, I was born and raised in northern Virginia. Like many young men at the time, I joined the military after 9/11. I was a sharpshooter with the 75th Rangers before being accepted into the Green Berets. Did three tours in Afghanistan, two more in Iraq. After that, I retired and got into more unconventional work."

"You got family?"

"No."

"You ever going to give me a real name?"

"No."

Henry chuckled. "So you're a ghost?"

"Officially speaking, I was killed by an IED just outside of Kabul six years ago."

"Of course you were. I'm sorry to hear that."

A.J. pulled out his cell phone and swiped the screen. "Your ride's here," he mumbled as he turned into the hallway.

"In case you're wondering," Henry shouted, "I found the spec sheet."

The declaration stopped A.J. in his tracks. "So you know what it is?"

"Yes."

"Good. Then I guess you're all caught up."

Henry flashed a tiny grin before pacing through the living room and out the front door.

* * *

Miles tapped his fingers against the table as Agent Harwick read through a stack of contact reports, each of which outlined his recent meetings with the informant previously known as the Shadowmaker.

After a few uncomfortable minutes, the NSA agent slung the paperwork across the table in disgust. "So he didn't mention anything about the research vessel?"

"Only that it had departed Brazil a month ago. He told me he wasn't sure what it was being used for."

"Bullshit!" Harwick exclaimed. "We have photos of Martović standing on the fucking pier with Anton Krunoslav! And I'm supposed to believe he had no idea what he was doing there?"

"I guess not."

"He was lying to you, Agent Brennan!"

"Perhaps."

"I really expected more. What an absolute waste of time and resources."

"While I appreciate the kind words, sir, I have years of solid intel from this guy on record. The information I gleaned from his meetings over the years has resulted in over a dozen arrests and quite possibly saved the lives of two federal judges. I'm sorry we're not able to see eye to eye."

"That's all well and good," Harwick said, his voice eerily calm. "But none of it matters now. He's dead."

"So where do you want me?"

"Get with Garza. He needs help trying to track down Henry Sirola. Krunoslav's preparing to make his move, this whole thing's about to come to a head and I'm sure Sirola will be there when it does."

"Why is Garza trying to track Sirola down? Didn't he return to his apartment?"

"Maybe he did, who the hell knows. Just get with Garza and sort it out. The kid's probably still shook up from the shooting, but he's been off the grid since yesterday."

"I'm right on it."

Harwick stood from the table and glared out the window at the Park Avenue building. "Why is Anton being so quiet?" he wondered into the glass.

"Well, one of his captains was just gunned down in a public park," said Miles. "He's reorganizing, preparing his team for whatever it is he's got coming in from Brazil."

"The research vessel returned to port three days ago."

"No shit?"

"Yep. Brazilian Customs apparently checked the ship, but they're probably in Krunoslav's pocket so I'm not holding my breath. Or maybe it was all a distraction—a wild goose chase."

"I don't think he'd spend that kind of coin just to distract us."

"I asked CIA to nab one of the crew, try to shake something loose."

"What'd they say?"

"They won't get involved unless one of the crew members steps foot on American soil. Which means there's no black site, no interrogation. Nothin'."

"Great," scoffed Miles. "So much for containment. We're five thousand miles away from a boat we've only seen through a monitor with no way of finding out what was on it. We should've had a team waiting for it when it pulled into port."

Harwick turned and headed for the exit. "Find Henry Sirola!" he shouted as he charged out of the room.

Miles slung his hands onto the armrests and leaned back in his chair. He stared out over the skyline at a set of clouds passing by in the distance.

Nearby, a young NSA analyst pegged away at his keyboard. "He seems fun to work with," the kid joked softly.

Miles turned his head and looked him over. "How long you been doing this?"

"Four years," remarked the young man. He had a thick head of dark hair and a wispy patch of growth where a goatee would someday be.

"What's our surveillance total at the moment?" Miles asked.

The kid continued typing. "Five: we've got full surveillance on Krunoslav from here; you and Garza are now assigned to Henry Sirola; we've also got a team watching Asa Petrovi; and a team on the warehouse off Krog Street."

"Good," replied Miles. "You'll feel the buzz when Anton's treasure arrives. They'll all start scurrying around like cockroaches."

"Yes, sir. We'll be ready."

The FBI agent stood from his chair and walked across the carpet. "Can I get you anything while I'm out?"

"No, sir. I'm all set here."

Miles left the room, and as he walked up the hallway toward the maintenance elevator, he pulled out his cell phone and dialed a number.

"Go ahead," a voice answered.

"Hey, Garza. Anything on Sirola?"

"Absolutely nothing," the DCIS officer replied. "His car hasn't left Scranton and Brooks since yesterday. He's not at his apartment either."

Miles winced with frustration. "Okay, where are you?"

"I'm back at the Forty West building just waiting for this little prick to show up."

"You're at the wrong location. Meet me at Scranton and Brooks in ten minutes."

CHAPTER 23

The rented minivan merged south onto the interstate. It was Monday afternoon and rush-hour traffic was already backing up.

"How'd everything go?" she asked. Henry glanced out the passenger window at a light fog gathering to the west. "Henry," she tried again. "Did something happen? Did you find anything?"

"No. Sorry, I just… didn't get much sleep."

"So what's on the laptop?"

"Darius has enough evidence to bring down the entire organization," he said ominously.

Isabell gripped the steering wheel tighter. "I still don't understand why we aren't setting that house on fire and burying A.J. in the backyard."

But Henry didn't answer. He continued to stare blankly into the passing landscape.

"Henry?" she asked. "What are you not telling me?"

He let out a deep exhale and shut his eyes. "Anton promoted me to captain."

"When?"

"The day before yesterday."

"Okay. And how does that change things?"

"I guess it doesn't."

"You haven't answered my question," she gently pressed. "What exactly is going on?"

"We're looking for answers, Isabell. Something about all of this made Darius want to turn on Anton. Somewhere on that laptop is evidence of something Anton did that was so fucked up, Darius was willing to burn him for it. Whatever it is, I intend to find it."

"And if you don't?"

"Then we'll destroy everything, cancel A.J., and pretend we were never there. Besides, we're on the verge of a deal that could change our lives forever, so it's not like I'm trying to ruin a good thing here."

"How is this deal still going through? Darius is dead, Hassani almost had us killed in Sorrento, and you've got a small army of feds watching your every move. There's no way we're still on track."

"I found more info on the asset."

"You did? What?"

"They launched a research boat from Brazil. Darius was there last month when it set sail from Porto Santos, but he didn't tell me about it."

"Why not?"

"Probably because it was the biggest haul Anton had ever gone after."

"You know what it is?"

He nodded spitefully. "I saw the spec sheet. It's the biggest diamond in existence."

Isabell darted her eyes from the road to Henry, then back to the road. "What are the specs?"

"Nine-sided, double-rose cut. One hundred and thirty-seven carats."

She couldn't help but laugh. "You're kidding me, right? That's not even possible, Henry. A diamond that size doesn't exist."

"What if it did?"

"What's that supposed to mean?"

"It means it's been sitting at the bottom of the ocean for the last five hundred years."

Isabell blinked in disbelief. "What? What are you talking about?"

"It's the Florentine Diamond."

"I don't believe you. There's no way you found it—it doesn't exist. Anton's full of shit."

Henry shook his head. "It would explain why Hassani reacted the way he did. Even he knows it's impossible."

"No offense, but you expect me to believe you didn't know anything about this?"

"I really didn't. I suspected Darius was in Brazil recently, but I never asked him about it. And then, when I met with Anton the other day, I asked him point blank what the asset was."

"What did he say?"

"He said I had to see it to believe it."

Isabell puffed out her cheeks and exhaled. "Okay, let's just pretend for a moment that Anton has recovered the Florentine Diamond. What's it worth?"

"It's priceless," Henry answered. "It was discovered in the fifteenth century in India. Charles the Bold was the first owner. He carried it with him into war against the Swiss, and when he was killed, he and the diamond lay on the battlefield field for several days before a soldier recovered it. By the mid-seventeenth century, the diamond was in the possession of the Medici family."

"How do you know all this?" she interrupted.

Henry turned up the corner of his mouth. "Because any good jewel thief knows the story of the Florentine Diamond; it's the most sought-after gem in the history of the world."

"When exactly did it go missing?"

"No one really knows for sure. After the fall of the Medici dynasty, it was stolen by the archduchess of Austria, who displayed it in Vienna for a while. After the First World War, her family was exiled to Switzerland. From there, nobody really knows what happened. Some stories say it was cut into smaller pieces and sold. Others say a servant pocketed it and fled to South America."

"What do you think happened to it?"

Henry puckered his lips and raised his brow. "I've never really thought much about it. It's a unicorn. Like you said, it doesn't exist. Or, at least, it's not supposed to exist."

"Did Anton say when this mysterious stone would arrive? Do we get to see it?"

"Next week sometime. I'm sure Asa will be securing it with a small army."

"Where would he possibly store something like that?"

"The vault."

"What vault?"

"We have a large safe for keeping valuables. A couple years ago, I lifted a British ceremonial crown that was on display in Los Angeles. Anton kept it in a secret vault beneath the Fox Theater until it was ready to be shipped to a buyer in Moscow."

"The Fox Theater?"

"Yeah, there's an old underground tunnel where the Confederate Army kept priceless works of art during the Battle of Atlanta. Anton updated the place with reinforced concrete and a steel vault."

"This is crazy," she grumbled. "You guys have gone too far this time."

"It can't be real. There's just no way."

"Well, if it is real, this thing's going to sell for a fortune. Listen, I know you're struggling with your moral compass and all, but *do not* mess this up with Anton until the deal's finished and I get paid."

But Henry was distracted—drifting in some obscure daze.

"Seriously," she tried. "We both need this. Afterwards, you can do whatever you want with all of Darius' evidence. You'll have enough money to create a whole new life—get a fresh start in a new place."

"Maybe I don't want a fresh start."

"Well, that's an option too," Isabell granted as the minivan cruised along the interstate. "Henry, I can't imagine how hard it was for you to watch Darius die. I know how much he meant to you. Please take some time to mourn, to wrap your head around everything before you decide to do something stupid."

"I miss him so much," he softly confessed.

"I know you do, sweetie. I know you do."

The van exited the interstate and continued to Sandy Springs MARTA station.

After pulling into the lot and parking at the curb, she reached for his hand. "Tell me you're going to be okay?"

"I'm going to be okay."

"Any word on the funeral?" she asked gently.

"I haven't checked my phone since yesterday morning. But I'll get in touch with Anton when I get home and let you know something."

"I'd appreciate that. Anything I can do for you in the meantime?"

He looked up, locking his gaze into hers. "Why did you lie to me about your boyfriend?"

"Excuse me?"

"Jacob—why did you lie to me about him?"

"I didn't."

"Yes, you did," he revealed calmly. "I know he doesn't exist."

Isabell searched for a way out. But there wasn't one. "I'm sorry, Henry. I only did it to keep a wedge between us."

"A wedge? Why do we need a wedge between us?"

"You know why. Don't make me say it."

Henry lowered his gaze. "Just say it, Isabell."

"We have history," she explained. "I wanted to keep everything professional. I didn't want old feelings boiling up, especially at a time when we're both vulnerable."

"I just want to trust you. I need to trust you."

"Look at me," she demanded. "You can trust me, Henry. I promise."

He put on his ball cap and reached for the door handle. "I truly appreciate everything. And for what it's worth, I do trust you."

"Please be safe, Henry."

He stepped out of the van and jogged away, into the station, fighting the urge to look back. He continued down the escalator and disappeared below ground.

The platform was nearly empty now. The stench of brake fluid and urine floated through the air as he stuffed his hands into his pockets and waited.

The next train brought him to Midtown, where he walked two blocks to Ammazza Trattoria and into the hidden tunnels.

Now standing in his office at Scranton and Brooks, Henry peered out the window in both directions. With no visible signs of federal agents, he made his way through the lobby and stepped out beneath a blanket of dark clouds. His Maserati darted out of the lot and continued northbound through the Old Fourth Ward, then Virginia Highlands.

As he crested over a small hill and into a busy intersection, a black Suburban cornered the street and casually fell in line several cars behind him.

Henry parked in the underground deck of the Forty West building and took the elevator to his penthouse. There, he slipped out of his dirty clothes and into a hot shower. He inhaled the steam and took a series of deep, calming breaths. As the water pounded against his chest, he heard a faint clank in the hallway. Startled, he stepped out of the shower with the water still running and placed his ear closer to the door.

For several seconds, he listened to the quiet. Finally, he wrapped his fingers around the doorknob and pulled it open.

He remembered setting his pistol on the entry table in the foyer.

With tightened fists, he charged up the hall in a naked dash for his gun. He snatched the pistol from the table and traced it across the penthouse, searching for signs of an intruder. His senses were suddenly heightened as his eyes narrowed toward the balcony. He trained his weapon and began a slow, methodical march through the kitchen.

He gently opened the sliding glass door and peered outside. The brisk air brushed across his body as he turned and retreated back to the hallway. He moved cautiously toward the study and pushed open the door. As he steadied his pistol and entered the dark room, he could see the silhouette of a man sitting behind his large oak desk.

"Put some clothes on, Henry," the deep, throaty voice instructed.

"Asa? Jesus Christ, you scared the living shit out of me!"

The figure sat motionless, his hands folded in his lap.

"Just give me a minute," Henry implored as he stormed out of the room. He returned a minute later in a light blue shirt and a pair of khakis. "Can I get you something to drink?" he offered as he clasped the cuffs of his shirt.

"Where have you been?" snapped Asa. "We've been worried about you."

Henry's mind searched for an answer. Surely Asa already knew that he hadn't gone to his Aunt Sara's. It was a trap.

"I was out," he finally answered.

"You told Anton you were going to your aunt's house."

"I changed my mind."

"So where were you?"

"I spent a couple nights with a friend."

"What kind of friend?" Asa pressed.

"A hooker," Henry confessed. "Happy now? I spent the weekend drinking and fucking. Now why the hell are you in my apartment?"

"You know, Henry, this is no time to be keeping secrets."

"Give me a break, Asa. Anton told me to take some time off. Besides, I didn't know I had to keep you informed of my whereabouts at all times."

Asa rose from the behind the desk and buttoned his jacket. "Don't play games with me. Anton wants to see you tonight. Six o'clock." With that, the stout Croatian showed himself into the hallway and onto the elevator.

Henry kept his eyes on the small screen mounted against the wall, watching as Asa rode the elevator to ground level and exited through the lobby.

Henry grabbed a gray wool coat from a hall tree in the foyer and slid his keys into his pocket. He hurried down to the parking deck, fired up the Italian twin-turbo engine, and tore out of the garage.

Through the rearview mirror, he could see the black Suburban doing its best to keep up. He pressed his foot on the gas pedal and slipped lanes before hanging a hard right onto Tenth Street. From there, he pushed the sportscar through two intersections and ducked into a parking lot behind an upscale bar on the east side.

He lunged out of the car and checked over each shoulder. Agent Brennan's Suburban was nowhere in sight.

Across the street, a family-owned deli was drawing a late lunch crowd. Henry broke into a light jog and stepped through the front door. He waited in line for several minutes before a man in a grease-stained white apron handed him a paper bag from behind the counter. Henry thanked him with a nod and pushed through the crowd to the sidewalk outside. With an anxious glance, he walked several blocks to a small community park and took a seat on a wooden bench.

He stared at the paper bag for a moment before opening it. Inside, there was a thick stack of bills accompanied by a single folded piece of notebook paper. He reached in and unfurled it.

Spartan has arrived.

He leaned back and gazed into the clouds. Three simple words told him that his paintings had arrived at the port in Savannah and been loaded onto a freighter—the first leg of its journey now complete. It was a handsome reward for months of planning and flawless execution.

Henry stuffed the cash into his coat pocket and stood from the bench. He tossed the paper bag into a trashcan and strolled along the sidewalk, up the alley, and to the parking lot.

The clouds had finally started to clear as a cool breeze came across the pavement. He climbed back into his Maserati and drove to the safe confines of Scranton and Brooks.

With the entire staff having left for the day, he unlocked the front door and hurried inside. He entered his office and brushed past his desk to a small safe hidden in the corner of the room beneath an antique telescope. After punching a five-digit code into the keypad, the little door sprang open. Henry pulled the wad of cash from his coat and tossed it inside. He then closed the safe and rushed out of the building, locking the door behind himself.

As he stepped out onto the sidewalk, he noticed it: the familiar pink-and-turquoise bicycle chained to the rack in front of Maggie's Coffee House across the street.

Miles had caught up.

With a concentrated gaze, he climbed into his Maserati and turned onto Irwin Street. He continued north to Little Five Points and parked his car at the old produce market. As a blanket of storm clouds hovered overhead, he got out and began his hike to Moreland Avenue.

Beneath the shade of a leaning oak, he sat down and waited patiently, until a large, disheveled man in torn jeans and a suede jacket lumbered up the street.

The agent sat down on the bench next to him and began thumbing through a newspaper. "Where have you been?" he asked quietly.

"Why does everyone keep asking me that? Besides, it's none of your damn business."

"I can't keep your little underground tunnel a secret if you're going to be so careless with it," Miles threatened. "At some point, the NSA is going to realize you're covertly traveling between locations. You'll make a fool out of me."

"I'll try to be more careful. Now what did you need to see me about?"

"I hear you're a captain now?"

"I am," Henry confirmed. "First day on the job."

"Congratulations. Now tell me what the hell you guys just pulled up from the Atlantic?"

"I think it's a pirate treasure."

The agent mocked him with a roll of his eyes. "Don't fuck with me, Henry. I'm not in the mood."

"All right then, Anton found some rare gems. But it's not like we stole it from anybody. It's ours. Besides, I told you not to jam me up on this one."

"Everything's changed, Henry. There's a lot of moving pieces. It's not just you and me playing cat and mouse anymore."

"Then I'll come up with something else to give you. But not this one."

"Those stones must be pretty valuable," Miles casually noted.

"I'm happy to gift you a little something for your trouble."

"Oh c'mon," the agent said with a chuckle. "You've known me for a long time. I've got everything I could ever want in life."

"You sure about that?" Henry challenged. "You couldn't use a new car? New house? A little something for the ex-wife?"

Miles clenched his lips, fighting the urge to smile. "Is Hassani still your buyer?"

"I have no idea. I'm meeting with Anton this evening. I'll know more afterwards."

"As soon as you confirm the arrival of your little pirate treasure, send a signal."

"I told you to leave this one alone."

"Listen, Henry, I can't help you, nor can I misdirect the NSA, if I don't even know what's going on. They already know about the shipment from Porto Santos. You can have this one, but I just need to know when it gets here so I can manage the situation."

"Fine. What's the signal?" asked Henry.

"The postal box outside First Presbyterian." Miles stood up and looked to the horizon. "Looks like more rain. I'd better get going."

CHAPTER 24

He wedged his fingertips beneath the window pane and gave it a gentle tug. The warm air from inside the house swept against his face as he shimmied his way in. Maneuvering through the darkness, Henry crept across the basement to the main breaker box that hung against a concrete wall. He gently ran his hand along the outside of the metal casing and waited for his eyes to adjust. With a light nudge, a hidden panel popped outward, revealing a small open crevice. He reached inside and pulled out a cell phone, a roll of cash, a US passport, and lastly, a small golden key.

He gave the key a curious look. There was an inscription lasered into its side— Banque Lyonnais 2291. With a furrowed brow, he quickly stuffed it into his right sneaker. The rest of the items were shoved into his coat pockets. He then closed the hidden compartment and carefully retreated into the shadows.

With calculated, muted steps, Henry tiptoed along the edge of the staircase to the main level into a long hallway. He reached Darius' bedroom and stopped at the door. He pushed it open and stepped inside.

A set of modern white furniture pieces sat eerily along the gray walls. Henry froze in the center of the room, casting his eyes to the walk-in closet, the bathroom, and then a bookshelf in the far corner. There, nestled on the shelf, was a framed photograph of him and Darius. The picture had been taken three years ago at a New Year's Eve party in Las Vegas, he remembered.

For a sobering moment, his mind drifted back in time—he could see Darius' broad smile and hear his booming laugh.

He grabbed the frame and yanked the photo from behind its glass and placed it in his pocket with the rest of his finds. He gave the room one last glance before slithering back down to the basement. Outside, he emerged from the window and landed in the lush green grass. He hustled through the woods along Ansley Park before surfacing in a small parking lot adjacent to the neighborhood tennis courts where his Maserati sat in the shade of a tall pine tree. Before leaving, he pulled the photograph from his coat pocket and set it in his lap, staring at it with a lifetime of memories.

The Maserati pulled away and darted north through the neighborhood and into Buckhead.

Under the watchful eye of Special Agent Brennan, Henry turned left and pulled into the Park Avenue building lot. He was fifteen minutes early.

The elevator took him to the forty-second floor, where Asa greeted him in the lobby and led him through the main hall into the study. Anton was waiting inside, dressed in a crisp black suit with a gray shirt and white tie. His eyes cut to the door as Henry entered.

"Good to see you, my boy! How are you feeling today?"

"Better. Much better," said Henry as he fell into Anton's waiting arms.

"I'm glad to hear it. You look well and rested."

"Asa said you wanted to see me."

Anton finally released Henry from his grasp. "Yes, I do. But I'd like for us to talk upstairs. It's more comfortable up there. Besides, I get cooped up in this office sometimes."

Anton guided him back to the foyer where Asa and two of his foot soldiers joined them in the elevator. They rode up to the next floor and stepped out onto a mosaic of polished Italian tile.

Henry had never been to the forty-third floor. He'd heard stories of a luxury spa, a grand dining hall, and a spacious lounge, all of which were typically reserved for entertaining senators, dignitaries, and heads of various criminal organizations.

As they walked deeper into the penthouse, it revealed a brilliant tapestry of medieval furniture, crystal chandeliers, and vaulted ceilings. Asa guided them past a marble fountain, which gave way to a set of thermal pools and steam rooms, before finally reaching what appeared to be an empty restaurant.

One of Asa's goons snuck behind the bar and began preparing drinks. The other remained at the entrance, standing guard like a stone watchman.

"You drink vodka?" Anton asked.

"A little," Henry said with a sly wink.

Three small glasses of vodka quickly appeared on the bar. Anton handed one to Henry, the other to Asa, then made his way to a set of black leather chairs perfectly nestled in front of a roaring fireplace.

As they settled in, Anton raised his glass. "To new beginnings," he toasted. Asa and Henry lifted their drinks into the air. "I want to welcome you to your new role," Anton continued. "This is a big step for you, Henry. And Ružaro is lucky to have you."

"I can't thank you enough, Anton."

"You've earned it, my boy."

Henry tasted his vodka and glanced over at Asa, who sat with a formidable grin.

"I want to discuss our next steps," said Anton. "Our prize arrives tomorrow. Is your team in place?"

"Yes, sir."

"And who is stepping in as your lieutenant?"

"Jack Veselko," Henry said pridefully.

Anton nodded his approval. "He's a very strong young man, much like you." He paused for a brief moment, then reached into his pocket and brought a cigar to his mouth. "We have discovered who was behind Darius' murder."

Henry's eyes grew wider. "Really? Who?"

"It was, as we all suspected, the Cardoso cartel. It was a revenge hit for stealing the diamond in Brazil."

"Are you sure? Do we have evidence to back that up?"

"Yes," Anton confirmed. "Arturo Cardoso and I have come to an agreement. And the man who pulled the trigger was carved into little pieces last night."

"He was a bit of a squirmer," Asa added. "It's always the little ones."

Henry stared into the palms of his hands and steadied his breathing. "That's great news, Anton." He wanted to ask why they weren't charging into South America, burning every Cardoso business to the ground, then lining up the entire cartel and putting bullets in their heads, but he didn't.

"I'm sure you would have preferred a more vengeful response," Anton said intuitively. "But this outcome is better for us in the long run. We have vested interests in some of our partnerships—"

"Those partnerships are sealed with Darius' blood," Henry interrupted. "Those goddamn pigs don't deserve to be let off the hook with this eye-for-an-eye bullshit."

Anton allowed the rant to hang in the air unchecked. "Are you done?" he asked.

Henry straightened himself in his chair. "Yes, sir. I'm done."

"Good," Anton replied as he lit his cigar. "Obviously, Darius' death was a setback. Asa seems to think we need a new buyer—that Darius' entire network may have been compromised. But my gut tells me to stick with Hassani."

"Hassani?" Henry screeched. "I didn't exactly think he was the best buyer to start with."

"Are you going against my instincts? And Darius' instincts?"

Henry shook his head. "No, not at all. Darius was planning to give Hassani some space, wait for him to reach out to us. But I just don't know if that's the best strategy."

"And why not?"

Henry wanted to reveal what had happened in Sorrento, but knew that Anton would just brush it off as typical behavior that came with the territory.

"Henry?" Asa prompted. "Is there something we should know?"

"No. I just don't trust Hassani, that's all."

Asa loosened his tie and scowled. "I agree with Henry. I say we scrap the lousy bastard."

"Now, now, boys," Anton interjected. "Hassani is the perfect buyer; he's got the network, he's got the appetite, and best of all, he has the money. What if we vetted him a bit more? Would that make you both feel better?" Henry shrugged it off and sipped his vodka. "Wonderful! It has been decided!" Anton continued in jest. "Now, let's set up our surveillance of him immediately."

"Do we even know where he is?" asked Henry.

Anton sat quietly for a moment, tapping his finger against his chin. "Not at the moment," he answered. "But we can find him. Asa, locate our Arab friend and get an LZ in place. Henry, put a surveillance team together. How long do you need?"

"At the very least, I can have an advance team ready to deploy in twelve hours," Henry assured.

"Very well. If Hassani checks out, I want you to deal with him directly."

"Yes, sir."

Anton blew a smoke ring into the air and leered into the crackling fireplace. "Whatever happens, whoever the buyer is, the final transaction is going to take place here in Atlanta. I want to oversee it myself."

Henry was stunned. The suggestion that Anton would be present at a handoff went against every protocol in the book. "Are you sure that's a good idea?" he asked cautiously.

"Yes. This is important to me."

"Understood," Henry conceded quickly.

"Perfect. Now, talk to me about the Montreal job. Where are we?"

Henry sat up and cleared his throat. "I received confirmation that the truck made it to Savannah—the paintings are probably charging through international waters as we speak. I received the down payment and I'll have the total balance by the end of next week. We'll funnel it all through Scranton and Brooks."

"That's great news," Anton noted through a cloud of smoke. "And speaking of the firm, it belonged to Darius."

"Yes, sir. I'm aware."

"Well, it's yours now. Update all of your cover docs and websites and whatever else you need to. You're the new president of Scranton and Brooks."

Henry nodded his appreciation. "Thank you, Anton. I'll have everything taken care of as soon as possible."

"Splendid. That's exactly why you're a captain now," granted Anton. "Get your surveillance team up and running. Asa will be in touch as soon as we have a location on Hassani."

Henry sipped the last of his vodka and set the glass on a small end table. "Consider it done."

"And one last thing. Darius' funeral is tomorrow morning."

Henry's face fell flush. "Where?"

"Cathedral of Christ. Nine o'clock. I'll have a car pick you up at eight."

"Thank you, sir. I'll be ready."

Anton placed his cigar in the ashtray and stood from his chair. "I appreciate everything you've done for this organization," he said with an extended palm.

Henry rose to his feet and shook Anton's hand, then Asa's. "See you both tomorrow morning," he promised.

CHAPTER 25

As a thin layer of fog fell over the city, a small crowd gathered inside the Cathedral of Christ church in downtown Atlanta. Henry wore a black suit with a black shirt and black tie. The morning service was solemn and respectful. And while he would never remember the words spoken by the priest, or the songs performed by the choir, it was a moment he would never forget.

The crowd eventually moved outside to the cemetery, where Henry stood at attention just behind Anton. As Darius' casket was lowered into the grave, Henry turned his eyes to Isabell, who stood on the opposite side of the plot with her head hung in grief.

After a few words by Father Horvat, Anton stepped to the head of his flock and offered words of strength. He spoke lovingly of Darius, and told the story of how he'd raised him to be a gifted, talented young man.

Following the burial, Henry lingered beside the freshly dug mound of earth as members of the syndicate, along with their families, slowly dispersed.

"How are you holding up?" Isabell asked as she approached.

"I'm good. I still can't believe he's gone."

She stood next to him and gently rubbed his arm. "I know he'd be proud of you right now, Henry."

"I wish I could believe that."

As their eyes met, Anton slipped away from a nearby group and joined them next to the grave. "Miss DiMarco, thank you for coming," he greeted.

"You have my deepest condolences, Mr. Krunoslav," she replied politely. "Darius was an amazing man—a true warrior."

"Yes, he was. And he will be sorely missed."

"Please let me know if there's anything I can do," she offered.

"I certainly appreciate that, Miss DiMarco." Anton reached down for her hand and held it softly. "Now, if you don't mind, I must get going. Henry, the car is waiting," he said as he turned and strode away.

"Any news on the asset?" Isabell asked quietly.

Henry waited for Anton to drift out of earshot. "It's arriving today," he revealed. "And get this; Anton wants to vet Hassani some more. We're trying to track him down and get a surveillance team in place."

"When will you be deploying?"

"I'm about to put my team on standby. As soon as Asa gives us a location, we're out." He lifted his gaze to the tall pines swaying against the horizon. "I'll need a tour guide."

"Of course," she said without hesitation.

"Good. Go ahead and get packed. I'll call you as soon as I hear something."

She dropped her eyes and nodded with conviction.

Henry leaned over and kissed her on the cheek before shuffling back to the limo, where he climbed into the back alongside Anton, Asa, and a bodyguard. The vehicle pulled away from the cemetery and made its way across town. Shortly after, they arrived at the underground parking deck of the Forty West building.

Henry fidgeted in his seat as the car came to a stop.

"Is everything all right, my boy?" Anton asked.

"Yes, sir. Of course it is. Just a tough day, that's all."

"It's a tough day for all of us," the old boss agreed. "I have something to tell you."

"What is it?"

"Henry, the item that's arriving today is a very special diamond."

"Of course, sir. I can assure you my team is taking every—"

"It's the Florentine Diamond, Henry."

He tried to act surprised. "That's incredible. But I don't understand. How did you ever find it?"

Anton grunted as his eyes grew cold and narrowed. "The diamond was shipwrecked in 1924," he began, "just beyond the continental shelf off South America. A historian in Uruguay handed me twenty years' worth of research… he'd gotten his projections down to a seven-mile radius, five thousand feet below the water."

"And you just, what… snatched it from the ocean floor?"

"Yes, my boy." Anton paused for a moment, then exhaled with consternation. "You're going to be very rich, Henry. I hope I can depend on your loyalty."

"Yes… my absolute loyalty," Henry promised. "You can always depend on me, Anton. Always."

"Good."

Henry stepped out of the black limo and stood dumbfounded on the curb, watching as the car sped out of the garage.

He floated up to his penthouse in a wonderous daze, trying his best to calculate the price of such a relic that had, until now, been lost to history. After a few sobering minutes, he began to move with purpose. He darted to his bedroom, then the closet, where he took off his black suit and donned a pair of jeans and a blue sweater. His shoes squeaked against the hardwood as he bolted for the elevator and descended to the main lobby.

He stepped outside and circled the block to Peachtree Street, where he pulled out his cell phone and quickly opened his inbox. With the steeple of First Presbyterian Church towering over him, Henry took a seat on a sidewalk bench and scrolled through several messages, responding only to the ones he deemed important. As a small crowd exited the church and gathered nearby, he stood and walked away. Behind him, scrawled onto a blue postal box, he'd left a short, thin chalk mark.

On his walk back to Forty West, a strange, high-pitched sound chirped from his front pocket. It was Darius' burner. Henry ripped it from his pants and pulled it to his ear. "Hello?"

"Hi there," a voice greeted. "I see you found the phone."

"I did. Listen, A.J., there's been some… revelations."

"Revelations?"

"Yeah, we're lining up a buyer for the diamond. I may be leaving soon."

"Is it still Hassani?"

"It appears that way. I'm heading up a surveillance team—probably be gone for a few days. Any updates on the laptop?"

"Nothing I'd consider Earth-shattering."

"All right, we'll catch up when I get back."

"Will do," promised A.J. "By the way, you've got international service on that burner so hit me up if you need anything."

"Thanks, A.J. Talk soon." Henry stuffed the phone back into his pocket. He then hailed a passing cab, which quickly landed at the curb in from of him.

He slumped inside and gave the driver an address in Grant Park.

Ten minutes later, the cab pulled up in front of a small brick home with black shutters and a wall of pink roses set against a wrap-around porch. He handed the driver a twenty-dollar bill and began striding up the walkway.

As he rushed up the stairs, the front door slowly opened.

Jack Veselko stepped onto the porch with a tight-lipped smile. His eyes beamed with surprise. "Well, well, well. Look what washed ashore," he joked.

"Sorry for the unannounced visit," said Henry. "Is there someplace we can talk?"

Jack looked his friend over and welcomed him into the house.

Henry stepped inside and peered around the living room. It was sterile and modern. An antelope skull hung eerily from the wall, its long antlers rising towards the vaulted ceiling. In the far corner, a glass display held crustacean fossils from the Jurassic period—an impressive collection of archaeological finds, thought Henry. He wondered for a moment if any of it had been acquired legally.

"Can I get you anything, Henry?" Jack asked nervously.

"No, I'm fine."

"Well, come on in and have a seat," Jack offered as he settled into his sofa. "I heard about Darius. I can't believe it. I mean, what the hell happened?"

"It was a mess, Jack. I'd rather not talk about it."

"Do we know who did it?"

Henry dropped into a plush club chair on the other side of the room and cleared his throat. "It was Cardoso."

"That's—that's crazy. I mean, how did they get an assassin here that fast? You think someone followed us home that day?"

"Who the fuck knows."

"Well, I'm sure everyone's scrambling right about now. Is there anything I can help out with?"

"Actually, there is," said Henry. "In the wake of Darius' death, I've been elevated to captain. I'll need someone to step in as my lieutenant."

Jack nodded awkwardly. "Sure, sure. You've got a hell of a team to choose from."

"I've chosen you."

"Me? You—you want me to step in?"

"Stop acting so goddamn surprised, Jack. You've earned it. You were an asset to us in Brazil, not to mention Los Angeles, Montreal, and everywhere in between. You're ready for this."

Jack shook his head with measured pride. "I would be absolutely honored, Henry. I—I don't even know what to say."

"You don't have to say anything. You just need to be prepared. I'm launching a surveillance op; I'd like you to lead the advance team."

"Sure thing. Where?"

"I don't have a location yet, but we should know something in the next few hours. I'll go ahead and begin notifying the crew."

"What kind of equipment do we need?"

Henry pondered the mission for a moment. "AV and counterintelligence should do it."

"You don't want any firepower?"

"Depends. How good are you with a long rifle?"

"I still hit the range from time to time."

"Good. I'll have a target package ready before you fly out."

"I'll be ready. Can you tell me who the target is?"

"A Qatari billionaire—Hamad Al Hassani. He's one of Anton's new buyers."

"You can count on me, Henry."

"I know I can, Jack. That's why I'm here." Henry stood from the couch and extended his hand to his new lieutenant. "If you don't hear from me directly, you'll hear from our tour guide, Isabell DiMarco. She'll get you squared away."

Jack met Henry's palm with a firm grip. "I'll start packing," he announced eagerly.

With that, Henry turned and let himself out the front door. He hustled to the curb, jumped back into the taxi, and disappeared.

The car wove through Grant Park and into Midtown before dropping Henry off at the entrance to his building. He continued across the lobby and into the elevator to the penthouse. There, he slinked into his couch and turned on the television.

He found a James Bond marathon playing on BBC and decided to settle in and order pizza. His jeans were quickly taken off, followed by his sweater, and he swapped them out for a pair of cotton pajama pants and a t-shirt.

The hours slowly passed, and as the end credits of *The Spy Who Loved Me* scrolled in the background, Henry reached over to the end table and pulled a small key from its drawer. He examined its engraving for a moment, remembering the time that Darius had bragged about having five million dollars in a security box in France. He was going to buy a small house on the ocean and a modest yacht, Henry recalled.

But more importantly, Henry knew that Banque Lyonnais was located in—of all places—Lyon, France.

As he stared at the key, intrigued, twirling it between his fingertips, the buzzer in the foyer began sounding off.

He quickly tucked the key back into the drawer and lumbered across the living room to the small monitor set within the wall. The grainy video showed two men standing downstairs in the lobby. It was Asa Petrovi and one of his henchmen. Henry pressed a button on the display, which sent the elevator down to get them. Minutes later, the door opened and Asa and his sidekick stepped into the foyer.

"Did we wake you up?" the general growled.

Henry leered at them for a moment, wondering why they'd chosen to come in person. "No. I was just watching a little TV. Please, come in."

"You remember Paul?" Asa asked as they traipsed into the living room.

"Yeah, sure. I think we've met once or twice." Paul was a grizzly bear of a man; Darius had once described him as an anvil stuffed into a suit. The man's droopy, lifeless eyes panned the penthouse with disgust. Henry grabbed the remote, turned off the television, and fell back onto his couch. "So did you find Hassani?"

Asa stood in the center of the room, his barrel chest puffed in front of him. "We did. He's in Zürich."

"Zürich?" Henry repeated with a raised brow. "I would've guessed Dubai or Amsterdam or something like that."

"Apparently, after your meeting in Sorrento, he spent some time in Positano, then Rome. Last week, he traveled by train to Zürich." Asa placed a manila envelope on the coffee table. "This is your target pack. Hotel info is inside, as well as photos of Hassani's entourage, his bio, and a map of the city with predetermined points of interest, extraction routes, and weapons caches."

Henry picked up the envelope and looked inside. "Thanks for putting this together, Asa."

"What's your plan?" the general asked sharply.

"Jack Veselko's going to lead the advance team. I'll have him and the other guys wheels up tonight. They'll set up surveillance before I arrive tomorrow with my tour guide."

"Fine. Don't stay too long," Asa insisted. "Four days, tops. Once you're comfortable enough to clear him, get in touch with us on the satellite phone."

"And then what? Are we making contact or just packing up and coming home?"

"Anton will make that decision once you have some intel for us. If Hassani checks out, I'm sure you'll get clearance to make an approach. We can handle all the arrangements from this end, but it would be nice to get a commitment out of this bastard."

Henry rocked his head in thought. "Okay, I can live with that."

"Good. Don't fuck this up," Asa warned as he turned and headed back to the elevator. Paul wobbled behind him, trying to keep up.

"Thanks for the vote of confidence, Asa!"

The two thugs stepped into the elevator and melted behind the shiny doors. Henry shoved a slice of cold pizza into his mouth as he dialed Jack's number. "Zürich," he broadly announced. "You guys fly out tonight."

"Roger that. We're packing up the gear now."

"I'm texting you our tour guide's contact info now. Send her a list of team members and she'll take care of the flights and hotel. I'll see you tomorrow."

"All over it, boss. Safe travels."

Henry hung up and swiped to an encrypted messaging screen. He brought Isabell's number into a new thread and began typing: INITIATE REDWOOD PROTOCOL. 4 ON ADVANCE. ZÜRICH.

Her reply came within seconds: RECEIVED. ETA 30 MIN.

Henry lumbered to his bedroom and pulled two empty bags from his closet. He packed his clothes first, then essentials—duct tape, a monocular scope, gloves, flashlight, satellite phone, and two packs of gum. Satisfied, he made his way to the foyer and set his bags next to the door.

He ran through a quick checklist in his head but was interrupted by the unmistakable sound of the buzzer. For a fleeting moment, a tiny grin appeared on his face as he watched her through the monitor.

With the press of a button, the elevator descended to the lobby and returned moments later.

Isabell stepped into the foyer and examined the penthouse. "Veselko sent me a list of passport names and I went ahead and booked all of our flights," she said as she slipped past him into the living room. "Where's Hassani's hotel?"

"Not sure. The target pack's on the coffee table," he said as he followed her.

Isabell sat on the couch and snatched the manila envelope into her lap. Her eyes zipped through the first couple of pages until she found the itinerary. "He's staying at the Baur au Loc in old town Zürich," she noted as she pulled her laptop from her bag. Her fingers worked the keyboard furiously. "Unfortunately, his room is facing the river."

"That's fine, we'll just get creative. Can you find us something across the water?"

Isabell continued to type. "Okay, there are three rooms available at the Park Hyatt." She narrowed her eyes with another tap, which showed an overhead satellite image of Zürich. "They face Hassani's room from the other side of the Limmat… but you're still about fifteen hundred feet away."

"That should work. We can get eyes on him from there."

"Perfect, I'm booking it," she said as she entered her credit card number. "So why the surveillance anyway? Anton doesn't trust Hassani?"

"No, I don't get the impression he does. He's really on edge right now."

Isabell took off her jacket and leaned back into the sofa. "And the diamond?"

"It arrived today. I haven't seen it, but Anton told me point blank that it is, in fact, the Florentine Diamond."

Her eyes revealed a hint of reservation. "This isn't going to end well, is it?"

Henry didn't have an answer. He took a seat next to her and clasped his hands in front of his face.

"The advance team is flying direct to Zürich in about two hours," she said. "But our flights are to Milan. We can rent a car and drive the rest of the way."

"What's with the additional measures? Why Milan?"

"Because the same black Suburban's been parked in front of your apartment since Darius' death. Don't pretend you don't know what I'm talking about."

"It's just the FBI," he retorted. "They can't follow us all the way to Europe."

"Either way, I'd rather be safe than sorry."

"Fine. What time do we leave?"

"Six o'clock tomorrow morning."

"Well, look at us," he teased. "Another romantic trip together abroad."

"You're awful," she said, smiling with reluctance.

He cut his eyes and fidgeted on the sofa. "I've enjoyed working with you," he confessed. "You're ridiculously good at what you do, you know that?"

"I appreciate it, I really do. So… what's the deal with A.J. and the secret room?"

"I don't know. I can't even think about it right now. Yet, at the same time, I can't *stop* thinking about it."

"Can I just ask again why it hasn't all been destroyed? I mean, what's the end game here, Henry?"

He stretched his legs out in front of himself and let out a deep groan. "I honestly don't even know where to begin, let alone what the end game is."

"Okay, then I guess my question is, why would you even consider bringing down the organization? What aren't you telling me?"

He shook his head profusely. "No. I'm… I'm…"

"What is it, Henry?"

"I just want to make sure no one gets hurt. And right now, all I see is a mountain of evidence that's going to get a lot of people I care about hurt. In fact, I'm pretty sure I'll go to jail if any of that shit sees the light of day."

"Then destroy it."

He leaned forward and rubbed his temples with his fingertips. "I haven't seen all of it yet. A.J. and I are categorizing the files. We're trying to get a bigger picture of what Darius had his hands on."

"So you and A.J. are pals now?"

"Something like that." He got up and made his way to the kitchen. "Do you want some coffee? Pizza?"

"No, thanks," she shouted. "I want you to check out these overhead images I pulled up on the laptop." Henry returned to the living room with a cup of coffee and sat down next to her. "This is Hassani's hotel," she began. "*This* is the Limmat River, and *this* is our hotel on the other side. You plan on getting bugs into his room?"

"Veselko will get us in there."

"Good. Then we should be all set." She scrolled the touchpad and zoomed in on a series of side streets west of their hotel. "These are our fastest escape routes. All three of these roads hit the main highway out of the city."

"You sure you're up for this?"

"Absolutely. There's too much money on the line and Mama needs a new car."

He allowed a light laugh. "All right then."

For the next hour, they scoured through satellite images and photos of known Hassani soldiers. They identified all the police precincts and checkpoints in and around Zürich, and assigned surveillance roles for Veselko and the other three operatives.

Midnight quickly approached and they began wrapping things up.

Isabell stuffed her laptop back into her messenger bag. "You good with everything?"

"Everything looks perfect. We should be in and out in a matter of days."

She slung the bag over her shoulder and sauntered to the elevator. "I'm heading home," she announced. "Pick me up around three thirty?"

"Sure thing. See you in a few hours."

<h1 style="text-align:center">CHAPTER 26</h1>

The next morning, Miles sat in David Tisdale's office. It was another cold, damp day, and the agent was physically and mentally exhausted. After a few minutes of awkward silence, Jonathan Harwick entered the room. "Sorry I'm late, gentlemen," the NSA agent offered as he set down his notepad and took a seat next to Miles. "I appreciate you both meeting with me on short notice."

"Not a problem. How's everything progressing?" Tisdale asked.

"Could be worse, but we seem to be connecting some dots. As you know, we lost Agent Brennan's informant."

"Yeah, that was a pretty big blow. Anything I can help with?" the special agent-in-charge asked.

Harwick shook his head. "Nothing at the moment. I just wanted to make sure everyone's on the same page before this thing steps into high gear."

"Miles tells me that whatever Anton plucked from the seabed may have arrived in Atlanta. Can we verify anything?"

Harwick exhaled with an irritable frustration. "It's been hard to pin down, David. The movement of Ružaro members over the last few days has been… sporadic at best. I believe you guys have some new intel on the matter?"

"Yes, sir," Miles acknowledged. "Yesterday, security cameras at Hartsfield-Jackson picked up four Ružaro members boarding an international flight. We identified them as fairly low-level guys, but one in particular caught our attention."

"And who was that?" asked Harwick.

"Jackson Veselko," Miles revealed. "We picked him up two years ago for a robbery at a Sony distribution warehouse in Charlotte. He eventually walked, but we believe he's a recon and demolition specialist."

Harwick crossed his arms. "Do we know where they were going?"

"No," said Tisdale. "It was several hours before the security footage was flagged. They were in the international terminal, but the cameras never picked them up at a specific gate."

"Flight logs? Passports?" Harwick pressed.

Tisdale rubbed his mustache with a few slow, methodical strokes. "They were probably using fake identities. But the whole thing seems a little odd. If Krunoslav is bringing in a new prize, he should be tightening his security, not sending it out of the country."

"That's not all," Miles added. "Henry Sirola skipped town this morning as well. I tailed him from his apartment to the airport."

"Interesting," Harwick noted. "Any idea where *he* was going?"

"He boarded a flight to Milan, had a layover at JFK. He's traveling with a woman."

"What woman?"

"Her name's Isabell DiMarco: thirty years old, honors graduate from Vanderbilt. She's a linguistics instructor for XT Security. Prior to that, she worked as a consultant, spent eighteen months in Italy as an advisor to Shaun Leffler."

"Shaun Leffler? The arms dealer?"

"That's the one."

Harwick lifted his eyebrows. "So what? She works for Ružaro now? What's her role?"

"She acts as a coordinator for teams that deploy abroad," Miles explained. "She knows the culture, knows the landscape—sorta like a babysitter for a bunch of wily animals."

Harwick was intrigued now. "And what's in Milan?"

"A buyer," Miles reasoned. "Like I said before, Martović and Sirola were tasked with setting up a fence. The four clowns who left yesterday were probably Sirola's advance team."

"And who was the buyer he met with in Sorrento last week?" asked Harwick.

"Hamad Al Hassani. He's a well-known real estate mogul from Qatar."

"You think he's meeting with him again in Milan?"

Miles cocked his head to the side. "Only one way to find out. We need to get eyes on Milan."

Harwick shot a glance to Tisdale, who pressed his elbows onto the desk. "The FBI doesn't have that kind of reach," Tisdale bluntly pointed out.

"Yeah, I know. Let me make a phone call, see if the NSA has an asset in the area. What time does Sirola's flight land?"

Miles checked his watch. "Three and a half hours."

* * *

A tall, slender American walked unnoticed through the parking lot. Milano Malpensa Airport was the largest in northern Italy, and on this brisk October afternoon, tourists were zooming in and out at dizzying speeds.

The American entered Terminal 1 through a sliding glass door and pushed across the pristine gray-and-white striped floor. He slipped his hands into the pockets of his wool peacoat and kept his head down as he walked.

He brushed past several retail shops—Gucci, Bulgari, Rolex—before stopping at a small bookstore to browse the new releases. After a quick inspection, he continued on to baggage claim.

As he walked slowly within a dense crowd, he glanced up at the flight board. Delta Flight 1795 from JFK would be arriving right on schedule.

* * *

The best he could do was try to calm her anxious nerves. As the plane prepared to land, Isabell's crippling fear took over. Henry reached down and slid his fingers into hers. "You okay?" he gently asked.

"You know I'm not. But I'll feel better when we're on the ground."

It was a soft landing, and like always, the Italians on board applauded the aerial achievement.

As they came to a stop outside the gate, Henry and Isabell grabbed their luggage and fell in line with the other passengers. They all rumbled through the jetway like a tired herd of cattle, then spilled into the terminal and fanned out in different directions.

Henry and Isabell pulled their travel cases behind them as they marched onward. A long hike up the corridor brought them to customs, where a young man in a white uniform waited behind a thick glass window. Henry handed their passports through a small slot and, after a thorough examination, the agent handed them back.

They continued on to baggage claim and waited for ten minutes until a black duffle bag dropped onto the belt and circled its way toward them. Henry snatched it up and pushed his way through a gathering crowd. "What now, princess?" he asked.

"There's a car waiting for us outside. Follow me," she ordered.

Henry slung the bag over his shoulder and grabbed the handle of his travel case.

Isabell led him up the escalator to a sprawling atrium, where the floor-to-ceiling windows offered a small glimpse of Milan's world-class museums, luxury hotels, and five-star restaurants. They continued outside into the cold night and dodged their way through a parade of oncoming cars. After crossing the street and taking the stairs down to level 2B, Isabell pulled a key fob from her purse and pointed it into the shadows. The chirp of an alarm and the flash of headlights revealed a black Audi A6 tucked along the far wall.

Their footsteps echoed across the deck as they hurried toward it. Isabell quickly opened the trunk and Henry tossed their bags inside.

A rush of foreboding adrenaline suddenly shot through his veins. It was a reaction he'd learned to respect—a survival mechanism that had been coded into his DNA. And as he scanned the parking garage, his instincts told him something was off.

"I think I left something inside," he said to her over the roof of the car.

Isabell could sense his trepidation. He never left anything behind. "All right," she replied nervously. She tried to keep her voice even. "Everything okay?"

"Yeah, just need to go back and look for something," he said as he broke into a light jog across the parking deck.

He reached the staircase and darted upwards, two steps at a time until he reached the top. As he crossed the street, he brushed past a tall, slender man in a gray peacoat. Their eyes locked briefly. Henry continued on into the building and across the atrium to a set of elevators in the northeast corner. He waited patiently for the doors to open, then rode down to the main level and began a steady walk toward baggage claim.

After years of training, he knew what to look for: the slick hair, the firm build, the beady, hunting eyes, and now, the gray peacoat.

With a firm breath, he arrived at baggage claim; the crowd had swelled considerably since he and Isabell had left only minutes ago. He barged his way through an irritable mob to the other end of the baggage carousel. He gazed out over the sea of travelers and noticed the beady, hunting eyes and gray peacoat as they rushed down a set of stairs toward him.

Henry flashed a devilish smirk and retreated down a narrow hallway leading to a stairwell. He scrambled back up to the main level and sprinted toward the exit. With his arms braced in front of him, he burst through the door and landed outside just beyond the transportation depot.

He calmly tugged at the collar of his jacket and began an easy stroll up the sidewalk. As he coasted along, he heard the utility door blow open behind him. He picked up his pace and continued across the street to the parking deck, only this time, he took the stairs to the top level. *The perfect hunting ground.*

As he reached the top of the staircase, he turned his eyes to a set of storm clouds gathering above. Then, with a formidable inhale, he vanished into a maze of parked cars.

The tall, lanky American eventually appeared. His dark eyes scanned the lot from one end to the other. Henry glided along the side of a large blue van, one foot at a time, until he was within feet of his prey. The American could sense him now—suddenly aware that he'd been lured into an ambush.

Henry steadied himself behind the van, then struck with lightning speed. He swept low with a kick that sent his target to the pavement. The man landed with a deep thud and a displaced kneecap. Henry followed up with a quick left jab, then a hard right to the jaw. The American now lay flat on his back, groaning in pain, semi-conscious.

Henry knelt down and began sifting through the man's pockets. After a quick search, he pulled out a passport and held it into the air.

"You have no idea what you're doing," the man snarled through blood-stained teeth.

Henry read the name on the passport: GERALD OLIVER. Surely a fake, he thought. He lifted himself to his feet and tossed the passport onto the guy's chest. As he made his way back to the staircase, he shook the sting from his right hand. He arrived at street level and shuffled toward the crosswalk, panning his eyes through the dark night.

Seconds later, a black Audi roared up and came to a stop. He slung open the passenger door and dipped inside.

"What the absolute hell was that?" Isabell asked as she stomped the gas pedal and accelerated past the terminal.

"We had a tail," he explained calmly.

"Jesus, Henry. I've never actually had to use the 'I left something behind' trick before. Are you sure you're feeling all right?"

"I'm fine. We picked up surveillance back at baggage claim. There was only one, which means he was sent on short notice." Henry turned his head and glanced out the back window. "It wasn't FBI this time either. That was national intelligence."

Isabell wove the sportscar through a small pocket of traffic and merged north onto SS336.

Henry slammed his fist into the dashboard. "Those fucking bastards," he growled.

"It's fine. Looks like we're all clear," she said as she peered into the rearview mirror. "But we need a new car. We have to assume they caught us on security cams."

"Oh, I'm pretty sure they did," he said sardonically.

"Henry, what did you do?"

"I lured our tail to the top of the parking deck. He needed to be disabled."

She snorted. "Well, there were definitely cameras up there. Was he armed?"

"No. Just a fake passport."

"All right," she exhaled, "we just need to find another rental car and we'll be all set."

The Audi pushed north through the darkness until they reached Lake Como. Isabell exited the highway at the small village of Lazzago, and they abandoned the car behind a vacant building. She tossed the keys into a trashcan as they hustled up the sidewalk on foot. After a rigorous uphill hike, they found a car rental place just beyond the main square.

Isabell took a moment to catch her breath, then stepped inside. Minutes later, she returned with a set of keys and a thin stack of paperwork. They made their way around the building to the back lot where a maroon Skoda Karoq SUV awaited them. Isabell climbed behind the wheel and started the engine.

"How much farther?" Henry asked as he climbed into the passenger seat.

"Maybe three hours. Why don't you try to get some rest?"

As she pulled the SUV out of the lot and merged onto E35 North toward Zürich, Henry closed his eyes and allowed the whooshing sound of pavement to lull him to sleep.

* * *

Harwick clenched his jaw and slammed his cell phone onto the table. From their observation post in Buckhead, he and Miles sat in front of the window, glaring out at Anton Krunoslav's residence. "We lost Sirola," the task force leader announced. "At the airport in Milan."

Miles hid his amusement with a cold stare. "What happened?"

"Our guy lost him. Sirola put him to sleep in the goddamn parking deck."

"Of course he did. You sent an NSA bag man to put a tail on a Ružaro captain. I'm surprised the guy even made it to the parking deck. Did we get anything from security cameras?"

"Yeah. Apparently, it shows Sirola beating the shit out of him, then getting into a black Audi."

"Was he driving?"

"No," Harwick snapped. "I'm guessing it was his chaperone or whatever."

"I told you these guys are tough, Agent Harwick. We can't just cut corners like this. If you don't have the resources to keep up with them, we're never going to get anywhere."

"That'll be enough, Brennan."

"I'm sorry, sir. It just feels like we weren't prepared for this type of scenario." Miles stood from the table and paced the floor. "Half of their operations are overseas. Meanwhile, we sit here with our thumbs up our asses watching an empty apartment. It's frustrating."

"I know it is. But it'll all come together soon. We just need to be in the right place at the right time."

"With all due respect, the right place is Milan!" Miles argued. "And the right time is now! How is a federal task force supposed to monitor an international crime ring if we can't leave the country?"

"We can still get some drones in the air, but we need a location," Harwick bargained. "And right now, I don't know if Sirola is staying in Milan or just using it as an entry point. For all we know, he could be halfway to Spain by now."

"For Christ's sake! This is a huge operational failure. So what now? We just sit and wait for Henry and his team to come home?"

"I've got an ancillary team on route to Milan."

"That doesn't do us any good. Sirola and the woman have already ditched the car."

"It doesn't matter. Our real target is here. In Atlanta."

Miles continued pacing the carpet. "If Sirola's out there setting up a buyer, we're missing a huge opportunity."

"Dually noted, Agent Brennan. Now why don't you go find a hot shower and a warm meal. You look like absolute shit."

Miles shook off the insult and barged out the door. Thanks to Henry's signal, he knew Anton's treasure had arrived the day before. And while his informant's mysterious trip to Milan was troubling, Miles assumed it had something to do with Hassani.

But that was the game. And that's how it was played.

CHAPTER 27

It was well past midnight as the Skoda Karoq swept along the 3W into downtown Zürich. A thick fog muted the street lights as Isabell turned left onto Dreikönigstrasse, then crept along the quiet street for several blocks before parking behind a delivery truck.

"This is it," she softly announced. "Our hotel is one block south of here."

Henry lifted his weary eyes and nodded.

They stepped out of the vehicle and scanned their surroundings. Henry lifted their luggage out of the back hatch and onto the sidewalk, where he took a knee and unzipped the large duffle bag. A small two-way radio was removed and with the turn of a knob, Henry brought the device to his mouth. "Tomahawk Two, this is Tomahawk One on approach."

"Copy that, Tomahawk One. Glad you made it, see you soon."

Henry stuffed the radio into his pocket and lifted the duffle bag onto his back. He and Isabell left the car and walked one block south before arriving at the Park Hyatt Hotel. They were greeted by a short brunette with big brown eyes and high cheek bones.

"*Guten abend,*" Isabell stated with authority. "We have reservations for Hailey."

"Thank you, *Fraülein.*" The woman began typing away on her keyboard, the smile still stuck to her flawless porcelain face. After a moment, she handed two room cards over the counter. "You'll be in rooms four seventy and four seventy-two. There are coffee machines at the end of each hall. Breakfast is available in our dining room every morning from six until nine."

"Thank you very much," Isabell replied as she grabbed the cards.

Henry followed her to the elevators. They got off at the fourth floor and turned left up the hall. Ahead of them, a stocky young man with dirty blond hair emerged wearing a pair of gray slacks and a black shirt.

It was Jack Veselko. "Look who showed up!" he called into the hallway.

A studious grin appeared on Henry's face. He dropped his duffle bag and shook hands with the young operator. "How's everything going?" he asked.

"Not bad. We're all set up—eyes locked in."

"Good. Have you met Isabell DiMarco?"

"Not in person. Nice to meet you, ma'am. I've heard wonderful things."

"Thank you," she replied with a straight face. "I look forward to working with you."

Jack ran a hand through his thick hair. "Listen, I'll let you two get settled in. We're right down the hall, come check it out when you get a chance."

Isabell allowed a bright smile. "Sounds good. Thanks, Jack."

The young operator quickly returned to his room and shut the door.

"Henry, I'm the next one up," she announced. "I'll catch up with you later, okay?"

"Yeah, no problem." He slipped his card into the reader for room four seventy. "Do you want to meet me in the ops room, say, thirty minutes?"

"No," she replied with a look of sheer exhaustion. "I'm going to get some sleep. I'll come see all your little gadgets in the morning."

"Sleep good," he said as he drifted into his room.

The place was cramped, but well-decorated, with two double beds, and a nightstand. He sat down on the bed and stretched his legs out across the quilted comforter. After a few minutes of decompression, he wandered into the bathroom. A cold shower brought his senses back to life, and once he was dressed, Henry marched into the hallway and up to the team's command center. He rapped his knuckles against the door and a moment later, Jack slung it open and welcomed him inside.

"How was your flight?"

"Not bad," said Henry. "Thanks for asking."

"So, you know everyone here, I assume?"

"Of course."

Henry leered at the other three members of his team. He knew the men well; they'd been Darius' best soldiers. Erik Durden, notorious getaway driver and former fighter pilot; Michael Janić, surveillance and weapons expert; and Davidov Malek, audio engineer and all-around tech geek.

Henry cast a proud gaze over his crew as he made his way around the room for some quick handshakes and fist bumps. "All right, boys, let's have some fun!" he proclaimed.

Jack straightened his shoulders and rubbed his palms excitedly. "We're all really thrilled to be working under you, Henry. I mean that."

"Yeah, yeah, don't overdo it," Henry bemoaned. "Now, everybody, listen up; you all know Jack's been promoted to lieutenant. He's done some great work for this organization over the years and he deserves your utmost loyalty and respect. Understood?" All three men confirmed with a nod. "Good. What do we have?"

Jack cleared his throat and took a seat at a small writing desk with an open laptop. He clicked a link that opened a video feed, then another one that synced the computer to the television on a nearby dresser. "All right, this is a look at the front door of Hassani's room," he began. "We lifted the feed from hotel security. And this second channel is from the lobby." The television quickly snapped into split screen. "We also have three feeds from the parking garage."

Henry glanced through the sliding glass doors into the darkness. "Are we able to see his balcony from here?"

"We are," Jack confirmed. "Lens is currently set for infrared mode." He brought another set of windows up on his screen.

Henry leaned in for a better look. The Baur au Lac Hotel was nearly a quarter mile from their position. Between the two locations was the Limmat, a slow-moving river that separated Old Town from the Left Shore.

The screen in front of them showed a dark hotel balcony and two silhouettes painted in shades of red and orange.

"Do we know who those guys are?" Henry asked.

"Based on size and stature, it looks like two of his bodyguards," said Jack. "We're keeping a running list of his entourage."

Henry nodded his approval. "Great work. How about audio?"

"Yes, sir," Davidov answered from a table at the far end of the room. "I was able to get a bug inside. It's underneath an end table in the living room." The audio engineer held a set of bulky headphones into the air. "Care to take a listen?"

"No, I'm good," Henry answered with a wave of his hand. "I'm thrilled to see everything in place so quickly though. And just to be clear, our mission is to find out if Hassani is in contact with law enforcement, intelligence, or military personnel from any country whatsoever. Asa and I have a bad feeling about this dude, and it's our job to clear him for future transactions. Everybody good?" The men nodded in unison. "So what are we doing when he's on the move?"

"He hasn't really gone far," reported Jack. "Last night, he left for a couple hours. Michael and Davidov followed on foot, Erik and I were in the car just in case he decided to hop a bus or something."

"Where'd he go?"

"He and two of his thugs went over to a bar on the opposite side of the bay. They ate dinner, laughed at themselves for a while, and returned to the hotel around nine thirty."

Henry tilted his head in thought. "Sounds thrilling. How about hardware?"

Jack reached over to the bed and retrieved a submachine gun, hoisting it proudly in his hand. "We hit a weapons cache on the way in—the marina in Old Town. There's also an emergency cache in the maintenance shed outside St. Andrew's Church. It's across town, along our exfil route in the event we need to reload, heaven forbid."

"I appreciate all the hard work, Jack. Looks like you guys have everything covered. You need anything from me?"

Jack tossed the gun back onto the bed. "Not at the moment. We're about to roll into shifts and get some shuteye. You look like you could use some yourself."

Henry nodded and turned, heading for the door. "I'll see everyone bright and early in the morning." He let himself out and trudged back to his room.

He lay in bed for over an hour, his thoughts bouncing from Darius to Anton, then to Hassani and the ridiculous notion that the Florentine Diamond had been salvaged from the bottom of the sea. It was enough to put his anxiety into overdrive.

Eventually, however, he succumbed to his fatigue and drifted into a light sleep.

Just before seven in the morning, Henry snapped his head from the pillow and rubbed his eyes. He threw on some clothes—a white shirt and charcoal slacks —and slipped his feet into a pair of black sneakers.

The elevator brought him downstairs, where Isabell sat alone in the dining hall.

"Good morning," he said as he approached her table.

"Good morning to you," she replied.

"May I?"

"Of course." She cut her eyes at the chair across from her.

Henry sat down as a waitress hurried to the table. He ordered a plate of scrambled eggs and marmalade toast and a hot cappuccino. As the waitress slipped away, Isabell picked at her fruit and coffee cake.

"Any big plans today?" he asked.

"Not really. I'm going to brief the team after breakfast, then get some fresh air and the lay of the land."

"Give me a break," he derided. "You already know this city inside and out."

"Things always change. How'd it go last night? Everyone all set?"

"Yeah. Jack runs a tight ship. Everyone's locked in."

"You need to be careful," she warned. "Hassani and his team know who you are, they know your face."

Henry's cappuccino appeared on the table. "We'll be fine," he assured quietly. "Just a simple vetting mission."

Isabell sipped her orange juice and eyed him tactfully. "Good. Just stay off the grid and off security cams. Your cover is an American manufacturing executive—you're celebrating your anniversary with your wife."

"I know. I read your operation brief."

"Okay, then what anniversary are we celebrating?" she challenged.

His eyes locked into hers. "It's our seventh wedding anniversary. We met at a conference nine years ago. We were married in Chicago, honeymooned in Paris."

"Well, well, well," she teased. "I shouldn't be impressed, but I am."

"Listen, you don't have to sit here with me. I just wanted to come down and say hello."

Isabell patted her mouth with her napkin, then set it on the table next to her plate. "I really don't mind. I can't get started upstairs without you anyways."

The waitress brought Henry's breakfast and set it on the table with a polite smile. He tore through his eggs and toast as Isabell entertained him with small talk: the weather, her thoughts on Swiss food, and a new Steinhauer novel she'd picked up from the airport. With a clean plate, Henry sipped the last of his cappuccino and stretched his arms.

"You ready?" she asked.

"Yep. Let's get to it."

They left the dining hall and crossed the lobby to the elevators. At the fourth floor, they got off and drifted up the hall to the command center.

"Good morning, gentlemen," Henry announced as they entered. "I'd like to introduce everyone to our tour guide, Isabell DiMarco." The four men stopped what they were doing and stared at the attractive, dainty brunette standing in the room. "You guys may remember her from some past operations," he continued. "You know the drill; she'll be in charge of logistics, transportation, and putting out any fires we start." The men each greeted her with a respectful nod. "Now that we're one big happy family, Miss DiMarco would like to give us a quick briefing before we start our day."

Isabell took a confident step toward the team. "All right, you all know the mission and you should have familiarized yourselves with exfil routes, extraction points, emergency rendezvous locations, and city transportation schedules. Are we good?"

A collective "yes, ma'am" resounded through the room.

"Perfect. Does anyone here speak German or Italian?"

Audio engineer Davidov Malek raised his hand. "*Jawohl*," he confirmed.

"*Ausgezeichnet*," she replied. "Now then, let's make sure Davidov is running point if there's any need to tail our target on foot." She moved to the opposite side of the room and stared out the glass window. "If anyone gets apprehended by local law enforcement for any reason, you do not speak to anyone. Not a word. We have attorneys that can be here within forty minutes, or if things escalate, a private jet can be fueled and on the runway at Kloten Airport within an hour. But please, for the love of everything good in this world, don't make us initiate either of those protocols."

"We'll be as careful as we can," Jack promised.

"Wonderful. That's all I've got. I just wanted to say hello and lay down some ground rules. I'll let you boys get back to work; call me if you need anything." Isabell scanned the faces in the room one last time before turning toward the exit.

"Thanks again," said Henry as he walked her to the door. "I'll touch base with you this afternoon."

"Just stay out of trouble," she warned.

CHAPTER 28

The days began blurring together. A greasy pizza box lay on the table next to a smoldering ashtray, set against the backdrop of a nearby window, where a row of distant street lights sparkled in the hazy night. Henry and Jack rested on a pair of recliners. Their eyelids fought to stay open as the television clamored against the wall.

"Who's the new guy?" Henry asked, leering at an orange silhouette on the screen.

"The driver," answered Jack. "He just parked the car. Looks like he picked up some dinner."

Henry heaved with boredom. "So, what do you think?"

"I think we've been here for three days and all Hassani's done is shop at expensive stores and eat expensive food. He's on vacation." Jack reached over and turned the volume up on the speakers. "See what I mean? They're sitting around talking about horse racing."

"Yeah, top-notch stuff. Any interesting phone calls today?"

"Nothing. He doesn't call or email anyone outside of his network. Clean as a whistle."

"All right," Henry relented. "Twenty-four more hours and we'll clear him."

Much like yesterday, and the day before that, the team watched and listened as Hassani and his men discussed meaningless topics, took long walks around the city, and used their cell phones to make museum and dinner reservations. And after all that, Hamad Al Hassani turned out to be exactly who they thought he was: an arrogant, corrupt billionaire leading an uneventful life abroad.

Henry leaned forward in his chair and rested his arms on his knees. "I need a drink."

"There's some beer in the fridge, liquor in the cabinet."

"No," he huffed, "I think I need to get some fresh air, then get a drink."

Jack let out a weary laugh. "I hear ya, amigo. Why don't you get out for a bit? I'll keep eyes on Hassani."

"Thanks, that'd be great," Henry said as he stood. "Wake one of these other guys up if you need to take a break."

"Will do. Just keep your head down and stay along the river—fewer cameras."

Henry walked to the foyer and grabbed his leather jacket from a hook before sneaking out the front door. As he shuffled up the hallway, he stopped at Isabell's room, then lightly knocked. "It's me," he called out.

Isabell opened the door and peered out at him. "Hey there," she greeted. "How's everything going?"

"It's good. Pretty sure we'll clear him by tomorrow."

"That's excellent news. Do you want to come in?"

"Actually, I was going out," he said with a mischievous glint in his eye. "Care to join me?"

She stared at him for a brief moment, tired and drained of energy. But before she could say no, a light smile unfolded on her face like the petals of a flower. "Sure," she finally allowed. "Give me ten minutes, I'll meet you downstairs."

"Perfect. I'll be waiting."

As she closed the door, he turned up the hall and hopped into the elevator. He waited at the hotel bar while a soccer game played silently on the overhead television. Just as he checked his watch, Isabell appeared in the lobby wearing a long green parka with an oversized fur hood. The soles of her white suede boots echoed across the floor as she approached.

"What'd you have in mind?" she asked. He fixated on her perfect, smoky eyes and soft, rosy lips. "Henry?"

"Yeah, I was thinking maybe some tapas and a drink?"

"I like that," she granted. "There's a nice little restaurant across the river."

"Sounds perfect."

They left the Hyatt Park and turned up the sidewalk toward the harbor, then crossed a small bridge over the river. The lights of the towering Opera House reflected off the glassy waters of Lake Zürich in the distance.

They trekked over another bridge overlooking a canal—this one much larger than the first—and continued along the harbor to an upscale café facing the waterfront. The revolving glass doors welcomed them into a dimly lit lobby, where a hostess was quick to usher them to a table in the back.

The walls were covered in light blue wallpaper emblazoned with a simple white pattern and hints of gold. Two napkins, folded into swans, rested on the white tablecloth.

Henry pulled a small handheld radio from his pocket, then slipped a tiny plug into his ear. He leaned his head down and spoke quietly. "Tomahawk Two, do you copy?"

"Copy that, Tomahawk One. Go ahead," Jack replied through the earpiece.

"I'm across the river at a place called Razzia. I've got Tinkerbell with me."

"Do you need cover?"

"Negative," Henry replied. "We're all set. I'll let you know as soon as we're inbound."

"Sounds good. Tomahawk Two out."

He removed the earpiece and placed it, along with the handheld device, back into his breast pocket.

"Well, isn't this nice?" Isabell remarked playfully.

"Yes. It is. What's good here?"

"Everything," she said bluntly.

"I find that hard to believe."

"I honestly don't remember each and every dish, Henry. But the chef is amazing."

They examined the menu as an older gentleman in a white double-breasted service jacket approached the table. Isabell ordered a watermelon salad with crumbled feta while Henry opted for kabeljou miso fish with white rice. As the waiter peeled away toward the kitchen, Henry took a sip of his red wine.

Suddenly, a group of men dressed in black suits and facemasks charged through the door with assault rifles drawn.

"Shit!" Henry hissed under his breath.

Isabell followed his eyes to the front of the restaurant. "What the hell is this?"

He quickly pulled the radio from his pocket. "Tomahawk Two, this is Tomahawk One. We have armed men entering the restaurant. Do you copy?"

"Copy that, Tomahawk One. How many?"

"I count seven," he said calmly. "Probably more outside."

"Sit tight, we're on our way."

The armed thugs were now shouting wildly in German, demanding everyone evacuate the restaurant immediately. Henry and Isabell sat motionless.

As more than a dozen diners raced for the exit, a second group of men entered the building.

"Great," Henry growled. "It's Hassani."

Isabell set down her silverware. "Well, this should be interesting."

"Hands up! Both of you!" one of the masked gunmen yelled. Henry and Isabell slowly raised their hands above the table. "Stand up!"

Henry stood first. The man charged over and patted him down. His wallet, sat phone, and two-way radio were all yanked from his pockets and tossed onto the table. Next, the man emptied Isabell's purse onto the floor as Hassani approached.

The billionaire seemed pleased with himself. "Mr. Sirola! Miss DiMarco! What an absolute pleasure! Talk about coincidences."

"This isn't a coincidence," Isabell snarled.

Hassani stared at her blankly. "Such a pretty face," he noted. "What a shame. I'm sorry it had to come to this."

"Come to what?" Henry asked.

"Mr. Sirola, I'm going to need you to call off your support team. Surely they're on their way here. We wouldn't want a war on the streets of such a fine city, would we?"

"Whatever happens from here, you've brought it on yourself," warned Henry.

Hassani lifted the small radio from the table and handed it to him. "Make the call. I won't ask again." A group of black-clad soldiers took a step forward and trained their weapons on Henry and Isabell.

After a moment of contemplation, he snatched the device from Hassani. "Tomahawk Two, I need you to stand down," he ordered.

"Bad copy, Tomahawk One. Please repeat."

"Shut it down, Tomahawk Two. Initiate exit plan… pack it all up. I'll see you boys back home."

"That's a negative, boss. I can't comply with that order."

"Goddammit, Tomahawk Two, get the hell out of here! Now!" Jack Veselko didn't reply. "Tomahawk Two, *do you copy?*"

Finally, Jack's voice crackled over the radio. "Roger that. Initiating exit protocol now. Tomahawk Two out."

Hassani beamed from the small victory. He took the radio from Henry and tossed it onto the table.

Henry lifted his brooding eyes. "What the fuck do you want?"

"Well, first and foremost, I hear you were promoted to captain. Congratulations!" Hassani cheered. "Now, what would a Ružaro captain be doing all the way over here in Switzerland?"

"Sightseeing."

"That's cute. This is your only opportunity to give me a straight answer, Mr. Sirola. What are you doing here?"

"Anton has the diamond," Henry confessed. "But he doesn't trust you. I came here to make sure you checked out. And in case you're wondering, we were getting ready to clear you tomorrow."

"Clear me for what, exactly?"

"To become our buyer," he answered after a slight pause.

"I see. And you say Anton has the diamond?"

"Yes."

"Where is it?"

"The deal's going down in Atlanta. It's non-negotiable."

"Says who? You?" Hassani playfully challenged.

"No. Anton."

"Call him," the stout Arab growled. "How do you contact him? This satellite phone here?"

"I can't call him, Hamad. If he finds out what's going on here, he'll completely lose his shit. I'm telling you, you'll screw this whole deal up if anything happens to me or my tour guide."

"That's funny. Because back in Sorrento, I remember you told me that the tour guide was no more than collateral damage."

"I lied."

Hassani let out a booming laugh. "Of course you did. Now call Anton before my patience runs out." As he snatched the phone from the table and held it in the air, one of his henchmen placed the barrel of his rifle against Henry's temple. "Call him, now!" Hassani roared.

Henry reached up and grasped the bulky plastic phone. He extended the rubber antenna and dialed a number from memory. "Anton. It's Henry."

"Put him on speakerphone," Hassani demanded. Henry pressed a button and set the device back on the table.

Anton's voice snapped through the tiny speaker. "Henry? Are you there?"

Hassani leaned closer. "Mr. Krunoslav, this is Hamad Al Hassani."

"What's going on over there, Hamad? Is everything all right?"

"No. Everything is not all right. Your captain says he's here to surveil me. Is that correct?"

"It is," confirmed Anton.

"Why would he be doing that?"

Anton's heavy breath sizzled through the phone. "Did you really think I wouldn't do a little background check? You're a potential buyer for the largest diamond in existence and I need assurance that you're not a threat to me or my organization. You've been in this game a long time, Hamad. I expected more from you."

"And I from you," Hassani replied gravely.

"The diamond is now in my possession," Anton assured. "If Mr. Sirola feels you have passed a thorough background check, I believe there's a way for us to move forward."

Hassani motioned toward Henry, then to the phone.

"He's clean," Henry called out. "We were going to clear him first thing in the morning."

"Very well," Anton replied. "Then I believe we should coordinate a transaction."

Hassani took a moment to consider his investment. "I'm eager to see it with my own eyes. But I am not comfortable traveling to the United States to make the deal, Mr. Krunoslav."

"You don't have a choice," Anton explained. "I have already taken the risk of not only retrieving the stone but bringing it here. I expect my buyer to take their fair share of risk as well."

Hassani hovered over Henry. His nostrils flared with each breath. "Very well. Four days from today. But, Anton?"

"Yes, Hamad?"

"I believe I've earned the right to teach your new captain a lesson. His work here has been quite careless and unprofessional."

A cloud of silence hung in the air. Henry tightened his brow, awaiting Anton's response.

"Do what you have to do," his boss finally stated.

With a tempestuous sneer, Hassani hung up the phone. His goons immediately rushed in and lifted Henry and Isabell from their seats, dragging them to the back of the restaurant and into the kitchen.

Hassani followed closely behind. "Separate them!" he instructed. "And when you're done with the tour guide, dump her on the filthy sidewalk out front."

"You can't do this!" Henry implored as the soldiers struggled to subdue him.

"Why of course I can," Hassani said calmly. "You heard Anton. We made an agreement."

"He didn't say anything about her! Leave her out of this!"

Hassani motioned his goons, who grabbed Isabell and dragged her out of the kitchen and into a nearby office. Henry was slammed into a chair, his mouth wrapped with duct tape. He could hear Isabell screaming his name and doing her best to fight off her assailants. Finally, her voice fell silent.

The men began circling Henry like a pack of hungry wolves. It started with a baton—a shot to his left hand, followed by several more to his torso. After that, the goons took turns with their bare knuckles, each one of them seemingly stronger than the one before.

After several minutes, Henry began to fade in and out of consciousness. He could no longer feel the pain, just the pressure of fists slamming into his rib cage and across his jaw. The cold flow of blood drained from his mouth as the world around him melted into darkness.

Eventually, his eyes closed and his body fell limp.

Nearly an hour later, he began to wake. It was a fleeting consciousness—just enough to see, through blurred vision, the rushing of street lights through a window, the opening of a car door, and feel the thud of concrete against his face.

He laid there for what seemed an eternity. Eventually, a set of headlights bore down on him through the murky night. Henry blinked, but his eyes refused to focus.

Isabell gasped as she saw his body slumped against the sidewalk of the Feldeggstrasse Bridge. The gentle waters of Lake Zürich splashed against a stone seawall below.

She'd been left outside the restaurant, battered and bruised, only to rush back to her hotel and grab their bags and then jump into the rented SUV. After racing back to Razzia, she'd waited in the shadows, patiently, until a black delivery van left the restaurant. A slow, methodical pursuit brought her here to a narrow side street that ran parallel to the marina on the east side of the lake. It was dark and desolate—the perfect location to dump a body.

She leapt from the vehicle and rushed toward him as fast as she could. His face was bloodied and swollen. Doing exactly as she'd been trained, Isabell stood at Henry's head and lifted him from beneath his arms. She pulled his body to the passenger side of the vehicle. After heaving his torso onto the seat, she reached down and grabbed his feet and slung them into the floorboard. Henry's face bobbed against the headrest, drenching its leather in blood. Seconds later, the SUV peeled away from the bridge and turned north onto Bellerivestrasse.

The shock began to wear off somewhere around the Bormio Mountains. A pitch-black drive through the Swiss Alps had never been on her bucket list, but Isabell soldiered on, navigating the slippery asphalt and hairpin turns with precision. With her eyes locked on the road, she reached over and held his face, stroking his bloodied cheek with her thumb.

"Henry?" she whispered.

"Yeah," he replied through labored breaths. "Where am I?"

"You're in a car, sweetie. You were beaten pretty badly."

"Where's Hassani?"

But before she could answer, his eyes closed and his head collapsed against the seat.

CHAPTER 29

Henry filled his lungs with a deep breath of mountain air. After a moment, he opened his eyes and sat up on his elbows. He was in a bed in a room with soft, yellow walls. Beside him, on top of a wooden nightstand, was a carafe of water, a dusty lamp, and a roll of gauze.

His clothes were neatly folded on a chair in the far corner of the room. A thick layer of gauze had been taped to his ribcage. His left hand was also wrapped and a brace held his index and middle fingers together. With his good hand, he rubbed his forehead and tried to remember. After a moment of brevity, the door to the room slowly opened.

"Henry?" she said tenderly. "How are you feeling?"

"Better, I think. Where are we?"

"We're just outside of Castelletto, Italy."

"Did Anton set this up?"

"No."

Henry shut his eyes and winced in pain. "This is your Italy network, isn't it?"

"Yeah," she smirked, "it's my Italy network."

"Who patched me up?"

"A friend of mine, Francesco. He's a doctor."

"Is this his place?"

"It is," she confirmed. "Hassani's men did quite a number on you. A concussion, fractured hand, and two broken ribs."

"How long have we been here?"

"Got in last night. But you need to rest. Francesco says you still have some swelling in your brain. It's not safe for you to fly yet and you don't have the strength to walk, so we're going to sit tight for now."

"Have you contacted Anton?"

"No," she replied. "Per protocol, I contacted Jack Veselko by encrypted email. I told him we went to ground."

"Good. Did you tell him where?"

"I don't exactly trust any of them right now, Henry."

He dropped his head back against the pillow. He could barely move a muscle and ached in places he didn't think were possible. "I kind of blacked out at the restaurant. Did they throw me out of a plane or something?"

"I'm afraid it was much worse than that," she mused. "Are you hungry?"

"No. I'm still a little nauseous."

"Well, at least have some water." She filled a glass from the carafe and handed it to him as she sat down on the edge of the bed.

Henry clasped the glass in his feeble hands and lifted it to his mouth. He then took a cautious yet eager sip and wiped his lips. Through a veil of intense pain, he glanced up to look at her. He could see now that she too had been beaten. Even with a black eye and a split lip, she somehow managed to look gorgeous, he thought.

"I'm so sorry, Izzy. Did they hurt you?"

"Of course they hurt me. But I'm chalking it up as an occupational hazard. No hard feelings."

He sat up and placed his palm against her face. Isabell shut her eyes and welcomed the comforting touch of his hand. If for only a moment, everything seemed peaceful. He slowly brought his face toward hers. Her chin quivered at the thought of him drawing closer. And then, their lips met.

Everything inside of him—the anger, the hopelessness, the desperation—slowly slipped away. As much as he'd tried to fight it, he missed the touch of her skin and the softness of her lips. It seemed like a lifetime ago since he'd last felt it.

Slowly, he opened his eyes and pulled his face from hers. "I'm sorry. I shouldn't have done that," he whispered.

She rose from the bed and brushed a hand through her tangled hair. "It's fine. I'm sure it's just the painkillers." After a gentle pause, she got up and left the room.

Henry turned up the corner of his mouth as his head returned to the pillow.

He spent the afternoon dozing in and out of sleep until he found the strength to lift himself out of bed. He stood in the middle of the room and gazed out the window. The sun was slowly setting behind a range of mountains to the west—the Dolomite Alps, he figured.

He turned and made his way to the door and continued into a short hallway that led to a kitchen. The place was old and musty, with rickety floors and overhead lightbulbs that flickered on, then off, then on again. He made it to the kitchen and propped himself against a wooden table.

"*Mio amico!*" a voice called from the next room. The man rushed toward him with concern. "*Siediti*! Please, *signore*, sit down."

"You must be Francesco," Henry mumbled as he dropped into a chair.

"Yes, I am Francesco. How are you feeling?"

"I'm okay."

The man was short in stature but didn't appear to have missed too many meals. His tattered wool sweater seamlessly blended into his thick gray beard. He placed a pair of bifocals over his eyes and examined his patient carefully, scanning Henry's retinas and feeling the base of his skull with his bony fingertips.

"The swelling has gone down," Francesco assessed in his best English. "You will survive."

"That's great news," Henry replied. "I'm suddenly very hungry. Is there anything to eat?"

"Eat? Yes, of course!" The man turned and rifled through a nearby cabinet. "*Mangiamo!*" he proclaimed as he dumped a bowl of chunky, dark soup into an iron cooking pot. "*Ribollita, sí?*"

Henry nodded. "Sure. Ribo-whatever." He looked over each shoulder, charting the layout of the old farmhouse.

"*Due minuti,*" Francesco called out, holding two fingers in the air.

"Great. Where's Isabell?"

"*Benzina,*" the old man replied. He took a moment, searching for a translation. "Gasoline? Petrol, yes?"

Henry nodded again. "Yes. Thank you… for taking care of me. *Grazie.*"

"*Prego,*" Francesco said pointedly. A thin smile sprouted from his beard.

As the soup began to simmer, Francesco spooned it into a bowl and set it down in front of Henry, who examined it closely.

"*Verduro è pollo,*" the doctor-chef asserted.

Henry brought the spoon to his lips and tasted the dark mixture of shredded chicken and vegetables. "This is very good," Henry admitted. "Very good indeed."

The grin on Francesco's face widened. "Yes. You must eat, friend. Strong, healthy man!"

Just then, Isabell charged through the back door and into the kitchen. "Hey there! Good to see you're eating. I guess you've met Francesco?"

"I have. He's my new best friend."

She stripped off her coat and hung it on the back of the door. "Well, I'm glad to hear it. I went ahead and filled up the car. Hopefully, we can get home tomorrow, but we'll see how you're doing."

"Yeah, that would be excellent. I'm still a little foggy though."

"It should wear off soon," she assured.

Henry set his spoon on the table and wiped his mouth. "Anton's going send a search party if he doesn't hear from me soon. And if he doesn't find me, he'll have Hassani murdered. Which means the entire deal goes to shit and we don't get paid."

"Paid?" she struck back. "Henry, your boss gave the go-ahead to have you tortured last night! Do you really think Anton is sending someone to find you?"

"Absolutely. Why wouldn't he?"

"Stop it! Just stop it! How do you know he doesn't have a hit out on you right now? You think Anton will let one of his captains get in the way of a deal this big? Because if this thing really is the Florentine Diamond, chances are we're all going to end up dead anyways."

"It's not like that, Isabell."

"You don't know for sure," she argued. "Darius was taken out and you wound up unconscious in a ditch in Zürich. I'm scared, Henry. I'm scared of what happens next. Because the fact is, it sounds like you're sitting on enough evidence to bring Anton to his knees and it's going to get you killed. It may very well have been enough to get Darius killed."

"Will you stop implying that?" he shot back.

But Isabell was done arguing. She stormed out of the kitchen and into a bedroom down the hall. The door slammed loudly behind her.

Henry cut his eyes across the table to the Italian doctor, who sat unfettered in his chair. "What do you think, Francesco?"

The man shrugged. "I think she cares very much for you."

"Yeah. I was afraid of that." Henry finished his soup in silence, then returned to his room. Francesco followed him in and redressed the bandages on his hand and torso.

As the daylight melted away, a soft, purple sky blanketed the mountains. There was a sense of seclusion around the old farmhouse, something that comforted Henry for reasons he was unsure of. Perhaps it was the quiet, he thought, or better yet, the separation from a world that had been turned upside down.

Isabell stood in the doorway, watching him daydream. "I'm sorry I lost my temper," she softly confessed.

"It's fine. I've already forgotten all about it."

She took a few steps forward and stood above him, her arms crossed in front of her. "I worry about you sometimes."

"I know you do. But I promise everything's going to be fine."

"We just need to be careful, that's all." She reached down and brushed the hair from his forehead.

"Thank you for coming back to get me in Zürich," he muttered. "No telling what would've happened to me if you hadn't been there."

"I was just doing my job. But now I need you to heal up so we can go home. We can figure it all out from there." She gazed at him for a few precious seconds before leaving the room.

He stared out the window at a patchwork of stars breaking through the dusk. Minutes later, his eyelids gently closed.

The next morning, he awoke to a rooster crowing in the backyard. He pulled himself from the bed and lumbered across the room. He looked at himself in a small mirror that hung against the wall, surprised at the extensive bruising around his eyes and nose. The stubble on his jaw and chin had grown out and his face looked pale and dehydrated.

He took off the musty brown sweater he'd loaned from Francesco and tossed it to the floor. He grabbed his white dress shirt from the chair and held it up in front of himself. It was covered in blood and dirt, completely unsalvageable, he thought.

The sound of Isabell's boots resonated up the hallway. Henry turned as she entered the room with a small plate of prosciutto and fruit. She set it on the nightstand and looked him over. "How are you feeling this morning?"

"I think I'm all right," he said. "I could use a shirt."

"Francesco, *una camicia?*" she shouted over her shoulder.

The old man grumbled incoherently from down the hall before appearing in the doorway with a blue cotton shirt. Henry nodded politely and put it on.

"Now eat your breakfast," Isabell sternly instructed.

Henry buttoned the front of the shirt and stretched his arms out in front of himself. The agonizing pain in his ribs wasn't quite as bad as yesterday, but they still hurt nonetheless. His mind was clearer now, and tiny fragments of the past few days began slowly coming together.

Isabell walked out of the room and returned seconds later with a steaming red mug. "Here, have some coffee," she offered.

Henry took the mug and dropped down onto the bed. He grabbed the plate and picked at fresh slices of melon and prosciutto, sipping his coffee between mouthfuls. When he was done, she took his dish to the kitchen, washed it by hand, and placed it into a cabinet.

Then, through a fog of silence, a strange sound rattled nearby.

"What is that?" Isabell asked as she followed the muffled buzzing toward Henry's room. "I thought Hassani took our phones and radio?"

Henry winced in pain as he reached down and pulled his bag onto the bed. He unzipped it and retrieved a small cell phone. "A.J. gave me a burner."

"A burner? For what?"

He ignored her question and brought it to his ear. "Hello?" he answered.

"Henry, it's me. How's everything going?"

"Good to hear from you, A.J. Things didn't go exactly as planned. I'm at a safe house in northern Italy."

"Everyone okay? Do I need to get on a flight?"

"No, everyone's fine. I'm with Isabell. We may try to jump a flight later this afternoon."

"Sounds good. Just let me know if there's anything I can do."

"I will. So what's happening on your end?"

There was a brief, troubling pause as A.J. cleared his throat. "Well, I found something. I thought you may want to take a look."

"What is it?"

"I'm sending it to that email address you gave me. It's secure, right?"

"Of course. Totally encrypted."

"Good."

Henry shifted his legs against the mattress, searching for a comfortable sitting position. "Can you not just tell me what it is over the phone? I'm not doing so hot right now."

"Just take a look whenever you get a minute. We'll catch up when you get home."

"Okay. Talk soon." Henry closed the phone and placed it back in the duffle bag.

"What's going on?" Isabell asked.

"I'm not exactly sure. I asked A.J. to sift through the laptop and help me organize some of the files. He must've found something."

"Well, it sounds like something you're not going to like."

"Do you still have your field laptop?"

"Yeah, I'll go grab it." She fled to the living room and quickly returned with the thick stainless-steel laptop, then set it on the bed next to him.

Henry dove into the keyboard and navigated his way to an online portal for ProtonMail. He typed in his username and password, then narrowed his eyes at the inbox before opening an email that had arrived only minutes before.

He clicked the attachment and a PDF file appeared on the screen.

Isabell drew her head back in bewilderment. "What am I looking at, Henry?" He didn't answer. His eyes fixated on the document, scanning it with purpose. "Is that in Croatian?" she asked over his shoulder.

"Yes." His eyes peeled from the monitor and stared blankly into the air.

"Say something, Henry," she pleaded.

"It's a military incident report. Issued by the Croatian Army, July 17, 1991."

"And what's it say?"

"It describes an attack on a small village by Serbian rebels. Any of these names look familiar?" He pointed to the bottom of the document.

She leaned in and squinted at the screen. "Those are your parents," she noted. "Želijko and Marija Sirola. It's from the day they were murdered, isn't it?"

"Yes."

"Why would Darius have a copy of this?"

"Because it details everything that happened in Krasno that day. And the people who were killed."

She brushed her hair from her face and sighed. "Wow. I'm sorry, Henry."

"That's not all. The report lists the names of the Serbian rebels who executed them and the man who was leading them that day."

"It gives *names*?"

"Yeah."

"Anyone you know?"

"Yes. Major Anton Krunoslav," he read aloud from the document.

Isabell gasped. "Oh my god! How is that possible?"

Henry was frozen in disbelief. His soul searched desperately for an emotion—a reaction appropriate enough for the moment. "I have to kill him," he declared quietly.

"Henry, I—I don't know what to say." Isabell's eyes darted nervously around the room. "This doesn't make any sense. I thought Anton had been a Croatian soldier?"

"He was. He fought with my Uncle Luka in the early days of the war. I've seen photographs of them together at military outposts."

"He must've defected at some point," she guessed. "Or he was some sort of double agent."

"I have no idea. But if this is true… then he wasn't helping everyone escape Krasno. He was saving his own ass."

"Henry, your Uncle Luka would've known about this. Why wouldn't he have said something?"

"I don't know. There's no telling what kind of hold Anton had on my family." He hung his head, holding it in his hands. "I need to get back to the States. How soon can we fly out?"

"Slow down," she warned. "You can't just… what are you going to do? Just walk in and shoot him?"

"Yes. That's exactly what I'm going to do."

"Henry, listen to me. I know you want revenge, but we need to be rational."

"Revenge seems pretty rational to me right about now."

Isabell wrapped her arms around him. A small tear fell on her cheek. "I'm so sorry, Henry. I don't know what to say."

He tightened his eyelids, fighting tears of his own. "I have something to tell you."

"What is it?"

His eyes wandered to the ceiling.

"Henry? What is it?" she asked again.

"I'm an FBI informant," he confessed.

Isabell's face was paralyzed in shock. She blinked, then blinked again.

"Say something, Izzy."

"Y-y-you… you're an FBI i-i-in-informant?" she stuttered.

Henry nodded pensively.

She began pacing the room in circles, shuffling her bare feet against the aging hardwood. "This can't be happening," she mumbled. "Henry, what have you gotten me into? What the fuck is really happening right now?"

"I never meant to—"

"You never meant to what? Drag me into your best friend's murder? Methodically lure me into a federal investigation?" Her face was burning with rage. "Or trick me into going to Zürich just to get my face beaten in?"

"Listen to me, you're wrong."

"Wrong about what?"

"None of this has anything to do with… who I am… or what I am. The stuff on Darius' laptop is just… I dunno, pure coincidence."

"What was pure coincidence?"

"That Darius was putting a case together for SOA. And that I just happen to be working with the FBI."

"This is insane, Henry! Does the FBI know about Darius' house in Waleska? All of the evidence?"

"No. They have no idea."

She patrolled the room with intensity, her hands gripped to her waist. "What if Anton already knows?"

"Just stop with that! He doesn't!"

"What if he finds out? He'll kill us both!"

"That's not gonna happen, Izzy. I promise. Anton has no idea."

"I'll bet Darius thought the same thing."

He slammed his fist against the wall. "Damn it! Stop saying that! Enough already! We're going home. Everything is perfectly normal. Anton's going to pat me on the back and tell me what a great job I did in Zürich and that what happened with Hassani was just the cost of doing business."

"And then what?"

Henry took a deep breath. "And then I'll put a bullet in his head."

"Or you give him up and watch him spend the rest of his miserable life behind bars," she reasoned.

"Are you kidding me? They'll treat him like a king in there. The man killed my parents! He needs to pay!"

"In blood?"

"Yes! In blood!"

Isabell froze in the center of the room. "Why didn't you tell me?"

"I couldn't. Not you, not Darius, not my Aunt Sara… nobody."

"How long?"

His mind wandered back through time. "About four years."

"Great. So while we were together, you were doing this? I was dating an FBI informant?"

"Yes."

"Did you ever wear a wire with me?"

"Of course not," he assured her calmly. "It was never like that. I just reported back to my handler with little bits of info on some of the other crews in the area. In return, he let me go about my business."

"What business?" she demanded.

"All of it."

"I don't understand, Henry. How did you get caught up in something like this?"

"I don't know. I was naïve and stupid. In hindsight, I'm not even sure I knew I was being groomed."

"Being groomed?"

"I kept getting brought in for questioning. It was always the same guy. A robbery would go down or a bunch of merchandise would go missing, and he'd bring me in for an interview. I always gave him just enough to keep him off my back, to keep my guys out of trouble."

"And then what?"

"Before I knew it, we were meeting for coffee, doing dead drops, exchanging intel. The relationship became beneficial for both of us; he got information, I got protection."

"What's his name?" she coldly asked.

"I can't tell you that."

"What's his name, Henry? If something ever happens to you, I… I need to know who to go to, what to do."

He took a few seconds to think it over. She was right. He needed to develop an insurance policy, just as Darius had. "Special Agent Miles Brennan," he finally revealed. "Show him everything."

"Jesus Christ, Henry. This is heavy." She took a moment to steady her breathing. "So what now? What happens next?"

"I already told you. We get on the next flight home. I need to pay Anton a visit."

"Good. So that gives me about twelve hours to talk you out of committing first-degree murder."

"Do you still have your fallback in place?"

Isabell darted her eyes at him. "Yes. Why?"

"Because you might need to use it."

Like most international operatives, Isabell had an emergency plan in place. Located in a storage unit just outside Macon, Georgia, was a car, fake passport, credit cards, disguises, and several thousand dollars—all waiting for her in the event she needed to disappear into thin air.

"Henry, is there anything else you're not telling me?"

"No." He exhaled. "That's everything."

She inched closer to him, then grasped his hand. "Listen to me," she instructed softly. "We need to take a deep breath and evaluate all reasonable options. For one, you can't just shoot Anton. He's guarded by a small army, you'll be killed on sight, and that doesn't work for me."

"I'm listening," he said. "What else?"

"You could have him assassinated, but the planning would take months. Your third option is to go home and turn everything over to the FBI. Then run like hell."

"Those aren't viable options, Isabell."

"All right, how about this," she tried. "You certainly can't try to overthrow Anton. Two weeks ago, you were a lieutenant. The Balkans would never go for it, and Asa and his little gladiators would eat you alive. Which leaves us with one final choice, the one you originally proposed; we go home and pretend everything's normal—you're not an FBI informant, Anton didn't murder your parents, and Darius wasn't working with SOA."

"So I just forget any of this happened?"

"No, Henry. But you hold all the cards. You have the resources to do whatever the hell you want. You want Anton dead? Put together a team and get it done. You want to put him in prison? You've got enough evidence to lock him away forever. And if this deal with Hassani goes down— provided Anton doesn't have you killed first—you'll have enough money to abscond to some exotic location and live out your days in complete bliss."

"Fiji," he whispered with a tiny grin.

"Excuse me?"

"Darius wanted to go to Fiji."

She dropped her eyes to the floor. "I know he did."

"But I agree, you're absolutely right. Let's go home and regroup."

"Then there it is, that's the plan," she declared. "You ready to move out, soldier?"

He let out a tiny laugh. "Yeah. Let's do it."

They quickly gathered their things and met Francesco in the garden outside.

"I can't thank you enough for your generosity," said Henry as he packed their bags into the SUV. "I'm going to repay you, Francesco. That's how this works, do you understand?"

The old Italian nodded fervently.

Isabell rushed over and pecked him on the cheek before piling into the Skoda. "*Ciao! Grazie di tutto!*" she shouted.

Francesco waved his hands clumsily into the air. "*Ciao, stai attento! Che dio vi benedica!*" he prattled as the SUV pulled away and rambled down the long winding drive.

At the far end of the property, Isabell veered onto a thin path that wove deeper into the forest. The trail emptied into a pasture where an old dilapidated outbuilding sat on a hill ahead of them. Its crumbling mortar revealed decades of use. She pulled the SUV into the old barn and parked it next to another vehicle resting beneath a weathered tarp.

"What's this? A change of cars?" Henry asked.

"Something like that." She got out and walked across the barn. With careful precision, she pulled away the old tarp, revealing a black BMW.

"How long has this been sitting here?"

"Three years," she replied. "I told Francesco he could use it whenever he wants, but I'm starting to think he doesn't know how to drive."

Isabell climbed behind the wheel of the BMW and fired up its engine—the headers of the turbocharged V6 purred like an old leopard waking from a long hibernation.

Henry grabbed their bags from the Skoda Karoq and transferred them to the trunk of the BMW. He then dropped into the passenger seat and buckled in as the sedan pulled out of the barn.

They emerged moments later on a scenic roadway and darted west through the mountains until they reached the countryside, where an endless array of rolling hills stretched beyond the horizon.

Milano Malpensa Airport was only three hours away.

CHAPTER 30

Just north of the airport, they ditched the BMW behind a chain-link fence on the side of the road. Henry suspected it was a drop point for Isabell's Italy network and that in the coming hours, the vehicle would be wiped clean and outfitted with a new plate, if not destroyed.

She led him south on foot along Via Liguria for several blocks before hailing a taxi. They rode in silence to the airport, then pulled their luggage from the back hatch. Henry slung the duffle bag over his shoulder and stood on the curb as the taxi disappeared into a sea of buses and vans.

Inside the terminal, an escalator brought them to the main level, where they purchased two tickets to Atlanta. They presented their passports at a security check before being herded toward the gate. After a quiet, thirty-minute lull among a crowd of anxious tourists, a loud speaker announced the first rows of boarding.

As they grabbed their bags and fell in line, Henry reached over and gently caressed Isabell's arm. "I want to apologize for yesterday."

"What about yesterday?"

"Kissing you like that. I'm sorry."

"Well, I'm not," she declared with authority.

Before he could respond, she turned and traipsed into the jetway.

"So what does that mean?" he asked as he hurried behind her.

She stopped in the narrow tunnel and turned to face him. "It means we're back together, Henry. Just don't get me killed."

His eyes lit up in his battered face. "I never agreed to that!"

"You didn't have to. I could feel it when you kissed me—it's something you've been fighting since the day we left for Sorrento. Admittedly, we both have, but I didn't want it to be real. Yet here we are."

With a small crowd of passengers bottling up behind them, Isabell stepped onto the plane and found her seat. Henry followed and sat down next to her.

Minutes later, KLM flight 6291 pulled away from the gate and began taxiing for takeoff. He entwined his fingers with hers and held them closely until the plane lifted off the runway, climbed through the clouds, and leveled off.

The hours passed under the light chatter of passengers and the warm smiles of flight attendants. As the Airbus streaked across the skies over Nova Scotia, Henry sipped his bottled water and set his head back against the seat.

"What's the most afraid you've ever been?" Isabell randomly asked him.

His eyes peeled open, then closed again. "Brazil."

"Your recent trip to Brazil?"

"Yeah, just before Darius was killed."

"What happened down there, Henry?"

He took a shallow breath. "Well, we broke into the Customs House at Porto Santos, but our package wasn't there. We tried to exfil as fast as possible, but I got hung up by a guard as I was trying to get over the fence."

"You were taken into custody?"

"Yeah. It got bad."

"How bad?"

"Like, sold-to-the-cartel-and-taken-out-to-the-ocean-to-be-executed bad."

"Henry! That's more than *bad*."

He snickered to himself and sat upright in his seat. "Anyways, these two Cardoso guys have me out on the water—middle of the night, miles from the shore—and they drop me to my knees and put a hood over my head."

Her eyes widened with disbelief. "Why didn't you bring me? I could've helped avoid something like that."

"You know why," he said cryptically. "This was top-level, covert shit. Ružaro only."

"I know. I've heard it all before."

"So I'm sitting there on the deck with a hood over my head, shitting my pants, when I hear the rack of a pistol slide. I'm thinking it's the end, this is it. And I gotta tell you, preparing yourself to die is a remarkably sobering thing."

"I'll bet."

"It's funny, in that one millisecond, I saw everything flash in front of me… just like people always say. It's like this pure, unrelenting sense of devastation that just washes over you. I can't explain it. It's the most empty thing I've ever felt."

"I can't imagine. What happened next?"

"Next thing I know, I hear two gunshots and I slump to the ground. For a second, I thought I was in shock and I just couldn't feel the bullets. But then I realized I hadn't been hit. So I start listening to what's going on and I could hear one of the guys being dragged to the edge of the boat and dumped into the water. Then the other guy yanks off my hood and takes me back to shore."

"Are you serious? Why did he do that?"

"Because Darius had offered a reward to save me." Henry took a moment to pause, remembering the absurdity of it all. "In the end, the one dude who was hired to blow my brains out is the one who wound up collecting the reward."

"Holy moly! I can't even… I mean, what the hell?"

Henry smirked. "Darius was always looking out for me. Always going out on some crazy limb to make sure I was okay. I seriously don't know what I'm going to do without him."

"I have to ask: how many times have you been in situations like that?"

The smile quickly slipped from his face. "Too many, I suppose."

"Yeah. It sounds like it." She reached over and placed her hand on top of his. "I don't want that for you anymore. We have a chance to erase all of this, Henry. A chance to start over."

"The Balkans will never let us start over, even if Anton's gone. They'll come for us. And they'll never stop."

"It's all profit based," she said as she nestled into his arm with a deep yawn. "They'll only come for you if finding you is more profitable than leaving you alone. Hunting you down like a wounded animal will take time and resources. The return on that investment has to be substantial, or they'll never sign off on it."

Henry steadied his breathing and prepared himself for what lay ahead. His body was sore and beaten, his soul reduced to a vulnerable shell. And he only had a few hours to turn it all around.

It was early afternoon in Atlanta when their plane touched down at Hartsfield-Jackson International. After a long wait at baggage claim, Henry and Isabell jumped into a waiting shuttle that took them to a hotel just up the highway.

His Maserati was still parked where he'd left it—around the back of the building beneath a lamp post. He threw his sunglasses over his eyes and their bags into the trunk.

"What now?" Isabell asked as they got into the car.

"I need to debrief with Asa. After that, I'll swing by your place."

The Maserati pulled out of the parking lot and raced northbound onto the interstate. Henry gripped the steering wheel as he hit the gas and pierced through a small pocket of traffic.

"Are you sure you want to go see Asa?" she asked.

"I don't have a choice. We agreed to keep our heads down and pretend everything's fine, right?"

"Yeah, I guess we did."

"Listen, I won't let anything happen. If any of Asa's thugs question you about our trip, just give them the details: the surveillance, Hassani, the ass beating, all of it. Just leave out the part about A.J.'s laptop… obviously."

"Obviously," she echoed sarcastically. "And you promise not to compromise Francesco?"

"I swear. The man saved my life."

"Good." She nodded thoughtfully, trying to convince herself everything was going to be okay.

As they pulled into her neighborhood and parked in the driveway, her big green eyes peered over at him. She leaned in and kissed him on the lips. "I know you're struggling with this, Henry. I know you'd rather put a bullet in Anton's head and never look back. But life's never that simple."

His eyes lifted to meet her gaze, as if pleading her to come up with a better solution. But he knew there wasn't one. He needed to be patient, and Isabell had proven, once again, to be the voice of reason.

They both got out and Henry lifted her luggage from the trunk and set it on the driveway. "I'll talk to you soon," he promised.

She wrapped her arms around his neck, then turned and walked to the front porch with her travel case rolling behind her.

* * *

Antonio Garza watched from a distance, tucked behind the wheel of his SUV. His eyes followed the Maserati as he lifted the radio to his mouth. "Phantom One, do you copy?"

The radio crackled for a moment before Miles' voice responded. "Copy that. What's up, Phantom Two?"

"Our mystery couple is back on the grid. Echo Target just dropped the woman off at her house. I'm tailing him now."

"Is that right?"

"Yep. He's probably heading back to Forty West."

"Thanks for the update, Phantom Two. Once you get there, hold your position. I'll swing by to relieve you in about two hours."

"Roger that." Garza set the radio back on the dash and veered onto the main road. He followed the Maserati back to Midtown, where it parked in the underground deck of Henry's building. After a brief twenty-minute lull, the sportscar reemerged and pulled out of the garage onto Twelfth Street.

Garza brought the radio back to his mouth. "Echo Target is on the move again. I repeat, Echo Target is on the move."

He threw the Tahoe into drive and pulled out into traffic, tailing his target from a safe distance. After weaving several blocks north into Buckhead, the Maserati pulled into the private entrance of the Park Avenue building. The Tahoe continued past. Garza circled the block and ducked into the lot behind the Marriott.

Miles' voice again shattered through the radio. "Phantom Two, where the hell is he?"

"Look out your window. He just pulled in. I'm on my way up."

* * *

Henry got out of his car and tightened his jacket against his chest. He toiled nervously with the bandages on his left hand as he paced toward the entrance.

A short, robust man in a black suit stood guard in the corridor. Clearly, Asa had increased his security measures.

"Hey there, Frank," Henry greeted.

"Good afternoon, Mr. Sirola."

"I'm here to see Asa."

"Yes, sir. I believe Mr. Petrovi is upstairs on forty-two." Frank leaned over and pressed the button on the wall.

Henry kept his eyes ahead of him and stepped onto the elevator. On the forty-second floor, he got off and continued through the foyer.

"Henry!" Asa shouted, his voice booming through the penthouse.

"Hello, Asa. My apologies for not getting in touch sooner. Hassani took our comms."

The aging general examined the bruises on Henry's face and the splint on his left hand. "I'm so sorry about Zürich," he said. "Looks like that bastard did a real number on you."

"I'm sure I'll live," Henry replied.

"Come inside. Let's talk." Asa led him back to a formal living room just off the grand hall. "Here, have a seat."

Henry unbuttoned his coat and sat down. "Did Veselko submit the surveillance reports?"

"Yes, yes, of course," Asa confirmed as he took a seat next to Henry. "I'm happy to hear everything checked out with Hassani. But something bothers me."

"And what's that?"

The general looked him over curiously. "Where have you been, Henry? The last two days after Zürich?"

"You already know, Asa. The tour guide and I went to ground."

"To where exactly?"

"Hassani took our cell phones, my radio, and the sat phone. And unfortunately, I was in no condition to fly."

"Just answer my question, Henry."

He took a moment to gather himself. "Isabell had a safehouse, just across the mountains, east of Liechtenstein."

"What village?"

"Davos," Henry said without hesitation. "Listen, Asa, I tried to keep everything undercover. I have no idea how they picked up our surveillance. But I can assure you, it won't happen again."

The general seemed amused. "Fair enough," he relented. "So tell me about the ambush at the restaurant."

Henry dove into a detailed account of what took place the night he and Isabell were having dinner at Razzia. He revealed everything that happened from the moment Hassani's men stormed the dining room until the moment he blacked out. Asa sat quietly, his legs crossed and his hands in his lap, as Henry finished his story.

"Did you schedule the handoff?" Asa asked coldly.

"Yes. Sunday night, nine o'clock."

"Where?"

"Brown Field."

Asa allowed a tight smile. "You did well, Henry. Everything's going to be fine. Anton and I were just worried about you, that's all. We don't like being worried. I'm sure you can understand."

"Of course."

"But I must admit, I'm growing tired of having to keep asking where you've been lately. Do we need to worry about you anymore, Henry?"

"No. Absolutely not."

"Excellent. Now let's discuss the handoff. Hudson Rukov's crew will deliver the diamond. But you're still in charge of the transaction."

"Asa, will all due respect, I'd feel better if my crew managed the delivery."

The general narrowed his eyes. "Listen to me closely," he began. "Hudson Rukov has been a Ružaro captain since I was teaching you and Darius how to tie your shoes. His crew is on delivery. Do we understand each other?"

"Yes, one hundred percent. You and Anton can count on me, I promise."

"Good. Now before I forget; I've brought you a new phone." Asa reached into his jacket and pulled out a shiny new cell phone, which he tossed to his captain. "Anton will be in touch soon. Try not to wander away this time."

Henry stuffed the device into his pocket and stood to shake Asa's hand. "I'll be ready," he promised.

CHAPTER 31

Miles sat quietly at the table against the window. He raised his arms with a deep yawn just as Garza burst through the door. "What'd I miss?" the DCIS officer asked with bated breath.

"Sirola just met with Asa Petrovi on forty-two. Probably a debrief after his trip to Milan."

Garza took a seat at the table. "Do we know if he met with Hassani while he was there?"

"No idea. He must be traveling covertly; we still haven't been able to pinpoint his location."

"That means Sirola could've been meeting with anyone."

Miles checked his wristwatch. It was nearly four o'clock. His eyes quickly returned to the Park Avenue building across the street, waiting for the Maserati to pull out of the lot.

Just then, Agent Harwick charged into the room with a set of files under his arm. "Afternoon, gentlemen," he greeted. "Get me up to speed. What are we looking at?"

From across the room, two young analysts peered up from their laptops. One of them raised his hand. It was a slender, clean-shaven guy with curly brown hair.

"What is it?" Harwick barked.

"We've picked up security footage from Hartsfield-Jackson with some of Krunoslav's men getting off a plane from Zürich the other day. One of them was Jack Veselko."

"Zürich?" Harwick asked, somewhat surprised.

"Yes, sir. We believe it was Henry Sirola's advance team."

"Thank you, Jeremy." Harwick turned to face Miles. "And you said Sirola returned today?"

Miles nodded. "Affirmative. I guess now we know where he went."

"What are they doing now?"

"Sirola just wrapped a debrief with Asa Petrovi. You got anything on Hudson Rukov?"

Harwick set his file folder on the table and opened it up. "Rukov and his crew set up shop at a welding facility off Krog Street. They've gathered a small army over there."

"Krunoslav's protecting whatever it is he pulled from the ocean," suggested Miles. "And I have reason to believe it's already been delivered. They're in the final stages."

"If Hassani's the buyer," Garza pointed out, "we have to get a track on him."

Miles glared out the window with uncertainty. "What if we missed it?"

"What do you mean?" asked Harwick.

"I mean, what if Sirola just made the fucking handoff in Zürich? It's almost too easy; he and the woman fly into Milan to throw us off, they drive to Zürich, where his security team is already in place, and he meets with Hassani for the handoff."

"What about Customs?" wondered Garza. "Whether it's a painting or a sculpture or a diamond, they're not getting it through Customs on a domestic flight. A private jet, maybe. But a domestic flight? Not a chance."

Harwich loosened his tie. "Let me see if I can get any accurate ISR data on Hassani. I can't imagine Krunoslav would put his prize possession in the hands of one of his captains and a four-man crew. It doesn't add up. It's not how these guys operate. When the deal goes down, we're going to see Hassani's top-level guys converge in the same place as Asa Petrovi and a swarm of Ružaro soldiers."

"Yeah, you're right," Miles agreed. "We need to clamp down on Sirola and Rukov. I think as long as we're being attentive here, we'll see the signs."

Harwick shuffled through his notes. "Agent Brennan, I have to ask: do you have any other touch-points within the Ružaro organization that we can utilize?"

Miles shook his head. "I don't think so… I've questioned at least a half dozen of those guys over the years, but Martović was the only one that ever panned out."

"I've seen the field reports," the NSA agent reminded him. "You've had contact with both of the current captains—Henry Sirola *and* Hudson Rukov."

"Well, yeah, I literally just took a witness statement from Sirola like a week ago."

Harwick sat frozen in thought, weighing his options. "Unfortunately, we don't have time to groom another resident. We just have to work with what we have." He stood from the table and paced the worn carpet. "Agent Brennan, stay on top of Sirola. Officer Garza, why don't you move on to Rukov's lieutenants. If his crew is guarding something at that welding shop, they'll be the first ones to move out."

"Roger that," said Garza. "Are you sure you want me and Brennan to split up?"

"Yes. We need to cover as much ground as possible right now." Harwick turned to the two analysts hiding behind their laptops. "Jeremy, Caleb, get a scan in place for all international flights in and out of Hartsfield. I also need a visual over Doha, Qatar. Do we have any drones operational in the area?"

"None of ours, sir. CIA has a fleet running sorties in the Gulf of Oman," Jeremy stated. "Should I try to coordinate something?"

"Fuck the CIA," Harwick growled. "Anything else?"

The analyst typed feverishly into his keyboard. "Yes, sir. There's a Russian satellite in low Earth orbit that'll be over the target in roughly six hours. Would you like me to intercept?"

"Yes."

"Sirola just left the Park Avenue building," Miles interrupted. He sprang from the table and dashed toward the door. "I'm out!"

"Keep your comms open, Brennan!" Harwick shouted as the agent disappeared out the door.

* * *

Henry drove back to the Forty West building and took the elevator up to his penthouse. He now stood on his balcony, mesmerized by a medley of pink clouds that melted into an orange sky as dusk fell over the city.

Surely Miles' team was out there, he thought. But there were things that needed to be coordinated, plans that needed to be put together, and the truth was, he'd lost precious time recuperating in Italy, and if he was going to make a move on Anton, it needed to be done quickly.

He wandered inside and took a hot shower. After cleaning his wounds, he slipped into an old pair of jeans and a t-shirt.

The searing pain in his left hand was impossible to ignore. He tried to wiggle his fingers, but every tiny movement felt like glass grating through his flesh. With a fortifying sigh, he wrapped it with gauze and secured it with medical tape. Satisfied, he made his way to the foyer, grabbed his keys and jacket, then bolted for the elevator.

Minutes later, his Maserati crept out of the garage as Henry scanned the street in each direction.

The drive out of the city took him to a quiet residential neighborhood, where he tucked the sportscar into a familiar driveway and cut the engine. He got out and glanced up the street, where he noticed a black Suburban cutting its lights as it parked on the curb behind an old pickup truck. With a smoldering grin, Henry stepped onto Isabell's front porch and knocked on the door.

She opened it up and greeted him with a bright smile before letting him in.

"I would've brought you flowers," he admitted. "But I've still got a tail."

"Of course you do. I'm just happy to see you." She leaned in and kissed him on the cheek, then the lips. "So? How'd everything go with Asa?"

"Not bad. We're just gearing up for the handoff Sunday."

Isabell turned and walked through the living room to the kitchen. Henry took off his jacket and followed her in. "Something to drink?" she offered.

"No. I'm fine, thanks."

She sat down at the dining table and looked him over. "So have you had a chance to think about A.J. and the laptop?"

"I have."

"And what did you come up with?"

"I'm going forward with the diamond handoff. Afterwards, we'll collect our money and get the hell out of here."

"And what about Darius' stash of evidence?"

"I'm sending it to my handler as soon as we're in the clear."

"I'm proud of you," she said as she grasped his hand. "I know this wasn't the solution you wanted."

"I just hope Anton has a miserable life in prison, rotting away like a rat," Henry confessed. "I'd be okay with that."

"Yeah, I think I could live with that too."

Henry reached into his pocket and pulled out the burner phone. "Do you mind if I make a quick call?"

"Not at all."

He put the phone on speaker and set it on the table. "Go ahead," a male voice answered.

"A.J., it's me. I'm here with Isabell."

"Hey there. Good to hear from you guys. I was starting to get worried."

"We're fine, just a few bumps and bruises. Listen, I appreciate you sending me that Croatian incident report."

A.J. sighed heavily into the phone. "I'm really sorry about that, Henry. But I believe that may have been what you were looking for."

Henry rubbed his brow. "Yeah… I think it was."

"So where's that leave us?"

"We're moving forward with Hassani."

"Okay. You sure about that?"

"You have to understand, A.J., there's a huge payday in this for us. All of us."

"You don't have to explain it to me, Henry."

"Good. The deal's going down the day after tomorrow. We'll just lay low until Anton gives me our cut. Then we're gone."

"And the laptop?"

"As soon as all three of us are safe and sound, I want you to ship it to Special Agent Miles Brennan at the FBI field office in Atlanta."

"Got it."

"All right, cover your six, A.J. I'll be in touch." Henry placed the phone back into his pocket.

Isabell reached over and gently squeezed his hand. "I promise you've made the right decision."

"I don't know about that. A stronger man would've done something different."

"And a weaker man would've ruined his entire life for a moment of revenge," she countered. "I admire you for withstanding the temptation."

"Don't make me change my mind."

She flashed him a devilish grin. "There's something sexy about you when you're being practical."

"Is that right?"

"Yes. I like it."

Henry's mind drifted to some long-lost memory. "What are we doing, Izzy?" he asked quietly.

"We're enjoying each other again, Henry."

"It's more than that, isn't it?"

"I'm sorry for what happened… for what I did to you back when we were dating. I was kind of hoping you'd gotten over it."

"I have. It was a long time ago."

"No. It wasn't," she corrected. "It was barely two years ago. And I hurt you. And I know it still bothers you."

He fought the instinct to remember. "So why'd you do it?"

She got up and yanked a bottle of red wine from the cabinet. "You want to know why I broke up with you?"

"Yes. I do."

She took a sip of merlot and floated her eyes away from him. "Believe it or not, I loved you very much, Henry. But things were crazy then. We were both trying to make something of ourselves, trying to advance our careers. It was just too much at once."

"I don't believe you," he challenged. "You promised we would tell each other the truth, so tell me what really happened."

"What do you want me to say, Henry? You were out putting your life in danger every night and I was helping an arms dealer build an empire. Then we'd hook up over the weekends and play boyfriend and girlfriend like everything was normal. We weren't normal. We still aren't."

"And we never will be," he added. "I'm okay with the fact that we'll never have a white picket fence or join the PTA or collect grocery coupons, but that doesn't mean people like us can't have some kind of relationship—feel something that makes us human. Am I wrong?"

"No, Henry. You're not wrong. It's just not easy sometimes, that's all."

He took a deep breath and sat down at the table. "So why couldn't we have had this conversation two years ago?"

She was uncomfortable now, questioning how far she was willing to go.

"Isabell?" he tried. "Why was this so hard? There's more you're not telling me. What the hell happened?"

"They warned me," she whispered.

"Warned you? *Who* warned you?"

She put her head in her hands and began to cry.

"Izzy? Talk to me. Please."

After a fleeting moment of regret, she lifted her face and wiped the tears from her eyes. "Asa and one of his little henchmen came to see me one night," she started with a whisper. "They told me how much they appreciated the work I'd done in Monaco—the Hotel Monte Carlo job."

"Yeah, I remember. So?"

"Henry, you almost got yourself killed. You put the whole operation in jeopardy. And all because of me. They were obviously upset about it."

He shook his head profusely. "That's not true. I made a split-second decision and I don't regret it. It was in the best interest of—"

"Stop, Henry," she interrupted. "Because that's not how Asa and Darius saw it."

"Darius? You mean Darius was with him?"

"No, not when Asa came to see me. But I know Darius felt the same way. They said I couldn't be with you anymore."

"You're fucking kidding me, right? You have to be kidding me!"

"I wish I was. Asa promised me you wouldn't be punished and that they'd sweep everything under the rug as long as I stopped seeing you. I was, apparently, a distraction. And they weren't wrong, Henry. You would never have advanced through the organization if you had stayed with me."

Henry stood from the table and ran a hand through his hair. He gazed vacantly across the room into a void of humiliation.

"I'm sorry," she offered, her eyes swollen and red. "I'm sorry for everything. None of this has been fair to you."

"You broke my heart," he finally said.

"I know I did. But I promise it won't happen again."

"Well, you're about to be a multi-millionaire," he pointed out. "Why even bother? You can go anywhere in the world and live a good life. You don't need me."

"I know I don't need you. But I want you," she said somberly. "I want to be with you when this is all over."

"Well, I'm happy to hear that. Because I want to be with you too."

Isabell set her glass on the table. She wrapped her arms around his neck and kissed him passionately. Henry's hands gently drifted to her waist, then her hips, exploring each curve with conviction. They slowly made their way to her bedroom, where their clothes fell to the cold, hardwood floor.

CHAPTER 32

Henry awoke to the faint sound of music. Contemporary classical, he noted. With a tired yawn, he got out from under the sheets and searched the room for his boxers. He then made his way up the hall and into the kitchen. Isabell waited at the table with a steaming cup of coffee.

"Have you been awake long?" he asked.

"A couple hours—long enough to brew a fresh pot."

He poured himself a cup, then sat down next to her. "Ludovico Einaudi?" he asked, motioning his eyes to the small speaker on the counter.

"Of course. Who else would it be?"

"Some things never change," he teased.

"The black Suburban finally left. Was that your handler?"

"Yeah. That's him." Henry brushed his thumb around the dark bruising on her eye, then kissed her softly on the cut below her lip.

"It'll heal," she promised. "I'm more worried about you though. How are those ribs feeling after last night?"

Henry smirked. "They hurt like crazy. But well worth it."

"Good. Can I make you some breakfast?"

"No, I'm fine. I'll pick something up on my way out. I need to get in touch with my guy today."

"You mean the FBI agent who was parked up the street a few hours ago? Why didn't you go talk to him last night?"

"It doesn't work like that," he informed her. "There's absolutely no direct contact in the open. We set everything up through dead drops and signals."

"Nice to know he's cautious, I guess. But does he always surveil you like this?"

"No. The feds have put together some kind of task force. They're watching all of us."

"Wonderful. So how do you expect to handoff a priceless diamond without them knowing? I mean, this is going to draw a lot of attention, don't you think?"

"There's an old Chinese proverb that says it's better to have a diamond with a flaw than a pebble without one."

"Please, spare me," she scoffed. "There's no good way to pull this off with a federal task force watching your every move."

"We just have to be careful. Very careful."

Isabell raised an eyebrow. "What is it with you guys? You just go charging into fires with abandon. It's crazy."

"I told you, it'll be fine," he assured her gently. "Agent Brennan won't let anything happen."

"Must be nice to have people covering your ass all the time. Do you plan on coming back here tonight?"

"If you'll have me."

"I think I'd like that." She leaned over and kissed him on the lips. "Please be careful today," she whispered.

"I will. I promise."

After a second cup of coffee, Henry hugged her goodbye and made his way out to the driveway. She watched through the window as the Maserati drifted away and careened around the block, disappearing behind a tall row of cypress trees.

Henry drove south toward the city and after several miles, pulled into the Druid Hill Dry Cleaners and parked in the front lot. The building was flanked by a diner on one side and a pawn shop on the other. Graffiti tags decorated its brick exterior and a neon sign in the window offered two shirts for eight dollars.

Henry sat in his car for a moment, paralyzed with apprehension. The impact of what he was about to do weighed on his aching shoulders.

With a calming breath, he got out of the car and hurried inside.

An old Vietnamese man sat behind the counter, hunched over a small cash register. He was short and frail and in no sort of hurry.

"Good morning," Henry mumbled as he entered.

The little man eyed him suspiciously.

Henry pulled a ticket from his pocket and handed it over the counter.

The man looked it over through his black button eyes and after a brief pause, disappeared behind a set of curtains.

Henry waited. He could hear voices coming from the other side of the wall but couldn't understand a word of it. The old man was speaking Vietnamese to someone—another chain in the protocol, he supposed.

Finally, after several minutes, the man returned. "Your pants will be ready in one hour," he assured.

"Thank you," replied Henry. He nodded politely and exited the shop.

It was a moment he'd hoped would never come. And in some bizarre way, it turned out to be less climactic than he'd envisioned.

He walked back to his car and started the engine. The Maserati darted back to the interstate and maneuvered through patches of midday traffic. He got off at Oakland City and turned right. It was a typical Tuesday morning on the west side and the crack dealers and sex workers were still posted up at their corners from the night before.

Henry crept the car past an abandoned industrial complex, then parked around the back of a package store. With his eyes glued to the pavement, he walked two blocks to a nearby bus stop and took the 83 Line north, where he got off at Campbellton Road and continued on foot to a nearby seafood market in a sketchy part of town.

He stuffed his hands into his pockets and entered the open-air market, weaving through an ocean of vendors who'd arrived early to set up their booths. As he reached the southwest corner, he ducked through a sheet hanging over an archway.

A dark, narrow corridor led him to a small, empty courtyard. There were shards of broken glass and cigarette butts scattered in the dirt at his feet.

It was Henry's least favorite spot—one they'd reserved only for emergencies.

He waited patiently at first, but as the minutes passed, his anxiety began to take over. He paced back and forth in the dirt. Waiting.

A man finally appeared from the corridor and stepped into the courtyard.

"Jesus, what happened to you?" asked Miles.

"You should see the other guys."

"I'll bet," the agent replied. "Trouble in Italy? Or was it Switzerland?"

Henry couldn't help but smirk. "A little bit of both, I guess."

"Another meeting with Hassani?"

"You know I'm not going to tell you that."

"What are we doing here, Henry?"

"Let's just say there have been some new developments."

"What kind of developments?"

"The organization's about to go dark, Miles."

The agent furrowed his brow. "What exactly does that mean?"

"It means you probably won't ever see me again. This is our last meeting."

"Is this about the Hassani deal? Am I supposed to believe Ružaro's going to close up shop after this?"

"Don't come looking for me," Henry warned.

"I don't think the organization's going dark. I think *you're* going dark. Am I right?" Henry shook his head defiantly. "You know I can't just let you slip away, Henry. But you're right about one thing: this is all coming to an end. The task force is already preparing for a takedown. It's over and there's nothing I can do to stop it."

"When?"

"The handoff," Miles revealed.

"I'm not letting you anywhere near the fucking handoff!" Henry struck. "You need to stand down, Miles. You promised me!"

Miles' face tightened with disappointment. "I'm telling you it's out of my hands, Henry."

"Fine. Then do one last thing for me."

"Sure. What is it?"

"When this is all over, you're going to receive a package."

"What kind of package?"

"The kind that could destroy the entire syndicate; the kind that makes you a hero."

Miles quickly connected the dots. "You're double-crossing him, aren't you?"

"I'm not double-crossing anyone. I'm taking my cut and disappearing."

"And you're going to what, leave me with evidence?"

"Something like that."

"You know, I can offer you a nice life here—in the States. A small town, someplace safe where nobody will ever find you."

Henry shuffled his feet in the dirt. "It's not that simple."

"Yeah." The agent sighed. "I guess it never is."

"I appreciate everything, Miles. I really do. It's been one hell of a ride."

"So this is it?"

Henry lifted his gaze. "This is it."

"You're a good guy, you know that? Now, I can't make any promises, but if this goes down the way you want it to and you beat me to the punch, I wish you nothing but the best."

"Have a nice life, Agent Brennan."

Miles squinted into the sun and grinned to himself. He shook Henry's hand, then watched as the greatest thief he'd ever known vanished into the shadows.

CHAPTER 33

Miles climbed back into his Suburban and drove away. He veered west through the housing projects of Oakland City, then north toward Midtown before stopping at the drive-thru of a locally owned burger joint. As his SUV pulled away, he unwrapped a greasy burger from its greasy wrapper and took a greasy bite. He wondered for a moment if Henry would actually follow through on his threat. Perhaps it was all for the best, he thought. Besides, the Shadowmaker was officially dead; any information gleaned from Henry at this point would be useless.

But Miles was a pragmatist. He was driven more by practical considerations than by any set of rules or ideals. And the fact was, he'd lied to the NSA about Henry because he didn't trust them. He knew that Agent Harwick was only in it for his own aspirations. It was the type of selfish leadership that often got people hurt, if not killed. He'd seen it his entire adult life—in the ranks of the FBI, on the battlefields of Iraq, in the streets of Atlanta.

He stuffed the last of his cheeseburger into his mouth and snatched the radio from the console. "Evergreen, this is Phantom One. Do you copy?"

"Full copy, Phantom One. Go ahead."

"I just followed Echo Target to Oakland City. He's coordinating with outside operatives. I believe it was the Dominicans."

"Copy that," Harwick answered. "What's your location?"

"Heading north, following him back to his apartment," said Miles. The lie felt easy.

"Do we have an ETA on the handoff?"

"It could be as early as tomorrow. Echo Target's making shady deals in every alley from Milan to Atlanta. They're definitely prepping for the handoff."

"Copy that, Phantom One. Stay on top of Echo Target and let me know if he runs any more errands."

"Any updates on the buyer?" asked Miles.

"Negative. He's in the wind again. Evergreen out."

The agent tossed the radio onto the passenger seat and continued north to Midtown. He pulled into the retail center across from Henry's penthouse and threw the SUV into park. Through a pair of dark sunglasses, he leered up at the Forty West building with a sense of unease.

He'd been working with Henry for years. The relationship had been beneficial to him, and in some strange way, Miles had grown to like his brash informant. But he knew this day would eventually come. Every residency had its end, and Henry's would be no different.

As Miles sat behind the wheel and contemplated his career, twenty-six stories up, Henry paced nervously in his living room. He checked his watch; it had been just over an hour since he'd left the dry cleaners, and surely his pants were ready for pickup.

In a flash of weakness, he stood frozen in place, wishing everything would go back to the way it was—when Darius was still alive and Anton was a protective father figure. He tried to picture himself sitting at Club Trinidad sipping vodka without a care in the world. But that life, he knew, was over.

He pulled his feet from the floor, took one small step forward, then another, until he reached the elevator. But instead of going to the lobby or the garage, he got off on the tenth floor and darted up a hallway to the emergency stairs. He rushed to the bottom and zig-zagged through a maze of corridors before bursting through a metal door to an outside maintenance lot.

He turned north and began hustling along the sidewalk, checking over his shoulder to make sure no one was following. At the corner of Fourteenth and Spring, he hopped a MARTA bus and rode north for twenty minutes before getting off at Druid Hills. After a three-block hike, he stepped off the sidewalk and into the dry cleaners.

The frail little Asian looked up from his register, then slipped behind the curtain. He returned moments later and motioned for his customer to follow. Henry accompanied the man through an entanglement of garments and conveyer lines to a small table against the back wall. A single cardboard box sat ominously on top.

"This is for you," the man said. "It is everything you requested."

Henry removed the lid and peered inside. All of the items seemed to be accounted for. He reached in and removed a keyring, followed by a stack of credit cards, birth certificates, and bank statements. Lastly, he pulled out a postcard and stared at it for a moment. On one side was an address in The Netherlands, and on the other was a photo of a small farmhouse set against a rolling green pasture. He stuffed it into the breast pocket of his jacket, then placed the credit cards, keyring, and other documents back onto the table.

The old man gathered the items and carefully placed them into the pockets of a pair of brown dress pants. He then set them onto a hanger and covered them with clear plastic.

Henry offered the man a grateful nod, then grabbed the pants and hastily left the building.

* * *

A.J. sat alone in a booth at Emily's Donuts, sipping hot coffee from a paper cup. He never liked venturing into Atlanta—something Darius had only asked of him a handful of times. But when he did, this was his spot. The donuts were second to none and the woman who ran the place—Emily—was always up for some innocent flirting. He waited patiently, picking at his blueberry donut, until Henry finally arrived. "Glad you could make it," he mumbled.

Henry sat down across from him. "Yeah. You too. How's everything going?"

"Not bad." He looked Henry over. "What happened to your hand?"

"Things in Zürich didn't quite go as planned."

"Obviously. That seems to be a theme with you lately."

Henry motioned for a cup of coffee. "But everything's still on track," he assured. "The deal with Hassani goes down tomorrow night."

Emily set another hot paper cup on the table, accompanied by a small plate of fresh eclairs. "I made a few extra this morning," she said with a wink. "On the house."

"Why thank you," A.J. replied.

Once she was out of earshot, Henry leaned in. "Did you bring what I asked?"

"I did." A.J. produced a small paper bag and placed it on the table. "Passport, credit card, driver's license, and a plane ticket. Congratulations, you are now Mr. Colton Sinclair."

"Among others," Henry quipped. "What about the laptop?"

"It's all packed up. So is the house."

"Good. Good."

"So where's the rendezvous?" asked A.J. "I fly out Thursday morning, it'd be nice to know where I need to be."

Henry scanned his eyes across the café. "Just outside of Brussels, a small town called Kortenberg. There's an old rundown pizza joint just across from the train station. Two weeks from tomorrow."

A.J. nodded over his coffee, then reached for an eclair and took a bite.

"I really appreciate everything," Henry continued. "I'm gonna make this right for you… financially speaking."

"There's no need for that, Henry."

"Yeah, well, I might need some help tying up a few loose ends. There's five million dollars in it for you if you show up."

A.J. didn't flinch. "That's a lot of money."

"Well, you've earned it."

"I'm smart enough to know that when a man promises you that kind of cash, you're likely to wind up dead. Am I going to wind up dead, Henry?"

"That's not how I do business. I'll see you at the rendezvous. Promise me you'll be there."

"Of course I'll be there. Anything I can do in the meantime?"

Henry shook his head. "Nothing more than what we've already discussed."

A.J. snatched another eclair from the plate and stood from the table. "Be safe," he muttered. He waved to the cute blonde as he passed the counter, then pushed through the front door and disappeared.

* * *

Miles pulled the Suburban into a condominium complex on the outskirts of East Atlanta and parked beneath a street light. He got out and hurried up a flight of stairs. His one-bedroom apartment was simple and cluttered, bearing all the hallmarks of an overworked bachelor. He opened a cold beer from the fridge and took a satisfying drink.

As the agent turned away, he noticed the television light flickering in the living room. He set the beer on the counter and pulled his .40 caliber from its holster.

He was certain he'd left the TV off. In fact, it hadn't been on in weeks. With a steady breath, he raised his pistol and slid up the hallway to the living room, where a shadowy figure waited against the wall.

"Don't shoot," the voice said calmly.

Miles approached slowly, squinting his eyes for a better look. "Jesus Christ, Harwick! What the fuck are you doing here?"

"My apologies," the NSA agent offered. "I didn't mean to startle you, Agent Brennan, but I'm not sure how comfortable I am waiting outside in this neighborhood."

"Well, you almost got yourself killed," Miles warned.

"Again, my apologies."

"I didn't know you made house calls. Can I get you a drink?"

"No, I'm fine, thanks."

Miles put his gun on the coffee table and dropped down in a recliner. "So, what exactly are you sneaking around my shitty apartment for?"

"There's something I need to speak with you about… away from the office."

"I see. It couldn't wait until tomorrow? Or better yet, a phone call?"

Harwick took his place on the loveseat across from Miles. "How was your shift today?" he smugly asked. "You were on Sirola, right?"

"Yep. I sure was."

"You know, Agent Brennan, I always knew we were going to have an issue with this whole Shadowmaker thing."

"You mean my informant? He's dead," snapped Miles.

"That's the thing—I don't believe you."

"What the hell's wrong with you, Harwick? You got some kind of problem I should know about? We both saw the Shadowmaker sitting in the goddamn morgue with his guts blown out."

"No, I saw Darius Martović sitting in the morgue. But I don't think Darius was your boy." Miles remained calm. His eyes bore into the NSA agent with resentment. "You met with Henry Sirola today," charged Harwick. "I saw it with my own eyes."

"So you have surveillance on me now?"

"Yes."

"Why? There's absolutely no fucking way you got a judge to sign off on that."

Harwick crossed his legs and produced a nine-millimeter from beneath his coat. The long steel silencer attached to the barrel hung steadily in the air.

"What the hell is this?" Miles said as he jolted upright in his recliner.

"This is your last chance to tell me who the Shadowmaker is."

But Miles wasn't ready to answer. He eyed his .40 caliber sitting on the coffee table.

Harwick lifted himself to his feet and took aim at Miles' chest. "Tell me, goddamn it!"

"Listen to me," Miles pleaded, his hands now raised in surrender. "We can work this out, Harwick. I only met with Sirola today because I'm trying to groom him as Darius' replacement."

"Don't bullshit me, Agent Brennan. We already determined that grooming a new resident wasn't an option." Harwick stepped closer and raised the gun to Miles' forehead. "Besides, that wasn't grooming I saw today. That was an agent meeting with his informant."

"All right, all right! Just put the gun down!"

"Tell me if Henry Sirola is the Shadowmaker!"

"Fine!" Miles frantically confessed. "Sirola's the Shadowmaker, okay! It's Henry. It's always been Henry."

"How long have you had him?"

"Just a few years."

"Be more specific," Harwick demanded.

"I don't know, a little over four years."

"You know, we could've avoided all this if you had just told me earlier. It's a shame, really."

Miles gazed up at the wily NSA agent. A firestorm of rage swelled within him. "I didn't tell you because I don't trust you. And I never will, you disgusting, hellbent asshole. And now that you've got your information, get the fuck out of my apartment!"

"Sadly, lying to me is going to be your last mistake," Harwick promised. "I'm sorry, Brennan. You were a good agent."

Miles raised his hand in front of him, but it was too late.

The bullet tore through his hand and into his forehead as his neck snapped back against the recliner. A cloud of red mist, bone, and brain matter painted the wall behind him.

Harwick slid the pistol back into its holster under his coat and retrieved a cell phone from his pocket. Dialing a number, he brought it to his ear. "It's done. Brennan's dead."

"Good," a cold, raspy voice replied. "And the informant?"

"Henry Sirola. They've been working together for just over four years."

Before Harwick got a response, the line went dead.

The NSA agent pulled a handkerchief from his back pocket and wiped down the living room before exiting through a back window, climbing down the fire escape, and retreating into the crisp, dark night.

CHAPTER 34

Henry glided his sportscar north along the interstate toward the suburbs. A gloomy haze hovered above as he exited into a maze of craftsman-style homes and perfectly edged sidewalks.

Isabell met him on the front porch. "Hey there, handsome, nice to see you," she greeted as they went into the living room and sat down on the sofa together. He slipped his arm behind her as she nestled into his shoulder and closed her eyes. "Tomorrow's a big day," she said with a sense of unease.

"I'm ready. Everything's going to be fine."

She wanted to believe him, but her instincts simply wouldn't allow it. "I think you need some good sleep tonight," she whispered.

He didn't argue. They enjoyed a quick nightcap before locking the doors and retiring to the bedroom. As she changed into a pair of cotton shorts and a t-shirt, Henry lay beneath the sheets, watching the ceiling fan whirling above him.

"Do you remember the first time we met?" he quietly asked.

"How could I forget?"

"I want you to meet me there when this is all over."

She shot him a dubious scowl and crawled into bed next to him. "You mean Kortenberg?"

"Yeah. That little pizza place. I'll have our money from the Hassani deal by Thursday. You need to be ready to board the first flight out Friday morning."

"I can't believe this is happening. It–it just all seems too sudden."

"It's going to be okay, Izzy. I promise. Where will you fly out of?"

"Probably Jacksonville or Savannah."

"Good," he said with a confident smile. "Two weeks from tomorrow. Kortenberg."

"And after that?"

"After that… we go wherever the wind takes us."

"Is there any place in particular you'd like to settle down when this is all over? Besides Fiji?"

"I've always wanted to see the Spanish coast," he said thoughtfully.

"It's beautiful there in the spring. You'll absolutely love it."

"I figure we'll buy a house somewhere. Stay off the radar… maybe start a garden or something."

"A garden?" she intoned. "You strike me as the type that would easily get bored with gardening. How do I know you won't sneak off and rob the nearest bank or art gallery?"

Henry chuckled. "I guess you don't."

"Well, you'll have an entire lifetime to figure it out," she said as she ran her fingernails along his chest.

"You know, it takes everything I have not to drive to Buckhead and wire Anton's penthouse with C4. Then find someplace to sit and watch as he and Asa and the whole lousy bunch get blown into a million little pieces."

"That sounds nice. But I still like the idea of him rotting away in prison better."

"Yeah, I know," Henry reluctantly agreed. "It's just not as dramatic."

"Funny how that works, isn't it?"

Henry pulled her closer. "I wish I could remember their faces," he said somberly.

"Whose faces?"

"My parents'."

Her face fell flush with grief. "I wish I could help bring closure to all of this, Henry. I wish I could make it all go away."

"Me too." His eyes remained locked on the ceiling fan. A lifetime of memories swirled within its blades, circling like an army of angry ghosts.

"I know you feel this aching desire to avenge them," she noted. "But you can't. I need you to promise me."

"I promise," he uttered. "I just want to get away from all this. There's another kind of life out there. I'd like to see what that's like. And I don't want to have to look over my shoulder every step of the way."

"I think you're going to like what you find, my love."

"I hope so. My Uncle Luka used to say, 'the world can be a wonderful place, you just have to know where to look.'"

"He's not wrong," she said with a light giggle.

Henry's mind began to wander. "Have I told you how much Anton is paying me on this deal?"

"No. How much?"

"Now that I'm a captain, my cut is seventy million. After squaring up my team and paying other expenses, there should be close to forty left over."

"That's an insane amount of money, Henry. How are you going to funnel all that into an account without Anton knowing about it?"

"It's already taken care of," he assured. "I've been opening a bunch of offshore accounts over the years—off the Ružaro books, all under different identities. That lowlife, murderous scumbag will never see me or my money again."

The thought of a life abroad—with a nearly endless supply of money—seemed to excite her. She carefully rolled over on top of him and pinned his wrists against the mattress. Then, after a long, passionate kiss, she made love to him.

The next morning, Henry awoke to the soft pulse of her breath against his neck. He gently caressed her arm and inhaled the scent of her hair. Soon, her eyes peeled open, gazing up at him with adoration.

"Morning, sunshine," he whispered.

She stretched her arms and wrapped them gingerly around his neck. "Well, good morning to you, handsome. Want some coffee?"

"That would be awesome, actually."

She kissed him on the lips and slowly crawled out of the bed. "I hate that I'm not going to see you for a couple weeks. I'll miss you fiercely."

"I'll miss you too," he replied as he put one leg into his pants, then the other.

"Let me make you some breakfast before you go." Isabell went to the kitchen and poured ready-make pancake batter onto one skillet and lined strips of bacon across another.

Henry finished getting dressed and joined her at the table. After a quiet breakfast, he helped clean the dishes, then grabbed his keys from the counter and kissed her on the forehead.

"Be careful today," she told him. "And I'll see you in Kortenberg."

He wrapped his arms around her one last time. "Please take care of yourself, Izzy. I'll be holding my breath until I see you again."

"Me too." She flashed him a loving grin as he stepped out the front door and climbed into his car.

He drove out of the suburbs and sped south toward downtown until he reached the small town of Chamblee. The Maserati veered into a MARTA station and parked in the main lot against a chain-link fence.

He stepped onto the pavement and began a light stroll toward the entrance. He scanned his transit card, pushed through the turnstiles, then took the escalator down to the gold line.

Henry now stood at the end of the platform. Minutes later, the train blasted up beside him and came to a loud, screeching halt. He examined the other passengers with a wary eye as he boarded. He could almost sense the presence of a federal task force—lurking somewhere in the shadows, tracking his every move. As the train pulled away and darted south, he held on to the grabrail and stared out at the passing concrete. A quiet hush fell over the subway car.

Henry sat motionless, his eyes locked ahead of him until, suddenly, he noticed someone moving toward him. He cut his gaze across his shoulder. The man was short and solid, wearing a brown coat and tan fedora. There was something familiar about the creases in his face and the sharpness of his eyes.

The stranger sat down behind Henry, then neatly folded his hands in his lap. "Do you know who I am?" he whispered from beneath the brim of his hat.

Henry chuckled to himself as the name finally came to him. "Officer Garza, is it?"

"Keep your eyes forward," the man instructed.

"Listen, buddy, this really isn't a good time—"

"You need to listen to me very closely," Garza interrupted. "Special Agent Brennan is dead." The words struck Henry like a bolt of lightning. He closed his eyes and tried to compose himself. "You're in danger, Mr. Sirola."

"I'm sorry, you must be mistaken. Why would I care about Agent Brennan?"

"Because I know he was your handler."

Henry shook his head. "That's not true."

"I know you're the Shadowmaker," Garza charged quietly. "I saw video of you two meeting yesterday over in Oakland City. Krunoslav must've gotten to him."

"I don't believe you. There's no way Agent Brennan is dead."

"I'm sorry, Henry. He's gone."

"When?"

"Last night. He was executed in his apartment."

Henry swallowed hard, pushing his emotions as far down as they would go. "That's uh… that's… really unfortunate. Any idea who did it?"

"We don't know yet. FBI is working on it."

"But you're not FBI," Henry noted, his eyes still glued ahead of him.

"No. I'm not."

"Then why are you telling me this?"

"Because if you really are the Shadowmaker, then you're our last chance of bringing down Krunoslav. The entire operation's been compromised. Everything's fucked."

Henry clenched his jaw as the train came to a hissing stop at Lindbergh Station. "Brown Field," he stated bitterly. "Nine o'clock. Bring a damn army."

Garza raised his eyebrows and looked away. "You're not safe here, Mr. Sirola. I suggest you go to ground." The officer got up and stepped off the train, disappearing into a platform full of waiting passengers.

Henry sat frozen as the doors closed and the train pulled away. He rode for several more stops before getting off at North Avenue Station and hustling up the stairs into the brisk morning air. As he strolled along the sidewalk, he tried to make sense of it all. His identity as the Shadowmaker was now compromised, and if Anton had a man on the inside, it would only be a matter of time before he was plucked off the streets and killed.

In a sudden panic, Henry broke into a light jog. He rounded the corner of an intersection and ducked into the front door of a Hertz rental office. Inside, a tall, lanky Hispanic guy stood behind the counter fiddling with the keyboard of an old desktop computer. "What can I do for you?"

"Yes, I'd like to rent a car," Henry stated casually.

"I can help you with that. All we need is a valid driver's license and proof of insurance."

Henry reached into his jacket pocket and produced a North Carolina driver's license and insurance card.

The man typed the info into the computer, then swiped Henry's credit card. Finally, a set of keys were handed over the counter.

With a pleasant smile, Henry made his way to the back lot and jumped behind the wheel of a Chevy Malibu. As he eased the sedan out of the lot and into traffic, he grabbed his burner and dialed a number. "Izzy!" he said excitedly.

"Hey, sweetie. Everything all right?"

"No, it's not. You need to listen to me. It's time to go, you need to pack your shit and—"

"Slow down, Henry! What are you talking about?"

"You don't have much time, babe. You need to sanitize, pack, and get your ass on a plane. Do you understand?"

"Yes, fine. But please calm down and tell me what happened."

"They killed him. They killed Brennan."

"Oh my god." She gasped. "Your handler?"

"Yeah. He's dead."

"Henry, you're in danger. Please tell me you're on your way out of the country."

He took a moment to catch his breath. "Kortenberg is still in play. But you need to leave now!"

"I'm leaving, I promise. I'm out the door in sixty seconds."

"I love you, Izzy. I'll see you in two weeks."

"I love you too, Henry."

As the car crested into Chelsea Heights, Henry ended the call and quickly dialed another number.

"Hello?" A.J. answered.

"A.J., it's me. We have a problem."

"What's goin' on, boss?"

"I need you to clean everything."

"You have to be kidding. Everything?"

"All of it. Destroy the laptop and every shred of evidence, even the backup file."

"This isn't what we talked about, Henry. What happened?"

Henry narrowed his eyes over the steering wheel. "There's been a change of plans."

CHAPTER 35

He peered into the rearview mirror, searching for ghosts that weren't there. At the end of a winding street in a quiet residential neighborhood, he pulled the Malibu into the driveway of a two-story white home with a neatly manicured yard.

An older woman stood outside in her flower bed, smiling from beneath a large straw hat. "Henry!" she shouted as he got out of the car.

"Aunt Sara, it's good to see you!"

"I didn't know you were coming by, I would've brewed some tea."

Henry gave her a warm hug, lightly pressing his temple against hers.

"Is everything all right?" she asked with a sharp Slavic accent.

He glanced down at the freshly planted tulips at her feet. "I wish it were," he confessed. "Unfortunately, something terrible has happened."

"I can sense that," she replied, eyeing the bruises on his face and neck. "I heard about Darius. I'm so sorry, Henry. I just can't believe it. Why don't you come inside and I'll make you something to eat."

"I've already had breakfast, Aunt Sara. But this isn't just about Darius. There's something more we need to talk about."

"Are you in trouble, Henry?"

"Yes," he said sheepishly.

"Well, you've been getting yourself into trouble since you were a little boy. What has Anton gotten you into now?"

"It's different this time," he warned. "We need to get some of your bags packed. It's time for us to leave."

She shook her head, disappointed. "Luka always said this day would come. I never believed him. I never thought I'd have to pack my things and flee my home again."

"I wish there was another way. I really do."

"Does Anton know we're leaving?" she asked.

"No, he doesn't."

"I see. Well, come inside. Let's talk this through."

"There isn't time, Aunt Sara."

"We have to leave right this very moment?" she asked suspiciously.

Henry nodded. "I'm afraid so."

"Fine. There are some bags in the pantry, why don't you go ahead and pack up all the pictures and things. I'll get some clothes."

He walked with her to the front door and into the house. It was a nice little place: clean, fragrant, and well decorated.

"You know, Henry, I'm just a harmless old widow. Why would anyone want to hurt me?"

"There are people who are going to come for me," Henry said pointedly. "And then they'll come for the ones I love, including you."

She stood firm with her hands on her hips, unrattled by the danger of it all. "Well, Anton doesn't scare me, and neither do those slouchy goons he runs with!"

"I'm sorry, Aunt Sara. But there's no other way."

"What have you done, Henry?"

He began gathering picture frames from the walls and bookshelves and stuffing them into plastic grocery bags.

"Henry!" she demanded. "Tell me what's happened?"

"Let's just say we've worn out our welcome."

"And where are we going?"

"I have some business to take care of in Europe. But you'll be going to Minnesota. One of the guys I went to school with lives up that way. You're going to stay with him for a while."

"It's cold in Minnesota," she objected. "And I don't know anyone there. What's this friend of yours do for a living?"

"He's, uh… well… he's in the laundry business."

She shot him a baleful glare. "Of course he is."

Henry stopped packing and went over to her. He placed his hands on her frail shoulders and stared affectionately into her eyes. "After a few weeks, I'll fly you out to Europe— anywhere you want."

"Are we driving all the way to Minnesota?"

"No, I'm taking you to the bus station. You'll go to Charlotte, then fly the rest of the way. I've got all your tickets already taken care of."

"Why can't I fly out of Atlanta?" she pried.

"It's just not safe right now. Which reminds me—you never saw me today, do you understand? If anyone asks, you took a cab to the bus station and you're heading to Minnesota to see an old friend."

"Where in Minnesota?"

"It's a small town called McGregor. It's nice and quiet. There's a garden for you to plant in."

"What's the point?" she complained. "It'll be too cold to put anything useful in the ground."

Henry let her grievance hang in the air, and for the next ten minutes, he packed her things and loaded the car.

As the Malibu pulled out of the neighborhood, Henry reached over and held her hand. "There's something I have to ask you, Aunt Sara," he said gently. "It's about Anton."

"All right. What is it?"

"When he and Uncle Luka were fighting in the war, did he ever… did he ever talk about defecting?"

"No, of course not!" she snapped.

"What about the day my parents were killed? Where was Anton that day?"

Sara's mind wandered back in time, to a place she'd tried hard to forget. "I don't know."

"Was he in the village?"

"No."

"Was Uncle Luka in the village?"

"Yes. You already know the story, Henry. Why are you asking me this?"

"Just entertain me for a minute. When the Serbs came for us, where was I? And where were my parents?"

"Your father and several of the other men, including Luka, tried to confront the soldiers as they entered the village," she explained. "Your mother rushed in to our home and thrust you into my arms. She told us to hide, then kissed you on the forehead and dashed out the front door. I never saw her again."

"And Luka?"

She clenched her eyes and shook her head. "The shooting started right away. It was very chaotic. Henry, this is all such a painful memory and I don't want to discuss it!"

"I'm so sorry," he said regretfully. "But I have to know what happened next."

The old woman grunted with contempt. "Fine. I remember Luka came running into the house. He had blood all over him. Your father had been captured, along with many of the other men. Those Serb bastards went door to door and rounded up the women too."

"… and shot them all in a field," Henry whispered.

"Yes. They were all shot to death while I held you in the basement, beneath the floorboards."

"It was Anton."

Her eyes fluttered beneath a ridged brow. "Why would you say such a thing?"

"Because I read the military incident report. He was a double agent working for the Serbs. He was there, and he ordered the execution of my parents."

"That's not true, Henry! There's no way I would ever believe that."

"Luka knew, didn't he?"

She shifted her gaze to the windshield, then began to cry.

"Aunt Sara, did Luka ever talk about Anton? Did he ever discuss what that monster did to us that day?"

"You don't understand what that war was like, Henry," she implored through a veil of tears. "We lived every waking hour in absolute terror. It destroyed us. It destroyed who we were. And there was nothing we could do! After everyone was murdered that day, our only choice was to go with Anton."

"So you knew?"

"Of course not! I had no idea what Anton was doing. We just knew that he had worked out some kind of deal. I only learned later on that he had threatened Luka and the other survivors if they ever spoke of it. We had two choices that day, Henry. We either went with Anton to America or we stayed and got slaughtered."

Henry gazed out at the highway. He suddenly realized that his entire life—everything he'd ever believed—had turned out to be a lie.

His breathing became labored and his vision blurred. He gripped the steering wheel as a bead of sweat ran down his forehead.

"This was never supposed to be talked about, Henry. It was buried in the past, where it belongs."

"Well, now I know. And I won't allow his crimes to go unanswered."

"What are you going to do?" she asked. "Why are we running?"

"I just need to take care of some things before I get out of this life for good."

"I never wanted you to work for Anton," she confessed. "I never wanted to see him again after that day. But he owned us, Henry. All of us who came over with him. He got us our citizenships, he bought our homes and our businesses. He gave our children jobs and made sure we all had nice lives."

"Well, that's all changed now. He doesn't own us anymore."

The distraught widow sighed with regret, clutching her purse in her lap.

There was nothing left to say. The truth of how their lives had transpired was now out in the open.

The Malibu barreled east along a desolate two-lane highway until they arrived in Athens, Georgia.

Henry skirted the car past a line of traffic and slipped into the parking lot of an old brick building. The silver icon of a greyhound hung above the entrance, frozen in mid-stride. Nearby, a row of rumbling chrome buses idled on the curb, waiting to haul passengers to a myriad of far-flung destinations.

Henry stepped out of the car and pulled Aunt Sara's luggage from the trunk—a single tote bag and a roller case. The overwhelming stench of diesel fuel festered in the air.

Sara climbed out of the car and cast her eyes across the lot. "I hate traveling by bus," she griped as she paced around to the backside of the car.

"You're going to do fine," he told her. "And I'll make sure all of your things are put into storage, including your picture frames."

"Oh, Henry, I'm sorry you have to do this. I should've raised you differently, taken you far away from all this nonsense."

"Please don't," he whispered. "Please don't say that. I'd be nothing without you, and soon, we'll be back on our feet again. I promise."

"You've always been such a sweet boy. Don't let them change you. Don't ever let them change you."

"I won't, Aunt Sara."

She took a moment to examine her surroundings. "Very well. You aren't coming inside with me, are you?"

"I'm sorry. You know I can't."

The old woman nodded.

Henry reached into his pocket and produced a thin stack of tickets. "This is everything you need," he told her. "Your bus ticket to Charlotte and a plane ticket to Duluth, Minnesota. My friend is going to be at the airport to pick you up. He'll be holding a sign that says Stanić. Can you remember all that?"

"I think so," she replied as she took the tickets from him. "Bus ticket, plane ticket, and a man in Minnesota with a sign for Stanić."

"That's perfect," he said through a tiny, sad smile. He leaned in and wrapped her in his arms, desperately hoping it wouldn't be the last time.

"I've loved you since you were a little boy," she said into his chest. "And your mother loved you as well. You were everything to her."

"I'm going to make this right. For you, for Luka, and for my mother and father, and everyone else who was murdered that day."

"They would have been very proud of you, Henry. You've grown into such an amazing young man. Please be safe."

"I love you, Aunt Sara. Take care of yourself, make sure you're eating and exercising and all of that. I promise to send for you in the spring."

"I'll look forward to it," she said as the smile drifted from her painted red lips. She turned and began a slow shuffle toward the station, her suitcase rolling effortlessly behind her.

Henry stood and watched until she turned one last time and waved. She then entered the station and disappeared from view.

CHAPTER 36

Isabell loaded the last of her bags. She took a final glance up and down the street before slamming the hatch and getting into her Pathfinder.

She pulled out of the driveway, then the neighborhood, and took the interstate south toward Macon. A thin patch of clouds drifted overhead as she accelerated into the fast lane. Ahead of her, the skyline of Atlanta rose ominously against the horizon.

She checked the rearview mirror. Then again. Her hands gripped the steering wheel tighter as the SUV sped through the Moreland Interchange and into downtown. Eventually, she reached the south end of the city and coasted past a series of overhead signs for the airport. As she exhaled a sigh of relief, the clouds above seemed to slip away, leaving nothing but a clear blue sky in her path.

The fallback plan was simple: from her storage unit outside Macon, she'd drive south to Jacksonville and board the next available flight to Italy, where a methodical network of transporters would be waiting to move her undetected throughout Europe.

It had all been carefully crafted and assembled years ago.

Under a mountain of anticipation, she drove south until she reached a visitor's center just outside Barnesville. The strategic pitstop offered her an opportunity to detect any potential followers.

Three vehicles exited just behind her.

She examined each one carefully: an older couple in a red coupe; a college-aged woman in a black Jeep; and a family of five crammed into a white minivan packed with luggage and sleeping bags.

The Pathfinder idled for another moment before she backed out of the space and returned to the interstate. For the next forty-five minutes, she rode in silence, listening only to the droning hum of the tires against the asphalt.

It was almost surreal—the whole concept of packing what few possessions she could and driving away from it all, never to return. She pushed the thought from her mind. There would be no second guessing or reevaluating, she reminded herself. That was the deal.

Just north of Macon, she got off the highway and turned west onto a desolate road, flanked on both sides by endless green pastures.

Isabell turned onto an old country road that took her further into the nothingness. As she peered through the windshield and squinted into the sun, a dingy white building appeared on the horizon. The SUV coasted another quarter mile before pulling into the driveway of a small storage facility, surrounded by chain-link fence.

She came to a stop in front of an old gate and a security keypad. She entered a four-digit code and the gate began dragging itself through the gravel, leaving behind chalky dust that floated weightlessly in the air. She pulled through the gate and slowly crept between two brick buildings that had been painted white, each lined with rows of blue garage doors—one after the other.

Isabell drove to the end of the units and came to a stop in front of door number 619. She got out and pulled a key from her purse—it was the one with no markings, and it fit perfectly into the deadbolt. She reached down and grabbed the bay door and lifted it over her head.

With the flick of a light switch, the room beamed to life, revealing a black sedan and a small metal safe resting on a table against the wall. She hurried to the safe and typed a code into the touchpad, which sprang the thick steel door open.

From inside, she pulled out a burgundy passport and two stacks of bills—one with hundreds and another containing smaller, easier-to-use denominations. She reached in and retrieved a compact nine-millimeter pistol and stuffed it into her purse.

The black sedan parked inside was covered in dust, just the way she'd left it. She took a moment to survey it—assessing whether it would be up to the task—then tossed her bag into the passenger seat and climbed behind the wheel.

With a nervous exhale, she reached into the glove box, pulled out another key, and set it into the ignition. The engine struggled to resurrect itself, but after a stammering purr, it growled to life. She inched the Buick out into the sunshine and parked it close by. She then raced over to her Pathfinder, parked it inside the storage unit, and shut the bay door behind herself.

As she returned to the Buick and dropped into the driver's seat, she heard it—the familiar sound of the chain-link gate grinding open on the other side of the property.

A silver Range Rover idled restlessly beyond the fence, waiting for it to open.

With a determined glare, Isabell gripped the wheel, promising herself she'd do whatever necessary to survive the day.

The Range Rover crept menacingly through the gate. She could now make out the silhouettes of two men sitting inside.

The vehicles stared each other down from fifty yards away. The thin driveway—bound by storage units on each side—created a gauntlet between them. She reached for her purse and the grip of the small pistol, clutching it in her hand as her pulse quickened.

You can do this, she told herself confidently. Whatever it takes.

Isabell dropped the Buick into drive and began pressing forward. The Range Rover mirrored her advance, slinking toward her along the gravel. As she continued on, her eyes locked on to what appeared to be an assault rifle being hoisted by one of the men.

In sheer panic, she stomped her foot on the brakes and threw the Buick into reverse, thrusting it backwards with a high-pitched squeal. With her foot pinned to the accelerator, she yanked the steering wheel and slung the car around. The sedan shot around the backside of the building and turned the corner through a cloud of dust.

The Range Rover bolted into pursuit, racing between the storage units to the rear of the property. As the SUV gained momentum, Isabell dropped all of her weight onto the gas pedal, blasting the old Buick through a chain-link fence and into an open grass field. She steadied the wheel and kept her foot to the floor. As the car sprinted onto the main road, a chunk of fencing broke loose from the front bumper and tumbled in her wake.

She shifted her eyes to the rearview mirror. Behind her, the Range Rover jumped onto the road and quickly closed in. She pushed the gas harder, but the engine simply didn't have the strength. Within seconds, the Range Rover caught up and rammed into the back of the sedan. The impact jolted her in her seat. It rammed her a second time, and a third.

The burst of an assault rifle cracked the air as her rear windshield shattered onto the back seat. Isabell let out a terrified scream.

With no way of outrunning them, she slammed the brakes and cut the wheel. The sedan skirted violently from the road and tore into a thick forest before crashing into the base of a large white oak. The Range Rover came to a skidding halt in the middle of the road. It backed up to the crash site and two large men in black suits emerged from either side.

With weapons drawn, they slowly approached. The front windshield of the Buick had been blown out and the hood was wrapped halfway around a tree. A white cloud of steam rose from the engine like a small smokestack. As they flanked the vehicle from both sides, they could now see that Isabell was no longer inside. Their eyes immediately darted to the surrounding brush.

The crash site fell eerily silent as the men fanned out with their guns at the ready.

She could feel the cool sensation of blood running from her forehead as she peered out at them from her hide—one had an assault rifle, the other a handgun.

Through the quiet hush of the forest, the crack of a nine-millimeter pierced the crisp air. One of the men fell to the ground with a thud. The earth underneath him rustled as he squirmed in the dirt, fighting for a breath that would never come.

She'd taken out the assault rifle first, which, in her mind, had leveled the playing field.

The second man scanned his eyes from tree to tree, his pistol in front of him.

A slight movement in his peripheral gave away her position and he unloaded a flurry of rounds into the hazy green woodland. Just as he was trained, the assassin followed the sound of crinkling leaves and the scent of fear.

As he closed in, Isabell crawled through a patchwork of wild grasses and boxwoods, struggling to return to the Buick's wreckage—the one place that offered her cover.

She reached the old sedan on her hands and knees and grabbed the passenger door handle. She tried to pull herself up but was suddenly paralyzed by the sound of snapping twigs.

Lacking the strength to stand, she twisted around and rested her back against the steel frame of the sedan, clutching the gunshot wound in her stomach.

The footsteps continued to draw closer until a tall, middle-aged man emerged from the trees.

With a painful wince, she wiped the blood from her mouth and gazed up at him. She could see him clearly now; his hair was tufted in places where it had once been combed and a pool of sweat gathered around his throat, soaking the white shirt beneath his black jacket.

He stepped forward and raised the pistol to her face.

She stared down its deep, cavernous barrel and managed a faint smile. As she closed her eyes, a gunshot shattered the silence, reverberating through the empty countryside.

The man fell to his knees, then collapsed facedown into the dirt.

Isabell lay motionless. A plume of gray smoke seeped from a tiny black hole in her purse, where her hand was still snuggly tucked inside.

The next several minutes seemed to pass in a peaceful, euphoric daze. Her vision began to blur. Her breaths became shorter and harder to manage.

Somewhere in the distance, beyond the rolling green hills, she could hear the blaring wail of sirens. They grew louder at first, then softer, until soon she couldn't hear them at all.

Isabell shut her eyes and fell unconscious against the car door.

CHAPTER 37

Henry exited the highway and blasted past a strip of retail outlets and car dealerships. Minutes later, he coasted into the fringes of East Atlanta. From there, he continued to the wealthy neighborhood of Oakhurst. It was a collection of renovated homes, locally owned coffee shops, and well-manicured parks.

The Malibu drifted several more blocks before parking in front of a single-story brick home with a black door and black shutters. Henry stepped out of the car and peeled the sunglasses from his eyes. He marched to the front door and knocked twice.

Seconds later, Jack Veselko's big brown eyes appeared in the doorway. "Great to see you, Henry! Come on in," he quickly offered.

Henry stepped inside and stood mawkishly in the center of the living room. "I appreciate you seeing me on short notice, Jack. It's been a difficult day, to say the least."

"So what's going on?" the young operator asked as he closed the door behind them. "You sounded a little panicked on the phone."

"The truth is, I could use some help."

"Anything for you, Henry." Jack led him into the kitchen, then grabbed a bottle of whiskey from the counter and two glasses from the cabinet. "Have a seat, boss. Tell me what's going on."

Henry trudged to the center island and dropped onto a barstool. "Listen, Jack, some new information has come to my attention," he began. "I've learned some things over the last few days. Things that put me in a very precarious position."

"Okay. I'm listening."

Henry downed his whiskey in a single gulp. "I need to get away for a while. Someplace nobody will find me."

"Why not go to Anton? I'm sure he could send you to ground."

"Because Anton's the one I need to get away from."

Jack wrinkled his forehead and straightened his back. "I know I'm supposed to report directly to you, Henry. But I'm a little concerned about keeping something like this from Anton. I can get in a lot of trouble for even having this conversation."

"I know, Jack. And I appreciate your loyalty—to me and the organization."

"You know, I can't imagine this has been easy for you," Jack allowed. "Darius' death, the new promotion… maybe we just need to take a step back and sort it all out."

Henry stared vacantly into the empty shot glass. He ran the tip of his index finger along the rim, debating how much he was willing to tell his new lieutenant. "I think I'm past the point of sorting it out," he said after a moment.

"There's nothing I wouldn't do for you, Henry. Just say the word." Jack chugged his whiskey and slammed the glass onto the counter. "I could probably get you to South America—Paraguay, middle of fuckin' nowhere."

Henry nodded. "Yeah. I think I'd like that. How soon could you set it up?"

"I could probably have something arranged in the next twelve hours. But you need to find someplace other than here to lay low until then."

"I can do that. How much?"

"Forty thousand. It's a guy out of Juarez. Twice a month he runs a fleet of single-engine Cessnas to Galveston and back."

"The drug cartels, huh?"

Jack gave a culpable glance. "Something like that."

"All right. I can have forty grand within the hour."

"You know, Henry, I know I shouldn't ask, but… what on God's green Earth is going on?"

Henry scoffed with amusement. "Well… let's just say I've uncovered a lot of secrets about my life—how I got here, what happened to my parents, and why I even became a member of Ružaro. It's all part of one big goddamn lie."

"And you think going to ground is the answer?"

"There's just something I have to do. And it's going to get me in a lot of trouble."

Jack hung his head and rose from his stool. "I really wish you hadn't told me that, Henry." The sound of footsteps echoed from the hallway, and then, as if out of nowhere, two figures appeared in the kitchen. "I'm sorry," said Jack. "I had no other choice."

Henry gazed up to see Asa and his grizzly-bear friend, Paul.

"Let's go," Asa instructed. "You know the drill."

Henry turned to his lieutenant, who silently shook his head, unable to find the words to defend himself.

"It's all right, Jack," Henry allowed. "You did the right thing. You're going to make one hell of a boss someday." He stood to his feet as Asa and Paul grabbed him by the arms and ushered him out of the house. They piled into a black Mercedes and sped out of the driveway.

"I thought I trained you better than this," Asa snarled from the front passenger seat.

"Where are we going?" asked Henry. "I want to talk to Anton."

"Oh, don't worry. You'll get to speak with Anton. I can assure you he's looking forward to it."

Henry understood the veiled threat. He knew the old man preferred to kill high-ranking traitors in person. As a wave of nausea washed over him, he stared through the window at the world outside—the mindless commuters, the playing children, the leaves blowing in the wind. It all suddenly seemed so virtuous. Yet beneath it all, he knew, buried in the concrete buildings and the mediocrity of everyday life, was a world where the wicked climbed to power on the backs of the innocent.

And in that moment, he was tired of it all: the corruption, the violence, the betrayal. With a sobering breath, he closed his eyes and thought of Isabell. He hoped she was hundreds of miles away by now, far from the reach of Asa and his murderous goons.

The Mercedes pulled down a narrow street, around the back of a massive warehouse. Henry knew the place well. "Anton's not coming, is he?" But Asa didn't answer. The car came to a gentle stop in front of the loading docks. "You know, Asa, you and I are like family. You practically raised me!"

Asa got out and opened the back door. "That's what makes all of this so hard," the general replied as he slung Henry out and guided him into the warehouse.

It took a moment for Henry's eyes to adjust to the darkness. Across the concrete floor, in a shadowy, damp corner, was a single foldout chair and a thick metal chain that draped from somewhere high above. A construction hook was mounted at the bottom, waiting for its next victim.

As Asa and Paul led him across the warehouse, five more men emerged from a nearby office and gathered around him like a pride of hungry lions. Henry knew each of them by name.

Asa was the first to step up—he threw a hard right into Henry's jaw, knocking him backward onto the ground.

Paul was next. He rolled up the sleeves of his neatly pressed shirt, then cracked his neck to each side. He picked Henry off the floor and set him down in the chair.

"Why were you trying to run off to Paraguay?" Asa asked from the shadows.

"I wanted to hide out for a while," Henry answered.

"For what?"

"It doesn't matter."

Paul slammed a fist into his gut.

"Why were you going to ground?" Asa asked again.

"Because I found out about Darius."

"And what exactly do you think you found out?"

"I know the Cardoso cartel didn't kill him." Henry was fishing now, doing anything he could to redirect Asa's attention.

"If you have information about Darius' death, I suggest you share it with me," the general warned.

"That's the problem. I don't know if I can trust you, Asa."

Paul delivered a hard right hook to his face, followed by a heavy uppercut. Henry recoiled for a moment, then spit a mouthful of blood onto the floor.

"Who do you think killed Darius?" Asa pressed.

"I think you killed him."

The general stepped closer. "Why on Earth would I do that? Have you gone mad?"

Henry's left eye began to swell. He stared blankly at the concrete beneath his feet.

"Regardless, the decision has already been made," Asa announced. "You've betrayed your family, Henry. And unfortunately, forgiveness is not an option." The old general turned and walked away, motioning to his men before disappearing into the darkness.

Henry's wrists were bound with rope, which hung from a large steel hook. He dangled there like a ragdoll, his toes squirming against the floor, trying to keep his shoulders from pulling out of their sockets.

The beating continued for well over an hour.

With their prisoner on the brink of unconsciousness, the men gave up and retreated into the far reaches of the warehouse.

He could still see out of one eye, but even that was blurred by a thin coat of blood. The faint voices of Asa's soldiers murmured from somewhere in the distance. Above him, through the fiberglass tile ceiling, the last glimmers of sunlight illuminated the clouds with a brilliant amber glow.

As darkness fell, a set of headlights pulled around the back of the building. The loud metallic slam of a door announced the return of Asa Petrovi. The general lumbered across the warehouse floor to examine his prisoner.

"All right, Henry!" he shouted. "Are you ready to see Anton?"

Henry lifted his head and squinted into the blackness. "I thought you'd never ask."

Paul and his crew returned from their break and cut Henry loose from the hook. His body collapsed to the ground with a deep thud.

"Pick him up!" Asa ordered. "And bring him to the car."

Half conscious, Henry was lifted and dragged across the concrete. He was brought to the outside parking lot, then shoved into the backseat of the Mercedes.

The black sedan thundered out of the lot and rushed west toward Buckhead. After a ten-minute drive, they pulled into the underground deck of the Park Avenue building. Asa got out and walked to the back of the car and popped the trunk. He retrieved a light blue dress shirt, then stepped to the back door and tossed it through the window.

"Put this on," he insisted. "We can't have you walking around like some wild, bloody animal."

Henry took off his shirt and put on the new one. He was then yanked from the back of the car and into the elevator.

Moments later, they stepped out into the lobby of Anton's penthouse. It seemed much colder than before, more foreboding. What was once a safe haven now felt like death row.

Paul shoved him through the archway and into the grand hall, where a half dozen men, each armed with an assault rifle, meandered around in a terrorizing silence.

Henry kept his chin up and walked under his own strength. As he stood breathless in the center of the hall, Asa brushed past him and swung open the doors to Anton's study.

"Henry's here to see you," the general announced. "We'll be right outside if you need us."

Henry inched his way into the study and the doors were quickly shut behind him.

There, sitting behind a large oak desk, was Anton. His fingers were tented at his lips. His eyes were pinched with anger. "Come. Have a seat, Henry."

Henry paced across the room and sat down in the chair across from his boss. Beneath his feet, a large plastic sheet had been laid across the ground, covering one of Anton's prized Persian rugs.

"I'm very disappointed in you," Anton leveled. He stood and clasped his hands behind his back.

"I don't know what they told you, Anton, but I'm sure this is all a misunderstanding."

"Oh, my boy, I wish it was. I really do. But I must say that I have never felt as betrayed as I do now. You've hurt me beyond belief."

"I feel the same way, Anton."

"Is that so?"

"Yes. I know what you've done."

Anton allowed a scant laugh. "And what exactly is it that I've done?"

"I know you were the one who ordered the hit on Darius."

Anton began pacing the room, deep in thought. "That's a very interesting theory. However, I don't care much for it."

"I know that he was an informant. He was SOA. And I think you found out about it."

"SOA?" Anton shook his head and sat back down. "No, no, no. He wasn't SOA. Although I did have suspicions he was working with the FBI just before his death. And if you must know the truth, it was actually Asa's idea to have him killed. He sent that stumpy little fucker, Paul, to do the job."

"So you admit it?"

"I admit nothing. Besides, I'm talking to a dead man."

"He was my best friend!" Henry yelled. "He was like a son to you! How could you do this?"

"As you know, every action has a reaction. And Asa can be difficult to manage sometimes. People often get hurt when he's around. You know how it is."

"You're nothing but a lowlife piece of fucking trash!"

"Henry, my boy, what you fail to realize is that *you* were the one who got Darius killed. Not me, not Asa… it was you."

Henry's mind spun frantically in circles, searching for a response that never came. His jaw tightened with anger.

Anton tapped his diamond-studded pinky ring against the armrest of his chair. "You see, Henry, when I first discovered there was an FBI informant within my ranks, all the evidence pointed to Darius. So, he wound up dead. And then, low and behold, I find out that it wasn't Darius after all. It was you."

Henry shifted in his seat, gripping the armrest firmly. "You're a monster, Anton."

"Am I? Let me ask you something, Henry. What would you call a man who turns his back on the people who gave him everything?"

Henry could feel the pit of his stomach churning like the pistons of a diesel engine.

"A coward!" Anton yelled. "That's what you call it! You, Henry, are a no-good fucking coward!"

Henry remained silent. There was a fire building inside him—a rush of white-hot rage swelled from deep within his soul. He steadied himself in the chair as a single tear rounded his eyelid and fell onto his cheek.

"I know what you did in Krasno," he revealed, almost inaudibly. Then, louder, "I know what you did to them."

Anton's face fell with shock. He reached into his desk drawer and pulled out a chrome-plated .38 revolver.

"They were innocent people," Henry continued. "And they were your people. How could you have done that to them?"

"You were always too soft for this business, Henry. You could never see the big picture."

"The *big picture*? Tell me what the big picture is, Anton! I'm dying to know."

Anton let the moment hang for a beat. "Survival. That's the big picture. You have no idea what that war did to us. Anyone who made it out alive was forever changed. There wasn't a single one of us who didn't sacrifice everything to survive that war! But in those days, when an opportunity to survive presented itself, you took it... and you didn't ask questions!"

In a sudden flash, Henry sprung from his chair and dove across the desk, taking both him and Anton to the floor. A single gunshot rang through the room.

Henry could feel the burning graze against his ribs.

With a violent thrust, he pinned Anton to the ground and swiped the revolver from his grasp, sending it spiraling across the hardwood floor. He then rolled himself into a mounted position and gripped the old warlord by the throat, choking him with everything he had.

Anton struggled for leverage, flailing his arms desperately in the air, clawing at Henry's face. But it was no use. Henry kept slamming the back of Anton's head against the floor, again and again—each time harder than the last.

"This is for my parents," he whispered into Anton's ear. "*Djavli te ponesli.*"

Anton wheezed, gasping for breath. His legs thrashed violently against the floor as he continued to reach for something to grab hold of.

Then, with a final recoil, his eyes rolled back in his head and his arms collapsed against the floor. His feet twitched for several seconds, then went completely still.

Henry lifted himself from the ground and gazed down at Anton's lifeless body. In the stillness of the moment, he felt absolutely nothing.

He stumbled over to a large mirror against the wall and used his hand to brush his hair back into place. He tugged the wrinkles from his shirt and straightened his shoulders.

Through a searing rush of adrenaline, Henry strode across the room and stood at the door, preparing himself for whatever awaited him on the other side. With a fortifying exhale, he reached down and wrapped his hand around the knob. As the door peeled open, he braced himself, then stepped into the grand hall.

There, strewn across the floor in small pools of blood, were Anton's goons, their weapons at their sides, still gripped in their hands. Further up the hall, seemingly frozen in an attempt to escape, was the crumpled body of Asa Petrovi.

Henry lifted his eyes from the floor and set his gaze on the only man still standing.

A.J.'s assault rifle dangled at his side. A steady stream of smoke seeped from the suppressor mounted to its barrel.

"They're all dead?" Henry asked.

"Yes."

"Good."

"You must be absolutely insane," A.J. noted as he examined the carnage.

Henry ambled across the room, stepping over the bodies in his path. "Yeah, I hear that from time to time."

"So where do we go from here, boss?"

Henry checked his watch. "I have thirty minutes to get to the handoff. You should probably get the hell out of Dodge. I'll take it from here."

"You sure about that?" A.J. asked as he handed Henry a nine-millimeter gun and its holster.

"Yeah, I'm sure." Henry made sure the holster was in its place, ejected the magazine to check the ammo before slamming it back in and chambering a round, and then placed the gun in the holster. "I owe you my life, A.J."

"You don't owe me anything. We made the world a better place tonight."

A sliver of pride appeared on Henry's battered face. "I hope so."

"Listen, I'll meet you at the rendezvous point in two weeks. We can sort it out then."

"Thank you again. For everything." Henry reached out and shook A.J.'s hand.

"No problem." And with that, the grizzled mercenary turned and walked up the hall and disappeared from sight.

Henry stood alone, staring down at the faces of the men he'd once called family. But he didn't feel remorse or guilt or even shame—any one of them would've killed him without question, he reminded himself.

With a heavy sigh, he made his way to the elevator and descended to the underground parking garage. He stepped out into the cold, concrete abyss and grabbed a set of keys from the wall. Behind him lay the lifeless body of Frank, the doorman who'd always greeted him with a smile. "*Pokoj mu duši*," Henry whispered.

He turned and marched into the shadows. With the press of a button, Asa's black Mercedes flashed its lights from across the garage.

CHAPTER 38

It was getting late, and the night shift was settling in at Coliseum Northside Hospital just outside Macon, Georgia.

Agent Jonathan Harwick stormed through the front doors and hurried across the waiting room to a long corridor. His eyes wandered the halls as he approached the nurses' station.

"I'm looking for the woman who was brought in with a gunshot wound," he said as he flashed his NSA card to the nurse at the counter.

The nurse looked up with surprise, then took a moment to examine the ID. "Yes, sir, she just came out of surgery an hour ago. She's in recovery, up the hall in 204."

Harwick turned and charged up the hallway. He barged through a set of swinging doors and made his way deeper into the unit, checking the room numbers as he went. He arrived at 204 and snatched the clipboard from the door. After a quick scan, he quietly slipped into the room. His eyes darted from the bed to the dresser, then to an IV bag hanging from a hook. In a fit of rage, he charged into the hallway and sprinted back to the nurses' station.

"Where the hell is she?" he shouted. "Why isn't there an officer guarding that room?"

The nurse sprang from her chair. "I—I don't know. There was a deputy monitoring the hallway not ten minutes ago. He must've gone to the cafeteria. But there's no way she could've gotten up and left; she was under heavy anesthesia."

Harwick slammed his fist against the counter. "Get security over here and have them lock down the entire building! Now!"

"Sir, we only have one security guard. But I'm telling you, there's a deputy around here somewhere if you can find him." She reached for a phone and began frantically dialing numbers.

Harwick turned and broke into a sprint toward the main entrance. As he rushed to find his target, a group of men swept through the doors ahead of him. The agent stopped in his tracks, his eyes locked on the tall, Black man lumbering toward him.

"Agent Harwick!" David Tisdale greeted sharply. "Just the man I was looking for!"

Harwick shook his head in astonishment. "What the hell are you doing here, David?"

A swarm of FBI agents circled him as Tisdale stood with his arms crossed against his broad chest. "Jonathan Harwick, you are under arrest for the murder of federal agent Miles Brennan."

"What the fuck are you talking about?" Harwick growled as his arms were forced behind his back. "You're making a huge mistake, David! I have a goddamn suspect on the loose… and we need to apprehend her *now*! It's the woman! Isabell DiMarco!"

"You have the right to remain silent," Tisdale continued. "Anything you say can and will be used against you in a court of law. You have the right to an attorney. If you cannot afford an attorney, one will be provided for you."

"You're gonna burn in hell for this, David. You have no idea who you're dealing with! They'll come for you! They'll come for your family!"

"Get this lousy piece of shit out of my sight," Tisdale ordered.

The agents ushered Harwick through the lobby and into the parking lot, where a black Suburban with flashing red and blue lights waited in the darkness.

CHAPTER 39

Henry pulled through the gates of Brown Field. Like most Sunday nights, the place was fairly quiet. The Mercedes crept through the shadows just beyond the runway. He cut the lights and pulled around the side of a large hangar. Two men in bomber jackets stood guard at the back door, their machine guns cradled in their arms. Henry got out of the car and waved at them as he approached.

"Good evening, Mr. Sirola," one of the men greeted.

"Evening, gentlemen. Everything going all right?"

"Yes, sir. The jet is on its final approach now. Should be here any minute."

Henry nodded with approval. "Good. Where's Rukov?"

"He's inside waiting, sir."

With a slight limp, he stepped through the door and into the sprawling hangar, where more armed men paced around on high alert.

"Henry!" a voice shouted. "Glad you could make it!"

Henry made his way across the polished floor, doing his best to mask the pain of each and every step.

"Where's Asa?" Hudson Rukov asked bluntly.

"He won't be able to make it tonight," Henry replied. "Something came up."

Rukov wasn't convinced. "What do you mean *something came up*? This is the biggest deal we've had in years."

"It's our biggest deal *ever*," Henry corrected. "But he and Anton had to take care of something. I'll be in charge tonight."

"Where's the rest of your crew?" Rukov pressed. "We're gonna be shorthanded. And I don't like being shorthanded."

"I told them to stand down. Hassani's already been spooked once; we can't afford to have him turn his plane around this late in the game."

Rukov raised his eyebrows with concern. "All right. I'll just give Asa a call and see what the hell's going on." He pulled out his cell phone and brought it to his ear. Henry held his breath as the line began to ring. After a few minutes, Rukov shoved the phone back into his pocket. "Asa's not answering."

"I already told you, Hudson, something came up. He and Anton are busy."

"What the fuck happened to your face?"

"It's been a long day, man. Don't even get me started on this bullshit."

"Nah, something's not right, Henry. The top brass is supposed to be here, but instead, you show up alone looking like you got hit by a train."

Henry allowed an easy grin. "You're not seeing it, are you?"

"Seeing what?"

"This is a huge opportunity for us, Hudson. Do you have any idea how good this is going to look if you and I manage to pull this off on our own? Do you not see the level of responsibility we've just been given?"

Rukov's eyes wandered the hangar.

"So just take a deep breath and relax," Henry continued. "I know everybody's on edge, but just stay on point and we'll be on our way home within the hour. Anton's got a bonus lined up for us if this thing goes off without a hitch. So are we cool here or what?"

"Yeah, I'm cool. I just don't like surprises." Rukov motioned to a nearby table resting in the center of the hangar floor. "Your asset's over there, the locks already been disengaged. Just remember to use hand signals if anything feels off."

As Henry gazed at the table and the suitcase resting on top of it, one of Rukov's men came rushing in from the runway. "They're here!" the young soldier announced.

Rukov broke away and whirled his finger into the air. "All right! Everyone into position!" He gave Henry one last glare before jogging off to his post at the front of the hangar.

Seconds later, a black Gulfstream G700 taxied the runway and emerged from the darkness. The jet came to a stop just outside the bay doors, its red navigation lights blinking from the tips of its wings. As the plane's engines came to a rest, a set of airstairs broke free from the fuselage and set down against the asphalt. Henry watched as a dozen armed men hustled down the steps and set up a perimeter around the jet.

Then, Hamad Al Hassani stepped into the cold, dark night. He was dressed in a perfectly pressed tan suit with an orange tie. A matching fedora rested on his head. With a small entourage in tow, he descended the staircase and walked across the tarmac and into the hangar.

Henry stood like a statue at the small table as Hassani approached.

"Mr. Sirola, very nice to see you again!" the billionaire shouted gleefully.

Henry peered down at the black suitcase resting in front of him. He reached down and lifted the top. "I hope your trip was pleasant," he offered dryly.

Hassani removed his hat and handed it to one of his men. "I was told Anton would be overseeing the handoff along with his general, Asa Petrovi. Where are they?"

"Anton sends his regards. But neither he nor the general will be able to make it tonight. You can either deal with me or get back on your little plane and fly home."

The Arab smiled precariously, then cut his eyes to the suitcase. "No hard feelings about Zürich?"

Henry shook his head. "None whatsoever."

"Very well. Let's get this over with, shall we?"

Henry reached into the suitcase and gently removed a black velvet pouch. As he slipped his hand inside, he could feel the pristine cuts and smooth edges against his fingertips.

With a slow reveal, he pulled the diamond out and cradled it in his palm.

Hassani stood speechless, his eyes fixated on its perfectly chiseled facets and golden shimmer.

"She's all yours, Mr. Hassani," Henry said as he handed over the stone.

The billionaire removed a small scope from his pocket and pressed it against the diamond, examining it with diligence. After a few seconds, he smiled to himself and returned it to the table, then motioned to one of his men, who rushed over and set a laptop down in front of him. As Hassani began typing his password into the keypad, the silence was shattered by a burst of gunfire and frantic shouting. Outside the hangar, Hassani's men were darting in every direction, firing their weapons blindly into the night.

Hassani shifted his eyes to Henry, then pulled a pistol from his jacket and took aim. "What the hell is this?" he sneered.

Henry carefully raised his hands. "I have no idea, Hamad. Now put the gun down. They must've tracked your flight."

Before Hassani could pull the trigger, Hudson Rukov shouldered his rifle and put a single bullet through his forehead. Hassani crumpled to the floor in a heap, his pistol still clutched in his hand.

As the perimeter team outside was being overrun, Rukov's soldiers strategically retreated to the center of the hangar. They waited with their weapons drawn as an eerie hush fell.

Then, without warning, a fleet of black SUVs roared up to the bay doors and a wave of armed federal agents spilled into the hangar. In a careful, methodical approach, they surrounded Rukov's men.

Henry kept calm, watching the scene unfold with bated breath. "Stand down!" he ordered.

Hudson Rukov and his men slowly set their rifles onto the ground and raised their hands in surrender.

Under the raucous shouting of federal agents, Henry placed his hands on top of his head. He stood there motionless until the agents rushed in and slammed him face down onto the table. With a defiant grin, he peered up at the Florentine Diamond, which rested just in front of him. Its yellow aura glistened across his face as he stared at it with unbridled appreciation. He could almost smell it now—the history, the mythology, the sheer impossibility of it all.

As he was lifted from the table, his holstered gun was removed and a set of plastic zip ties were placed around his wrists. Across the hangar, a group of men in suits marched toward him. A familiar face emerged from the pack—Antonio Garza.

The DCIS officer came to a stop with his hands clasped to his hips. "I wasn't sure you'd make it," he greeted.

"You and me both," Henry replied.

Garza inhaled the fresh scent of gunpowder and jet fuel. He cast his eyes around the hangar, then back to Henry. "I'd like to introduce you to Special Agent David Tisdale with the FBI."

A tall, muscle-bound Black man in a navy-blue windbreaker stood like a giant. "Nice to finally meet you. I worked closely with Miles Brennan," Tisdale revealed.

"Tonight, we took an NSA agent into custody for his murder. We believe the guy was working for Anton Krunoslav."

"What's his name?" Henry asked.

"It doesn't matter."

Henry nodded. "Thank you, Special Agent Tisdale. Miles was a good man."

But the agent was in no mood for conversation. He quickly turned away and began shouting orders to his men.

"You made the right call tonight," Garza quietly noted. "Miles would be proud."

Henry stood still, his hands bound behind his back. "So what happens now?"

"We've got a team surrounding Krunoslav's residence. I'll be joining Tisdale and his men when we're done here. We're taking him down, Henry. Tonight."

"And what about me?"

"You have an opportunity to play a huge role in this. And if you're willing to testify, we can put you into a relocation program and protect you until the trials are over."

"It'll never be over, Officer Garza. They'll never stop."

"Don't be so pessimistic, Henry. This deal alone breaks a litany of international, state, and federal laws. And if we can manage to coordinate with outside agencies, we'll have the entire syndicate sitting in prison before Christmas."

Henry was speechless. He peered out across the hangar as Rukov and his men were taken into custody and shoved into a fleet of SUVs. After a moment of consideration, he nodded grudgingly. "Yeah. I'll testify if it means putting all these assholes in a deep, dark pit somewhere."

"Good. In that case, I'm turning you over to these US Marshals. They'll get you settled in someplace until we're ready for you."

Henry glanced up at the two men in blue jackets and ball caps.

"Take care of yourself," Garza said with finality. "I'll see you soon."

Henry fought the urge to snicker. "Just make sure you give Anton my best."

"You got it." Garza turned and broke into a light jog across the hangar. He climbed into the back of a Suburban and sped away.

The two marshals grabbed Henry by his arms and escorted him outside, where a dark blue pickup truck waited on the tarmac. They opened the back passenger door and shoved their prisoner inside.

As the truck pulled away from the hangar and raced across the runway, the driver removed his ball cap and tossed it onto the dashboard.

"Thank you, Jack," Henry mumbled from the back seat.

Jack Veselko glanced at his captain through the rearview mirror. "A deal's a deal, boss. Don't get all emotional on me."

Henry leaned back against the headrest. "Don't worry, I won't. It's not my style."

"You know, I thought you were crazy when you called me this morning," Jack confessed. "I thought for sure I was sending you to your death."

"You were," Henry allowed with a rigid smile.

The nameless operative sitting next to him pulled out a switchblade and cut the zip ties from his wrists, then chucked them onto the floorboard.

"So, where to?" Jack asked as he pulled the truck through the gates and onto the main road.

"Anywhere but here."

They continued for several miles in a deafening silence. Along a stretch of dark, abandoned industrial buildings, the pickup truck pulled off the road and came to a stop in a small patch of gravel.

Henry slipped a piece of paper from his pocket and set it on the center console.

"This is the account number, Jack. It's in your name. My entire life savings has been transferred into it—three and half million dollars."

Jack took the paper from the console and pulled out his cell phone. He typed in the account number and his password, then waited patiently for the website to load. Satisfied, he swiped his finger and closed the screen.

"All right, Henry, we're all set. Will I ever see you again?"

Henry shook his head. "I'm afraid not."

"Ah, you never know, man. Maybe we'll find ourselves on another job together someday."

Henry scoffed at the insinuation. "I have a feeling you've got a lot of work ahead of you, Jack. But whatever happens, don't come looking for me. You won't like what you find."

Jack understood the veiled threat—any search for Henry Sirola would come at a cost.

With a triumphant glance, Henry opened the back door and got out.

As he stepped away, the truck spun its tires in the loose gravel and bolted into the darkness. He lifted his gaze to the night sky and thought of Isabell. It had been such a long, winding, calculated road, and he yearned for her tender touch and the scent of her skin—seeing her again, being in her company was his reward for overcoming such remarkable odds.

Under a brilliant tapestry of stars, Henry stood alone in the deserted lot, unsure of what obstacles lay ahead. He reached into his pocket and wriggled something out of it.

As his hand emerged, the large yellow diamond glistened in his palm.

With a slow grin, he shoved it back into his pocket and began an easy stroll along the roadside until his silhouette ultimately vanished into the cold night.

EPILOGUE

A light rain pelted against the hull of a massive freighter as it slipped away from its dock. The ship glided through the calm waters, inching its way further from the towering lights that lined the port. Deep below deck, a team of men gathered around a table under a flickering light, speaking in hushed Italian as they desperately tried to find a vein in the woman's arm. A thick needle was driven into the top of her hand and an IV bag was raised above her head. A stream of saline rushed through a thin tube and into her bloodstream.

"*Antibiotici, morfina. Fretta!*" the oldest of the men ordered.

Isabell lay unconscious on the steel table. Her breath slipped between her lips in tiny waves. A small pool of blood collected around her wound, staining the gauze that had been taped to her stomach.

A young man rushed to the table and handed a syringe to the physician. The others stood frozen, watching with anxious hope as the needle was injected into one of the ports along the IV tube. The men waited with agitation, pacing the room with muted faces, waiting for her to open her eyes.

"Henry?" she quietly whispered.

The Italians exchanged looks of curiosity. They'd been given strict orders to keep her alive at all costs. And now, they waited for the strange woman to utter something more—anything that would give them an indication of what had happened to her. But nothing else came.

As the ship coasted through the dark waters and slipped further away from the lights of Savannah, the men stood over her and offered a silent prayer, clinging to the hope she would survive the night. Having done everything they could, they gathered their tools and quietly left the cabin.

The antibiotics and morphine coursed through Isabell's veins. Her legs twitched in tiny bursts and her heartbeat reduced to a shallow pulse.

Then, with a soft exhale, she relaxed her body against the cold steel table and drifted into unconsciousness.

For More News About T.J. Champitto,
Signup For Our Newsletter:

http://wbp.bz/newsletter

Word-of-mouth is critical to an author's long-term success. If you appreciated this book please leave a review on the Amazon sales page:

http://wbp.bz/shadowmaker